DINNER WITH A MA

She had tried to be a good hostess to Tiny Tim. But after all, what did one say? Had any good books read to you lately? What's your opinion of this season's "Sesame Street"?

"You like strawberries, don't you, Adam?" She apportioned the dessert. While she assumed normal children enjoyed whipped cream as well, she wasn't miffed when he scraped it to one side of his dish.

"I hereby appropriate Adam's share." Coby reached for the dish.

At precisely the same moment, Adam grabbed for his milk.

Suzannah watched with dull horror as Coby's forearm knocked a taper, unbalancing its pottery holder. A lime candle nose-dived to the cloth. She didn't have to worry about that fire, because the Mexican candelabra and Adam's Baccarat both self-destructed on impact, releasing a flood of milk onto the flame.

"I think," Suzannah said after an intensive survey, "I think we'll have our coffee elsewhere."

EASY ANSWERS

Judith Greber

FAWCETT CREST • NEW YORK

All characters in this book are
fictitious, and any resemblance
to actual persons living or dead
is entirely coincidental.

A Fawcett Crest Book
Published by Ballantine Books
Copyright © 1982 by Judith Greber

Library of Congress Catalog Card Number: 81-43371
ISBN 0-449-20269-0
This edition published by arrangement with Doubleday & Company, Inc.

Manufactured in the United States of America

First Ballantine Books Edition: September 1983

This book is for Robert Greber, patron saint of would-be writers and best friend.

The first step often felt as if it were over a chasm, and only a great many helping hands made it possible. Therefore, to Leonardo Bercovici, Jerry DiPego, Allyn Freeman, Howard Pearlstein, Joyce Sparling and Jane Walsh, all of whom are not only splendid writers but also excellent readers and teachers, to Maggie Field, who was right about everything, to Jean Naggar and Kate Medina, who made the magic happen, to my father, Martin Pearlstein, for an early and abiding love of books and to my sons, Matt and Jon, for not interrupting my "typing"— many, many thanks.

One

She spent too much of her time proving things to people who didn't matter, didn't notice and didn't care.

She also spent a great deal of time denying this.

Sometimes, late at night, Suzannah envisioned herself on-stage, pirouetting wildly, breath held in anxious anticipation of one definitive burst of cosmic applause.

She didn't like the image or the need that provoked it. Suzannah was not overfond of fantasies, even her own. But at twenty-nine, the vision of the dancer was as much a part of her, loved or unloved, as were her ten extra pounds, her shoulders' spray of freckles and the small bump on her nose from a childhood fall. She'd made tentative peace with all her unsatisfactory parts.

She shivered as she pushed the bell of the townhouse again, surreptitiously wiped her nose on the shoulder of her cape and sneezed as fur migrated to her nasal passages.

She stamped fresh snow off her feet, then looked at her juli-enned alligator slippers and cursed her vanity. At the tag end of December, in Philadelphia, even Cinderella would have worn boots.

Suzannah jiggled the knob, banged on the brass knocker and rang two more times. The party was one story up, above her host's psychiatric offices, and its congested babble, audible even outside, was undoubtedly drowning out her ringings and pound-ings.

Irritably, she pushed the bell once more.

The wind whined, imitating her mother's voice. "It's your own fault. You're so late, no wonder they locked up."

Why stay? She could be alone New Year's Eve. She'd been at this party before, at previous years' versions. The shape of the hours ahead was predictable, almost palpable. A weightless holi-day ornament of a night. Nothing, encased in lacquer.

She didn't have to stay and prove she was perfectly fine. Prove she'd been correct to leave Christopher Barnes. She didn't have to prove anything. To anyone. Ever.

Decision made, she turned away.

"I *thought* I heard the bell. Stop playing orphan of the storm and get in here."

So much for decisions. More than ethics, Suzannah needed warmth.

Abigail Newhouse closed the front door and lounged against it. "You're lucky nature called me to the only uncrowded john in this house. Follow me. You can use the sacred shrinking grounds for repair work." She sucked herself off the door, tucked a wandering breast edge into its silky hammock and led Suzannah through the office, into a starkly functional cubicle.

Abby sighed. "What a depressing refuge for his patients with anal fixations."

Suzannah frowned at her mirror image. Her face was too pastel, too soft, its skeletal supports hidden under faintly tinted flesh. Her eyes hovered between gray and tawny, her hair between blond and brown. She'd been designed by an artist with too much water, too little pigment and no guts. "I'm a blurry, pale haze," she complained. "I blend into the upholstery. Have to find very interested or very nearsighted men. I wish—I've always wished I had some of your drama."

Abigail Song Newhouse stared, her almond eyes wide, eyebrows meeting the fringe of jet bangs above them. "Too late, cookie. Your daddy forgot to impregnate anyone in Korea." She stretched her voluptuous frame. Suzannah considered Abby a gold and black, scarlet and ivory plea for world unity. "I didn't think you'd be here," Abby added. "Particularly solo. Did Hedy dare you? Why'd you come?"

"Why did you?"

"Is standing in the shrink's bathroom making you talk like one? I asked first."

Suzannah began another protest, then shrugged. "I give up. You've known me too long. I dared myself and I'd better get the show on the road before I realize how stupid I am." She tossed her cape onto the analytic couch. "I wish I were thinner," she muttered as they left the office.

Mid-stairs, Suzannah's sleeve was yanked. She turned to a plump woman masquerading as Dorothy Lamour in sarong and orchids. ''I can't believe how *good* you look!'' the woman said, sounding acutely disappointed.

Abby continued upstairs while Suzannah, trapped by the woman's grip and social convention, stayed and tried to remember what name accompanied the frosted hair and scarlet lips.

''How *are* you, though? I mean *really*.'' Her voice had the unwholesome passion of a reporter at the scene of a disaster.

''Fine,'' Suzannah said.

The stranger scowled, forming small fissures in her makeup. ''I might have known.'' Her voice was now flat with disdain. ''Nothing gets you. You're the toughest one of us.''

Us? What sorority had secretly initiated Suzannah and this ersatz South Sea Islander?

''When Ridge and I split, I fell apart.'' She sounded proud. ''Of course, I had a child.''

Suzannah had no such thing. But what was this equation? Why the interest? Why so many scorekeepers watching since Suzannah quit the game?

The attention surprised her. As yet another divorcée, she was ordinariness personified, a speck on a statistical bar graph. Still, her married friends probed, seeking assurance they wouldn't commit her stupid errors. Single friends studied her like a text and a warning, and ex-marrieds played duplicate divorce, insisting their deals had been worse.

Suzannah had nothing to share, so she smiled and politely excused herself.

At the top of the stairs she took inventory. This was her fifth New Year's at Hedy and Gabriel Mishlove's. The first alone. The last she planned to attend. The guests, overflowing the high-ceilinged living room, leaking into the study and halls, up onto the third-floor stairway, looked and sounded familiar, even if many were strangers. New names and faces, but the same script resumed after a 365-day intermission. The same players and the same play, the leads given to the liberal, the artsy, the verbal and the trendy, and bit parts to exotics—blue collar workers, old folks and unfashionable minorities.

A cross section was well and good, but there was something strained about Hedy's prepackaged New Year's mix, as if each guest filled an official slot on a master requisition list. One Innovative Artist. One Political Hopeful with Interesting Theories. Two Second-trimester Pregnancies . . .

Suzannah wasn't certain how her ticket of admission read. Perhaps she was a leftover, the remnant of a stale marriage included for old time's sake.

Or worse. She was Hedy's holiday charity. Remember the Needy.

Suzannah's cheeks burned. She clenched the newel post. Nobody turned to look her way. Nobody welcomed her. There was no easy entry into the party and she was back at terrible junior high dances when, sandy-haired and soft, bookish and shy, she had floated at the edge, a pale, unassimilated blob of flour in the gravy.

"Hey! Broker-lady! Get over here!"

The sound of Randy Smith was generally a signal to head the other way. But definitely not this time.

"Give us a kiss, Suzannah." He puckered his mouth, which lacked a noticeable upper lip and reminded Suzannah of a ventriloquist's dummy.

"RANNNNNdy!" Letty Smith's voice clanked, as if she dragged her irritations through a steel-lined throat. "*Really,* Randy!"

"Loosen up! It's New Year's." Randy hugged Suzannah, bruising her ribs and sensibilities, but he had pulled her into the party and she owed him. She stayed in his straggly circle through bad jokes and boring anecdotes, intermittently spotting and discreetly signaling friends across the room.

Then, head swiveled, a smile still on her lips, she stopped her general survey and stared at a new face, an unfamiliar face. But not one of Hedy's predictable types. Not one designed to fit a vacated space on Hedy's party roster. Suzannah couldn't understand how it had taken her a quarter of an hour to notice him.

He was put together the right way, seemed brighter than the rest, as if more attention had been given his fashioning. She felt an instant fizz of pleasure, liking his size, his colors, his dark mop of hair, his fair skin and flushed, prominent cheeks. She liked the large eyes behind the glasses and the intelligence they suggested.

For a second, he appeared startled, as if she had shocked him. Then he pushed his glasses up the bridge of his small nose, stared again and began moving towards her until someone touched his arm and he turned to respond.

Suzannah was no longer sorry she'd accepted Hedy's invitation.

"Excuse me, miss?" Suzannah swiveled to face a young twosome in construction worker disguise. The female half giggled. "My mistake, miss. Straight city, aren't you?"

Her male clone scowled. "Stop asking my mother's friends, stupid. Old people aren't into dope." They wandered away.

Suzannah bristled. Old? She yearned for a gold spoon or track marks as credentials. Old? How dare they reclassify her prematurely?

"Hey—Suzannah! Don't wander off without giving me a hot tip on the market!"

"RANNNNNdy! It's rude to talk about money at a party."

Suzannah ignored Letty's aluminum voice and searched for the man with the glasses, the green sweater and the face. She wanted to know if she could again affect him so mysteriously and profoundly.

She could not.

He was sculpted into a lean line of attention, bending to listen to a diminutive woman holding his arm. Disappointed, but safe from return scrutiny, Suzannah studied him openly.

He smiled at the small woman and Suzannah felt her own lips mime his delight. He nodded emphatically and said something, touching the woman's shoulder as he answered, his body readjusting to make contact.

His graceful, unconscious gesture sent pinpricks of pain through Suzannah. She caressed the flesh of her own shoulder and moved into his range. Then she stopped. He was engrossed in his conversation. Better to wait for a lull.

The little woman kept talking, tying him with a rope of words. Suzannah observed and waited, full of confidence. Her competition was small and plain, makeup poorly applied, bright caftan a sad attempt to hide plumpness. Nothing special and nothing to fear.

The man smiled and spoke pleasantly, comfortably. He nodded at what Suzannah felt was a shared reminiscence. He patted the woman's arm, adding a few words to her anecdote.

Suzannah became wary.

The way they stood, loosely but together, the very manner in which they spoke, they appeared comrades who'd shared a long, not always easy, history. The little dove of a woman didn't look like, couldn't be, a date. She looked and acted like a wife.

Suzannah pulled herself out of the man's magnetic field.

Scratch him. Scratch all married men. Married man meant schedules. Married man meant listening to long stories. Married man meant holidays spent alone. Otherwise, Michael Tully would be here with her, not home with his wife and baby.

She turned back to the dreadful Smiths, faced Letty and asked the obligatory "How are the children? Bet they keep you busy."

"I'll say!" And Letty did. Interminably. Her pasty face became animated as her metallic voice sparked off great moments in maternal history. "Busy! You wouldn't believe it!"

Suzannah retreated inside her head, listening to Letty only when necessary.

I believe it, Letty. You told me last year and the year before that.

"So I'm room mother to an overcrowded second grade . . ."

But *my* life is bleak, right? Because I haven't fulfilled my biological destiny. Because I permit sex without procreation.

". . . and we raised $2,000! Imagine, from castoffs . . ."

But when I make money, it's tainted because I do it for myself. Ah yes, and for the capitalization of world industry. But you produce consumers, Letty, and that's noble.

Letty completed her single song and clamped her mouth shut.

Suzannah smiled. Gracious behavior was easy when the end was in sight. "You do so much," she purred. "Now, if you'll excuse me, I need to find our hostess and a drink."

She kissed and chatted with a series of friends. She couldn't find Hedy Mishlove, but the invisible hostess' ragout simmered on, comforting in its predictable bubbles of sound.

". . . anything but starches. Fourteen pounds in five—"

"—and I say their quarterback can't—"

"We're looking further out. Prices here are completely—"

"The intermediate trail, see? And this shushboomer—"

It was atonal, but harmonious. In half an hour they'd join for "Auld Lang Syne," then splinter again, this time discarding diets, sports and real estate for arias more basic, songs of lust and money and who was cheating whom.

As if on cue in some miserable farce, Suzannah saw the redhead, a woman she'd thought of simply as "her" since last New Year's Eve.

The redhead smiled timidly, a cowed animal offering its neck as appeasement. Suzannah remained impassive until the redhead, blushing slightly, looked away. A hollow victory. Suzannah couldn't justify a grudge against the woman whose freckled cleavage and small belly had done nothing more than signal enough was enough. But seeing her turned Suzannah's mind directly towards Chris.

And she missed him. Like a gangrenous limb finally amputated, he was invisibly present and her mind tracked still on the missing nerve paths.

Chris had made Hedy's parties fun with his ruthless predawn dissection. Late, during their doomed attempts to stay up for the Mummers' Parade the next morning, Suzannah would chuckle as Chris MC'd The Ceremony, merging the worst of Oscar and Miss America.

"Ladies and gentlemen, the Sominex award this year goes to the single most soporific sentence of the night. The envelope, please? Ahhh . . . to Burton Beck. Mr. Beck would be here in person, but unfortunately, he's still in Hedy's dining room, trying to reach the punch line of his story. Accepting for him is his wife, no slouch at catatonia herself."

Chris had undoubtedly won Best Performance by a Consenting Male last year. Only they hadn't played The Ceremony. They'd spent the dawn snarling and hissing instead.

What a burlesque the night had been. Hedy had wanted Suzannah to see a Nigerian totem. Randy Smith lumbered along for reasons known to himself. By the time they reached the master bedroom, an unknown drunk lurched in their small parade.

They opened the door and entered, none but Suzannah registering the twosome sunk in the coats and scarves on the bed.

The thing that continued to rankle was that she had not been able to stop watching. Or to quell a rising tide of excitement.

The redhead's dress was unbuttoned, a freckled breast and stretch of abdomen exposed. And Chris's hand cupped the breast, then stroked it slowly, his fingers tracing its contours, learning and loving its swell. His head moved slowly on the other breast.

They looked timeless, as silent as a held breath as they lazily loved in their nest of fur.

Suzannah had watched the redhead arch towards Chris. His hand leisurely skimmed the surface of the breast, moved below it. And even watching, Suzannah felt the small of her back tighten, push, felt her nipples grow taut, her breath shallow.

And she shuddered. Her mind screamed.

We are all alike.

She wasn't sure if she spoke out loud. It didn't matter. She felt herself evaporate, become transparent, a different casing for the redhead's central nervous system. Chris's hand knew where to stroke, what to touch and it didn't matter what the receiver called herself.

I am her. She is me. There is no difference. I am not special.

And then the redhead moaned, Hedy turned from her dresser, Randy shouted whathefuckinhell and the drunk laughed hysterically.

"Christ on a crutch," he said between hiccups, "just like in the movies." He stumbled towards the bed, staring at the redhead as she buttoned her dress. "You're Frank's wife!" he shouted, pointing at the terrified woman.

Suzannah could play it through in slow motion, even though it had been small-scale chaos with the drunk and the woman, with Hedy's fevered attempts to pull the drunk away from her, to block Suzannah's line of vision and to stop Randy's threatened emasculation of Chris.

Only Chris had remained serene, buttoning his shirt carefully, readjusting his belt and helping the redhead off the mountains of fur.

"Sorry," he'd said, apologizing to his hostess. "I thought this was the maid's room."

And it was over. With a quip and a snip of the dry umbilical cord that bound them so loosely and had so long outlived its function. Whoever they were, whatever they did was singularly unoriginal. She couldn't think of a thing that was theirs except a desiccated legal definition.

She'd grinned rather foolishly, walked into the master bath, thrown up calmly and returned to the party, joining the dust motes, specks of nothing floating through the crowd.

Randy indignantly spread the news. The redhead's husband raced for coats and the exit and Hedy produced another round of hors d'oeuvres.

And through it all, Suzannah moved, impervious because nonexistent. And everyone agreed she was made of steel.

Including Chris, who never understood.

He didn't understand days later while she sorted household goods and emotions. "I still don't get it. For Christ's sake, Suzannah—a kiss at a party! What did I do?"

"What you did doesn't matter!"

"Then what does?" For once, Christopher Barnes, *bon vivant* and man of nonviolent passions, showed symptoms of incipient rage. "Does who keeps the original cast recording of A *Chorus Line* matter?" He snapped it in two.

"*I* matter. I have to! I—" But there was no language for what she felt. She knew she'd had an allergic reaction to conditions she had formerly tolerated. She knew she'd abruptly changed their ground rules, but she didn't know why and she didn't even know if there were twentieth-century terms for the archaic, primitive shock of betrayal and rage she'd felt in Hedy's bedroom.

Then she'd have to terminate—without an explanation—what Abby had called the wittiest marriage in Philadelphia. Good-by Mr. Wrong. For each girl child, as certain as the curse of a jealous witch, a Mr. Wrong. Hers, her Chris, had materialized one autumn, brighter than the burnt orange leaves, glimmering and glistening, the rainbow and pot of gold in one. The prince who conquered the tall thickets and found her, proving she must indeed be a princess.

Suzannah had never risked telling Chris she saw him as Prince Charming. They seldom used words like love, so how could she mention his rainbow aura, the spectrum wrapped around his person?

And it was just as well because the light and the rainbow faded. Despite the fine sound of their theory of nonpossessiveness, it hurt like hell hearing of Chris's outlandish and public escapades. The more she studied Prince Charming, the more he flattened into gold paint, rich pigment and slick high-gloss stock. An illustration as thin and insubstantial as the paper carrying it.

"What is suddenly wrong with us?" he had asked that night.

Months later, she wrote her answer on a ladies' room wall. "In life's exams, charm, wit and style do not fulfill minimum requirements. Final grade: Incomplete." She wrote her graffiti in pencil, in case it wasn't true.

But that night she had tripped over words and surprised herself with tears. "I want more. Something special. And if that doesn't exist, if nobody gets that, then I don't want anything. Nothing. No games." She looked up at the ceiling and blinked. "I don't feel free. I feel tied up by our new rules. There are so many, there's no meaning left.''

She admitted that their *détente* was her fault. That she'd begun hoping for a sort of sharing. A wholeness. A set-apartness. Maybe something impossible to achieve, but still . . . "God, it's embarrassing saying words like commitment,'' she said, ''but somehow, I—" Her words dried into silence when she saw Chris's face and felt his amusement.

''Aren't you continuing?" he asked.

She shook her head.

''Pity. It was marvelous. Like a drugstore romance—the sort with the heroine's cleavage on the cover. Oh, the tears and handwringing, the language, the ideas. Love's Fatuous Flatulence.''

She stopped explaining and never again tried grafting fairy-tale images onto real life tales.

She hated thinking about it and hated missing Chris although it perversely continued to happen. She shook herself back to the party and the present and realized a toothy male was blocking her way.

''I've been watching you,'' he said. ''You with anybody?''

She shook her head.

''So,'' he said, leaning into her face. ''What's your story? Like what do you do?'' He smelled of macho after-shave and girlie magazines.

''I'm a stockbroker.''

''Fan-TAS-tic!''

She despised him. She had a long list of qualities she abhorred in men. Fish-belly skin. Round stomachs. Skeletons that seemed brittle. Men waiting to be toppled.

She was a toppler, but the act was pleasureless, mechanical, like pushing aside a swinging door.

Men with hair on their shoulders. Men who perspired inappropriately. Man who laughed at their own jokes. Men who didn't laugh at hers. Men who laughed too much at hers.

This man.

''You sure don't look like a stockbroker.'' He snorted and wagged a finger. ''No, you don't.'' He touched the gold chain at his neck and patted his expensive precision-cut hair. ''Now me, what do you think I am?''

A schmuck, she wanted to answer, but instead she studied his

Mexican wedding shirt, rich with embroidery, his designer jeans and turquoise-embedded moccasins. "A C.P.A."

His face fell. "Howja know?"

"Lucky guess." She spotted Abby and waved, as if in reply, then excused herself.

"Where have you been?" Abby demanded. "Meet Tonio and don't be sanctimonious. He becomes taller when he stands on his money."

Suzannah looked down at a small male made even more diminutive by his grand European bow. Abby's man of the week.

Suzannah had earlier questioned the relationship. Tonio possessed thirty-eight years' seniority, one wife, five children and thirteen grandchildren in Italy. To balance such dubious assets, he lacked size and English.

"He's clean, unkinky and generous," Abby had answered with a shrug. "What more can a woman hope for?"

A high school teacher had once labeled the two girls "the ant and the grasshopper." "You have nothing in common with that Abby," she had sanctimoniously informed Suzannah, the ant. "Nothing." That teacher had been correct, if years of friendship and mutual need were considered "nothing."

Tonio completed his bow with the smallest of heel clicks. Suzannah tried to exude an international language of good will, but leaping across linguistic barriers was exhausting, and whenever Tonio was responding, enthusiastically and unintelligibly, she let her eyes wander around the room.

And they found him again, the green sweater highlighting the face, the face, alas, smiling at the dreary wife.

Her hostess, Hedy Mishlove, materialized and diverted Suzannah's attention. "Darling," she said, rubbing cheeks and making kissing sounds. "Forgive. So busy with the cheese puffs. How are you?"

Suzannah side-stepped the question. Hedy meant it. She had Gabriel's wedding band, children and, she believed, knowledge. Freud, Jung and Reich, absorbed by insemination.

Luckily, tonight Hedy was consumed with party giving. "Are you having a good time? Eaten yet? Beautiful dress you're wearing. I like that peach shade. Have you met the fellow who makes collages from exposed film? Or the Afghan? Or my cousin?"

The year before, Suzannah spent an agonizing half-hour with a

Rumanian pole-vaulter and, in the year since, too many hours with people's cousins.

"Better find somebody," Hedy said, winking. "It's nearly midnight, you know."

"I'll see what I can find. If nothing else, a drink." Suddenly, Suzannah really needed something to wash away a wad of misery in her throat. New Year's Eve mattered after all. She believed, rationally or not, that what one did at the stroke of midnight shaped the coming months.

A year ago, she'd been dazed, acknowledging the death of her marriage. Ringing out the old. And the year that followed had taken the pain and confusion of that moment as its leitmotif, playing it back, amplifying it, working variations on its themes.

Suzannah had come here to prove she was fine on her own. Hedy and Gabriel and their guests would pair off, seal midnight and shape the year with kisses. Suzannah would watch, turning inside out to whisper sweet promises in her own ear.

She went in search of the bar cart.

He pushed his glasses up the bridge of his nose.

"I love this sweater, Jacob," Rachel said. He watched her small hand flutter and land on his arm. "This shade of green reminds me of August in the Poconos. And makes me thirsty. Can I trouble you for a refill?"

She held up her glass so winsomely, adding so many unspoken requests, that he smiled and set out for the bar, upset again, unable again to ask why tonight she'd switched to Jacob instead of Coby, which everyone, including Rachel, called him.

Who was Jacob Waldemar? A distant ancestor? A dear little man in suspenders humming Yiddish tunes as he measured groats in a shtetl market.

He was Coby, even if Rachel made "Jacob" sound a secret name, a password for intimates.

She was so nervous, this new Rachel. So pathetically jolly. What had happened to sane Rachel the psychology professor who car-pooled from Narberth to Temple University with him?

She'd seemed normal enough when he'd invited her. He'd explained that one of his night school students had invited him, that he'd like her to come with him. He'd thought Rachel a wise choice, the invitation another bond in their friendship.

But the moment he'd arrived at her house, he'd seen the mutation. It wasn't her perfume, the filigreed earrings or unfamiliar makeup. It was an almost visible quiver of expectation, a giddy silliness draping her more completely than her caftan. He hadn't meant tonight as prelude to anything, but she'd obviously interpreted it that way and he liked her too much to hurt her by explaining.

This was really going to screw up their car-pooling.

He neared the crowded bar cart and waited his turn, in no hurry to rejoin the disappointing party. Hedy had promised a smorgasbord of appealing women. He had to disagree.

There's been one, though. The one who reminded him of Dana. God it had startled him, suddenly seeing that hair, that same small definite chin, the coloring and the smile. But whoever she was seemed to disappear when he sought her out and to turn from his glance when he did find her.

His head hurt. The music blared out of a nearby speaker, and people shouted above it. Music or talk, Coby believed, but not both fighting for air time at once. He turned his back to the speaker.

And found himself facing her. The small firm chin, the mellow hair, the gray-gold eyes, the radiant face itself.

And most of all, the smile. The smile beaming at him.

During his depressed teens, he had been periodically flooded with a manic wave of hope and happiness. His mother's sigh, her "Coby's flying again," would dampen and define his seizure.

He felt it happening now. He was lifting off. If not yet airborne, then at least racing towards cliff edge, arms flapping wildly. He moved closer to her. "Hi," he said.

Her smile froze. "Hi," she replied with no interest. She directed her attention back to the bar, smiled broadly again and giggled.

Her smile had been for the bartender. Coby was no more than an unwelcome intrusion, a break in her laughter.

He skidded to a stop, tottered at the edge of the ravine, let his arms hang limp.

"What else?" he heard her say and her voice delighted him with its throatiness, its low timbre. "You're lucky nobody had a heart attack! Pretending to shoot somebody! Hiring people to stage a dangerous thing like that!"

The bartender held up his hand, keeping her near while he worked. "Help you, sir?"

Coby put the empty glasses on the cart. "I need white wine and . . ."

The girl glanced his way, her gray and gold-flecked eyes wide. He loved her silky hair, her skin, the dress clinging to her curves, all of her.

"Sir?" the bartender prompted, pouring wine.

"A . . ." What the hell was Rachel drinking? Why had he brought her here, anyway?

The girl waited to resume her tête-à-tête with the bartender. Coby was annoying her. "Ummmm . . . ahh . . ." He needed to fill the yawning silence. "Ur . . . ahm . . ." He couldn't remember what in God's name Rachel looked like, let alone drank.

"Must have suffered a stroke," he said. "Part of my brain died. Amnesia, just like that." He snapped his fingers and could have amputated them instantly, for confirming that he was a fool, a buffoon.

She didn't seem to find his antics charming or even vaguely interesting. She gestured at the empty glass on the bar cart. "She obviously drinks liquor, not wine." Her voice was cool, as effective as a poker held straight to keep him at his distance.

The bartender and the girl exchanged a quick glance. "Take all the time you need, sir," the man behind the cart said, then he resumed his conversation. "One party, I don't know it, see, but they hire a couple." He kept his voice low and confidential.

"Scotch," Coby said abruptly. They looked at him blankly. "Please?"

The bartender nodded and poured. "So after dinner, this couple starts making it. Pull off every stitch, but slow like, taking their sweet time, messing around. Then right there on the carpet, between people's feet, they do it."

He handed the glass to Coby.

"What did the other guests do?" the girl asked.

"Water," Coby said.

"Water? I don't get it."

"Water." Coby's voice croaked. Dirges for bullfrogs. "She likes water in her scotch."

There was a moment's merriment at his expense in the girl's eyes. The bartender took back the glass and resumed his story. "Nothing. Nobody even says what you doin' down there? They pretend like they're not watching. But my business is sure slow during it. Then, when they're done, they get dressed and start mingling like nothing happened. Everybody else starts talking and drinking again.''

Coby accepted the scotch and water but refused to leave. If he held his ground, maybe he'd figure out how to distract a woman who wouldn't notice him from a story about a couple fucking their brains out in the middle of a party. But he doubted it.

"At Hedy's," the girl said, "I think a few souls would join in. A few would call the cops. And Gabriel and his buddies would crouch down and suggest the couple work through their exhibitionist compulsions."

Coby smiled, silently applauding her wit, her sound, her style. She observed his smile, then let her eyes linger on his hands and the drinks. "The ice in your lady's drink will melt," she said. Then she glided away.

What had he done or not done to be so ignorable?

"Beautiful, ain't she?" the bartender said, man-to-man style. He gazed at the cart as if sorry there was no sweep of mahogany to wipe down. "But tough."

"Confusing," Coby murmured, nodding farewell.

"Jacob! I've been looking for you!" Rachel visibly relaxed as she neared him. She accepted her drink and linked her arm in his.

He spotted her again, the "ice" girl. He smiled again, and she smiled back, but wryly, subtly shaking her head "no." As if he were asking old questions and she were giving old answers. "No." Again. And you should have known. But also, it was okay to have asked.

Rachel steered him into the living room. "Our hostess has a request," she said.

Hedy raked her hands through her wild, witchy hair. "I can't find my record of 'Auld Lang Syne,' " she said. "I know it's an imposition, but could you play it on the piano at midnight? Would you?"

"Sure," Coby answered. "Why not?"

If nothing else, it would save him the embarrassment of Rachel's upturned face. He'd seat her beside him on the bench and give her a friendly car-pooler's peck at midnight. That was definitely all.

She turned away. The man in the green sweater was again glued to his little woman and Suzannah would never encourage him to pull free.

There was no such thing as a free, as a clean, break. Men stumbled away from familiar supports, messed with wet cement, mucking all they touched with the sticky ends of their histories.

Sad sagas lasted longer than sex. The trade-off wasn't worth it.

She wished it were as easy to dismiss her other irritants. Something had gone askew in the last half-hour. Her wine tasted sour as did the party, which had been intended as her triumphal march.

She didn't know why. She knew she looked good—maybe no longer post-divorce mannequin thin, but good enough. And she was good. She'd made $45,000 before taxes and that was a beginning only, her first full year with Sherwood Hastings. She had loyal clients, an antique Aubusson on her living room floor and a very ambitious future she knew she'd realize.

There were no rust spots in her armor. She had men. After Chris, she'd proven her attractiveness with a string of them. And if they'd been nothing special, well that's how most men were.

However. She'd come to make this evening hers, to wipe away the last trace of Chris, but his ghost hovered by her elbow, chortling. He'd been fun, her Chris, and she missed that. She wanted to laugh, in bed and out. Wanted the nooks and crannies of the world brightly painted without having to make every brush stroke herself.

She wanted what never had been to return.

Abby, with her mysterious radar—her Eastern legacy, she'd once explained—was suddenly by her side. "Don't." She put her hand on Suzannah's shoulder. "Wherever you are, come back. Be with us. Rub Tonio's head at midnight for luck."

Suzannah hugged her.

"Meanwhile," Abby continued, "there's this Afghan person here. Back home, he's a jock—plays a game called *buzkashi.*"

A swarthy man beamed at them both.

"Hey, Abdur, tell Suzannah how you get on horseback and drag a dead calf across the goal line."

"Haven't they discovered the ball yet?" Suzannah said.

"Ask him. Do you speak much Pushto?"

People were studying watches, finding each other. Suzannah moved closer to Tonio. She would not usher in a year with a Pushto-speaking calf-dragger. God alone knew what that could forebode.

"Is there a Suzannah Barnes here?" One of the teen-age construction workers shouted down from the staircase. "Phone for a Suzannah Barnes."

Suzannah anxiously made her way to the staircase. Was her mother finally forsaking hypochondria for real illness? Was her father abruptly remembering her existence?

She nervously settled on the pile of coats in Hedy's bedroom and felt furious with herself. She could have used the kitchen extension. There was no need to revisit this bed, to make a pilgrimage to the spot.

"Yes?" she said, tensing.

"Happy New Year, my love." The voice was overly careful, a bit drunk, more than a bit unhappy. "Don't hang up. I had to call you. I'm having the worse New Year's of my life. The worst year. I need you."

"Don't do this, Chris."

"You must feel it, too. You must! We were special together. I can't stop thinking of you, whoever I'm with."

"If you were with me, you'd be able to."

Downstairs, the stereo became silent. "Midnight!" somebody shouted. "Happy New Year!" in ragged chorus. "Happy New Year!"

"You never understood me. But you loved me, Suzannah. You did. I remember every detail and I know what was real . . ."

Chris continued, stamping the new year his, using up the special moment the calendar was flipped and everything changed. Below, piano chords, false starts, shreds of "Auld Lang Syne." The chorus, thin and punctuated by laughter and shouts, made its way up the stairs into the bedroom.

" 'Should auld acquaintance be forgot . . .' "

"Chris, stop. I won't play this game any more."

" '. . . a-yund never brought to mind . . .' "

"Where in that hard shell are you hiding, Suzannah? You can't be happy. You must still feel something. Don't you? Don't you feel anything?"

" '. . . weel drinka cuppa kindness then . . .' "

"I can't feel anything any more, Chris. I don't want to feel anything any more."

"I wanted you at midnight."

"I know. You almost always did." She hung up the phone, no longer hearing music.

* * *

Coby watched his fingers move over the keys with a life and intelligence of their own. Beside him, Rachel all but purred.

It hadn't been a peck at all. He'd forgotten that the music started after the bewitching moment, that even the piano player was given time with a woman.

It had been unexpectedly pleasant. Tentative, promising, frightened, but all the same, warm and comforting. Maybe not wrong for now.

Last New Year's Eve he'd wound up in the Emergency Room at Lankenau Hospital, a bloody drunk with a lacerated right hand. He'd been out of his mind, squeezing his champagne glass until it splintered and became part of him, then driving through the night alone, shouting curses, glass spikes spearing his palm, his mind frozen with the possibility that he'd ruined his hand and his chance to make music.

But he had not. The surgeon stitched up his spell of doing damage, and only a star-burst scar remained.

He played another chorus, pouring his energy into his fingers, and the people around him responded with still more gusto.

"You really do make music," Rachel said. "Would you play more?"

"Anything," the group said. "Anything we can sing to."

Coby felt a surge of love for the faces around the piano, and play he did, request after request, improvising when he wasn't sure, creating wild variations when he was. And eventually, memories slid away as did midnight, and he was buoyant on an ocean of notes.

He scanned the circle as he played, wondering if the woman in the peach dress, the ice maiden, would relent and join him in even a peripheral way.

" *'Sorode Jamhouriat'* ?" a swarthy man asked. "Afghan song."

"Can you hum a bar or two?"

Welcome back, Coby, he thought as he and the Afghan poked and laughed their way through a skewed series of notes.

Rachel tilted towards him, touched shoulders, laughed.

But why hadn't the ice maiden come over, taken notice? What was so wrong with him?

He played a resounding finale. "Enough!" he announced. "I'll be back." What was wrong with him was that he hadn't asked, hadn't found out why the hell she was so distant. But dammit, he would now. He most certainly didn't react that way to a face, a voice and chemistry often enough to be blasé about it.

He scanned the room, ready and confident.

She was nowhere in sight.

"Are you lost, piano man?"

It was the Eurasian, her almond eyes almost on a level with his. She was gorgeous, but she wasn't the one.

"Do you know a girl wearing a kind of pink dress? About this tall, with odd-blond hair, grayish eyes?"

Abby grinned as if he'd said a great deal. "Suzannah Barnes? Sure. I've known her since Miss Popper's preschool."

He was tempted to pause for a full biography of the newly identified Suzannah. "Do you know where she is?"

Abby shrugged, nearly springing a breast from its halter. "She had a call. Maybe she's still upstairs."

Even better. She'd be alone. Coby took the steps two at a time. He tried a door, interrupted two naked teen-agers.

"Jesus, man! People knock!" the boy-half shouted.

He found the phone in the last room down the hall, but he did not find Suzannah.

The bathroom was open and empty. It seemed ridiculous, even to Coby, to begin checking closets. He walked back down the hall, this time slowly.

Abigail Newhouse wafted by the foot of the staircase. "Somebody saw Suzannah leave right after midnight. Sorry."

"Oh. Well. Sure. It doesn't matter."

Rachel approached and put a small hand on his sleeve. "I promised Nancy I'd take her to the Mummers' Parade tomorrow, and it's getting late, so maybe we should . . ."

"Oh," he said again. "Well. Sure."

Out in the quiet, frosted street, Rachel tilted her head. "Did you say something, Jacob?"

He shook his head. "Only that for a musician, I have the worst sense of timing imaginable. And, Rachel, could you call me Coby? It's more . . . comfortable."

He put his arm around her shoulder and walked her to his car and into a comfortable and pleasant, if somewhat pallid, new year.

Two

Suzannah's mouth shaped a scream. Her heart raced.

It had happened again.

The dream was so familiar, replayed so often, that whenever it began, she heard warnings and cries of alarm.

But she always brushed them aside and glided through mist to a doorway, to a resplendent guard waiting, nodding, his uniform's gold trim gleaming through the fog. "You," he'd murmur. "Yes. They'll love you."

"Love you," he repeated, caressing and guiding her.

They would. She knew they'd love her. She'd practiced so hard, learned so many special steps, they'd have to love her.

She whirled into the blinding spotlight blowing kisses, pirouetting, leaping. The pale, dimly seen audience applauded lightly, politely, so she leaped higher, redoubling her efforts to find and force out the love. Every muscle straining, she leaped again—and soared—flew—up above the stage, up, up into the wires and secret spots no one had seen before.

She waited.

So did the audience, pallid, heavy and bored.

And into the silence rushed the warnings she had brushed aside. "Stop!" they cried. "They don't want—they only want—don't try—stop—they—"

"No!" she howled, for they were death. *"No!"* But terror held her fast, paralyzed her at the high mark of her leap. And she saw, from up high, the audience become alert and bend forward as one.

From behind the spotlights came a guttural hum of anticipation. Lips smacking.

"No!" She looked for help in the wings, but the golden guard had gone. "No!" She tried to hide near the roof, but the audience, growing pinker, laughed, then laughed again, harder and louder, their hot breath engulfing her, swallowing her.

She knew she couldn't hold on, knew she must fall, would fall. *Did* fall—tumbling and spinning, down, endlessly, plummeting forever, over and over, until finally, there was a bottom and an end.

"No!" she screamed a last time, smashing into the floor boards, breaking, cracking, crashing, shattering, snapping her brittle bones.

Bits of herself littered the stage like rubbish.

And the audience inhaled and expanded, became thunderously alive, turning rosy, then crimson, laughing, applauding.

She shriveled, dissolved, became transparent and fragmented and that made them laugh all the harder.

This was what they had craved. Not her dance, but her humiliation. A failure feast.

They drooled. They salivated, they approached with hot breath, rooting, snuffling, grunting, closer and closer until she smelled the stench of their appetites, until she felt their power grow as they mutated, fusing into one hideous mouth whose bloated lips searched the stage, whose fangs ripped at the bits and pieces, shreds and small screams that were all that remained of Suzannah. She gasped for breath—

And sat up in bed, in a real night, in her own room. Alive, but with the sour taste of the dream hot on her tongue. Breathing heavily, she touched squares of antique fabric like the beads of a rosary. Her comforter's patchwork was made of souvenirs of luxurious, long-ago lives. Sometimes, after the nightmare, Suzannah held the satin, velvet and lace and envied the original owners their lives. Their crinolines and fans, hope chests and tapestry lessons. Their clear rules, set manners and safety. Most of all, their being taken care of.

But only sometimes.

Michael Tully slept on his side of the bed. Awake, his eyes often struck something dissonant. They were close-set and edged with tension. But asleep, one arm flung up, almost touching the brass headboard, Tully, if not Suzannah, found peace.

She edged off the bed, found her robe and went to the kitchen, trying to leave the dream and her anxiety behind.

But her anxiety persisted and multiplied. She knew she

couldn't truly lose it, that over the last few weeks it had metasta-sized and replaced the healthy cells of her brain and body.

The oven clock read four fifty-three.

She went into the living room and lit a cigarette. If only she believed in magic, she'd insist that Chris had cast an evil spell New Year's Eve. He'd appropriated midnight and its potential and nothing had gone well for her since.

All over the world there were take-overs, tender offers, mer-gers and splits. All over the world money spilled from its con-tainers, falling into waiting hands. But not hers. At some point the bandwagon had departed without her, and it wouldn't slow down no matter how fast she tried racing behind it.

She was going to lose some of her best customers if she didn't come up with something bright, and soon. Twice now her goddamn selfish pig of an office manager had distributed new of-ferings to his cronies, the office stars, telling Suzannah he was sorry, but.

Some clients weren't even bothering to call her about exciting offerings. They called other houses instead.

She stubbed out her cigarette and smiled ironically. There was one client she'd never lose, unfortunately. Potter Alexander, who'd awakened her at 11:37 P.M. tonight, who'd called sixteen other times during the past twenty-four hours. Potter Alexander, portfolio manager for a small mutual fund, he of the facial tic and nervous hiccups, would never desert Suzannah. Potter trusted her and no one else.

And if Potter's nervous system lay on top of his skin and audi-bly short-circuited all day and night, then she'd think instead of the commission dollars he generated. The way things were going, she had no choice.

She walked to the window, hugging herself and staring into the night. It was still difficult to breathe easily. The day, the days, the night and nights, had been too much.

There's been Olive Watkins, so eager to believe her hairdress-er's hot tip, she was risking her entire portfolio. And Suzannah, unless she took elaborate legal cover, would eventually be sued, charged with ruining the widow woman's life.

The day, with Potter's calls, with her office manager's eva-sions, with her growing sense of confusion and loss—the god-damned day had so weakened her that she'd made it worse by twice agreeing to perform onerous tasks. First, a Patty Luboff had tooled in from suburbia and weasled Suzannah into participating in a study of women in the financial world. Patty wanted a Ph.D. Suzannah didn't care. So Patty waved a red flag—said something incredible about her professor's contempt for businesswomen, a species he called "cold-blooded mutations" who'd never help a poor graduate student find her data. And naturally, Suzannah jumped for the bait and insisted she'd prove that chauvinist scholar was dead wrong.

Lucky Suzannah. She was really showing him—by having to fill out one hundred and seventeen questions on twenty typed pages.

Then, kicking the victim while she was still down, Suzannah's sister Josie had phoned and conned her into visiting their mother this coming night.

She took a deep breath and shook her head. After the dreaded maternal visitation, she had a class to teach, and she was no teacher.

She felt near tears. It was all too much. Too complicated. Too difficult.

She looked outside, suddenly aware of an overwhelming stillness. The world five stories down was white and silent, not yet disturbed by plows or the clank of chained wheels. An enchanted etching, black trees against the white, a moonlit wash from starry skies. Across the wide parkway, the art museum's buff glow warmed the virginal night, classical lines dominating its hill, east and west wings spread to embrace the now-soft contours of its staircase.

She stood by the window wishing she could sink into the whiteness, become the snow.

Tully wheezed and snorted inside her bedroom, shattering the stillness.

She didn't want him here any more. Didn't want to share the silence now or breakfast coffee later.

Time to bid adieu.

Once, it had felt close to spontaneous, having him ring her doorbell, wake her as his needs dictated, and to return to her still-warm bed, to sink half back into sleep in his embrace.

Tully's timing had been right. He'd appeared, ready to listen and console when she was raw from her break. Through the hours after midnight, they had talked and made love, both actions binding Suzannah's wounds and helping Tully unravel a hopelessly snarled marriage.

But Suzannah's marriage was now ancient history and Tully's ongoing domestic woes and jokes had become stale.

And more important, now she needed all her energy for her work. She couldn't keep sapping it with distractions like men and night games.

Time to simplify life.

Suzannah walked into the kitchen and poured herself a glass of wine. The dream still clung faintly, small talons scratching her shoulders and glassy fears bobbing like jellyfish in the surf.

She became impatient with herself. She couldn't keep pacing and palpitating, yearning for something good miraculously to appear. She had to do something, keep busy, at least seem to be making progress.

She returned to the living room and gathered up her class notes, pausing to view again the unnaturally peaceful cityscape below. Nature triumphant, concrete conquered, a pastoral overlay so oddly seductive, she decided to work away from it, in the kitchen.

She padded quietly back on tiptoe.

And Tully snored. Loudly, jaggedly.

Enough of intruders and intrusions, distractions and annoyances.

She turned on the light and the radio, then slammed the louvered kitchen door with such force it snapped into rigidity with a resounding thwack. She heard Tully inhale and say "Whazza?" and she felt oddly proud, as if she'd done something difficult.

"Zannah?" Then a mighty set of yawns, knee and arm joints creaking, thud of feet and the kitchen door again bending back. "What are you doing up?" He yawned and rubbed his swell of stomach.

He was naked and shivering, his pale torso a goose-bumped plastic baby-doll's. He was an attractive man, but there was something not yet fully molded about him that never would reach completion because he was subtly decaying in his mid-thirties.

"Sorry I woke you," she muttered.

"Z'all right." He squinted at the oven clock, then padded out of the room, returning wrapped in her comforter, carrying cigarettes. He put the kettle on the range and searched her cabinets for instant coffee.

She usually ground beans and brewed her favorite blend, but she sat on the stool doing nothing because she didn't care about quality control for the last cup they'd share.

Tully lit a cigarette and suddenly, Suzannah became her normal self, a person who abhorred cigarette smoke before morning coffee. She waved at the air in front of her. Tully, watching the kettle, was oblivious to her silent protests. She decided she couldn't stand him.

"Haven't been sleeping well myself," he said. He raked his fingers through his pale hair.

"Tully, have you had your eyes checked lately?"

"Why?"

"You always squint."

He shrugged. The comforter slipped down his pale shoulders. "What are you doing with those papers?"

"I'm starting a second career. Moonlighting as a teacher, starting tonight. I hear it's a great way to drum up business." She waited until he filled two cups with powder and boiling water and was seated on the stool next to hers. "Tully," she began, "this might not be the right time, but I don't know when will be."

He pulled the comforter tighter.

"This isn't good for either of us. You'll have to resolve Marietta one way or the other yourself. And this late-night business is exhausting me. You said you'd be here at a decent hour, but midnight isn't decent."

"I was tied up."

"That's not the point. I don't think we're good for each other any more. Not even as holding actions."

"Holding actions? What are you saying? What's going on?" He inhaled deeply on his cigarette and coughed, shaking his cocoon.

"We're stale. I think it's time to, ah . . ."

"Since when?" He became guarded. "What are you suddenly not getting from me?"

"It isn't that." She put her hand on his cushioned shoulder. "I simply can't function on three hours' sleep. I'm falling apart."

"For God's sake, I'm not here every night."

She sighed with exasperation. Why wouldn't he bow out gracefully? "I work late other nights, have business dinners."

"So cut back there. Sleep those nights."

"Dammit, Tully, don't be so dense! We didn't have some major thing and I don't have to justify my priorities to you!"

He nodded, silently acknowledging her message. "You don't even have to mention your priorities," he eventually said, his voice frozen solid. "There's only one. Money. When we were still that minor thing, it was our guilty little joke, wasn't it? We were soul mates." He stood up, then cleared his throat. "I, ah, I want to get this straight because I thought we . . . I was under the impression that the touching, the being together, the talking, the . . . I thought it was pretty important. I mean not very long ago, in your bedroom—"

"Don't."

"You're—you're serious, then? This is it? Now? Like this?" She nodded.

He whistled softly. "Christ." He picked up his cigarettes and wrapped the comforter under his arm. Caesar in padded toga. "Decent of you to allow naps before execution. Is that your standard procedure? And are the condemned allowed a final wash-up in the shower?"

"I wish you wouldn't act this way."

"I'm showing admirable dignity for the man who just fucked Lizzie Borden." He left the kitchen.

Suzannah tried to work on her class notes. She heard a gush of water hit the shower curtain and she waited for Tully to begin singing his predictable *Man of La Mancha* selections. But this morning, he remained silent.

She felt a twinge of guilt. Five hours earlier he'd arrived, snow on his hair, shaking himself dry like a puppy. They'd shared brandy, talk and her bed. Nothing had changed but Suzannah, and even so, efficiency, not brutality, had been her object. She'd botched it.

She would make an act of contrition. She'd listen. Tully might lavishly praise her body, but it was her ears he coveted, her receptivity as listener, not lover.

Meanwhile, she wrote Roman numerals on a clean sheet of paper and thought about her class. Before she touched on pragmatic investment decisions, she'd link her women to the concept of economics. "Ladies," she could say, "it matters which toilet paper you squeeze."

No. She would not be patronizing. Maybe she'd simply ask what issues bothered them, show how everything affected the flow of money around the globe. She could only hope that something besides menopause and marital busts troubled their heads.

The shower sounds stopped. She stood and put a filter in the Melita, ground beans and boiled water.

Tully, reassembled in soft blue shirt, dark suit and calm expression, eventually re-entered the kitchen and stood, squinting. Something in his stance frightened her, and she spoke quickly. "Stay, Tully. I'm making real coffee. I didn't mean to hand you eviction papers, just . . ." She put her hands up in mock despair. "Can't think of a suitable metaphor."

He sat down and she readied herself for news of his wife.

"One cup," he said. "I'm really beat. This thing at work . . ."

"What thing?" The coffee aroma filled the small kitchen. If someone grew a bean that tasted the way it smelled, she'd be the first to invest in its stock.

"Chemfax. The take-over. Didn't I mention it earlier? I'm sure it's only a rumor." He sipped coffee.

"What take-over? Chemfax taking over what?"

"You mean you haven't heard anything? My firm. Tydings and Roy. My honored employers."

"Haven't heard a thing. Ignore it. There are always rumors. Means nothing."

"But, Jesus, dinner tonight made me so jumpy. Everybody's scared. There's talk Chemfax will bring in their own people, maybe relocate the whole place, incorporate our jobs into positions they already have. A job like mine—they have their own public relations people, for Christ's sake. It scares the shit out of me."

"Who'd you have dinner with?"

"Fellow named Gregory Fine. Guys from my office. Why?"

"Who is this Fine?"

"He's with Chemfax. In development. Supposedly we were talking about an industrial park. But after he left, I needed five Mylanta."

"Why?"

"It felt like he was digesting us, not the lobster tails. Something's happening, Suzannah."

"It's your imagination."

"No, people talk specifics. People say a take-over by March, people say Chemfax is going to do half a share for one of ours. People—''

"People always talk. Ignore it."

"And with Marietta threatening to take every cent . . .''

Suzannah made sympathetic noises, her mind firmly lodged on his professional woes, not his personal. She felt a rising excitement. To be in at the beginning!

"She's growing leeches in the basement, the better to bleed me dry." He stopped, checking on Suzannah's attention. "I'll be a pauper. An unemployed pauper."

She shook her head and sipped coffee. He gulped the rest of his down, then stood. "I can't relax, might as well go in early and see what I can do to save my ass."

He went in search of his topcoat. She remained at the counter, doodling concentric circles on her notes.

A take-over.

He returned and kissed her cheek and she put her head against his chest. "Listen, Tully, we had some fine times. I didn't mean to negate them."

"Sure," he said. "I know."

She heard the distant whine of heavy motors. The snowplows were out. "Drive carefully. The side streets will be tricky."

"Right."

She followed him to the front door and unlocked several sets of chains and bars. He paused in his exit and spoke, sounding uncomfortable. "Ah, about the . . . the rumors? I shouldn't have said anything. If any of this leaked, well you know . . .''

"Tully! We're friends, remember? You can count on me."

He smiled and said nothing.

"Keep in touch, Tully," she said, and she locked the door. She had time to shower and wash her hair. To drink more coffee, think and plan.

She walked aimlessly around the living room, trailing her fingers over the sand linen of the sofa. The room was spacious but seemed enormous because of its sparse furnishings. The Aubusson's shell pink and pale turquoise glowed in the white light of dawn.

Absently, she lit another cigarette and seated herself on the sofa. In front of her the coffee table held a malachite cigarette box, an ashtray, a nest made of a web of gilt filaments holding a golden egg, a bronze unicorn engraved with mysterious inscrip-

tions and a stack of *Architectural Digests*. Suzannah thumbed
through one of them, then let it sit open on her lap. Generally,
when she had leisure, she studied them, then haunted auction
houses and fine shops, ferreting out the best, only as she could
afford it. The corners of the room would be filled in, but never
with substitutes, never with imitations or approximations of what
she desired. It was best to deny admission to such things. The
second-rate had a way of latching hold, wheedling its owners
into acceptance.

This particular dawn didn't feel like leisure time. Her muscles
twitched for activity. She replayed Tully's conversation, weigh-
ing its potential worth, him, his possible motives, reasons for
sharing such valuable news.

She believed that everyone was given two or three chances a
lifetime, chances that were proffered without fanfare or hidden
out of sight, wedged into cracks in the sidewalk.

Most pedestrians walked blindly by or saw the possibility as an
obstruction to be kicked aside. They plodded for life.

But for those with quick vision and, more important, the heart
and strength to force it free, the potential was limitless.

Only two or three times per lifetime.

This chance was hers.

She filled with the heat of certainty and smiled. Tully was a
fool, easily distracted by attention. He had no ulterior motives.
Thinking only of his miseries, he'd gushed too freely and shared
what should have been kept secret. He was undoubtedly parlay-
ing his information into cash himself, and there was no reason
she shouldn't do the same.

She squelched a momentary twinge of conscience. Ridiculous.
Acting on inside information was illegal—but only if someone
could prove she was doing so. And she wasn't. Not really. She
had, more or less, overheard something worth further investigation. Been given a lead to follow. So it really wasn't as if she
were contemplating a crime. She wouldn't so much act on inside
information as on what she could find to corroborate it.

It was, perhaps, a question of ethics, but who was she to debate such issues at dawn? The fools who dithered and delayed
that way missed every chance and never knew why they were
losers. The earth the meek inherited was dry, dusty and empty.

She breathed deeply and thought again about Tully's information. If she found evidence backing it—and she was certain she

would—she'd behave with perfect decorum. She would love, honor and obey the Securities and Exchange Commission's rules as well as those of all the other governmental and industry regulatory bodies. They said she couldn't act on inside information, so she wouldn't. They said she couldn't disseminate rumor, so again, she would not. She would disseminate her own opinions, based on her own research.

No evildoer, she. No criminal. But no fool, either.

Ah but this was a glorious dawn. She smiled in grateful memory of Tully's generosity. Nobody had ever given her such a lavish farewell gift. Certainly not at five in the morning.

Three

Nick DiRuggio held a steaming styrofoam cup, using both hands as if presenting a chalice. "Here," he said to Suzannah. "You've been too busy to find your own, and your dissipated face keeps me from my work." He returned to his side of the Plexiglas desk divider.

"Thanks, but of what relevance is my appearance?"

"I sit here wondering. Who is it that keeps her up all night? What is it he does? Why won't she let me do it?"

"Why does she have to remind him about his wife?"

"She doesn't. I remember Amelia. I love Amelia. I'd never be emotionally unfaithful to her. All I want is some tawdry, meaningless sex."

Suzannah grinned as she dialed her phone.

"Hey," Nick called over. "What's your sign?"

"This isn't a singles' bar, Nick."

"Isn't your birthday around Valentine's Day? Couple weeks from now?"

She nodded. A prim telephone voice issued from the receiver. "Dr. Locker's office," it said, stepping gingerly around the syllables. "I'll see if Doctor is free."

It was a mystery, the affectation that made M.D. and dental staffs fastidiously drop "the" when referring to their employers.

"Then you're Aquarius, Suze," from behind the Plexiglas. "Your horoscope says, 'Know what good friends expect and try to please as much as you can.' "

Suzannah's receiver played pasteurized recorded music.

"I'm your good friend, right?" Nick continued. "You could please me. I'm thinking of getting into adultery."

Suzannah giggled and cupped her hand over her musical mouthpiece. "Don't. Not until you lose your Holy Child High vocabulary. Adultery!" She chuckled again, then stopped as the prim voice replaced the musical pap.

"Doctor will be with you in a moment. Will you hold?"

"Certainly. For *the* doctor." Suzannah had something to distract Richard Locker's attention from rotten gum sockets. Tully's fears of a take-over seemed grounded in reality.

Tydings and Roy Development had enjoyed an interesting month. For years undervalued, it had hovered near 5 or 6 and moved roughly 5,000 shares a week. Nothing. Until one month ago when it began humming and shaking. By a week ago Monday, 2,500 shares were traded. Wednesday, 3,000 shares changed hands and Friday's trading alone almost equaled its former weekly total. The selling price was currently 8.

Her Quotron showed yesterday's action at about that level, the price still creeping up. Something was happening.

A bass boomed from the receiver. "Suzannah, what can we do for one another?"

"Tydings and Roy, Richard. A land development company. It's suddenly active after years in a coma."

She listened as he rumbled a series of questions and, mindful of his patient's mouth stretched over a rubber bite piece, she answered quickly. "It's undervalued. T&R bought large blocks of land in the development boom of the sixties and early seventies. Then the bottom fell out and the street forgot about them. Meanwhile, the cities expanded and what was once the boonies became prime suburban real estate. T&R has parcels all over the mid-Atlantic. Their book value's worth more than the price of the stock, and—"

"Sorry, Suzannah, my hygienist had a problem. Where were we?"

"I was saying that T&R's cheap. Their land is worth more

than the value of their outstanding shares, and you're not paying a thing for future earnings. I think it's a good investment for a large company and the individual investor. I'm buying it myself.''

The doctor was in. He ordered 500 shares and wanted to watch it the next few days.

By eleven forty-five, Mrs. Wallenstein also owned 500, Francis X. Toogood had 1,000 and Jessica Orkin 250 shares. Three other clients wanted to think about it, there being no real rush, and five others weren't interested, but had other issues they did want to discuss or buy.

The morning felt good. Redemptive. She tallied the transactions. She'd earned $450 gross commission dollars this morning. At roughtly 30 percent payout, she'd take home around $135. Not bad. Not a fortune, but not a bad two or three hours.

And she'd been honest, avoiding the rumor, certainly not disseminating it, admitting that T&R was speculative, that she had no proof of anything's happening, and that she was purchasing the stock herself, which she did at eleven forty-seven, investing her $8,000 savings, doubling it through margin, and ordering 2,000 shares in her name. For starters.

She checked the market again. Chemfax was still selling at 52. Looking great. If Tully was right and Chemfax traded one half a share of their stock for one share of T&R, then . . . she grinned happily. If, say, they did so this very day . . .

Suzannah could easily do the math in her head, but she enjoyed the sight of crisp numbers when they sumbolized profit for herself.

She lifted her pencil and wrote again. She now had 2,000 shares of T&R at 8. Neatly, she drew an equal sign and wrote $16,000. Chemfax was 52. At one half a share of theirs for one of hers, she'd have 1,000 Chemfax shares . . . each worth $52. Again she wrote the equal sign, the dollar sign and now, 52,000. She underlined it.

Absolutely lovely. She would show a $36,000 profit for being in the right place at the right time.

Of course, the take-over wasn't happening today but in a few weeks. And by then, T&R would surely be up because of increased interest in it. She had probably helped push it up today. And Chemfax might fall a point or two.

But the real point was that there were delicious profits ahead.

She couldn't wait to buy more T&R, to enlarge her portion of the pie before it was dished out.

Her phone rang and she answered it, smiling. She murmured greetings to Leonard Hardy, her caller, and flipped through her daybook to his page.

"So," Leonard said in his nasal voice, "should I sell Saskatoon Petrol?"

Suzannah scanned his page. It listed dates and prices for every transaction he'd made—with her. There was no Saskatoon, although she'd advised him to buy it six weeks earlier and sent him all the research he requested. Furthermore, she'd been correct. Saskatoon climbed 30 per cent in the month and a half.

"Leonard," she said coolly, the smile gone even from her voice. "Where did you buy the Canadian oil?"

"Oh. I . . ."

"You went to a discount firm again, didn't you? After I advised the purchase and had researched it for you."

"I . . . I saved 50 percent in commissions. You'd cost me twice as much, Suzannah." He was whining.

"You want cheap? Then use the cheap brand's research department, Leonard. Use Brand X's brokers, not me!"

Discounters be damned! Not that long ago, the industry had unity, dignity, a solid front backed by a uniform commission rate. You could buy from company A or B, but you paid the same amount in commissions. Rates were almost sacred, one of life's givens.

Then tradition and history were overturned almost as if Wall Street felt compelled to be a part of the tumultuous early seventies. Commissions became negotiable. To Suzannah, her industry became, for a while, like used car salesmen on the "Late Show." Houses hawked their own specials of the day, claiming better deals, lower prices, undercutting each other even if it meant losing money. And into this new world of aggressive capitalism was born the stepchild, the bargain basement of the industry, the discount house.

Discounters took orders. The process wasn't that different from phoning Sears and ordering what you'd already selected from their catalogue. Investment counseling, advice and information, research, were all discarded in favor of low prices.

Leonard Hardy had been silent a long time.

"Well, Leonard," she prodded, "will you do that for me? Pick cheapo's brains next time, not mine?"

"Oh, you know . . . they don't give opinions . . ."

"Correct, Leonard. And you know why? Because they are robots, not thinking, sentient humans. Cheap is cheap, brother. You don't get what you don't pay for. But if you want *me*—if you want my brains and my ability and my company's research staff, then you'll have to pay. You are not my favorite charity, Leonard. You understand?"

"The Saskatoon," he whispered. "Should I sell it? Through *you*, of course. I promise I won't . . . only through you. And I won't . . . do that any more."

He was a creep. Sounded like somebody failing potty training and placating his mom. But she had no further quarrel with him.

"Sure," she said, and then she did smile, but with no hint of warmth. "And, Leonard? While I have you, there's a land development company . . ."

She wrote up both sales with satisfaction. Nobody better think he could use her without paying for it.

Time for her weekly lunch with Abby. But she decided on one more shot before it, and dialed Carl Diamond, a retiree who was generally home at lunch time.

She felt oppressively warm. The first floor of the building was overly air-conditioned in summer, overly heated in winter, consistently winning an unfair share of the high-rise's controlled atmosphere.

Today the trading room smelled of coats and boots shoved in corners. Suzannah looked out the window as she waited. She hated the unwilling light of winter, the gray stone, gray sky, gray glass. She thought of the tropics where blazing light cut sharp divisions on bright stucco and tile.

In Philadelphia, God gave an annual sermon on mortality. The only visible life was in the single passer-by's struggle with the wind and slush.

Above him, the sky had the texture of depression. Thick, sullen, insistent. The climate itself was hostile to dreams. It made her work more difficult, because dreams were the real commodity she peddled.

No wonder people with time and airfare ran away. It was difficult fighting the urge to hibernate, to doze through the dead time.

Or to turn inward, unearthing clots of misery that matched the heavens' mood.

And, hearing the telephone ring and ring, she belatedly remembered that Carl and his wife were among the lucky escapees. There was a new grandchild in Arizona he had told her about. She replaced her receiver.

So did Nick. "Simultaneous termination," he said. "Either a new sex objective or an old Busby Berkeley number. And now a-one and a-two, let's lift 'em up again. Ours is not to reason why, ours is just to sell and buy."

"No," she said. "Time for lunch, which I've earned."

"I'm leaving," she told June, the sales assistant she shared with Nick. She never mentioned meals or anything edible to the woman who had once erupted into a tirade against poisonous "public" food. Only the gray yoghurt and exotic legumes June toted in Mason jars were nontoxic.

Bravely, Suzannah set off for the public food that would turn her into a killer or cripple or, as June had confided in a loud whisper, "a queer, if you catch my drift. It's the artificial colors, you know."

The spectator's gallery, Sherwood Hastings' Retirement Village, was taking a working lunch while continuing to study the ticker tape. Old Man Zicker snuggled in his plush theater seat and Suzannah waved to him as he happily munched his sandwich. Zicker was as much a fixture of the office as were the desks, the Quotrons, the Standard and Poor volumes and the telephones. He was diminutive and jovial, always wearing a brown suit, white shirt and one of three plaid bow ties. He picnicked on tuna sandwiches and the pungent aroma of his unchanging noon meal clung to his shiny suit and to "his" seat in front of the Translux screen.

Nobody objected. Zicker had never put stock in dress or cuisine. Instead, he'd favored Xerox when it was a fledgling copy-machine company. He'd been intrigued when gadgets called computers were developed. Sufficiently intrigued to back several firms developing them. Later, he'd surveyed his seven children and decided the pharmaceutical company making pills to prevent such excess had an interesting idea. And so on.

Not his broker, not his children or grandchildren and not anyone who valued his job at Sherwood Hastings ever objected to

Zicker's fishy smell. It was overpowered by the sweet perfume of his portfolio.

Near Zicker, a newcomer fastidiously unwrapped herself. Carefully, the old woman removed a tasseled stocking cap, a pair of purple mittens, a rusty black coat, a gray cardigan and a patchwork knit vest. She smoothed the bosom of her long dress, but she was still lumpy, as if concealing several undershirts. She put her carpetbag on the floor and sat down. "Hi, fellas," she said. "Sara's back."

She smiled at Suzannah endearingly, crinkling a face as wrinkled as a well-worn dollar bill. "Went out for a hot dog and couldn't wait to get back. This is fun!"

Suzannah stopped walking. "Is this your first visit?"

The woman nodded. "My late husband, Mr. Pratt, is gone. I have to take care of the money things now." One of her white anklets slipped and she bent over, groaning a little, to pull it up.

"My name's Suzannah Barnes, Mrs. Pratt. If you have any questions, my desk is right there by the window."

"You're a broker?"

"And a good one." Suzannah winked and walked to the lobby door. If the old lady didn't question her during the afternoon, she'd check back herself. Zicker had appeared in the same unheralded fashion and had eventually fixated on Billy Firestein. Billy had since added the Zicker wing to his home and the Marvin Zicker tennis court to his garden.

"Mizz Barnes?" Suzannah turned around. Sara Pratt, a bit flushed, approached her. "Mizz Barnes, I have a question right now."

"Shoot."

"The man with the tuna fish—is he married?"

"Mr. Zicker? Unfortunately, yes."

Sara pleated her long skirt with two fingers. "Good ones always are, don't you think?"

"Almost," Suzannah agreed.

"Well," Sara said, smoothing out the pleat she'd made, "I'll just have to lay it on heavier, that's all." She winked and sauntered back, moving as seductively as someone in ankle socks and three undershirts can.

Suzannah left for lunch feeling more than merely good.

Four

"Thank you. Oh, I don't know how to thank you, Dr. Walde-mar." Missy McClennahan patted her typed pages back into a square, licking her lips as she concentrated.

Her brain, beautifully masked by a fresh young face, had proven incapable of absorbing Coby's subject. But her voice was music itself.

Coby drifted in her rhythms, eyes skidding over blond curls, thin yellow sweater.

"Most students are so immaTURE, but I find your subject so INTEResting. So STIMulating. A whole PART of me has OPENED."

He tried not to think of her parts, open or shut. It was sufficiently difficult sitting knee to knee in the cramped office, controlling glances at the lush chest that was coated, not covered, by the buttery knit. He wished students would wear bras during conferences.

"Miss McClennahan, if I've answered your questions . . ."

"OH!" She stood up swiftly, pressing her knees against his, dropping her reassembled papers on him and the floor. "I'm so SORRY!" She reached for the pages and Coby hastily handed over those on his lap. He tried not to watch her bend for the others.

Papers reclaimed, she slowed down, changed meter and much too deliberately stretched her right arm back and into the sleeve of her down jacket. Her body was unbearably outlined. Coby studied the lithograph of Brahms above his desk.

"You think I'm a fool, don't you?" she said softly.

"Not at all." He considered her baklava, his generic term for the oversweet, flaky confections who decorated his classroom. But a fool? Never. She possessed an ageless, awesome wisdom.

She put her hand on his arm. He stood up, backing away, and nearly fell over his chair.

"I'm slow. With books. But you've . . . stirred me up so that . . . you've . . . I want to share, to experience . . . everything. Do you understand?"

He understood that she was his student, that she was sixteen years younger than he, that she was standing too close for academic discussion and that her motives were as base and basic as a passing grade. He walked around her and opened the door.

"Ah," she said. "I nearly forgot. I heard you write songs and well, my uncle's something with a record company. I mean maybe we could help each other? Be friends?"

He made soothing noises of thanks, nonacceptance and farewell and returned to his desk, leaving the door open to air out the office.

"Would it be a major offense, God, to shelve moral scruples and accept her offers? Energetic sex, a passing grade, my music seen by her uncle?" He looked up at the unsmiling gaze of Brahms. "God," he said, punching his desk, "I'm not Job. It isn't fair."

"Who said it should be?"

Coby swiveled around. "Harvey. What a letdown. I thought God was finally answering me."

"Did I interrupt a prayer service?"

"Nope. Cleaning the desk and going home."

"Know what, Heathcliff? Entirely too many nubile students confer with you each week." They left the room together. "Can you come to dinner tonight?" Harvey asked as they walked down the stairs. "Nina's making sauerbraten."

"I'd love to, but I teach Tuesdays. Another time?"

"Sure. But if I'm not bringing you, I'll have to bring answers. Number one: are you still playing?"

"Music?"

"The field. Aside from student-groupies."

"I see. Which of Nina's dear friends was recently divorced? Answer is yes. Guess you could call it playing."

"You don't sound wildly enthusiastic." Harvey braced himself and pushed the metal firebreak at the exit. "Does surviving this each year make us better people? I smell more snow coming." He glanced over at Coby, who walked naturally, his suede coat unbuttoned. "You don't feel it, do you? Superman. Speaking of whom, Paul Phelps will be in from the Coast next week. Want me to—''

"No. You know his act? Last time he asked me to pimp for him. To find juicy college girls. I'll stay with my unmiraculous local contacts.''

They reached the parking structure. "I didn't service Phelps," Coby added. "But someone else did. The worst part was, every coed he approached accepted.''

"Ah, it's that L.A. razzmatazz. You find it threatening, Heathcliff?''

Coby smiled and waved good-by. They'd never returned to whether or not he enjoyed what Harvey called playing.

Which was for the good. The possibilities of what could be wrong with the chemistry and/or timing between Coby and a woman were staggering. He'd never, through his years of bliss-ful inattention to the subject, suspected how populous was the world of wrong choices.

He was slowly combing through his friends' files. Two of the worst recommendations had been belligerent, ready to prove him a stinking male like the one who'd caused their inexhaustible misery. Another was a one-woman brass band, her laugh the clang of cymbals, her idea of fun congested bars where he was deafened by a cacophonous jumble, by her. There'd been a vapid wisp who became a marine drill sergeant, barking orders, turning her bed into boot camp. A hard-edged glossy one whose obses-sive chatter pinged off brand names, restaurants, people, design-ers, spas Coby had never heard of. And a dull one with a face like a cement sidewalk, all the wildness paved over.

But worst were those who, like Coby, had missed the much touted sexual revolution and found themselves back on the playing grounds, unsure of the new rules. Sometimes there was fear in the bedroom, or resentment, or a numbing sense of dutiful payment for the steak, the wine, the company. Bodies were time-worn, children slept behind thin walls, ghosts of unmet expecta-tions lay on pillows. Too much had and had not happened to both Coby and the woman and all of it still clung, gouging, scratch-ing, nipping at their tender spots.

And now there was Rachel, who, if not precisely wrong, was not right, either. Since New Year's Eve, their friendship had ex-tended into Rachel's pastel bedroom. Her sturdy body offered solace but he was certain, if he were ever again to be himself, solace was insufficient.

Coby never wanted to hurt Rachel, yet they'd created a situation where he feared he someday would.

She was in his VW now. "Sorry I'm late," he said. "Student conference ran over."

"No problem. I'm redoing a lecture. We became sidetracked today."

For most of the ride they were silent. Coby concentrated on avoiding both potholes and his fellow urban escapees. No one on the expressway looked happy.

As they reached Narberth, Scriabin's Fourth Symphony, *Poem of Ecstasy*, swirled out of the radio, filling the round interior of his car with its metaphysical enigmas. Coby listened carefully, trying to really understand the composer's five motifs. The flute played the Motive of Yearning.

Above it he heard the soft screech of Rachel's felt-tip marker. He glanced over as she highlighted her notes, drew a blue asterisk next to a paragraph, scratched a shrieking arrow down to the section below it.

Scriabin's Motive of Self-assertion trumpeted out of the radio. Rachel looked up. "Finished. Oh! I'm home. Want to come in and have lunch?" She waited a moment, then spoke again. "Nancy won't be home from school for hours."

"Ah . . . I'd like to, but . . . I mean, I think—"

Rachel interrupted, waving him to silence. "Coby, I think it's time for a sort of speech." She inhaled and began. "In my family, I was the smart one. My sister was the pretty one. I knew I wasn't hideous. But I wasn't first choice, either. I was sort of the good wool cardigan in the dating wardrobe—nothing special, but not rags to be ashamed of."

Her fingers twirled her sand and salt hair. The gray sprinkles made her look older, and Coby wondered why she didn't color them. But except for New Year's Eve, Rachel seldom decorated herself and her forthright plainness was part of the honesty he admired.

"David was more or less my equivalent. Like seeks like, you know. Anyway, once I was married, I decided those terrible feelings of inadequacy were adolescent. Silly."

"Rachel, there's no need to—"

"I knew you'd say that, but there is a need. Look, David

didn't simply pack up and leave me. He needed to wreck the past, demolish me first. Professionally, I understand defense mechanisms and why he had to dredge up all my old fears and insist they were justified. David was a man of fierce ethical standards and he needed to feel he was discarding garbage, not something worth while. I understood. But it hurt like hell. Worse, I accepted his judgments.''

Her small face was serious. ''I've seen a therapist for two years. She's helped enormously. But there weren't many men. I'm not the sort who attracts many men. I've stopped seeing the therapist because of you. The theory and the practice have come together and I honestly feel good about myself. Not only with students and patients but with men, the real toughies. And with myself, and this time, the feeling will last.''

She looked away. ''What I wanted to say is that I don't mind being your good wool cardigan. Everybody needs something to keep away the chill. That can be enough, for both of us, until it isn't. And then we'll still be friends.''

She looked back at him shyly. ''I only mean, Coby, that you can stop agonizing over every invitation to share lunch. Or anything.''

''Rachel, you're—''

''Amazing, right?''

''Precisely.'' He turned off Scriabin's mysteries and the car's motor and accepted her many invitations.

Five

The delicatessen was crowded and Suzannah joined those waiting by the door until she saw Abby's long arm wave wildly from a distant booth.

''I've been under siege. Two crones told me it was a criminal offense to occupy a table and not eat. I had to order.'' She slouched against the vinyl banquette, stroking the binding of her embroidered jacket. A salad sat in front of her.

Suzannah shoved her fur cape into the corner of the booth and straightened the cuffs of her suede suit. She'd loved it the moment she found it, ordered two, a fawn and a rust. Its designer understood her business closet, a narrow area walled by unprofessional voluptuousness on the left, sexless conservatism on the right. Yet the purple and green dragons on Abby's jacket made Suzannah feel constricted and too safely clothed.

An emaciated waitress placed water on the table and tensed. "Your order?" she whispered.

"Is the corned beef lean?"

The waitress' eyes reddened. "I don't know what you'd consider lean." Her voice quavered with fear.

"Never mind. The corned beef special and tea."

"And you have everything already, miss, right?"

"Me?" Abby looked astounded. "Hardly. Oh—you mean food. Sure."

"Poor woman," Suzannah said when she left. "Probably has six kids, a husband who skipped with a magician's assistant and no education past seventh grade when she was knocked up."

"Wrong. She's a Harvard Ph.D. in Plasma Physics. Can't find a tenured position and is going mad slicing pastrami."

Suzannah took a cigarette from her alligator case. "How is your Tonio the small?"

"Fine, presumably, and back home in Genoa." She drummed scarlet nails on the laminated table top. "I'm going to travel myself."

"Where?"

"Anywhere. South America sounds warm enough. I'm sick of planning trips for other people. I signed a man for China today, and I wanted to snatch the ticket out of his undeserving hands. The Great Wall, all those miniature me's tooling around on bikes. But I'd feel oversized."

"And in South America?"

"I'd feel oversized. But they don't look like me. I'd be a foreigner. An American. Maybe Africa . . . Masai warriors . . ."

"How's your dad and Lucinda?"

"The Masai remind you of those pale Anglo-Saxons?" She frowned and tapped a soft code on the table with the balls of her fingers.

It hadn't been the Masai, but the self-identification as "an American" that triggered thoughts of Abby's family. In third grade, Suzannah had lost a recess contest of double Dutch, stepping on the jump rope when she had heard the taunts.

"Chink! Chink!" a circle of children had screamed.

"I'm an American!" Abby had screamed back from their center.

"You're *nothing!* My mother and everybody says so! Just a dirty, lousy, slant-eyed chink!" Lucy Davis had danced close to her prey, yanked her hair and spit in Abby's face.

Suzannah had stormed the circle and kicked Lucy's crotch. "Abby's my friend. She's smarter and prettier than any of you!" And she had dragged Abby out and insisted they play jacks through that recess and many others during a long term of ostracism.

Some of the third grade's fathers had come back from Korea in boxes, Suzannah's father had explained. And they still blamed it on people who looked like Abby and her mother. People with straight black hair and tilted eyes. They were wrong, but perhaps understandable, he had said. Suzannah never had understood or forgiven.

Who cared if they weren't popular? the girls asked each other. Suzannah, the chubby scholar, and Abby, the porcelain doll misplaced in a Quaker cupboard, were the two top students in their class.

In seventh grade, Abby had grown. Not simply up, but conspicuously out in front. The seventh-grade boys had surveyed the Eurasian mammaries set precisely at their eye level and their owner's time of being ignored was over.

From then on, the only subject that had interested Abby was how her imagination could best fulfill other people's fantasies.

The waitress slipped Suzannah's food on the table and skittered off.

Abby pronged lettuce with a fork. "How's Tully? How's business? Your mom, Josie, Chris, I.B.M.?"

Suzannah lifted her sandwich with two fingers, minimizing contact with at least 3,000 calories. "Gone. Fine. Who knows and—what were the others?"

"Hold on—gone? Tully? But why?"

"But why not?" Suzannah savored the rich Russian dressing,

the salt bite of corned beef, the chewy tang of Jewish rye and the added spice of guilt.

Abby shrugged, accepting her friend's decision. "I'm involved with a pedagogue now. Instructor at the Health Farm. His I.Q. is smaller than his biceps, but his biceps are impressive. Actually, his age and his I.Q. are both nineteen."

"A half-century leap from Tonio to muscles? And neither has language skills?"

"For somebody who mostly only reads the bottom line, you're an intellectual snob."

Eighth grade had been a series of strange seasons, a time when their separate stories had locked them close forever.

That October, Suzannah's father and the woman four houses down had packed suitcases and departed.

Why did she remember it as Hallowe'en? Envision herself pushing doorbells, having her mask pulled off and treats withheld because her father had been there first and tricked them all? It hadn't been Hallowe'en. She knew it, but her memory contradicted her each time.

She had waited months of nights, but the real trick was, that time, he stayed gone.

And her mother, first that night, then from time to time, would muse almost proudly on the farewell note he'd left propped on the mantelpiece. "Just like in a movie," she'd say. She had preserved the note in a plastic protector sheet and begun watching television even more intently, awaiting the reruns of her life.

That same year, Abby's mother had also departed. But alone, except for an antique carving knife and the bathtub where she had performed her bloody hara-kiri. Abby had discovered her remains after school.

"She knew I would," she'd told Suzannah in early spring. "I was always the first one home. Why would she do that to me?"

"She wasn't thinking. She loved you. She wasn't thinking."

They had never discussed Suzannah's father. There was nothing corporeal to analyze or dispel. Nothing but a thin trail of musk.

One drunken night, years later, Abby had announced the end of a game they'd invented and played since high school. It was called "Shit Lines" and to win, a player had to find recent words or deeds of singular, exemplary cruelty, preferably of the domesticated sort that never made headlines. "I've always held the trump," Abby said, enunciating with difficulty.

"Impossible. We named Mrs. Diener All-time Champion after she asked the school counselor, in front of everybody, how to stop Donny from masturbating so much."

Abby shrugged. "Decide for yourself. My snotty cousin Harris told me a family story about when Daddy introduced his pregnant Korean souvenir to the family. Even though it was obvious, my grandfather informed the tribe that their stock was being mongrelized. And then he turned to my father and lost his genteel reserve. 'God damn it straight to hell, son!' he is quoted as saying. 'I wish you'd brought home the clap instead!' "

Now, Suzannah reached for saccharin, curling her mouth at this dietary self-deception. Inside, the Russian dressing oozed through her system, seeking fellow fat deposits, hipside retirement havens.

Abby sipped black coffee. She never needed to diet, was deaf to the siren song of bittersweet chocolate, flaky croissants, soft puddles of butter. Abby actually enjoyed lettuce, meant it when she declined dessert as too rich. Nothing, in honesty, was "too rich" for Suzannah. Abby, without effort, stayed round only where men had decided roundness was fine. Suzannah sighed.

"That sigh for the lost Tully?"

"For the lost thinness. I can't wear anything I bought last year."

"It was too small, then. Listen, Suze, you were trying to die. Shutting all your openings. I watched you gag over a grain of rice. You're too old for anorexia."

"Yes, but there's nothing like severe depression. Only time in my life everybody said I looked stunning."

"That's their problem. Who says we're supposed to look like boys with vaginas, that we shouldn't upset some pattern by being soft? Why do we have to fight our own bodies to fit the ideal of the month?"

"You're in no position to defend the misshapen."

"Oh no? You ever shop for dresses with a D-cup stitched to your chest? They don't make things to cover it. Maybe they want us to stay naked, or wear shrouds like women in Iran."

"They are not called shrouds."

"Who cares what they call them? That's what they are. Anyway, who's replacing Tully?"

"You think I have a list on a clipboard? Call in the understudy, the lead's fired?"

"You could audition new talent."

"Too much trouble. Prince Charming's dead. The woods are full of frogs. It's a waste of time."

"Who's talking about princes? You had Biology I. Remember those filmstrips? Plumbing diagrams of our cute insides? Sperm paddling upstream to spawn?"

"God knows I'm not looking to make meaningful contact with sperm."

"I'm talking about biology. Find a vasectomy, but you'll need to find something sooner or later, won't you?"

"There is the option of celibacy."

"Too chic. Too boring."

"No more boring than most men. Particularly in bed. I'm going to write a best seller. *The Book of Lousy Lays: A Hundred and One Nights of—*"

"It'll never sell. Who needs to buy it? I dare you to stand up and ask this randomly selected group if they'd like you to tell them how a man can be lousy in bed. And I'll wager heavy stakes that every single woman in here, including our depressed waitress, would shout, 'No! Me first! Let me tell *you!*' "

"Remember Freud's famous question? 'Vat iss it a vooman vants?' Dumb chauvinist—did he *ask* a woman? Why doesn't history record her answer? Why didn't he ask me?"

"I know what I'd have said." Abby smiled subtly. "Better than boring, at least, Sigmund. And then, what every woman wants. Someone I can share my interests with. Somebody interested in the same things I am."

"Such as . . . ?"

"Such as me. I want someone fascinated by the only thing that really intrigues me, which is me. I want him to whisper perceptive, insightful things . . . about me. I want him to travel the world over to find gifts and trinkets created for me. I want to be someone's life project. Now, do you want to discuss what I'd settle for?"

The frail waitress approached. "Dessert?" she whispered.

Suzannah glanced at the pies on the counter, then forced herself to look away and shake her head "no" as Abby did, even though she did not, almost never did, feel full.

The waitress backed off to tally their bill privately.

"While on the subject of sex, Suze, did that guy hunting for you New Year's Eve ever call?"

"I have absolutely no idea who you're talking about."

"I don't know his name, but you couldn't have missed him. Tall, dark curly hair, great bod, glasses. Offbeat, sexy face."

Suzannah shrugged.

"I refuse to believe you didn't even notice him. He played the piano, does that help?"

Suzannah remembered her early exit. The man in the green sweater had been playing the piano as she raced down the two flights of stairs. "Okay," she said. "I know who you mean, but he didn't call me and I'm glad."

"Why? He's gorgeous."

"And married."

"I didn't know you were up for eternal bliss, the cottage with picket fence. I was talking about biology. About getting it off. Happily."

"What's so happy about unhappily married men? They have too many problems."

"What else is there? Quirky bachelors? Divorcés? There's a reason for their prior failure. Beautiful gays? Vibrators? The best men are always married."

"You're the second person to say that today."

"That makes it gospel truth. Anyway, the piano player looked like one of the best. Worth a try, don't you think so?"

"Maybe."

"Maybe? Has your libido atrophied?"

"Listen, he didn't call so this is irrelevant."

"But if he did?"

"Would he have a written guarantee?"

"Did you listen to him play that piano? I've found a strong correlation between the way men pull music out of something and what they can do to me. It's a clue. Second only to the way they eat. That's the first major one."

"Oh, you never really know."

"You do so. There's something just this side of scary. A heat, an interest, a spark. A way they move, hold their head, look at you. A feeling they breathe. That they enjoy themselves and, more important, that they enjoy women, that they aren't posing, aren't pretending."

"Listen, Abby, I don't even want something good. The bad

ones are a pain in the ass and the good ones are maybe worse, interfering and draining energy.''

"The stockbroker-nun speaks."

"Why don't we talk about you instead, about *your* love life. What's going on, Ab? I mean to you—men are major things in your life, but you find such . . . Tonio, this moronic gymnast, the others . . . why? You deserve so much more.''

Abby looked at Suzannah with hooded eyes, a sudden flush on her cheeks. Her lips moved, curling around words that never made it into sound. She shrugged and counted out change.

"You're so hidden, lately. What's wrong, Abby?"

"Nothing." She made tidy piles of quarters and dimes. "The weather makes me edgy. So dead out there.'' She picked at woven dragon fire on her sleeve. "You remember my mother?"

"Of course!"

"Oh. Sure. Well, I . . . I keep . . . thinking about her lately. Isn't that odd?"

"Abby, please let me—''

"I think I need a change of scene." Abby stood and pulled on a floor-length white wool coat.

Outside, she turned back to Suzannah after having waved good-by. "Want to take a trip together? I don't much care where."

"I can't now. I'm up to here with work. Would you settle for a movie this Saturday night? A travelogue, maybe?"

Abby shook her head. "I'm not entering the convent with you. I'll see you next Tuesday."

She turned and Suzannah watched her saunter off, watched male heads swivel automatically to form a slowly dissolving honor guard of admirers.

During the afternoon, she took orders, answered calls, caught up on paper work and thought about buying more T&R. The future waved merrily and whispered sweet promises and, at the very end of the day, presented a bonus gift.

"This is Elaine Weiner," her caller said. Not "my name is," but "this is." It felt an important distinction. "You've been recommended as a crackerjack professional and I prefer dealing with women. I'm unhappy with my present broker and I'd like to discuss my portfolio. Could we arrange that?"

"Of course." What a foolish question.

"I'll warn you—it won't make your fortune yet. There's a quarter million or so to invest because I put most of my cash back into my business. But my goal—our goal—should be to increase that speedily. I'll mail you a list of my holdings today."

"That's the most self-satisfied grin," Nick said as they walked outside together. "Did you win the lottery?"

"Nope, but I've been given a chance on Elaine Weiner."

"The discount queen? The merchant princess?"

"None other. The creator of bargain haute couture."

"I'll bet she's a bitch."

"*Why?* Because she did it herself? Because Mr. Weiner didn't start or finance them? Why are men tough and women bitches?"

"Listen, if you're running with her money, get your facts straight. Her mister has a different last name. She bought him after she was rich."

"*Bought* him! Jesus, Nick, you're out of the Dark Ages!"

"Correct. And I say thank God there's some of us left. Remember me when you're tired of your washed-out contemporaries."

Six

The housekeeper, Mrs. Jennings, sat in the kitchen, working a crossword puzzle. "Boy's upstairs," she told Coby, shaking her head at a set of blanks.

The house was silent. Mrs. Jennings wasn't one for background music or TV. "Mean-looking outside," she added.

"Will you be able to get here tomorrow?"

"Dr. Waldemar! I'm Vermont born and bred!"

He smiled apologetically. She was a gentle bulldozer, and she'd be where she was expected, and on time. He flipped through his mail. Only one envelope intrigued him because of its mysterious acronym. "MOFS." Multinational? Orchestra? Margaret Olivia Franklyn-Smythe? Many Of us Fall Short?

Inside, a self-mailer contained fifty-five questions in microscopic print and a decoding of the initials. "Multiple Options For Singles."

He scanned a paragraph that urged him to answer a "compatibility guide" and find his heart's delight, a female who was even now marking "x" under "all the time" or "never" for "Do you enjoy retelling 'Good Jokes'?" And "Do you believe your life is ruled by a Supreme Being?"

Maybe it didn't have to be female. Question 36 asked, "Do you prefer the company of Your Own Sex?" There honestly were multiple options offered between horrible cutesy capitals and quotation marks.

"Is it right to be 'Intimate' without 'Wedlock'?"

"Is your idea of 'fun' a 'Wholesome Outing' with a 'Good Friend'? Are Most People too 'Uptight' for you?"

He couldn't see how anyone could answer those questions in a way he'd find compatible. He tossed the mailer into the trash.

Mrs. Jennings looked up from her crossword puzzle. "The boy lost a mitten today. Been Real cheery lately. Takes getting to know each other, that's all."

Coby liked the way she labeled Adam "the boy." It had a fine Vermont stability and permanence. Coby was, in turn, "the father," and this rock-bottom clarification of roles pleased him.

Upstairs, "the boy" sat cross-legged on his bed, copper curls bent low over a paper. He shared the bedspread with a mass of crayons and one asthmatic beagle named Boots. ("The dog," Coby mentally registered, completing the dramatis personae.)

"Daddy! I didn't hear you!" Adam dropped his crayon and reached to hug Coby mightily. Then he pulled back and studied his father.

Coby looked into Adam's enormous dark eyes. Their slate blue irises and shape were his, but the rest of his face and coloring was Dana's.

"I practiced my 'v's.' " Adam held up a sheet with somewhat undulating letters.

"Hey, that's really fine."

"Miss Plotnick says I'm sloppy."

Coby stifled a disparaging noise. He tried avoiding conflict between home and school, but Plotnick infuriated him, picking and niggling, ignoring and certainly never nurturing that which was positive in a child's achievement.

Plotnick was young, newly minted but still, an anachronism designed by an old-fashioned cartoonist. She lacked only a hickory stick.

She was not the teacher Coby would have designed for any child, let alone one he passionately loved. But Adam was doing Plotnick-well, scoring considerably above the average. If only Coby respected standardized indexes of success.

Adam took a deep breath, then spoke. "I had to sit in the thinking chair. I talked in line."

Coby bit his lip to keep his opinions subdued and not encourage delinquency. Fathers, one heard, were supposed to endorse and represent the rules of civilization.

"I said 'scuse me' because I bumped into Leslie Farber. But she said, 'Adam talked! Adam bumped me!' "

"And you were busted?"

Adam nodded. "I thought you should say 'scuse me' if you bump."

Coby sat down beside Adam. "I think so too. But every so often, you wind up with a Miss Plotnick running the show and then, nothing's what you expect and you're kind of stuck in the crazy house. But it isn't forever. After a year with Miss Plotnick, you'll be stronger for it. Something like that."

"But I'll probably still have Leslie Farber next year."

"Yeah." They sat side by side. Coby remembered the Leslie Farbers of his childhood, girls born smug, hair neatly braided, notepaper reinforced around each and every ring-hole. Had they ever been punished for their inborn nastiness, for their quick flips of ponytails and upturned noses and hands eagerly waving for every answer? Or did they grow into Plotnicks and torment whole classrooms?

"We gonna leave now, Daddy?"

"For where?"

"The doctor's."

Coby shook his head. "That's tomorrow. Wednesdays, remember?"

"What's tonight?" Adam suddenly looked older than his six years.

"I told you, I'm starting another term at the night school. But

I'll have dinner with you first, and Mrs. Jennings will be with you, of course.''

Adam put down a crayon and squeezed his lips into a crooked frown. ''Dad,'' he said softly. ''I like it better when . . .''

Coby didn't need to hear the completed sentence. He knew every permutation of the long history that had evolved into this mild and controlled response. Thank God and Adam's therapist for the ending of tantrums and near hysteria on every leave-taking. For no longer feeling a traitor every evening out. For wounds that were healing, leaving only this thin frown as a scar. For no longer seeing his son's small, prematurely wizened face peering out a window whenever he drove up. No longer hearing shudders of relief when he reappeared after any and all separations. For fewer shrieks and sobs in the night, less checking that Coby was home and still existed.

There were still problems. But there was also wholeness or its possibility reappearing. For both of them.

''I like it best when I'm with you, too,'' Coby said. ''But I have my work just as you have yours at school. And sometimes, I have to play, the way you and your friends do.''

''I know.''

''I know you know. We don't always get first choice. It isn't always easy, but we—''

''—gotta do what we gotta do.''

Sometimes in the dusk, as now, Coby felt the empty spaces in his home acutely, dry sockets with the pain still raw. There should be womansounds, other children's high voices, stories spinning simultaneously in many rooms. Laughter, music, an abundance of noise and people. Home sounds.

But he and Adam had been handed a different script with a different score. They were a new experiment in coupling, an avant-garde minimal family unit with Coby improvising all adult roles without benefit of rehearsal or coaching.

''What would you like to do before dinner?'' he asked Adam.

''Watch TV.''

''Oh, I don't think—''

'' ' Sesame Street.' Educational. You said so.''

''Trapped myself, huh? Okay. I'll be right down.''

The dog wheezed out behind Adam. They were the picture of Norman Rockwell happy-normal.

Coby carried Adam's drawing to the window. He pulled back

the red and white curtain Dana had lovingly stitched for her infant. Its edge was frayed.

Coby looked at his son's artwork. Another family complete with square, grinning Boots. The man, woman and child wore bright clothing painstakingly detailed, colored and outlined in black. The man smiled and wore glasses. The boy beamed so brightly his lips almost touched his curly red hair.

It was the woman, though. It was always the woman and still the woman who had no face. Never did. Only an angry orange scribble inside a black oval.

Many times he'd asked Adam why. Adam answered with an anxious peer, a set of his lips and a shrug. Coby stopped asking. Someday, blocked memories would surface, exhaled with the final gasp of Adam's anger. The last muddled resentment, the still unarticulated feelings of betrayal and abandonment would be released and then, a mother face might appear in the drawings. Then Adam might stop silencing discussions of Dana, might stop turning from her photographs, claiming he didn't know who she was.

The loudness of his own sigh surprised Coby. How solemnly dramatic. Perhaps he *was* becoming Heathcliff! And then he laughed. Heathcliff, indeed! Roaming the moors with a red-haired boy who'd interrupt dark musings with skips and pebble-tosses, riddles and requests for bubble gum.

Nope. Literary romantics were solitary travelers. He'd never make it into their ranks. Let Heathcliff have his moors and misery. Let him, if any way possible, also have the landscape Coby saw at the moment. Heathcliff might enjoy it.

At the side of the lawn the rosebushes stood, skeletal stumps in frozen snow, fading as the daylight died, squeezed under a leaden sky. The bay windows across the street glowed until someone closed the drapes, conserving warmth.

In summer, leaves curtained the view. Now, Coby could see through power lines and bare shivering trees to the blinking neon of a distant gas station.

He let the red and white curtain cover the glass and turned. Carefully, respectfully, he folded his son's work of a winter evening.

Seven

Suzannah drove reluctantly. The only value in visiting her mother was to place her own options in bas-relief from the recesses in which Benita Miller lived. Everything about the woman was sedentary and scared, including the Danish Modern living room suite that was devotedly preserved, even if the marriage wasn't, from the fifties, when they both were new.

Suzannah's hopes bore no resemblance to her mother's stunted dreams, her mother's terminal inertia.

She parked her weathered brown Mercedes on the blacktop and walked to the squat, pragmatic building's entry. Suzannah would never let herself live this way. Suzannah wanted more. Much, much more. And, her mind prompted, perhaps T&R, Chemfax and that take-over were her yellow brick road to that someplace as far as possible from here.

If she were to build a sizable stake, she'd need more capital than she'd saved. She could borrow on a building she and Chris still held jointly, but that would mean seeing her ex-husband again. She wasn't certain if the idea pleased or terrified her.

She pushed the buzzer next to "Miller, B."

"Who is it?"

"Me, Mom."

"Who is that?"

"Me! Mom, is it a grammatical problem? It is I. Suzannah, your daughter. Remember me? Christ, I'm freezing!"

A long angry-sounding buzz answered.

Benita Miller stood dourly at her apartment door, her expression suggesting that a clever rapist had discovered her daughter's name and disguised his voice in order to savage her droopy body.

"You didn't have to snap at me." She accepted Suzannah's kiss and a box of take-out chicken purchased on the drive over, then double-bolted the door and returned to "her" chair, a black plastic recliner in front of the television. "Guess what, Isobel," she called out. "My long-lost daughter has finally reappeared."

"Aunt Isobel's here?" Suzannah's tension lessened. Isobel's eighty-six years of wisdom, of tolerance, would smooth over some of the shards of old anger that surfaced during every visit, no matter how long the time elapsed between.

"I'm making tea, Suzannah," her great-aunt called from the kitchen. "Want some?"

"Love it. I'm frozen."

"So." Her mother's eyes, hidden behind thick glasses, pointed at the air above Suzannah's shoulder. "How did Josie blackmail you into visiting me?"

By sounding hysterical and scaring me. By saying she couldn't handle much of anything, but certainly not you right now, Suzannah could have said. But she said instead, "Could we turn the TV off and talk?"

"The news is on," Benita Miller said. She stared at Suzannah a moment. "I see you've gained back all that weight and then some." Then she swiveled her attention back to the newscast.

Once upon a time, Benita Miller could have had a brilliant career. But the Third Reich's experiments with pain thresholds flowered on foreign soil and Benita wasn't one for travel. In her homeland, and long after the war, she extracted nerves and twanged them, but only as a pastime, with no ideology or real sense of direction.

"How are you feeling?" Suzannah asked politely.

"I was sick. I was nearly hospitalized."

"Why didn't you call me?"

Isobel entered with the tea and Suzannah busied herself with the mechanics of dunking a teabag, trying not to listen to or become angry with her mother's interminable and self-designed life as an invalid. Benita crippled herself by insisting on illness despite every medical report. If not transported by Josie, she sat in place, her apartment walls her prison. Her dizzy spells, palpitations and sick headaches were probably protests from an organism protesting premature burial, but Benita had faith in her "condition" and worshiped it religiously.

"*If* you were still married," Benita said. "*If* you were settled down, I would have called you for help. But you're so busy with work and men . . . besides, if you're too busy ever to phone me,

I assume you're too busy for me to bother you. And who *knows* what I'd interrupt if I called?''

Zow. Pow. Whammy. Did her mother rehearse or were these barbs instinctive, to be tossed over the shoulder like grenades even while watching the next day's weather forecast.

"How are you, Suzannah?" Isobel asked. "You're glowing."

"It's the cold. I never glow when I'm warm. But you look wonderfully well. How's the leg?"

The old woman smiled. "Still attached to the rest of me. Are you happy, child?"

The question sounded alien, a foreign idiom inserted midsentence, scrambling the language of this household.

"Happy? Well yes. Yes, I am. I'm doing well at work, and today, I—"

"I think we should eat now." From the woman in the front row, watching an account of domestic tragedy in Iowa.

Suzannah stood up promptly. Interesting how her mother's appetite was never impaired when someone else prepared the food.

Benita's kitchen was orderly because she never truly cooked. Still, the apartment's scent pervaded the shiny counters and intensified as the oven heated the room. Suzannah didn't know what to call the ancient odor. Fatigue, perhaps. Dusty shadows of old emotions coloring corners no one had the energy to reach any more.

Once in summer, Suzannah had found the dried husk of a grasshopper. "Neee-tah" its juiceless shell seemed to squeak. "Neee-tah." She'd kept it on her table by her bed, hoping for revelation. But it hid its secrets under dead wings and the real Nita found it and swept it into oblivion.

"Nee-tah!" Her father called her that, coming home, flinging his hat on the sofa and whirling his daughters around while Nita dusted his hat with her palm and carefully placed it on the hall closet shelf.

Neetah. What a fine name for a woman who labeled cobwebs and dust her life's enemies. "You can't let it take over," she insisted, pushing cloths across wood, scrubbing floor molding, packing away Suzannah's plaster of paris molds, her tile-cutter and stamp collection, because they were the enemy's asymmetrical, confusing weaponry. Having Cat killed.

God, she thought she'd forgotten Cat, removed to the animal

shelter by Nita while Suzannah was at school because he'd ripped the edge of a chair. For months, Suzannah had nightmares that resounded with ghostly mewls. During the days, her throat painful as if she were getting flu, she'd wonder if he blamed her, fully understood her inability to be a caretaker. She never once believed he'd beaten the odds and been saved.

No other pets ever entered the house. The family unraveled, the marriage shredded, but nothing but time harmed the furniture.

Benita Miller, code named Neater. Super agent in the war against "it."

Suzannah returned to the living room. "One more minute."

"You're teaching a class about money?" her aunt asked.

Her mother shook her cap of crimped curls. "If you'd stuck your marriage out, you wouldn't have to kill yourself moonlighting."

"I'm not!"

"No marriage is perfect. At least I tried to save mine. At least I wasn't the one who walked out and called it quits."

Isobel ran interference. "Shh, Nita. Suzannah's better off. Chris was no good. Sexy," she winked at Suzannah, "but no good."

"Well?" Nita said. "Don't I know the playboy type? Didn't I live with one? But what can you expect from men? They're nothing but children."

Suzannah ignored her mother and watched Isobel. Lovable, wonderful Isobel who believed in happiness and found it. Isobel's only son had died of rheumatic fever and Josie and Suzannah had become stand-ins for unborn grandchildren. She taught them to bake and knit, gave them their first sips of champagne, crafted Christmas ornaments and hid Easter chicks in her apartment. But her nieces never needed to provide her with a life. Widowed, now retired from a lamp factory, she was an active member of the Gray Panthers, crusading loudly for senior rights. Isobel traveled. Isobel read the "Current and Choice" shelf at the library with the help of a magnifying glass. Isobel was rumored to be involved with a younger man, a beau of only seventy-five. You could almost hear her blood beating urgently beneath the nearly transparent skin.

Suzannah and Isobel clandestinely met for lunch and movies and never told Benita.

Benita sighed loudly. "It isn't easy being a woman."

For once, Suzannah was in agreement with her mother.

"But still," Benita continued, "Chris is a gem compared with what's around. You should see what other women put up with. *They* don't just—"

"Who? Who are they?"

"Oh . . ." Nita waved vaguely in the direction of the TV.

"Soap opera heroines? Mom, this is my real life. Who gives a damn what make-believe women do? They're paid enormous salaries to act like fools!"

Suzannah used her mother's stunned silence as time to retreat, to stalk into the kitchen and arrange the chicken. She pulled out a childhood conviction that the woman in the living room was an impostor. Surely not someone whose flesh and spirit had created Suzannah.

"Your father spoiled you," Benita said between bites of chicken. "That's why you expect too much."

No. She wasn't spoiled. Not by him. Yes, there'd been whirling dances, hugs and snowball fights and late-night talks. Then silence and the enduring pain of abandonment, of not being remembered for so long that Suzannah couldn't believe he'd ever really held her special. She visited him, reminded him of her continued existence and he seemed pleased and a bit surprised each time. And after she left, he forgot her again. Certainly not spoiled.

The muddled sense of betrayal was Suzannah's secret. She never shared it with her mother, who wrapped her own misery around her like a mourner's veil, obscuring all else.

Benita pulled up the skirt of her housedress, revealing a green blot on her flabby thigh. "Fell on the ice," she said. "If I were a well woman, know what I'd do? I'd go to California and get on a quiz show and never come back to the cold. I'd win." She waited for some expected response, but none was forthcoming. "I know you think I'm dumb, but I'm not, Suzannah. I know more than practically all those contestants. I know almost all the answers."

"Great, Mom."

"I'd win trips. To Tahiti. Or Mexico."

"Do it, Mom. But right now, I have to go teach in Merion. Aunt Isobel, do you want a lift?"

"Or the Caribbean. The kind of places you went when you

were married to Chris.'' Her mother aimed her thick glasses at the ceiling. "He calls me, you know."

She had not known.

"He misses you."

"Oh, Mom, I—"

"He's in Hawaii, or he was."

"I wish he wouldn't call you. It isn't fair."

"Why not? I had no quarrel with him."

"If you're serious about the lift," Isobel said, "I accept."

Suzannah nodded and reached for her satchel, a soft leather combination purse and briefcase. "I almost forgot." She unzipped the briefcase side. "I brought you a present. *My Cousin Rachel* in large type. It won't strain your eyes."

Her mother put it on the table beside a pot of plastic philodendron. "Thank you," she said.

It would still be there, dusted, when Suzannah next visited.

"I'll call," Suzannah promised.

Another round of dry kisses. Another slow unbolting of the door, another hallway peer as Suzannah and Isobel walked to the lobby around the corridor's bend.

The worst part, Suzannah thought, helping her aunt into the car, was that to her mother, they'd had a completely satisfying visit. Benita Miller's impaired vision perceived only the most primitive distinctions. People were well or ailing. Events were "nice" or "so-so." Excursions were "fine" or "not worth it."

Tonight, her daughter provided chicken, a gift book and an audience to hear the bleak facts of her life. What else was humanly possible?

"It's thoughtful of you, visiting Mother," Suzannah said after she and Isobel discussed a recent novel and the speech Isobel was scheduled to deliver at City Hall courtyard.

"I worry about your mother. She's so removed from life. So locked up and scared. Such a waste." Isobel hesitated a moment, then spoke even more deliberately. "I worry about you, too, Suzannah."

"Me? Why on earth?"

"Because I love you. I don't want to see you become just like her."

The words moved slowly towards Suzannah, then red-hot scarlet, they dropped on her and branded her flesh. It was a while before she trusted herself to speak. Even then, her voice was strained and harsh. "*Why?* Why would you *say* that? I'm the *opposite* of her! Great God, the woman's never done a damned thing! Never worked, or achieved, never even dreamed! She's missing her own life! Oh, Aunt Isobel—don't waste fear on me. On that."

Isobel patted Suzannah's right hand. "Forgive me. Forgive an old lady. My mind's beginning to wander, but my mouth keeps going." She settled back and said no more.

Eight

Suzannah was late. She ran from the parking lot across the high school campus, praying the rubber grids on her boots would protect her balance.

Once inside Building C, she raced past a busy kitchen, a roomful of sewing machines and women, all noisy, and a lecturer pointing at a map.

She skidded to a stop. "Sorry I'm late," she said. A chorus excused her tardiness as she breathed heavily, threw her cape on the desk and pulled out her notes.

Huffing, gasping, she introduced herself and listed her credentials. "I think"—Puff—"what we'll do is"—Wheeze—"begin with the basics of economics before considering investments."

Poor Isobel was become senile. What an insane thing to say! That Suzannah was scared? Anything at all like her mother? So ugly, so unexpected from Isobel! Like bending to pat the family dog and finding it with ears flat, fangs bared.

Poor, poor Isobel. Well, she'd had eighty-six good years. Time now for Suzannah to pay attention to her nervous class. She inhaled deeply like a diva, faced the twenty waiting women and began.

"The dictionary defines economics as 'the science that deals with the production, distribution and consumption of commodities.' A commodity is anything useful that can be turned to commercial or other advantage.''

Definitions were such clean, self-satisfied items. She felt a proper teacher having dragged out a duo.

"Economics is about money, about what you need, what you have, what you can get for it. It's about the business of life. What concerns you? Not for or about this class, but in your daily life. What do you worry about? Think about?''

Silence. Suzannah studied them. They were almost all in their late thirties or forties. She suspected many ruptured marriages, much belated panic about how the world worked.

Someone finally spoke. "Inflation worries me.'' She giggled as if her concern were wildly idiosyncratic.

"Energy.''

"The music blaring through the wall.''

"It is loud,'' Suzannah agreed. "But irrelevant.''

"Are housing costs part of inflation?''

"Car pools.''

The class glared at the frivolous offender.

"War.''

"Pollution.''

"The breakup of the family.''

A wake of silence followed this. "Yes,'' Suzannah said softly. "A very real current concern. Any more?''

They sighed and then called out world starvation, nuclear holocaust, ecological destruction, un- and underemployment, leisure time concerns.

"Fine. There's not a thing you mentioned—including car pools—that doesn't relate back to the market place, doesn't affect consumer behavior, governmental action, international trade, changing demographics—''

"Oh yeah?'' A gum chewer in the third row folded her hands across her chest. "Tell me how my husband's mid-life crisis is part of economics.''

"Really?''

The woman snapped her gum as a challenge.

"Is he still home?''

"Nope. The bastard took off.''

"In the family station wagon?''

"Not that creep. In a brand-new Porsche.''

"And he's living apart, necessitating an additional housing unit. Buying pots and pans, a stereo. But who cares about him?"

"Not me, that son of a bitch."

"Let's talk about you. You're probably contemplating a return to work. But you have children, obligations. Maybe you'll hire someone to drive and baby-sit and you'll thereby add to someone else's disposable income. You'll change your habits, cook less from scratch, buy whatever saves time and energy, use more gasoline or public transportation, wear and rip more stockings, look for vacation spots with congenial, single souls—"

"I get it," the woman said.

"Good. The point is, we're already a part of the economic process—the part at the bottom of the economic ladder, the lightweight on the pay scale. Half the time, women work for no pay, staffing schools and hospitals and charities as volunteers. And if they are paid, and if they're in a traditionally female job— teaching, secretarial work, nursing—anything to do with child care, of course—they are paid low wages and given low status. But that can change. What we need to do is learn how to accumulate capital, become functioning parts of the capitalist system. We need to understand the meaning of all those concerns you mentioned, comprehend the processes they involve and, most of all, then we need to use them to our advantage. You see—"

"That is morally offensive! Repulsive!" A woman with henna hair and a tiger-skin coat—both synthetic—interrupted Suzannah loudly. "It is *immoral*. It is *wrong* to profit from human misery. Starvation and nuclear catastrophe and even husbands running off. Those are *tragedies!* It is wrong to make money from suffering! *Wrong!*" She slapped her desk for emphasis.

The class seemed stunned, but after a moment, they murmured cautious agreement.

"It's a question of *honor!* Women are the conscience, the soul of mankind." Tiger-woman folded her hands on the desk.

No, Suzannah thought. It wasn't a question of honor, but of why women forged chastity belts of moral scruples to keep themselves from fucking around with the real world.

She didn't know how to begin answering, how to share her perceptions of history, philosophy, female psychology and just plain real life with these strangers. Dimly, then consciously, she became aware of the Chopin seeping through the back wall.

"You hear that waltz?" she asked. "Sweet and lovely—and very old-fashioned. Not destined for today's top forty, right? I—"

"You hate Chopin or something?" The hennaed tiger was invincible. "Or do you hate morality, and honor?"

"No!" Why was everything so difficult? Why didn't anyone understand what she said? "I *like* Chopin," she said. She felt exhausted. "I meant to give an example of something appealing, but outdated, like the attitudes . . ." She sighed. "Let's skip my bad analogies. They aren't working. I simply don't want to see an entire sex—my sex—remain the poor people of this country. Men don't worry that way. That's why they own the entire world—all except the mountains of guilt they've given us to mine. We're so used to wearing guilt we think of it as our special, womanly gift. We rename it sensitivity, compassion, conscience, femininity—"

Tiger-woman gasped. "*Now* you're saying it's wrong to be a decent human being!"

"No I'm not!"

"And that we should become just as rotten as men are!"

"That's ridiculous! I never said or meant that!" Her head felt clogged. How to explain, to make clear? How to define rules in a time without them? "I'm merely suggesting that certain traditional value judgments and role expectations might have to be reevaluated if you want independence or power of any kind."

"Power?" It wasn't the carnivorous redhead this time, but a young woman who appeared honestly confused. Suzannah opened her mouth to answer, but the redhead, sensing a possible second line of attack, shouted over her.

"Yeah—this is supposed to be a course about money. Not Chopin and power."

Was a night school teacher allowed to expel a student? "This course is indeed about money," Suzannah said, keeping her eyes away from the woman. "About money and power because they amount to the same thing. If you're talking about one, you're talking about the other, whether it's world politics or your living room."

"At home?" The woman shook her head. "Not at home. That's not really fair . . ."

"Then let's test it out. You and your husband are both watching the tube. You've both put in long days—his at the office, yours with the kids. If you both want coffee—who gets up to wait on the other? The one who earns the least, right? Money is power. Money is freedom and independence and liberation and equality."

The tigress was miffed. "*Ms.* Barnes," she growled, "you've switched the topic to avoid answering me."

One more peaceful try before Suzannah disciplined her student by smashing a chair over her dyed head. "Your—our—moral problems are part of the equipment of the powerless, and part of what will continue to *keep* us powerless. We want money and power, but *getting* it seems *nasty*. Men don't quibble that way, so the world is theirs. And they intend to keep it. They'll fight us for it, and they'll fight dirty. They'll call us ball-busters, try to bully us back into our dainty corners. We can't be squeamish, we can't let them keep it all forever, can we?"

"Do we want to *be* like them, though? Personally, I say if it means compromising my principles, then—"

"Shhh, Franny." A placater, a peacemaker, a real woman, patted the redhead's arm, then spoke in her behalf to the class. "Franny means that if a company makes money from, say, apartheid, then she wouldn't want to invest in it."

"Sure," Franny said. "But *she's* saying that when it comes to money, there's no right or wrong."

"I never said that!" Suzannah stopped. Is that what she sounded like? She was too confused to unsnarl her ideas, clarify herself, make sense. "I . . . I didn't mean to . . . I wanted . . ." She decided she could lose not only tonight's campaign but the entire war if she didn't change tactics. No more headlong charges down the hill. Time to retreat and retrench, to approach with stealth and discretion.

She had a lot to learn about teaching. It wasn't as simple as she'd expected. Wasn't a matter of dispensing information to grateful listeners like Lady Bountiful and her humble peasants.

"Whatever I said or meant to say, I certainly didn't say it well. We'll inevitably touch back on the subject—but not tonight. Tonight we'll discuss economics. How about if we break for coffee, then return and I'll use the outline I prepared. I might be more comprehensible with a script to follow. Take ten, okay?"

That pleased everyone except tiger-woman, who preserved her virtue and Suzannah's sanity by dropping out of the course on the spot, not even bothering to stay for the second half.

The hallway was congested. Suzannah decided to schedule her class break either earlier or later in the future and avoid the crush.

"Mind if I join you, Ms. Barnes? I'm Myrna Tucker."

Her student was small and wiry, feisty in her tight jeans and fisherman's sweater. She swaggered, eyes directly ahead.

"I'm a career gal. Run my own gift shop. Naturally, in that game, everything hinges on the economy. I've been thinking I should diversify."

Myrna had not paid for private consultations. "We'll discuss that sort of issue in class, or you could call my—"

Myrna kept her eyes front. "So, I figure that energy is always important. People need it, you see?" She turned her whole body to Suzannah, eyes glittering with revelation. "Isn't it a great idea?" She moved backwards down the hallway, eyes riveted on Suzannah.

"Well, everybody knows that—hey, watch where you're going!" Suzannah cried.

But Myrna couldn't, and Myrna consequently crashed. Only then did she turn to face a corduroy jacket with coffee dribbling down it. "I'm so sorry!" she said. "I'll buy you more coffee, I'll pay for dry cleaning, I'll—" She waved her arms around, unable to brush a stain so near a stranger's fly.

"No need," he said. He pushed his glasses up the bridge of his nose and registered surprise. "I know you."

"From my store, Myrna's Treasures, in Paoli, I'll bet."

"Hedy Mishlove's New Year's Eve."

Myrna finally noticed the angle of his eyes, stared as her teacher smiled and extended her hand.

"I'm Suzannah—"

"Barnes," he said. "I know."

"My teacher," Myrna added.

He shook Suzannah's hand. "I'm Coby Waldemar."

The piano player discussed over lunch. Embarrassing.

"She teaches money," Myrna said.

Abby was probably right. There was something glad and alive about this man. Suzannah remembered the first time she'd seen him, how intensely he'd been touching, connecting. With the little woman. Ah well, there might be exceptions. Men worth coping with extraneous domestic ties for.

A matron pushed through. "Dr. Waldemar, break's up."

"Doctor!" Myrna crooned.

"In music. Doctorate. No help during flu season. I'll be right there," he told the waiting woman.

Myrna pointed an accusing finger. "Music? You must be in the next room. We can hear your class."

"My apologies. The acoustics aren't the best."

"We'll survive," Suzannah said.

He smiled. "Please excuse me now. Nice meeting you, Myrna. And you, again, Suzannah Barnes." He smiled, his face crinkling delightfully. "We're whizzing through history tonight. In class, I mean. I'll keep Stravinsky under control if I can." He nodded and left.

A music teacher. Jesus. She passed a cup of coffee to Myrna, put change in the machine for another. He certainly wasn't her conception of a music teacher. She'd always envisioned anyone with that title as a meek, wistful sort, rapping children's knuckles, chewing breath sweeteners, living in dark, Dostoevskian basements.

At nine twenty-five, Suzannah paced the front of the room, tapping her palm with her other hand. "Adam Smith's theory held that the motivating force in the economic system was self-interest." She grinned. "Let's not challenge the morality of that again tonight. Anyway, by combining everyone's self-interest, the common interest is served, guided by what Smith called an invisible hand. Minimal governmental intervention and a free and self-regulatory market."

His hands, very visible, were slender with long tapering fingers. Perfect for a musician. A music teacher.

At nine thirty-six, Suzannah moved toward the present. "The equilibrium became very shaky during the Great Depression. There was still a balance, but a terribly diminished one. Less employment, less income, less investment capital, less savings to enable further development. Along came John Maynard Keynes, a name you'll still see. He advocated large-scale governmental planning to promote employment."

His eyes were enormous. Amazing. Dark blue and liquid, heavily lashed. Startling when his glasses slid down his small nose.

"Unfortunately, at that time no one, including Keynes, was concerned with inflation. Now, of course, everyone is. Which is not to say that concern has led to a solution."

Myrna called out. "What's stagflation?"

"A new coinage to describe our combination of inflation and unemployment. This creates what a colleague of mine calls a steer market—a bull market with its balls cut off. I, however, don't favor the constant equation of having balls with having vitality. In fact, I don't like the word stagflation. It sounds perverse, like something done in the men's room at singles' bars."

At nine fifty-eight, she stopped talking about macroeconomics. "Next week we'll begin our real topic, your options in the market place. Let's break on time even if we did begin late."

Myrna hovered at the door while the room emptied. "I'm into cards." She fell into step beside Suzannah.

"Pardon me?"

"Cards." Myrna stuck her hand out like a storm trooper and pushed the outside door. "Greeting cards. Old ones. My mom's, mostly. Cute. Quaint. And not a big collector thing yet like comics are."

The parking lot was arctic, the wind racing across its crusted expanse. Suzannah thought fondly of her sealed apartment, of the city's density and of well-trafficked streets defying all but the most adamant of storms.

"My car's over there," Myrna said. "Where's yours?"

Suzannah couldn't remember. She scanned the lot.

He was under an arc light. She was certain it was the music teacher, puffing and tamping his pipe, his hands in thick gloves, his body hunched against the wind.

He looked up, and Suzannah knew by the pause of his gloved hand, the tilt of his head, the frozen moment, that he was waiting for her.

She remembered now. Her car was to the right, near the Phys. Ed. building, but she gestured to where he stood, now straight and relaxed as if insulated. "I'll see you next week, Myrna. Nice meeting you."

"I'll walk you. I want to talk about the cards. Besides, I know karate. Just let anybody get smart with me." Myrna slashed the air.

"Hey—I'll see you next Tuesday."

Myrna interrupted her grunts and knee bends to look at Suzannah. Then she peered around, caught the figure under the lamp and shook her head. "You wouldn't—"

"Next week?"

"Talk about asking for trouble! A stranger! He could be a pervert! Listen, kick him you-know-where if he—"

"Next week." Suzannah walked away, sandwiched between the stares of the little woman behind her, the man ahead. She stepped carefully. Snow melted in sunshine had refrozen into transparent skins, and Suzannah had a terror of slipping.

"Yes?" she said when she was near him. Then she flushed with embarrassment. What if he wasn't waiting for her? What if a cooking teacher or slimnastics student was behind her, walking briskly to the tall man? How would she explain the summons she'd felt?

And why had she answered it? To hear variation seven thousand on how a well-intentioned marriage failed? She backed off a pace.

"I thought," he said, pipe smoke and frozen breath merging, "you might like coffee. There's a place nearby."

Suzannah frowned. Dumb. She should have stayed away. "Thanks, but I'm tired. I've had too long a day already and the last thing I need is more caffeine."

"Then Sanka." His voice was too loud.

"Some other time?"

No. He was not going to let that happen. No. He didn't believe in an open-ended series of other times. What if there were a blizzard? Classes canceled? What if she moved? Invited guest lecturers to cover for her? No. Twice now he'd known she was different. She was no compromise. All that he knew of her was right, the sweet curve of chin, the shine in her hair, her walk, her colors, her voice. He needed a chance to know more.

"No," he said. "I mean please? A cup of anything. No cups. Any excuse to spend time with you."

"You're certainly forthright."

"I am that. And trustworthy. And bad at beginnings. But I don't want you to disappear. It's only ten o'clock. Give us one cup of coffee's time. I'll drive, I'll bring you back safely. This is important, don't you know that? I want to get past the beginning."

A late-breaking class erupted from a far building. Suzannah heard a burst of chatter as twenty or so women advanced towards them.

"You're shaking," he said. "Are you afraid of me?"

"No. I'm freezing."

"Then come with me. Defrost."

"My car has a fine heating system, thank you."

"Mine doesn't." He appeared inordinately depressed. "I'm sorry."

"About your car heater?"

"About me. I didn't mean to be obnoxious. In fact, I hoped to be charming. Irresistible. I wrongly assumed matters would progress smoothly after 'how about coffee.' I'll see you next week. I will undoubtedly even try again."

"Well . . ."

They were in the crossfire of shouted farewells as the tardy class found its cars. She looked at him closely. His ruddy cheeks were rubbed to an even brighter intensity by the wind. Behind the glasses, his dark eyes looked at the ground, then at her, waiting.

"One cup."

He grinned, rearranging the planes of his face into a design that echoed and enlarged the gleam of teeth, the appealing curl of his full lips. "And talk," he said. "The purpose of this meeting is talk."

She followed him to his car, a burgundy VW, and entered it quickly, as if hiding from the matrons on the parking lot.

Nelly's Deli was brilliantly lit and loud with voices, not the least of which belonged to Nelson the Salami Man. He shouted at his customers, deriding them, their orders and pleas for service. And yet people came, needing to exorcise a masochistic gnaw.

"Two—no, one coffee, one Sanka," Coby told Nelson.

"That's it, sport? No blintzes? Cheesecake? Danish?" Nelson wiped a beefy hand on his stained apron. "Big spenders!" he shouted, and stomped off.

"How's your class?" they asked in unison.

They laughed.

"Nothing changes," Coby said. "My adolescent overtures began with questions about classes. 'How'dya do in the hourly? What's your major?' Now we're the teachers and we still start with them."

"You didn't. As I recall, you said you wanted to get past the beginning. That's different."

"It worked. But how do you like your class?"

She shrugged. "This is the first time I've tried teaching. So far, it feels like force-feeding a goose."

"It's fun, if you encourage them to share, be real participants. I've been teaching that course for years, and only because it's fun. After all, they're there for the learning, not for grades or degrees."

"What do you do in the daytime?"

"Same thing, but with degrees and grades. Teach. Play music, write some. And you?"

"I'm a stockbroker. With Sherwood Hastings, downtown."

He laughed out loud. "I never would have guessed."

He had exceptionally high cheekbones, as if he'd been sculpted by a modernist whose art was based on exaggeration. When he was silent, listening, his face was almost ascetic, saintly were it not for the constant play of emotions. But when he smiled, the face became all delight, laughed all over the high flushed cheeks, the hollows beneath them. It was a face to study. It was many faces. A warm center of joy expanded in her midsection.

"Why are you surprised? You know I'm teaching a course about money."

"I thought you did something with the theory of it. I don't know. You look otherworldly, like a Renaissance painting."

She watched him talk, hearing nothing. And it didn't matter. These words were fillers, planks pushed across the table until they formed a bridge they could cross. He gestured, held something invisible in the air as he spoke. She liked his movements, the long rangy exclamation point of his body, the highlights in his hair. His emotions, which seemed abundant and close to the surface. His voice. The secrets in his face. She wondered how his lips would feel.

She had her list of what she didn't like in men. But she'd never defined what it was she liked or wanted. Whatever it was, the man across from her had it.

"Sorry," she said. "What did you say?"

"Do you like it? Your job? I mean do you *enjoy* doing it?" He appeared dubious.

She nodded. Why did people come on this way? As if she handled tainted goods, as if liking her job meant she was depraved. They'd be satisfied only if she donned a nurse's uniform, held a teacher's pointer. Only if she accepted low wages, took care of someone and played female. "I *enjoy* it," she said. "I *like* it," she added, her defenses gathered. "I *like* riding hunches, using my brains, taking risks, talking to people, learning. I *like* action and excitement. I *like* challenges.''

Scratch the music teacher, his face and lips, if he launched into a hackneyed sermon on materialism, on sweet Renaissance females, on anything. She peered around high battlements, waiting.

"Look," he said, putting down his mug. "I'm doing this wrong. I want to know you, that's all. Where's the best place to start?"

Oh, Coby—and what sort of name is that—Waldemar. Six-two, mid-thirties, can this be the first time you're leaving the mortgaged nest to fly again? Am I supposed to teach yet another adult education course?

Ah, but he was attractive. And seemed a quick study. She smiled. "I think standard procedure is to begin with superficial biographies, not to probe psyches. So, I am Suzannah Miller Barnes. Haverford High, Bryn Mawr, Wharton. Twenty-nine, one marriage down the tubes, two jobs. I'm one of two children, have no allergies or debilitating defects. But I do have a tendency to be materialistic, self-serving and goal-directed, which is why I'm likely to be a success. I'm moody, unreliable lots of ways, overly fond of food and consequently oversized. I don't jog or play tennis. I'm a lousy daughter and I—''

"No you're not."

"I'll let you fight it out with my mother."

"Oversized. You aren't. You're perfect. Beautiful.''

She lifted her cup and gulped coffee.

"And you have trouble accepting compliments and only feel secure talking about measurable accomplishments. You were probably summa cum laude at Bryn Mawr and you don't do anything if you can't do it well.''

"I thought we wouldn't probe—''

"I'm Jacob no middle name Waldemar, called Coby. Troy High, Syracuse U., Ph.D. in Music from Columbia since you rank degrees up there with the most urgent information. Good but not great musician. Unhappy second son of the sole proprietors of Waldemar's Fruit and Produce. Unhappy because for years I was as tall as I am now, but I weighed 152 pounds. I have since gained weight and respectability. I love music, horses, camping, walking tours of old cities and . . . people say I'm too intense, but I don't understand what they mean.''

Nelson's enormous apron billowed up beside their table. "Anything else, sport?" Coby shook his head. "How'm I gonna pay my rent, cheapskate?" Nelson slammed the bill on the table.

Outside, the air sliced through Suzannah. Coby didn't bother to button his coat. Nor, she acknowledged with some regret, had he bothered to include his wife in his biography. He was treating her like a fool. Good-by, C. Waldemar, but first, understand I am not that stupid. "Coby?" she asked coolly, "didn't you skip a relevant statistic? Like your wife?"

He waited until they were inside, the ignition and headlights on before he spoke. "I was married for twelve years. I have a six-year-old son."

"Was?"

"She's dead."

"I'm sorry," Suzannah whispered, ashamed and confused.

He said nothing, driving back to the high school lot, pulling next to the only car left. "I never know how to broach it." He put the car into neutral. "It still isn't easy to blurt out, and people react so . . . I mean lots of people aren't married any more, but that doesn't make us alike." He looked at Suzannah intently. "I didn't mention it, maybe because I didn't want this. I don't want anything to intrude. I want a fair start, that's all."

He smelled of the cold, of pipe tobacco and lemony after-shave. His dark curls nearly touched the roof. There wasn't room for the dead woman or the past. There was only the icy still night and their small sealed enclosure.

"Coby," she said quietly. She touched the softness of his hair, ran her fingers down the planes of his face. He lifted her hand and kissed her finger tips.

Outside, an owl hoot sounded and echoed.

Suzannah remembered a time when hours and seconds were charged, when every moment counted and possibility was a cut crystal pendulum, suspended motionless and heavy, reflecting, suggesting, waiting.

"You're beautiful," he murmured, putting his hand behind her neck, drawing her towards him.

His lips were as she'd hoped they'd be, imagined them, warm and full, touching softly, tentatively at first. She could feel their shape, the swoop of the bow, the uptilt at the corners, the rich fullness of the lower lip.

His hand moved around her, under her cape. She drank in the male smell of him, heightened by the cold. He moved closer.

"Aaaagh!" he shouted, pulling back. "The gearshift!" Then he laughed, and she loved the sound that welled from deep inside, filling the car until she had to join in.

"Didn't it used to work in cars?" he said.

"Not in VW bugs." His hand still played with the collar of her silk shirt. "I don't live far," she said softly. "Just off the parkway."

"I can't." He freed his hand and put it on the steering wheel. "My kid's sitter . . ."

"I'm not planning to move. I'm in the book. S. Barnes, to deter cranks."

She could wait. She could always wait for anything she wanted, could even manage to enjoy the wait. S. Barnes was nothing if not goal-directed.

He smiled. Then he contorted his body, avoiding the gearshift to hold her close, kissing her this time with urgency. She could no longer feel the curl of his lips, only their pressure and need and something in herself struggling to meet it.

"I'll remember that, S. Barnes."

"Good. And, Coby? You've achieved your goal. We're definitely past the beginning. Of something."

Nine

The telephone rang inside Apartment 523. Suzannah jammed her key in the lock, kicked the door, cursed, raced through the living room, tripped over the Aubusson, twisted her left ankle and hopped, painfully, to the kitchen.

The phone stopped ringing.

She kicked a kitchen cabinet with her right toe, cried out, bent to rub both feet and hobbled into the living room to pour herself a brandy.

Carrying it as fortification, she returned to the phone. Nine-thirty P.M. Thursday. One more workday left. Before her resolve weakened, she must phone Chris.

His voice was mellow, pleasantly surprised.

"I have something to discuss, Chris. Nothing personal. It's—"

"Don't spoil my fantasies. How about lunch at André's tomorrow?"

"We could handle this at your office or mine."

"Suzannah, you're in danger of becoming a pragmatic creep. Don't reduce everything to its essentials. You love André's ratatouille, anyway."

"But I'd rather not go to someplace so—"

"And I love André's sole amandine."

"Fine. It's not worth a discussion."

Afterwards, she nervously sipped brandy, angry at having capitulated to his sentimental choice of restaurants, nervous about how to spend the evening ahead of her. She wasn't tired, and even when she was, she resisted sleep. She checked that the loan papers were in her briefcase, then pulled out notes she'd made at dinner. They were as boring as Hadley Lawrence and the heavy meal had been.

Business completed, she'd listened, stifling yawns while Hadley catalogued the merits of his children's schools, of his children themselves and of his civic-minded wife.

She found his monologues tedious, his motives amusing. Hadley couldn't assimilate the concept that Suzannah was first, last and solely his broker. While discussing offshore drilling companies, his glance repeatedly lost its moorings and slid to her breasts. Then he'd crawl behind his eyeballs and dredge them up, shoring them with a recitation of his credentials as a family man. He seemed happiest when he reassured himself that he wouldn't, accidentally, jump on her.

She went into her bedroom. She'd based today's clothing on Hadley, and she pulled off the cashmere turtleneck. Severe, but soft and snug, it had served her well. Hadley optically roller-coasted so often, he doubled his order.

Tomorrow she'd dress for Chris, giving no reason for his glance or conversation to ease onto anything but the loan papers.

She studied her body in the mirror and frowned, rearranging herself so that her weight was on one leg. After a twist of the waist, a thrust of the pelvis, one hipbone surfaced. But barely. She sighed and turned around. No visible spinal column. She was completely out of fashion, altogether too soft. She bent low, forcing her spine to the surface, craning at the mirror over her shoulder. When she was nearly touching the floor, she saw a hint of skeletal bumps low on her back. But she also, much more clearly, saw a roll of belly fat.

She stood straight, hands above head, then slowly pirouetted. That wasn't horrible. Clothed, her body always seemed in a battle with the angular dreams of designers. But naked wasn't awful at all. Naked, she seemed relatively well designed. Each part flowed into the next. Her skin fit perfectly.

She studied her image, attempting objectivity. How did she look, would she look, that awkward first time, to a man? When he really looked, when he had to notice the too-large thighs, the boneless hips, the spineless back—how did she appear?

As an adolescent, standing before other mirrors, she'd mentally jump-cut from a fully clothed kiss to herself, discreetly sheltered by a blanket, waiting for her handsome lover.

But real life didn't work that way. There were all those intermediate frames. The graceless undressing, the pulled-in stomach, pretended oblivion while he looked and she prayed he could barely perceive her through a red haze of lust.

I should find me a blind lover, she thought, going into the shower. I'm not bad in braille.

Coby wore glasses. Maybe without them, he wouldn't see. If he called. Which he hadn't. Which surprised her. It had only been two days, and it didn't matter, but still . . .

What the hell. There were more pressing matters, such as tomorrow's wardrobe, armament against Chris. The black number, she decided. Her heavy-duty camouflage for desiccated bankers, suspicious wives and terminated lovers.

She rinsed and left the steamy shower, pulling on a thick terry robe. It was still too early for bed. She checked television listings, flipped through an old *Architectural Digest* and reluctantly retrieved Patty Luboff's omnipresent questionnaire. She had reached a section concerned with commuting time, office politics and family planning.

Suzannah despised multiple choice questions. The only answer that ever seemed applicable was "none of the above." How did questionnaire writers live? And where? Nothing Suzannah had ever experienced suggested that life held tidy, clearly differentiated alternatives. She skipped to an easier "yes-no" section.

"Do you have or plan to have children?" "No." Nice. No shilly-shallying, no haggling with multiple options.

Her firm negative allowed her to skip ten questions concerning day care, time-sharing and other lifelines for working mothers. Permission to leap ahead imbued her stance with righteousness.

However, helping Patty Luboff win her Ph.D. was no way to spend an evening. Suzannah put away the pages designed for mothers and reconsidered her own large, albeit unpregnant, body.

The time was as ripe as she was for a long-deferred self-improvement program. Tomorrow she'd sign up for exercise class.

No. Tomorrow was already marred by lunch with Chris. Then Monday, an apt day to grunt and groan.

So much for *corpore sano*. What about the *mens sana?* There was more to the intellectual life than the collected questions of Patty Luboff.

Proust. Of course. In French. She had an appointment with a bookseller tomorrow anyway. They'd discuss selected stocks and *Á La Recherche du Temps Perdu*. Knock him dead with the Barnes double-whammy, street-smarts and *sagacité*.

And tonight, easing into the Redevelopment Program, she'd pluck her eyebrows, another hateful task.

She felt noble, well on her way to perfection as she tweaked misplaced hairs. Her eyes teared and she heard buzzing.

She stopped tweaking. The buzz continued. It dawned on her that it was not the sound of her martyrdom, but of her intercom.

"Who is it?" She was not fearful of late-night slashers, but of someone appealing who'd see her red, newly plucked brow.

"Suzannah? It's Josie. Can I come up?"

Her sister entered nonchalantly, as if such visits were commonplace. She kicked off her shoes, seated herself on the sofa and curled her feet under her, waving at Suzannah's brandy. "Any more of that around?"

"Sure. And let me take your coat."

The Miller girls didn't resemble each other although relatives tried forcing an analogy. It bothered cousins and aunts that Suzannah was four inches taller, that Josie's skin tended toward olive, Suzannah's to ivory, that the nine years separating their births had produced a new strain of Miller.

"It's so orderly here," Josie murmured.

"The maid was in today."

"Not that kind of orderly. I mean somebody's orders. Yours. You're so obviously in control, as usual." She sighed. "I surprised you, didn't I? Appearing this way?"

"Since it's the first time ever, yes."

"Good." Josie lit a cigarette. "It's nice to surprise someone." She bobbled her cigarette on the edge of the green ashtray. "I was scurrying home, programmed the way I always am. And all of a sudden, I couldn't figure out why I have to always, always have a boomerang on my back."

"What were you scurrying home from?"

Josie's hand froze a few inches from her mouth. "What do you mean?"

"Nothing. Chitchat. You said you were somewhere, I asked where."

"Dinner. With a friend. Ben's in a class Thursdays, so I . . . go out, you know?"

And now it was Suzannah's turn to methodically remove a cigarette from the malachite box, eyes nowhere near her sister's. A friend? Unnamed? No further description? That was standard code for . . . but Josie? Impossible. Of course, even PTA presidents played around. But Josie? One half of Josie and Ben, one of the world's ten happy marriages?

She thought hard before saying another word. First, she had to reshuffle all her mental pictures of her sister. She had always envisioned Josie in soft focus, sailing through life with a nine-year head start. Never making waves, placidly drifting through boys and school until she disappeared over the horizon. Anchored, married, a mother.

Suzannah had memories of big sister Josie taking time to pass along information on how boys were, how girls should be and where one actually inserted the tampon. Friendly acts, but never a friend.

Perhaps Josie wanted to change that. Perhaps that's why she was here. Until that was certain, Suzannah would select her words so that neither singly nor in syntax did they cast shadows, create new barriers.

"How was your dinner?" she asked politely.

"What stinks about being a wife and mother is that there are no official holidays, no legal recuperation time."

So much for exquisite politeness. "Do you need to talk?" Suzannah asked. "I'm a good listener."

Josie stood and walked to the large window overlooking the parkway. She sipped brandy, shaking her head against an interior argument. "I'd like to talk, but . . ." She wheeled around, knuckles white around her snifter. "How could you understand? You—your whole life *you've* decided what happened to you. Look at this place, the way you live! My house—there's everybody's droppings. Three kids. Dogs. A husband. The TV plays, the stereo blares, the dogs bark, Ben talks, the kids fight. For Christ's sake, we live on separate planets, Suzannah. You don't let things intrude or confuse you. You never have. You'd never understand me, not in a thousand years!"

Suzannah mentally blew up the bridge she'd intended to build. "Why did you come here? To attack me and the way I choose to live? What did I do to you?"

Josie's voice lost its anger and emerged thin and shaky. "I came here because I don't want to go home and I don't have anywhere else to go." Tears streamed down her face. "I'm so mixed up. I'm sorry. It isn't your fault. But it makes it worse that I had to come here and that I can't expect you to understand." She wiped a hand across her nose. "I'm jealous of you. I want to be the tough one, the grabber, the one who doesn't care. I want to be the kid who makes the mess, not the one who cleans it up. Remember?" She tried to smile. "Remember how if toys didn't work right away, you smashed them? I've always been Goody Two-shoes. The patsy! I *hate* me! I want to be *you!*"

"Somehow, that doesn't feel complimentary."

Josie, snuffling, went to the bar cart to refill her snifter. "I love you, Suze. But you treat me like something a few years out of style. Which I guess I am."

Suzannah walked to her sister and put out her hand. "How about a truce? How about we pretend we never met before?"

Suzannah noticed the fine network of lines around her sister's pale gray eyes. It was, she realized, the first time she was noticing Josie as anything but "the other" daughter, the well-behaved model to whom she was unfavorably compared.

Josie said nothing, searching until she found tissues in her pocket, then loudly, repeatedly, blowing her nose and dabbing her eyes. A smudge of mascara streaked her cheek.

"It isn't that I don't want to talk." She sat down heavily. "I . . . don't know *how*." She focused her gaze on the smoke alarm in the ceiling, then looked again at Suzannah. "Forgive me. This is nothing. Following the script. I'm supposed to have a mid-life crisis, aren't I? I've always done what's expected. When it was time to learn, I made the honor roll. When it was time to marry, I wed. When it was time to reproduce, I was so good, I tried to have 2.3 babies. Now, I hear, it's time to weep." She blew her nose again, then lit another cigarette. "Everybody I know is falling apart. This is so . . . damned . . . ordinary!"

Suzannah opened her mouth to console.

"No! Don't say anything. I'm not ready for a quick solution, even if this is standard. I don't know if I want to be the middle-aged lady with the book bag, or divorce papers, or a boutique or a shrink."

"I only thought—"

"No you didn't. Be honest. You don't think about me. I'm an unresearched topic, and not only for you."

Suzannah took her sister's hand. Josie sniffled, shook her head and pulled another clump of tissues from her pocket. "Boy, do I need to cry. I'm great at self-pity lately."

Suzannah waited. Finally, her sister inhaled deeply like an exhausted swimmer. "I wish my period were due. I wish I could blame something on that. I wish I didn't have to think I was having a nervous breakdown. I was afraid to go home because part of me wants to wreck everything, start my life over, unencumbered. Find out. But the other part knows that's crazy. I think I'm schizophrenic. Can you catch it, like a cold? I better leave. It's late. They'll worry."

"Oh, Josie, not yet. Phone home instead."

Suzannah waited while Josie called from the kitchen and quickly returned. "Mind if I pour another?" Josie asked. "I'm edgy when Betsy sits. She's good, for fifteen, but she doesn't always do her homework if I—" She clapped her hand over her mouth. "I *hate* sounding that way! That's the programmed lady I despise!"

She sat down and stared at her brandy, then jumped, her olive skin blanching as the phone rang.

It was Potter Alexander, hiccuping with anxiety. Should he

change his whole portfolio because some antsy V.P. who—

"Potter, I can't talk. I thought you were the paramedics. Emergency here right now."

"—so if I go ahead like a—"

Suzannah hung up.

"Who was that?" Josie asked the question before Suzannah was back in the living room.

"A lunatic. A client."

Josie flicked her cigarette repeatedly until the burning tip fell into the ashtray. "I thought Ben was checking up on me."

"Is . . . is this about the . . . friend?"

"God, but I'd hate Ben to find out. God, but I want him to." She began weeping again.

"All right," Suzannah said firmly. "Time for the real stuff, my antidepressants." She returned from the kitchen with a plastic bag. "Best bakery in town."

"Cookies?"

"My drug of choice is chocolate."

Josie munched slowly. "Want to know what started my whatever this is?" She washed each cookie down with brandy. "Last spring, I was going to bed, checking Ben's morning appointments, whether Betsy had early gymnastics, and it hit me. For years—forever, I'd set my alarm for other people's schedules. I don't even wake up to my own timetable, let alone live by it. And everything fell apart."

She swigged brandy and broke a cookie into three pieces. "Promise you won't laugh?"

Suzannah promised.

"I rebelled. My way. Oh, I was sneaky. A guerilla sniping at the house that Josie built. I bought cereals with preservatives. I overslept. I packed roast beef for Betsy, who was in a vegetarian phase. I told the laundry to starch Ben's shirts."

She stood and stretched her petite frame, waving her now-empty snifter. "Good God, I thought of myself as a wild-eyed assassin, lurking around the palace. When they were away, I'd laugh hysterically. I washed Ben's maroon sweater in hot water and bleach. I served frozen pizza three times one week."

She crept behind the sofa. "I left the salt out of the soup. I didn't pay library fines. I missed David's Peewee games. I napped through Kim's teacher conference, left stains on the kitchen table, didn't use cents-off coupons at the supermarket."

She walked, a bit too carefully, to the bar cart and refilled her glass, then held it aloft like the Statue of Liberty's beacon. "I watched game shows. I didn't exercise. I bought single-ply toilet paper!"

Josie lowered her torch, sipped, then went back to her sofa perch and ate more cookies. "Know what happened?"

Suzannah shook her head.

"Nobody noticed." Josie waited, then squinted in Suzannah's direction. "Go ahead," she said. "Laugh. It deserves it."

"No. I know it's serious."

"Yeah. But pathetic, too. Other women storm out of the house, abandon their kids, take on armies of lovers, murder someone! But I . . . I . . ." She ate more cookies, drank more brandy. "No. It wasn't funny and it didn't work. I didn't get a kick out of it or anything else. It's like someone turned off the color in the TV, you know? The same picture, but gray. I want the colors back and I don't know how to fix the set." She rubbed her forehead. "Why am I telling you this?" She put her head in her hands and sniffled.

Suzannah solemnly regarded the crumb-filled plastic bag. "C'mon, Josie, we need another fix."

They emptied the kitchen of edibles. Josie lined cardboard, plastic and cellophane containers on the counter, then stepped back to survey.

"Fucking neurotic feast," she said, weaving slightly as she waved at the counter. "What first? Peanuts? Fudge sauce? Cold macaroni? Pineapple chunks? Camembert? Triscuits?"

"I never heard you say 'fuck' before."

"Yeah. Bet you thought I didn't do it, either. I wasn't sure myself. Oh, I did, but in my whole entire life, only with Benjamin. Wasn't sure I did it right."

She swayed, then grabbed the counter top with both hands and carefully seated herself on the barstool. "Know what? My—" She released one hand to tap herself on the chest dramatically. "My generation, the good ones like me, the ones who bought it all, we were orange juice cans." She looked very pleased with herself. "What d'you think of that, huh?"

"Of what?"

"OR-ange juice cans." She waited. "Dontcha get it? The *label*—keep frozen until used. Get it? That was *me*. All of us. Until at *least* you had the engagement ring." She giggled, then opened containers, dipping a finger into the fudge sauce, picking up pineapple chunks and topping them with peanuts. "This is fun, you know? This is good. Maybe we could—that Betty Crontest? That Crock—that *contest?* Enter this? Call it the Miller Girls' Surprise?"

"I wouldn't eat anything with surprise in its name."

"Wise. You astound me. Very, very, very wise."

"You want coffee? You're tilting."

"No. Definitely no. I hate sober. I hate good." She chuckled, low in her throat. "I'm bad now. Having an affair. Sneaking, lying. The big time. The mainstream."

"Ah, Josie, why? I thought you were the happiest woman on earth."

"I *am.* That's what's awful." She pounded her fist on the counter, then sniffed and wiped away tears.

"You've a unique way of showing it."

Josie ate more of her peanut-pineapple-fudge confection. "I love Ben. That's a problem. Love the kids. Another problem. Lots of times, love being a Home Maker. It's a real thing, you know? Hated the way it was for us kids. I wanted to make . . . the opposite. Love, warm . . . for sixteen years . . ." She cradled her chin on her hand, looking miserable.

"You've done it."

Josie spoke with difficulty. "Wish I wasn't so *happy* . . ."

"Having an affair doesn't mean the end of a marriage."

"I didn't even mean to have this one."

"This one? Josie—there've been others?"

"Only one. Last summer. Because of the juice can." She pushed herself off the stool. "Let me get brandy for sad stories." She bumped into the louvered door, backed off apologetically and left, returning with the entire bottle. "Saves time," she said, pouring. "A sleazy summertime story. Beach bum, you know? Bulging muscles, bulging bathing suit. Beautiful. Red-gold hair . . ." She belched.

"What happened?"

"Same things that happen with Ben. Only Ben's more fun. This was . . . like making it with the Pope, you know?"

"No. Believe it or not, I don't have carnal knowledge of everyone. Certainly not His Holiness."

"Well, it was like being *honored.* I mean I was supposed to be thrilled because he *allowed* me to *share* him. Boring, you know?

The chocolate sauce is making me sick.'' She lit another cigarette and gulped.

"Josie, listen. You can't let sex, however fine—" The phone rang. Josie gasped. "Don't panic," Suzannah said. "You're where you said you were." She lifted the receiver.

Her brother-in-law's voice was anxious. "I just got in. Is Josie still there? It's late, and I—"

Beside Suzannah, Josie rocked gently, tears leaking down both cheeks. Her cigarette lay ignored in the chocolate sauce.

"Ben," Suzannah said, "I'm afraid I corrupted her. I offered her brandy, and she's zonked. Want me to wake her?"

"No," he said softly. "Tell her—have her spend the night, get a good rest. I'll—I'll get the kids off to school. Is she—"

"Yes?"

"Nothing."

When Suzannah hung up, she found Josie examining her dripping cigarette. "Can't smoke chocolate," Josie said gravely. "I don't want to hurt him. Sixteen years. Like you said, even great sex . . . no orgasm lasts sixteen years . . ." She turned to face Suzannah, but swiveling was obviously too demanding and she slid from her stool. "Ol' chocolate sauce got me," she said from the floor. "S'okay. Never get sick. Too *good* to make messes . . ."

Suzannah guided her out of the room, into the bedroom and off with her skirt. Then she covered her with the comforter. Josie drifted off immediately, then opened wild eyes. "Whirlies!" she gasped. "Talk to me, okay?" She blinked, forcing her eyes open. " 'Bout Stephen?" She labored to make each word clear, shook her head when Suzannah made soothing noises, and refused to stop. "Stephen. Divorced. So sad. Tried to be . . . friend."

"Shhh. It's all right."

"Plain. No redgold. Talk, though. Feelings. Felt so close . . ." She became quiet, closed her eyes. Suzannah tiptoed away. "You know?" sounded from the bed. "Not a body. A man . . ."

Her eyes still closed, Josie's mouth moved, sometimes emitting sound, sometimes not. She resembled a corpse, only her lips sporadically set in motion. "Too late for . . . have Ben . . . but, Suze? I want . . . it all.''

Suzannah bent and kissed her. "Nothing's ruined, can you understand me? Nothing is ruined."

"Want the colors back. With Stephen, but Ben—"

"They'll come back home." She felt like a parent lulling away nightmares, lying about the possibility of ugly endings and unhappiness. She kissed Josie's temple again, heard a sigh that sounded final and left the room.

She washed the snifters, reshelved the peanuts and pineapple and sat eating chocolate sauce with her index finger as spoon. Poor Josie, working so hard and long, planting a garden of sturdy perennials that now leached her strength into its deep roots.

She shook her head, looked at her chocolate-covered finger and at the counter, where she'd absently traced a pattern with the sauce. It gleamed on the white formica, rich and sticky. She sponged it away and flipped off the kitchen lights, deciding that she was the only woman she knew who wasn't falling apart.

Once beside her softly snoring sister, Suzannah thought back to her early teens when she'd studied the romantic rituals between lovable Benjamin and her grown-up sister. How closely she'd monitored them, memorizing the rules and rewards of adult life. Vicarious lessons then. And now.

And she knew, fleetingly, right before she fell asleep, that it was for the best that Coby hadn't called. He was too attractive. Too dangerous. Let him stay far away.

Ten

Suzannah studied her ex-husband's face, searching for what saved it from blandness. His tan added to his monochromatic appearance, blending waxy unlined skin into buff hair. His eyes were slightly darker. Wet sand. But, as with a characterless newborn, some primordial optimism, a belief he was intrinsically valuable and deserving of love, colored Chris, convinced his audience that he was, indeed, quite special.

Whatever it was, it remained powerful enough to produce pain in Suzannah.

"Well, now, what is the solemn purpose of this meeting?" Chris lit a cigarette. He sucked in the smoke, savoring it as he would his sole amandine, the body of his current woman, the ambiguous atmosphere of this lunch.

"I want to borrow on my half of the Spruce Street building." Suzannah's voice was harsher than intended.

"My, my," he drawled. "You're pressed for pocket money? Why? Have your customers forsaken you?"

"I'm making an investment. I need your signature. not your approval."

He lounged in his chair gracefully, his custom-made shirt hugging him. Chris's clothing always seemed designed by hands which had stroked him to learn his measurements. "Why so hostile? Why this grim neutered look? Not even a scarf or earrings. Hair pulled back like Miss Grundy. Are you afraid I'll remember how soft and smooth you are? Suzannah, I never forgot."

"We're off the subject."

"Wrong. I was summoned by my ex-wife, who reveres all contracts except the one with 'till death do us' in small print. Or maybe this dried-up look of yours means you're dying."

"I'm the same as always. I never appreciated your unsolicited analyses of my motives or self. I still don't."

"I agree that you haven't changed." He acknowledged the arrival of his lunch with an approving smile. "I think," he continued after the waiter bowed off, "you're Suzannah still and you're scared to death because it's there between us, even now. I can see it under your disguise. I can feel it myself. All over me."

"Maybe it's body lice. You know, we might be friends if you'd drop the routine. This is a business lunch. Talk business."

Instead, he ate intently, giving his full attention to the delicate white fish, the crisp almond slices.

She had the disquieting sensation of tasting what went into his mouth, living inside his body, being Chris, whom she'd once literally thought her other half, a half that provided her missing parts, could wander free and be what she was not.

But they'd never been joined, and anyway, the concept was incorrect. Believing in future completion meant believing in prior insufficiency.

"Chilly woman, you are. Like mother, like daughter."

"My mother? Your telephone pal? I wish you'd stop calling her, interfering—"

"With what? She's happy I care about her."

"You call because you don't believe in holding firm or letting go, not because you care."

"What's your business deal?"

His sidesteps in any sparring match never failed to surprise, infuriate and sometimes delight her.

"Why? Are you interested?"

He shook his head. "It comes in, it goes out. I'm happy as long as there's enough, and there is."

There always had been a fat cushion to elevate Chris above greed. He quoted Wordsworth, disparaging the getting and spending that directed most lives because his getting was effortless, his spending almost unconscious.

And as long as Barnes Realty handled most of the city's commerical leases, Chris had no need to worry.

Sometimes the spending achieved its own glory. Once, an hour after reminiscing about a café in San Francisco, they were aboard a plane. Several hours later they found their Irish coffees at the end of the Hyde Street cable line and enjoyed them thoroughly, then returned to the airport and the City of Brotherly Love.

What a Chris time that had been, jumbling geography and priorities for the sake of an urge.

"What do you want, Suzannah?"

"I want to borrow half my equity in the building. I want thirty thousand dollars. And your signature." She pulled the loan papers out.

"That isn't what I meant." But he signed on the line with the blue "x." His eyes skimmed the fine print as he spoke. "Remember the last time we had lunch here? Remember leaving the food untouched? Running home? You were really something."

"That was a long time ago." She kept her eyes on the papers, on his scrawled signature.

"You were great at lust. Do you know your lips swell when you're excited? Yes, you must know it because you suck in the bottom one, moisten it with your tongue. Like now."

She forced her lips into rigidity.

He handed her the papers. "So now money does it for you. Or is there a real live human being somewhere?"

She wanted to lie, to invent a passionate lover, a weapon to wound Chris, who'd been her man, her child, her father, her lover and who'd failed in each and every role.

"*Is* there?" Horror lurked in his voice, outrage at betrayal, at the obscene idea she might ever feel something for someone else.

She sighed. "No. I work, read and teach. Dull, huh? It's calm and organized and it makes me happy."

He relaxed, then reached into his breast pocket. "Brought you a token of my affection. Souvenir of Hawaii."

"I don't want your gifts."

"Do you think I'm seducing the Iron Maiden of Finance with a trinket? It's something I knew was designed for you the minute I saw it. I had to bring it back to you."

He held a lovely ring of gold and carved coral. A bouquet of pale, almost translucent roses trailed from a spun-gold chain. "Put it on," he whispered.

She slipped it on her right ring finger. The blossoms glowed as if they'd rooted in her veins.

"I knew it'd look like that. I remembered your delicate fingers. I remember everything."

"Thank you," she said quietly. "It's lovely." Then she looked directly into his sandy eyes. "I remember everything, too. How many of these rings did you buy?"

He laughed and slapped the table. "That's why you're irreplaceable! You're the only one who'd . . . I bought quite a few, actually. Never know when they'll be handy." He reached for the check.

"No," she said. "It's *my* lunch."

"You get a charge writing me off, don't you?" He waited. "Smile, Suzannah. It was a terrible pun."

He helped her up and ushered her out of the small blue and white room. Outside he faced her, took her hands. "We'll be together again, you'll see. When you're ready, we'll be together again. I'm your fate, Suzannah."

After lunch, she visited the loan officer at the bank, then spent forty-five minutes with her prospective client, the bookseller. By the time she returned to her office, she had Proust and possibly Mark Kaye, the bookseller, as new possessions.

Back at her desk, she pulled out research reports, underlining significant ideas, writing notes in the margins. "Mark," she penned carefully, "I think you may have meant this." She drew an arrow to a circled paragraph and did the same on two other reports, underlining pros and cons in two ink colors, personalizing her soft but adamant sell. She put the envelope in the day's outgoing mail as her phone rang.

"It's Katie MacPherson and I'm ready to roll," the crackling old-lady voice said. "I know the market's closed for the weekend, but let's hit Monday's opening, okay?"

Suzannah hummed as she wrote the ticket, the first of what she anticipated as many to be barked out by the salty widow who'd first called three days ago.

But Katie MacPherson was the only one to disturb late Friday afternoon. Without a next day's promised action, broker minds, always geared to the moment beyond this, lost interest. What loomed in the near future was home, and getting there.

The men of the office stalled Friday commutes with drinks at a bar next door. There, they rehashed the week and discussed everything except why they were reluctant to go home.

Suzannah wasn't one of "the guys." After a few attempts, she withdrew, realizing her presence inhibited their jokes, flattened the taste of their drinks, warped their ritual circle.

Still, they asked. And quickly accepted her excuses.

"Coming along?" Nick flicked eraser specks off his desk.

She shook her head. "I'm working on Elaine Weiner's portfolio."

"Can't it wait? Amelia won't have dinner ready for hours. Baby Nicky's chicken pox kept her busy all day."

"Sorry about that."

"Don't be. There aren't many childhood ailments left. If Amelia didn't have lousy days taking care of a sick kid, what would she reminisce about in her sunset years? She's happy. Nicky's happy. That leaves us. What should we do to be happy?"

She smiled sweetly. "Last Friday was so special, why not repeat it? Let's do absolutely nothing one more time."

"It isn't healthy repressing lust. That's how women wind up cruising the street with a shopping bag, twitchy and spastic and mumbling."

"Are you saying bag ladies search for sex in trash cans?"

He nodded gravely. "I can't reach everyone in time." He

picked up his briefcase. "How about if I swear I won't touch below the waist?"

"Go keep your kid from scratching his pox."

"The world's really changed. That line worked like a charm at Holy Child High. Well, have a good weekend. Just do not enter this room Monday looking satiated."

She wrote notes on a yellow legal pad. Elaine Weiner's portfolio was delightfully wrong, a sitting duck of a target. She scribbled away, smiling.

Eventually, only two brokers, both beginners, and the secretaries were left. Suzannah decided to continue working at home. She bent sideways to lock up her daybook and sensed a shadow on her desk.

"Can I help—you?"

Coby grinned, his hands pushed deep into the pockets of his unbuttoned sheepskin-lined coat. Under it he wore a nubby heather turtleneck. He regarded the hot, silent room with detached interest, a tourist from a foreign country. Or an invader. Despite his smile, his relaxed stance, dangerous.

"I was downtown," he said, "and I remembered where you worked." He pulled his hands out of his coat pockets. "Untrue. I never forgot where you worked. I've called you at home, but you weren't in. However, Adam's away."

Adam? Ah, his child. He hadn't named him before.

"—and I hoped you wouldn't be upset at my plowing in this way. That if not upset, you were also not occupied for the next few hours. And if not upset and not occupied, that you'd spend them with me." He put his hands back into his pockets. "Aren't you going to say anything?"

"When?" She stood up.

"Oh. Okay. I'm not talking now. So now. Say something. I'm not as confident or casual as I'm trying to appear."

She looked down at the volumes of Proust, at her briefcase.

He noticed. "Guess I should have called you here, but I hate phones. They're not the next best thing to being there. There is no next best thing."

She clutched Proust to her bosom.

"You look different today."

Ah. Almost forgotten, the stiff black suit, Victorian blouse, center-parted and pulled-back hair. She put the book back on the desk. In junior high she'd shielded herself with notebooks and texts, but why the devil now? Why did this man disturb her so? What couldn't she handle? Why see him emitting danger signals? Lurking? Ready to do her subtle harm? For God's sake, to flutter between a sexy, living male and Proust. *Proust!*

"I'm not occupied," she said firmly. "Nor am I upset. Give me a moment. I'll be right back."

There was little she could do about her buttoned-tight costume, but she removed the pins from her hair and let it fall free. She stared at herself in the bathroom mirror. How ridiculous to think about danger. She rubbed on blusher, found her revised image more acceptable and returned to him.

"You want me to carry that?" Coby pointed at her bulging briefcase-pocketbook. "Or is that a wrong question? Insensitive to your independence and strength?"

"A bit unenlightened, but kind. My shoulder sometimes kills me. All the same, I'll carry it myself. But thanks."

They entered the yellow-gray light of the dying week and wandered toward Chestnut Street. Suzannah shivered. She hated the premature dusks of February.

The street resembled a faded black and white photo. Even the walkway's brick trim dulled to sepia under the clouds.

"Every Wednesday Adam has a doctor's appointment right around the corner from here, on Eighteenth Street," Coby said. "Sometimes I spend the hour in there." He waved at an Art Deco façade. "It's pretentious, unimaginative and inhospitable, but it's therefore also unpopular and uncrowded. Plus, they have a great heating system."

Inside, while settling into the dark leather booth, Suzannah became mesmerized by one of the very few other patrons, a young man, his back to her, seated at the bar. The cut of his suit and its texture signaled success. He held a cigarette and smoke curled above his beautifully sculpted blond hair. In the bar's mirror, far away, Suzannah saw the stony set of his features, his silent and private focus.

A girl next to him waited, watching his profile. Then she spoke softly. He ignored her, pulled further away without visible motion and continued silent communion with himself.

The girl held his arm a moment, then disengaged and dropped her hand as if it carried weights. She bit her bottom lip and resumed contemplation of the half of his face she could see.

Suzannah breathed in softly, her eyes wide. The taste of the drama across the room was depressingly familiar. She looked at the woman, the once and future loser, and shook her head. Soft things never won.

"Is something upsetting you?" Coby asked.

She fiddled with the coral roses on her hand. "The couple at the bar, or the day. I don't know."

He glanced over. The girl's back was slumped, her head bowed. The man blindly studied the mirror while next to him, the girl's shoulders shook. Coby turned back to Suzannah. "I'm not whoever, whatever you're remembering. Don't mix me up with anyone else and I'll try to do the same."

She smiled. "Forgive me. It's been an odd day. I'm somehow . . ."

"How about idle conversation? Innocuous topics." He proceeded to tell her about music he'd written, about a disagreement with a friend who wanted to change lyrics which weren't Coby's but Ranier Maria Rilke's.

"Some specifics," Suzannah said, trying to ignore the couple at the bar.

"Well, the translation I used begins, 'Out of infinite yearnings rise finite deeds like feeble fountains.' And he wants it to be, 'I wanna be Niagara Falls instead of your bathroom faucet.' "

"I think there's cause to keep haggling. Have you written many songs?"

He nodded. "I bet you have a great alto voice. It would be fun hearing you sing my songs."

She felt heat stain her face. The exchange of her voice for his music was too intimate and out of bounds. She put a hand to her cheek and felt it burn, began to laugh but heard it emerge a nervous titter.

"Do I—do I frighten you?" Coby asked.

"Well! That's ridiculous! Why *would* you? I mean for heaven's *sake!*"

"Because you frighten me."

"Me?"

"Maybe not you, but well, possibilities do. The other night—there are so many forgettable, ordinary experiences."

"Yes."

"That wasn't one."

"No."

"I don't understand it."

"Neither do I."

"So I'm a little frightened. But I'm not a coward, Suzannah."

He slid through the syllables in her name as if caressing them. She felt herself shiver.

"Neither am I." She was not at all certain she spoke the truth.

"Are you hungry?"

She shook her head.

"Then, perhaps . . . ?"

"Yes."

Outside, he took her hand and they walked, hunched together against the wind. She didn't need to give directions or warnings of future turns and short cuts. He sensed her pauses, shared her stride, stopping only to smile, press closer for a moment. At a traffic light, he let go of her hand, put both of his on her face and kissed her. Then he took back her hand, put it in his fleece-lined pocket and walked on without a word.

They passed gated shops, cold dead windows, leftover Christmas lights on struggling city trees, small crusts of snow refreezing on the night-cold curbs. Finally, they crossed the parkway. Her crescent-shaped building was awash in light and silence. Still holding hands, still smiling, they rode quietly up the five stories.

She turned on the lamp by the sofa, put Proust on the coffee table and let her briefcase drop.

"To courage," she said, lifting an imaginary wineglass. "In the face of what might be."

"To what might be." He clicked his phantom glass against hers.

Her bedroom was dark, textured with white wool and velvet jewel tones, pale gauze and silk. Distant light filtered in from the living room, burnishing the brass headboard. She removed her black jacket, let it fall to the floor. She reached for the button of her high-collared blouse and he moved towards her and slowly, together, they unwrapped her disguise until there was simply Suzannah, pulling towards his heather sweater.

He held her away, looked at her, but with such gladness that she felt none of the fear, the anxiety of other times, other men. She felt a stirring within, a nameless thing she might have called, if she'd named it, acceptance. Even love. Of herself and what she became through his eyes.

"Suzannah," he murmured, and again as he said her name

she wondered at the pleasure it produced. Did other men avoid it? Say it differently?

She looked at him, all light and shadow, tension and grace, skin taut over muscles gently rippling his chest, his stomach, his upper arms, a shadow of ribs at his side, strong, long legs.

She touched the spray of dark curls on his chest, traced the downy line trailing over his flat stomach.

Remember this, she told herself as he led her to the bed. Remember, she repeated, her finger tips and palms enjoying the sharp, flat pull over his pelvic bones.

Save this for later, when it's over. Most time tumbled, flattening past images beneath newly fallen layers. But some could be preserved. Remember, her mind said as he touched and outlined the whole of her, remaking her, affirming her specialness, her wholeness and ability to delight.

Remember.

And then the voice sighed and stopped. There were no words, no warnings, no questions. Only sensation and the white sound of joy, and the unspoken knowledge that something long separated had fused within her, that her flesh no longer seemed a casing she carried like a half-welcome burden.

There was only Suzannah, deep, endless and whole. Suzannah, the way he said it. And then, not her, but them.

And she didn't care how good it would be because it already was. She wanted to be who she now was, with this man. What was happening, what would happen, what might happen in a believable future was enough, even if chemistry or timing or newness would make the moves and tastes and sounds less than wonderful. It didn't have to be wonderful.

Except it was.

She sprawled on the comforter for a long time, her breath catching as echoes of pleasure pealed, trilled softly and faded.

Then she turned and found him propped on one elbow, smiling at her.

"Nothing to fear," he said, leaning to kiss her, "but fear itself. As they say."

"They say wonderful things. Brilliant things. Like I never dreamed it could . . ."

"I did."

"I know. That's somehow part of it."

He looked at her. His dark-framed glasses lay on the night

table. Without them, his eyes were vulnerable and exposed. What does he see? she wondered.

"I could fall in love with you," he said. "I'm halfway there already. Have been since I first saw you. Be so advised and forewarned."

"You don't frighten me." It was the second time she'd told him that, the second time she wasn't sure if she spoke the truth. "What's your secret?" she asked him, only half-joking.

"You are." He smiled. "Oh, if there is a secret, maybe it's the degree of wanting. I wanted you—extraordinarily much. It couldn't have been ordinary, that's all." He bent and kissed her forehead, stroked her hair near her temples. "Well," he said, "I do have a secret." His head traveled over her, kissing between words. "It is," he said softly, pressing against her, fitting himself to her, "a fantastic . . ." He was quiet for a while and when he spoke again, she heard him distantly, and she didn't care about his secret, she wanted only to share it.

"Imagination." And he proved it. And the first time became only the working of the clay, fingers and bodies warming and molding until ready for definition, for becoming.

Only much later, when he was still locked to her, neither willing to break away, did he speak again. "More questions?"

She shook her head.

"Then let's find dinner. We have the potential here for dying of starvation."

When she finally pulled away and stood up, unsteadily, knees buckling, she watched Coby and saw nothing but pleasure and the promise of more. Why back off? Why fear it? Why dwell on it? Why not, instead, consider only the man and where to find dinner.

She loved the way he ate. He didn't stoke himself as if fulfilling a necessary bodily function. He hadn't frowned over the Szechuan menu, or become nervous when she ordered a dish he'd never tasted. He didn't rush through the meal as if meeting a deadline.

He ate with gusto, without the need to discuss his reasons for enjoyment. With curiosity and delight and appetite. Without shame or explanations or indigestion looming.

He ate the way he made love.

She thought of the conversation with Abby. The keys to deciphering a man's possibilities. "I'd like to hear your music," she said.

"So be it." He tapped a chopstick on the table, then conducted an *a cappella* concert. "I wanna be . . . Niagara Falls . . . instead of . . . your bathroom faucet!"

"*Your* music, and I didn't mean now, I meant . . . whenever."

He accepted her gift of future with half a bow. "You don't have a piano," he said, lifting the last bit of beef.

"I have a guitar. Relic of my youth."

"Adam's with his grandparents."

"How's that?"

"Thought you might be interested."

"Well, I . . . why?"

"No curfew. I don't have a sitter waiting."

"Ah."

"He's staying over."

"How lovely for him. Do you want dessert? Or just a fortune cookie?"

"You aren't interested?"

"In Adam's whereabouts?"

"In my continued availability."

"Forgive me. I haven't been trained to consider a baby-sitter's requirements when planning my nights. I must seem dim-witted and slow."

"You seem evasive. You interested?"

"I get it. You, too, want to stay over somewhere?"

"I might have phrased it somewhat more subtly."

"Phrase it any way you like but be my guest."

"Good. I already hired the kid next door to feed and walk the dog tomorrow."

"What's good is that I don't insist on spontaneity. Seems a great deal was planned in advance."

"Not planned. Hoped for."

A crockery saucer was placed between them. They each took a cookie.

Coby snorted. "I am fortune's fool. Listen—'Enjoy another oriental repast soon.' "

"Rip-off," he told the waiter, who interpreted the words as an order and hastily tore the check off the pad.

Suzannah regarded her fortune. "Mine was written by the

same burned-out case. But I like it." She cleared her throat and read, " 'The near future may bring everything you have always wanted. Then again, it may not.'

"What I like are firm convictions," she said, crumpling the paper, then retrieving it from the table and putting it into her wallet. "Onwards and upwards. Who needs a handle on the future, anyway?"

"You see," he said in the dark at 3 A.M. "Imagination is all. It's how my sex life moved out of neutral in the first place."

"You fantasized?"

"Other people did. In eleventh grade, there was this girl Jennie. She told her parents I'd impregnated her. I don't know how she made her selection. Naming me was more or less like claiming immaculate conception. I, with my customary lack of smarts, went around denying it, scared shitless I'd have to marry her. Anyway, she was banished to live with relatives, and I was left in town, the guy that mothers warned their daughters about. I was bad. Wicked. Wild, dangerous! Me! I became a status symbol, a rite of passage. It was wonderful. Nobody noticed how inept I was and then, eventually, after much tutoring, I guess I wasn't . . ."

Saturday morning, 10:30 A.M., after toasted bagels and cream cheese, crumpled sheets lit by brilliant light pouring from behind the bedroom's sheer curtains . . .

"You're perfect," he said. "All curves. There isn't a dull spot on you."

"It's an archaic body."

"Classic stays in style. It's woman."

She said nothing. But she smiled.

"Aha! Progress. I think you've accepted a compliment."

The blue-white light turned green in the fronds of the fern by the window, gold on the brass headboard and where it splashed onto them. "Gorgeous day," Coby said. "Want to race down the parkway or something?"

"Jesus, that's disgusting."

"I forgot. You mentioned in your basic dossier that you didn't jog or play tennis."

"Or anything. Why? Are you a closet jock? How do you keep your body so firm?"

"I walk. I ride horses. I swim."

"On a team?"

"Alone. Or with friends."

"Then you pass."

"I take it you're not excessively athletic?"

"It's my thirty-second major fault."

"You number them?"

"I'm an organized person."

"What's . . . seven?"

"My left eyebrow. See how it trails into nothingness? It's wishy-washy. My whole face is wishy-washy, but each part has its own number."

"For God's sake, I don't think I can spend time with someone who cares about eyebrows, let alone catalogues their structural defects."

"Well, I'm thorough. See, you begin with externals, your greeting to the world. Face, hips—my hips are number one. Then you reach personality defects, things you can hide."

"Poor Suzannah. Do you have a list of what's good about yourself? What you like?"

She shook her head.

"Then let's begin one. I'll instruct. You ready?"

"Now?"

"I think it's an emergency. Lesson one. Right here, this part is spectacular. Notice its molding, fine lines, exquisitely functional form. However, this part yonder is mind-boggling and could also be a contender for number-one spot. But my personal favorite, actually, is right here. Deceptively simple, this has endless potential. Tricky design, see, because—stop laughing. I need your full cooperation. Good. Ah, that's very good. This may take time because I want you to fully consider the possibilities before placing anything on a list. So let's begin with this area, from here to . . ."

"So there are two physical things you do," he said later, outside in the crisp air. "You also walk."

"That doesn't count."

"Come on, count it. It won't tarnish your image. Walk." He viewed the traffic pouring into the circle in front of the art museum. "Maybe, this once, run like hell."

Inside, he led her up the wide central staircase, then around a corridor to show her a work he'd thought of the first time he saw her, at Hedy's.

"This is it?" she asked when they'd stopped in front of a glass case. "I remind you of a plate?"

"A Della Robbia relief."

She tilted her head. "I don't get it. You saw me as the Virgin? Worshiping my child?"

"No. Forget labels. That virgin story isn't part of my ethnic folklore, anyway. Look at her, at the way she glows. Look at her features."

She looked at an ornamental dish with a border of lush fruit and delicate blossoms. The center was deep blue, against which the Virgin, pure white, kneeled and prayed before her equally pale and glistening child. "Nope," she said. "I can't see why you'd . . . nope."

"You were the entire thing. The face, the lushness, the profusion—"

"My lush, profuse hips, is that it?"

"Stop that. I don't know why you act that way, why you think you're too large when you're *right*. Why you want to minimize yourself, tailor yourself down. Anyway, the plate. You were all of it, including her. You look like her for starters. Your nose, your chin. Can't you see it? And glazed some way. Impenetrable. Glowing but private. Lush but pristine." He waited. "You don't understand, do you?"

"Nope."

"It isn't supposed to work this way. You're supposed to intuitively understand and be thrilled. There's a swell of music and you throw your arms around me."

"Make that fault thirty-three. Failure to comprehend."

They continued down the hall, pausing now and then. She was particularly attracted to an obscure painting of a ballerina on tiptoe, straining towards the heavens. It was silly, self-conscious and unduly solemn, yet Suzannah studied it for some time.

Then they entered a wood-ceilinged room, spacious under its decorated beams. Coby read from a brass plaque near the entry. "This was the main reception hall of the Palace of Duke Chao. Must have been beautiful once."

"Very, very sane, though. You could o.d. on sanity." She gestured at the lacquered columns, the wide painted throne at the back of the room. "And on serenity. This room is unreasonably serene."

"Its owner was the Chief Eunuch of the Emperor. That makes serenity and sanity major accomplishments. Poor sucker, what a nonlife."

"At least he was chief, and he lived in a pretty palace."

"Suzannah, my dear, you have a warped value system."

"I'm pragmatic. If I were a Chinese duke without balls, I'd appreciate comfort and a solid title. You want to make something of it?"

"No. I want out. I want people. Loud, uncastrated, unserene, shouting people. Follow me."

Several bus rides and roughly twenty-five blocks away, Coby and Suzannah were surrounded by the requested bedlam. Della Robbia's decorative bounty was replaced by pushcarts and stalls brimful of juicy tomatoes, pyramids of oranges, zucchinis and brussels sprouts. Above the cries of the vendors, the loud conversations and energetic haggling of shoppers, Suzannah heard the squawks of ducks, the calls of caged chickens. She looked away from a hutch with a red-eyed rabbit inside.

The Italian Market blazed with life in the bright, cold sun.

"Now." Coby lifted his arms as if to orchestrate the scene. "We shall shop for a picnic dinner to be enjoyed in front of your fireplace."

"I don't have one."

"No? Why did I . . . well, we'll open the oven and pretend."

"Best squash on Ninth Street," the vendor next to Coby said, flapping open a paper bag. "Amerigo around the corner picks up what falls to the ground. Buy from me. Don't waste time looking."

"I don't need squash. I was only—"

"How much did Amerigo say he'd charge?"

"I didn't ask. I'm only—"

"Two for sixty-nine, right? I'll give two and a half."

Coby smiled, shook his head and walked away. From behind them, the vendor shouted, "Three for sixty-nine, then! Three for sixty-five!"

They entered a cubicle flooded with the pungent aroma of cheese. The shop glowed in the collected light of amber wheels, goldenrod blocks, cream-filled pots, buff wedges and bright yellow globes tied in red string. A woman with skin like aging mozzarella waited on them and they left, arms laden with small paper parcels.

"And now," Coby said, "for some meats." He led Suzannah to the corner, then stopped abruptly. "I never asked if you had other plans. It'll be Saturday night soon. Do you?"

She shook her head. "Don't you?"

"No. Why?"

"Adam." His name intruded, a lump of sound breaking their lazy rhythm.

"He's with his grandparents until tomorrow."

"Mmmmm."

"He goes there once a month. In between, we visit for dinner, or he spends a few hours on Saturday. Adam's, well, he needs a certain structure in his . . . . I'd like you to meet him. Maybe one Wednesday, after his appointment, maybe we could all have junk food somewhere. The doctor's office is near yours, and—"

Suzannah was examining a street vendor's glass bracelets. She realized Coby's voice had stopped. "What's that?" she asked.

He appeared troubled.

"Something wrong?"

"No. Well, I was trying to exp . . ." He shook his head. "Nothing whatsoever."

"Did you tell the kid next door to feed the dog tomorrow, too?"

There was a short, confusing pause, and then he nodded. "I told him to check whether I was back."

"I'm awed by your foresight."

He grinned. "And my ability to whip up a meal, right? This is my specialty, delicatessen take-out."

She watched him survey the butcher's cases. Some man, she heard herself think. She reviewed her fresh store of memories. Last night, this morning, his body on hers, in hers, under hers, next to hers, until pleasure, pure and acute, remembered and now anticipated as well, flooded her, seemed to slide inside and remain, very alive.

"Buy the meats quickly," she whispered. "I'm suffering a sort of sexual hang-over. Need the hair of the dog. Let's get home of I'll create a scandal in the market place."

Coby looked bemused. "Think pure thoughts."

"I don't want to."

"Then think smutty thoughts."

"It's uncomfortable to walk."

"We need bread and olives and patience, Suzannah."

"And don't say my name. I don't know what you do, but it slithers through me."

"My, my." He tried controlling a smile.

"Yes. Well don't be smug."

"Do you cook?" he asked after they'd bought bread. "We don't know a thing about each other, do we?"

"Nothing but essentials. Anyway, yes. Not often, but when the mood strikes, I'm good, actually."

"That confirms my theory. Women who enjoy sex, enjoy food. They like touching it, smelling it, sampling its tastes, licking it, kneading it—"

"You're a sadistic bastard."

"You're a sick person. Look at that woman buying vegetables. Is she panting? Is she overwhelmed? Does she consider food shopping orgasmic?"

"How would I know? She looks happy. And she's—look—she's fondling and patting that goddamn eggplant as if—for God's sake, Coby—she's *stroking* it. Oh, Lord, I—"

"Avert your eyes and follow me. We still need olives."

She stood in the tiny shop, a long loaf of bread propped against her shoulder, her vital organs thrumming. A veritable genius coined the term "turned on," she decided. A switch she'd never noticed had been flicked, her being set into perpetual motion.

The walls of the store were lined with wooden cases, each divided into bins for spices and herbs. Suzannah surveyed the range of earth tones, appreciating their harmony and organization.

Her life could have an equally pleasant, equally varied and controlled pattern. Monday through Friday filled to overflowing with the crackling high of tension and mental gymnastics. Then a separate container for weekends. Exotic flavors, different colors. Cinnamon. Saffron. Coriander. Coby.

She liked her dream calendar's syncopated time.

Fridays she could leave her office, throw the switch and . . . She frowned. Things could become complicated with kids and sitters, but she didn't want to think about that now. She didn't want either of their other lives leaking into what they were creating. Keep it clean and pure, she thought. Virginal popped into her mind and she laughed out loud. A virginal affair, indeed. Well, what the hell? If he saw her as Mother Mary on a plate with angels, then why not?

The entire ride home, Suzannah could not distinguish between the rumbles and vibrations of the bus's motor and her own. "Once upstairs," she said as they entered the lobby of her building, "I will explicitly demonstrate the erotic potential of x-rated produce."

She stretched her naked legs and leaned against the sofa. A rumpled tablecloth lay on the parquetry floor, the remnants of their meal scattered on it. The carpet was stubbly beneath her, but not unpleasantly so. She sipped red wine.

The windows and corners of the room were dark, the picnic lit by the pink glow of the lamp in the center of the room. Suzannah felt insulated and safe in a sky-high castle without moats or drawbridges.

"Would you play now, if I found my guitar?" she asked lazily.

While she rummaged at the back of her closet, Coby, standing at its door, blinked myopically. "Do you live with someone else? I like whoever uses the right side of the closet best. Tropical. But the left side looks like a Greek widow's wardrobe."

She pulled aside a carton of school papers and small objects she could neither discard nor display. "People want deadly seriousness when their money's at stake. Hence, funereal attire. Here's the guitar."

He strummed and frowned and left for the living room where he tuned it. Suzannah settled against the sofa, her eyes half closed. "Could I hear your song. About infinite whatever?"

He strummed, tuned a string more finely and positioned his hands, then concentrated on a space beyond her shoulder. "I told you those lines to pull you out of your funk. There's no quarrel about the lyrics because they don't work either way. But I did write music that sounds, to me, the way the words feel."

Over a series of minor chords he hummed an introduction, harmonizing a third, then a fourth above a wistful melody the guitar sang softly. She listened as he switched from his hum to wordless sound, surprised by his singing voice, a fiber spun of many filaments, with a strong center.

There was something Slavic about the melody he played and

harmonized against. Something vaguely mournful, a yearning in the notes themselves, their progressions and intervals powerfully evocative without language intruding.

Someone had once told her there was a word "toska" that meant nostalgia for what was never to be known. She never heard of it again, couldn't find it in the dictionary, but she knew there should be such a word for there were such feelings.

She listened to his wordless song as his voice left the notes his hands played to sing above them, to float and fly free.

"That was lovely," she whispered when he was through.

"Do you know Rilke's poetry?" He leaned over and lifted the brass unicorn from the coffee table. "He has one about this fellow, one of my favorites:

> *"This is the creature there never has been.*
> *They never knew it, and yet, none the less,*
> *they loved the way it moved, its suppleness,*
> *its neck, its very gaze, mild and serene.*
>
> *Not there, because they loved it, it behaved*
> *as though it were. They always left some space.*
> *And in that clear unpeopled space they saved*
> *it lightly reared its head, with scarce a trace*
>
> *of not being there. They fed it, not with corn,*
> *but only with the possibility*
> *of being. And—"*

He broke off his recitation. "I love that line, 'fed with the possibility of being.' It's true, and not only for unicorns. And, having given myself that lead—I sound ready for an interview show—yes, Johnny, that is the title of my new album. 'Not Only for Unicorns.' "

He put the carved figure back on the coffee table and strummed quietly. "There's another one." He played a series of soft chords that melted one into the other, then spoke.

> *"And you wait, are awaiting the one thing*
> *That will infinitely increase your life;*
> *the powerful, the uncommon,*
> *the awakening of stones . . ."*

"He's terribly romantic, isn't he, your Rilke? The idea that any one thing could matter that much? That wanting can make something happen?"

Coby looked at her. "Romantic as in foolish, old-fashioned, sophomoric, infantile?"

"Well, I didn't mean . . . well, I guess so. It has the lovely sound of all make-believe. Unicorns and heroism and fairy godmothers who make sure your life works out right . . ." Coby's eyebrow was raised. "You believe in it, don't you?" she asked. "You believe in the one thing."

"I believe in the possibility of being. However, for now, Rilke is wrong. Wrong mood and wrong century and wrong emotions. Watch, madam. Watch how music can manipulate emotions. We now leave pre-Freudian romance for the here and now." He played a bold major chord, then picked and strummed, brushing his fingers over the neck of the guitar, fingers playing and palm dropping to punctuate hillbilly chords.

"This one couldn't have been written last century," he said, picking and playing all the while. "This is up to date, a song of the expressway, a lament for the tragedies of rush hour."

His fingers completed a frantic series of chord progressions. "There was a redhead, see? We had names for her kind in high school, but a man's pretty helpless at five-thirty on the crawlway.

> *"Pushin' through the traffic*
> *Doin' legal fifty-five*
> *When her taillights winked a greeting*
> *And I had the urge to drive*
>
> *Right on top her trunk before me*
> *Right in through that shiny steel*
> *'Cause I taste what's in there waiting*
> *Better than my dinner meal . . ."*

His hands danced, flew over strings, pulled out a whirlwind of sound. "Sexist lyrics," Suzannah murmured. "Possibly offensive."

He nodded happily.

> *"O commuter, why'd you signal*
> *Put my gear in overdrive?*

How's a man supposed to hustle
If he's stuck at fifty-five?

There's a cop car near my fender
Dragon-wagons breathing smoke
See you lookin' in your mirror
Thinkin' this is all a joke.

O commuter, here's my exit
Who knows where you're headin' for
I've got people waitin' for me
But I'd make a huge detour

If you'd only—"

He stopped, listening.

For a moment, Suzannah couldn't identify the repetitive, discordant note. "Damn phone!" she finally said.

"You could let it ring."

She sighed. "No. I've tried, but I simply cannot."

She, who spent five days a week and too many nights with her ear and a phone in suction, had forgotten that avenue of access. An impervious castle indeed. To each era its drawbridge.

He picked and strummed as she went into the kitchen, reluctantly lifting the phone, angry when she heard Tully.

"Can we talk, old friend?" he said.

"Well, it's Saturday night, and I'm a little busy. Is something up?"

"Not really. But I'm getting my shit together."

By now, Tully had gotten together so much shit he could start a fertilizer franchise. Suzannah checked the clock. The phone company considered three minutes basic and sufficient and who was Suzannah to quibble with Ma Bell? Tully had two minutes and seventeen seconds to go.

From the living room, a voice, strums. "Answer machines don't cost a fortune." Musical improvisations on the joys of phone interceptors. "Not only coitus should be uninterruptus."

Tully, on his end, describing his wife's most recent offenses.

"You don't do business on weekends, do you?" Coby. "Why not tell them you aren't home?"

Tully could hear either Coby's shouts or Suzannah's meter

running. "I won't keep you," he said. "But have you noticed what's happening at Tydings and Roy?"

Her heart pounded. "Not really, why?"

"Stock's moving up. I'm sure I was right. I hear it'll be two shares of T&R for one Chemfax. But don't say I said anything. I think I'm going to buy, what do you think?"

"You sound bored," Coby, from behind the kitchen wall.

"Gee, Tully, I'd have to study it before I could say."

Had he called to see if she was using or misusing his slip of the tongue? But how could he check? And why?

Coby stood at the kitchen entry, testing the atmosphere. She rolled her eyes to communicate boredom.

"I could lose my job in the take-over, so I figure to hedge, make a bundle to tide me over. You interested?"

More missed heartbeats. "You mean interested in handling your buys? Sure. I'm a broker. I'm always interested."

Tully hesitated a second. "Sure. That's what I meant."

Coby moved close and nibbled her cheek and neck.

"Hope you don't mind my calling," Tully said.

Coby expanded his area of interest.

"Happy you did. Let's have lunch soon." She sounded as insincere and disinterested as she was.

"For sure," Tully answered.

Coby silently put his hands under her arms, lifted and seated her on the counter.

Babble, babble, came through the receiver as C. Waldemar made his own message abundantly clear. Her eyes widened. He stopped, tilted his head, understood that widened eyes expressed surprise, not censure, and returned to his explorations.

"Tully," she said, somewhat more urgently, "as much as I enjoy talking—" She gasped. ". . . this really isn't . . . I can't—"

"Sure you can," Coby whispered.

"Sure, sure," Tully echoed. "Well, then, see you soon?"

"Very soon," Suzannah said.

"Not too soon," Coby whispered again. "No hurry."

She hung up the phone, gasped, arched her back and gasped again. "Wrong," she said shortly. "Very soon was accurate."

"It didn't seem an interesting phone call," Coby said. "Hope you didn't mind the intrusion." He helped her off the counter.

* * *

"When I was small," she said Sunday morning, smoothing the patchwork around them more tightly, "I wanted to become a cat."

"I was wondering when we'd leave the here and now and begin histories. Why a cat?"

"Because I knew instinctively that whatever made a cat purr felt terrific and wasn't mild."

"Then you aren't as goal-directed as you claim. If you were, you'd have ears and a long tail sticking up. You'd have transformed yourself by now."

"But I have. Can't you hear the purr?"

He laid his head on her chest. "Amazing."

"Feels like I thought it would. Kind of a sexy tickle all through my body."

"Do tomcats purr?"

"Are you kidding? That's what they sit on fences and howl for."

"Could I skip the fence sitting? It's colder than hell outside."

"You can even skip the preliminary howls."

In the shower, she slathered his back, sliding suds forward to his rib cage. "It's been my experience that jocks—even the spectator variety—dissipate their energy foolishly. You, on the other hand, conserve and invest it wisely."

They toweled each other dry.

"Next weekend?" Coby asked. "Or do you have plans?"

"I'm making plans right now. Let's begin Friday with a feast. I'll sniff and taste and do all the things you said, working myself into a frenzy."

"I'll have a curfew again. The sitter won't—"

"Then I'll do a fast frenzy."

"See, her husband becomes jumpy if—" There was a sudden loss of animation. "You don't care why, do you?"

"What I care about is what will cover you while we spin-dry your garments. Your body's gorgeous, but it's chilly today."

"I understand the rationale for work songs," she said, scraping egg yolk from a plate. "Moves the slaves along lickety clop and makes the buggers happy about it." She smiled as he played and she scrubbed the counter. Her apartment had been transformed by Coby, as if hues and heat raced from his guitar and mouth and coated, colored and charged the atmosphere, washing its contents to newness.

Her dishes were sudden wonders of symmetry, triumphs of geometry. The yellow of the yolk stain became an abstract blaze of light, as exciting as a Picasso. She'd never before truly appreciated the intricate brilliance of the carvings on her silverware. She'd never noticed how clearly etched were the edges of saucepans, the corners of cupboards.

Coby sang a funny tune about a boy and a bumblebee and she closed the dishwasher and lounged against it.

"You know," she said when the music had ended, "the songs you write have a specific internal rhythm. It's you, Coby. Your body's secret tempo. The same as in bed. I'm happy you compose. That way, there's a continuum. When I can't feel your rhythm, I can hear it. Aural sex, sort of."

Coby sat on a high kitchen stool, wearing Suzannah's white terry robe, which reached mid-thigh. His hands moved idly over the strings as he regarded her, almost abstractly, through his glasses. "I feel as if I'd always known you," he said.

"Well, if not forever, then certainly often, in the biblical sense."

"I was imagining you as a child, as a teen-ager."

"Don't. I was an introverted blob. The pale type, reading a book. You wouldn't have liked me."

"Impossible. What's your family like?"

"If you're bent on discovering a meaningful past, you'll be disappointed. My father skipped and my mother sulked. Now you know the whole story."

"People write three-volume epics based on that."

"Possibly, but this person won't. I don't enjoy that business. Early traumas, how I suffered. It's disgusting, in fact, to play with one's psyche in public. Endless self-stimulation in disguise as conversation. Getting off on sorrow. It's not conversation—it's mastversation."

"Aren't you a tad overemotional about a few innocent questions?"

"I'm always overly something. I thought that was one of my charms. Let's forget it."

"I feel as if you're saying 'don't get personal' and frankly, that's nuts at this point."

"Ridiculous! You want information? Question away."

"What about your ex-husband?"

"Chris? Why would he interest you?"

"For starters, I can't imagine why anyone would let go of you."

"Aw shucks."

He left his perch and they went into the living room. "Why did it end? Was there another woman?"

She pulled him close. "How quaint. But I guess there was. I was the other woman. I wasn't ever *the* woman, never that central. He—we—had a weird kind of marriage."

"He was a fool."

"He is *gone*. Must we discuss him?" She kept her tone light, but she was troubled, unwilling to exchange biographies. Despite her harangue, she was used to playing the mutual misery game with men, claiming Guinness book standards for record-breaking insults to her person. But Coby was different. Coby listened. Things meant something to him. It was a different game and she wasn't sure she could play.

"Not now, all right?" she whispered. "You're leaving soon. I need to memorize you." And she began, strong with new magic, for she reached through his beautiful flesh, stroked and fondled his heart, his lungs, his most secret parts as he also did to her.

"You were right," he said later. "There are better methods of communication than talk. It's your rightness in general that's disorienting me. I've lost my sense of space, of time, of whether this had a beginning. Are you always so right, Suzannah?"

"Of course."

"But I was right, too. He was a fool to let go of you."

"Back to him? We were both fools. He wanted too little and I wanted too much."

He nodded, encouraging her as he pulled the terry robe around himself.

"I went through a pretty neurotic phase. I craved total commitment, a fifties kind of thing—togetherness. I wanted to be half of something. Half a 'we,' half a unit, half a couple. God, it's embarrassing to even talk about it! Anyway, when I was divorced, forced into independence, I realized Chris had been right. I'd wanted the impossible, wanted him to make me happy. People can't make other people happy. I was hiding behind that, shuffling along, begging, wanting, needing . . ."

"Crap! That's pure, unadulterated crap!"

"Hey, you wanted this talk, not me. See what I mean? It's stupid—causes problems. It's finished."

"No," he said more softly, but with equal force. "People talk so they can know each other."

"Knowing you think my opinions are crap is not a plus."

"I'm sorry for my choice of words. You wanted Chris to love you is what I meant. To love you the way you deserve, the way anyone deserves. You wanted him to pay attention, for God's sake. That's what love is *for*. To acknowledge someone else's uniqueness. To say that people, bodies, aren't interchangeable. To affirm a belief in someone's value."

"People have to value themselves."

"Don't give me Psych I. Of course they do. You do—you *did*— that's why you pulled out of that sick nonmarriage. So don't rewrite it, don't decide you were wrong because you were right."

She shook her head. "No. Now I am. Now I make myself happy. I'm finally a whole—"

"Oh, please. Not you. Not that stinking pop psychology way of being whole like a goddamned jelly bean. A hard, encapsulated bright-colored ball. Bouncing against the other beans but only touching, rubbing. You can't want that, Suzannah." His face was unaccountably angry.

"I do," she insisted. "I don't mean a person can't have a satisfactory relationship—"

"Relationship!" He spat the word out so violently she expected to see its syllables shatter against the wall. "I hate that word! What's a quote relationship unquote? I have a relationship with my barber, with my senile great-uncle who can't remember who I am. With God. With my music. It's a word to use when you don't know what the fuck's between you and something else."

"You don't understand."

"I guess I don't. I'm sorry. I'm overreacting for a change, but that word is so bland. So is 'satisfactory.' Not great, not special. Enough, that's all."

"Maybe there's another term."

"Everything else is charged. Like love, passion, giving, yearning, hurting and yes, your detested word, 'needing,' too."

He stood up, put on his glasses and looked down at her. "Suzannah," he said, "I *need,* and if you can't even understand . . ."

She stopped listening, heard only a voice calling from inside.

This is it? Fireworks, then this fizzle? What of the future, the dream calendar, the syncopated weeks?

She studied a cuticle and finally, as the inner voice prompted her to try something, anything, she looked up.

And laughed. "Forgive me," she said a moment later. "But you look so . . . scholarly. And *silly!*"

The white robe hung open over his nakedness. He pushed his glasses back up from their customary slide and flapped his terry cloth arms in frustration.

She giggled again.

He shook his head, then grinned. "Hell, I won't make it as orator in this costume. Well, then. I apologize, or whatever's appropriate. Don't really know what that was about."

"I think it was a case of premature expostulation."

"You and your word games."

"You and yours."

He kissed her as he was leaving, then kissed her again. "I'll see you Tuesday night," he said, "and Friday." Midway down the hall, he called back. "After facing the dread unknown for forty-eight hours, are you still scared?"

"Who, me? Are you kidding?" She pounded her chest, shook her head and grinned. But she closed the door and leaned against it, wondering on Sunday as she had Friday, if her answer was true.

Eleven

Nick DiRuggio clutched his heart as if in pain. His shoulders were hunched, his voice squeezed through his nose. He was the Godfather in perfectly tailored pinstripes. "I warned you. But you're glowing. On Monday. You've pushed me too far this time, Suzannah. What does this work frenzy, this energy mean?''

"This means I'm meeting Elaine Weiner tonight and I didn't work on her portfolio this weekend.''

He leaned over menacingly, put his hands on her littered desk and spread his fingers over the yellow papers. "What *did* you do?''

She smirked.

"All weekend?''

She maintained her smirk.

"Jesus.'' He went to his own desk.

Suzannah handed Elaine Weiner's redesigned portfolio to June for typing. June sipped a malodorous brew.

"Shall I mail out this material to prospects with your card?'' June asked.

"No. If I don't add the Barnes touch, they won't know they're panting for my personal attentions.''

Suzannah underlined, circled and wrote her marginal notes, subliminally telegraphing a need for Superbroker, whose card she now clipped to the brochure. She hummed while she worked.

"You are definitely not your usual self today,'' Nick said.

"Well, I feel different. You know how you wake up and there's a split second of neutrality, then whop! You remember something awful? A final you didn't study for—even when you're not in school? And the feeling stays, like mental heartburn?''

"So?'' he prompted.

"Well, it didn't thud onto me today. It's taken a while to realize it. I probably just look relieved.''

Nick tilted his swivel chair back and studied her, running a hand over an imaginary goatee. "My child,'' he said gravely, "I believe I recognize the syndrome. You perhaps felt glad to be alive?''

She nodded and addressed an envelope.

"Didn't mind our lousy weather? Smiled as you brushed your teeth? Maybe?''

"Maybe.''

"Ahhh, yes. What you've caught is rare, but not unheard of. It's called happiness.''

"Silly. I wasn't unhappy before.''

"Play semantic games, but I'm convinced you've caught galloping happiness. Congratulations. Hope it's terminal."

"You're okay, Nick."

"Careful! One of the most common symptoms is affection for the human race. Next you'll become a humanitarian."

"Don't count on it."

He straightened his chair. "Enjoy it all the same. If I but wore one, I'd doff my hat to the man who filled your weekend."

"Why do you assume that my happiness could only be caused by a man?"

He looked up from his daybook with interest. "A woman, then? So that's why you resisted my charms. What a relief!"

"How's your son?"

"Bumpy, but more important, that's the second time in as many minutes you've shown concern. Be careful."

She glanced at the clock. Five of ten. Her muscles tightened, adrenalin pumped.

Across the room, Sara Pratt settled into her plush seat. Sara now toted her own paper bag, and Suzannah suspected that it contained tuna fish. Well, in the past, stranger things than shared interests and similar palates had caused the redistribution of community property.

The large board room murmured as human engines tuned themselves. Two rows over, George Newhall held his head and prayed. George functioned through a thunderstorm of migraines and he now moved his lips and counted his private rosary, a row of pill bottles near his phone.

Teddy Dieter strutted and pranced in front of the newest of the sales assistants. She followed him with her eyes after he returned to his desk and propped his feet on it, his receiver on his shoulder for action.

Teddy had an impressive sales technique. It worked on customers and the shifting population of sales assistants. The last time he'd involved a ninny, she'd lost her job because, according to Stewart Masterman, office manager, "that sort of unwholesome fraternization" was "counterproductive" and therefore intolerable to Sherwood and Hastings and Masterman as well. Chucking the secretary instead of the broker was sexist, biased, practical and irrevocable. Suzannah had bowed out of Masterman's office and stopped protesting.

The ticker started. Suzannah watched it a moment, checking

Tydings and Roy. It opened at 8¾. Chemfax had dropped a point to 51, but still, if Tully was right, at half a share, at 25½ for 8¾ . . .

Her phone rang. "Good morning," she heard. "This is your friendly operations manager. Your client, Stan Fisher, has not yet paid, despite being duly warned. Either a cashier's check by noon or we sell him out. Want to know which event I predict?"

Damn and double-damn. Of course Fisher had sworn the check was in the mail. One of the world's three great lies. The check's in the mail, I won't come in your mouth and . . . she couldn't remember the third, and it wasn't relevant, anyway.

"He lost five hundred dollars," the operations manager continued. "Or we have. Plus commissions. Plus your pound of flesh. Figure a hundred-dollar fine, but maybe you can sweet-talk Masterman out of charging you the rest of the loss."

"Sweet-talk's not my style, and anyway, I'm not sure it's worth suffering through another know-your-client speech."

She replaced the receiver and glared, then took a deep breath and tried to make up for lost revenues and time. She flipped through Friday's tickets, looked again at the tape, checked her daybook and made four calls. She set a date to discuss tax shelters, confirmed a price for casino shares, discussed Krugerrands and explained her firm's research opinion of a water reclamation firm. She also won three of the four customers over to T&R.

She began feeling recharged, and lifted her ringing phone with great energy and excitement.

"S'donalyere," she heard, and grimaced. That slovenly slur belonged to Keith Donaldson's receptionist. Suzannah suspected the woman was open to more than incoming calls or she'd have long since been on unemployment. She waited until Keith himself spoke.

"Hey, hey, Suzy!" he said, and she closed her eyes in silent protest. "I've been watching Stellercom, Suzy-Q, and I want five hundred at 19½."

She pushed her Quotron. "It's 19¾ now, Keith; it's been climbing for a long time, and I don't think it'll—"

"I know you can get it for me at 19½, Suzy. I know you. And if you knew Suzy, like I know Suzy—"

"Fine," she said, writing a ticket that would mean a sale only if Stellercom dropped back to Keith's limit.

"Oh! Oh! Oh! What a gal . . ."

The next call was straightforward and relatively pleasant. Carl Diamond, warmed by his grandbaby and the sunshine of Phoenix, wanted fifty more shares of Xerox.

"How's that baby doing?" Suzannah asked.

Nick muttered audibly. "Careful, kiddo, you're leaking the milk of human kindness again. It'll ruin the finish on your desk."

Carl Diamond described what sunshine, cacti and his newest grandchild looked like while another button on Suzannah's phone pulsed.

"Sorry to keep you waiting," she finally said.

The voice at the other end had atrophied. It cleared itself and experimented with low sounds while Suzannah wrote Carl's order and waited, puzzled.

"This is Zachary Caldwell," it finally managed. "Of Mission, Stoddard, West and Wallace, Attorneys at Law."

She became wary.

"I'm counsel for the MacPherson family, and we have a small problem, Ms. Barnes."

Small. The man said small.

"Ah . . . I understand Mrs. MacPherson placed an order last Friday?" His voice was studied and inherently snide. English by aspiration. Funny, raunchy Katie MacPherson hadn't sounded the sort who'd want ersatz Eton as counsel.

Caldwell again cleared his throat, allowing freer passage of his prep school vowels. "A trifle awkward, shall we say? Mrs. MacPherson should not have been encouraged to—"

"Mr. Caldwell, I'm confused. Mrs. MacPherson is an adult. The bank assured me she has a six-figure balance. Are you therefore implying that the transaction was unwise?"

"Not necessarily in the manner you might—"

"Or that I encouraged an irresponsible transaction?"

"I never—"

"Because Mrs. MacPherson researched and selected the stock herself, but it was, incidentally, recommended by our own research department, so I—"

"What . . . what precisely did she purchase?"

"Hold on. You're challenging something you know nothing about?"

"Well, I—what did she buy?"

"If she wants you to know, she'll tell you."

He coughed and cleared. "The issue before us is . . . Mrs. MacPherson isn't allowed to buy stock."

"Allowed? What nonsense is that? *Allowed?* Mr. Caldwell, you said you're her lawyer?"

"Ah, no. I'm counsel to the family."

"I think you're out of bounds."

He emitted a wiggly sigh. "You're complicating what is basically a—"

"I intend to make more and more complications unless you make your message clear."

He chipped at his consonants with even greater precision. "I am attorney for her son, Scott Daniel MacPherson. He has power of attorney for his mother."

"Power of—are you saying Katie MacPherson's bonkers?"

"Hardly. Never would. Kyle Tavis was a wizard."

"Was? Kyle *who?* Who is this conversation about?"

"His widow, Catherine. K.T. left her a substantial fortune. Alas, time takes its toll, all that sort of—"

"This Catherine—does anyone call her Katie?"

"No." He sounded unutterably depressed. "No one except Catherine herself."

Suzannah inhaled several times. "Are you then saying that Catherine MacPherson is nuts?"

"It would scarcely behoove me to employ terminology such—"

"Screw your behooves. Anyway, I spoke with her four times. She was completely lucid."

"Yes. She—in her own way—it's part of the . . . Ms. Barnes, I cannot violate family trust and be more explicit."

"I expect something and I expect it quickly. First and foremost, I expect payment or I'll take you to court."

"Oh. Not court—that would be out of the . . ." A resigned wheeze filled the receiver. "I—this is dreadfully awkward, but perhaps I must explain, then, in confidence. Some people think they're Napoleon. Mrs. MacPherson believes she's her dead husband, K.T. She, ah, smokes rather large cigars, wears his old clothing and places orders. Her nurse pretends to be her secretary. Humors her. Regrettably, Catherine placed these orders while her nurse was away from the room."

"I see."

He was heartened by her words and his voice surged to new

levels of Anglo-confidence. "Then you must also see how foolish, how futile, litigation would be. I'm certain you'll discreetly handle this on your own."

"You're not paying. Is that it?"

"Well, you accepted an order from a . . . an impaired caller. I believe it's the broker's responsibility to know his, or her, as the case may be—"

"What's Scott MacPherson's phone number?"

Zachery Caldwell suddenly sounded as if he were strangling. "*Don't* trouble him," he said, words tripping one over the other. "Busy man, hates disturbances. Surely the two of us can manage this entire—"

"Wrong." She hung up.

MacPherson Stretch Socks had upgraded its image by renaming itself Suburban Textiles. That was no problem. Reaching the man who controlled it was. Suzannah had to browbeat three protective females and stay on hold for thirteen minutes before MacPherson lifted his phone.

She began politely. There were solutions for civilized people. Then, too, Scott MacPherson might be so won over by her lucidity and persuasiveness, he'd include Suzannah in his personal roster of brokers.

But he interrupted immediately. "Miss Barnes, we're wasting time. This isn't my problem. It's yours. Next time be more cautious, more professional." His voice was a snarl.

"Hold *on* there!" she said loudly, junking courtesy as a viable option. "Your mother defrauded my firm!" There. The facts, plain and simple.

"I will not be spoken to that way!" he said loudly.

"What way? It's true your mother has—"

"Miss Barnes—"

"Ms.!"

"Missss Barnesss. Do you want to be the laughingstock of this city? If so, take this to court. Mother will be declared medically unable to testify."

"But then you, as her—"

"I won't discuss this any longer. You're becoming hysterical. Transfer this call to Stewart."

She hesitated. "Stewart? You mean my office manager?"

"Yes. Met him at the club. Decent fellow. He'll put things into perspective, handle this in a civilized way. I—"

Stewart? She cracked a pencil in half. Stewart, huh? Fellow initiate of the old boys' club? A series of snapshots raced through her mind. Civilized snaps. Society page photos. The sort Stewart Masterman and his horse-faced wife appeared in. The sort also lately featuring Scott MacPherson in tuxedo, a buffalo in black bow tie.

"Mr. MacPherson, excuse me, but could I—"

He never stopped talking, simply became louder. "Some things are best handled man to man anyway. I'm not saying you girls shouldn't have your equal rights, your women's lib, mind you, but the business world is no place for certain female emotional traits that—"

That did it. She upended the negotiating table and pulled both guns out of their holsters.

"Perhaps," she said, forcing him into silence, "perhaps before either one of us takes action, we should more thoroughly discuss your delicate mama and laughingstocks in this city. How many of your pals know about her Groucho Marx imitations? How many know she's the reincarnation of your late lamented papa?"

"What—you—what is this?"

"I hear she's happiest in drag."

"Miss Barnes—"

"Ms.! Ms.!"

"—my personal life is none of your—"

"It doesn't interest me. I imagine it's stultifying. And rather anxious. Listen, I like your mother and her earthy expressions. But I'm not part of the civilized, decent set you're climbing into and maybe they wouldn't find her as appealing as I do."

"That has absolutely no relevance to—"

"Are you certain?" Suzannah's voice became a lullaby sung by someone intent on infanticide. Nick turned to watch her.

"Those folks," she trilled softly, "the sponsors of horse shows and such, they care terribly about breeding, don't they? I mean breaking into that fossilized set is rough. Particularly for the son of the reborn panty hose king."

"You're libelous, Miss—"

"Truth is not libelous." She poured still more sugar into her voice. "Therefore, you wouldn't mind if I passed the truth on to

my friend at the *Inquirer?* I owe Peepsie a favor, and your
mama's quirks would make such an amusing human interest
story. The tough old lady escapes her keeper and rips off my firm
for a few grand.''

Nick stared. MacPherson said nothing.

"Maybe a photo in Papa's old three-piece pinstripe? Puffing
and placing fraudulent orders?''

"What do you suggest as an alternative?'' MacPherson
sounded considerably subdued.

"How do I even know your song and dance is true? Prove you
have power of attorney, and if you can do that, then bring along a
check to cover her purchase. I'll wait until market closing today.
If you don't show up, if it's going to cost me money, then I can at
least repay a favor and call Peepsie.''

"Who do you think you are?''

"I'm Suzannah Barnes and I'm not your patsy. I will not
quietly absorb one cent's loss to cover your family problems. Be
here this afternoon. And don't send a flunky.'' She hung up.

"Jesus,'' Nick said with a soft whistle. "You can be scary.''

"That miserable wretch! That arrogant creep!''

"Suze, who's Peepsie?''

She laughed out loud. "A diminutive. For Samuel, and it's
spelled P-e-p-y-s. Remember him from Senior English? Seven-
teenth-century diarist. Quite good. I tried to think of a journal-
ist's name. Even that bloated egotist couldn't believe Woodward
and Bernstein would want the scoop on his mother. Anyway,
Peepsie, then. And Peepsie sounded so horribly Main Line nick-
namish.'' She laughed again. "You think anyone at the *Inquirer*
gives a damn about his mother?''

Nick shook his head.

"Neither do I. But *he* does! That sniveling, self-important
asshole!'' She put both hands above her head and clasped them.
"One round for the kid!''

At 12:05, Stan Fisher's unpaid-for stock was sold, Suzannah
automatically lost money and Patty Luboff called. The sequence
of events didn't produce jubilation. Suzannah glanced guiltily at
her "pending" box, where the incomplete questionnaire was
again shelved.

"Wanted to know how it's going.'' Patty had lived in the suburbs too long. Her voice was a singsong, like a nursery school teacher's or the hostess of a clubwoman's lunch.

Suzannah became defensive. "It's so *long*. It's so overwhelming. I mean questions about *everything*, my personal life, my childhood, my aims, my philosophy. *Why?*"

"Well mostly because I—"

"And I can't even understand what the word on the upper corners *means*. 'Events.' What does that *mean?* I can't—"

"I'll explain if you let me."

Suzannah let her.

"There's a quote," Patty said, "in a Hawthorne novel. I'm using it at the beginning of my paper. It says, 'Did you ever see a happy woman in your life? . . . How can she be happy after discovering that fate has assigned her but one single event, which she must contrive to make the substance of her whole life? A man has his choice of innumerable events.' "

"I see," Suzannah said. "I think."

"I memorized it," Patty said.

"Great."

"A hundred years after he wrote that, with lots of what he'd call events and we call choices, alternatives—"

"You're looking for a happy woman."

"I wouldn't put it that way. Looking for lots of things, like definitions of success and correlations between success as perceived and happiness as perceived, factors leading to both, whatever. Don't bother yourself with that. That word 'events' is kind of a stupid joke, my title. And listen, if you're worried because maybe some questions are too personal, don't be. I have respondents all over the country. Nobody will ever know who said what. You're all anonymous, typically representative corporate women. Period."

Suzannah thought of her carbon copies. Clones from coast to coast. Nameless, faceless sisters. She was revolted by the idea.

At twelve-seventeen, while Suzannah ate a soggy bacon, lettuce and tomato sandwich, the bank called. Her loan had cleared and she had thirty thousand dollars to play with, to double through margin if she so desired, and she did.

"Your interest will be two above the prime. Couldn't get you a fixed rate."

"But the prime's crazy!"

"Best we can do. It's a nonessential loan, and you're an odds player anyway, aren't you?"

"Guess I'd better be. Thanks for taking care of it quickly."

She spit out a fatty piece of bacon. Perhaps she shouldn't rush into anything. Perhaps she should hold on to the money, test the waters a bit longer. Two above the prime with the prime heaving, receding, doing whatever it damned well pleased . . . two above the prime was nothing to ignore.

Maybe tomorrow she'd feel that warm rush. Maybe tomorrow she'd feel an all-clear. Meanwhile, she picked at the damp bread and watched the tape whir until her phone again rang.

"Josie! I've called, but you were out."

"No matter. Wanted to firm up the thirtieth annual celebration of your birth. How's a week from Friday at Mama's?"

"Fine, but I want to talk about you."

"I am well. I had the worst hang-over after your—"

"Josie, I'm talking about—"

"I know. About what I'll do with the rest of my life. Mostly, now, I'm thinking about it. But I have to run."

Suzannah listened to the phone click. The world seemed to be gently collapsing, like an underdone cake.

Scott MacPherson smacked papers onto her desk. She glanced at the power of attorney and the cashier's check.

"I assume this terminates our association," he said, his fleshy face mauve.

She nodded.

He glanced towards the office manager's closed door. "Then I see no need to trouble anyone else about this matter."

She deliberately placed her morning *Inquirer* in a conspicuous center spot on her desk. "Nor do I," she purred.

He turned royal purple, then wheeled and walked away.

"Have a nice day!" she chirruped.

Nick whistled softly. "I'll never again accuse you of becoming mellow."

Twelve

*Elaine Weiner was the sort of woman described as handsome, al-*though probably not before time softened the rugged planes of her face and definitely not before she learned to dress so assertively she defied a viewer to ignore her or consider her plain.

Tonight, her rail-thin body modeled a bias-cut jersey in tangerine and moss. "Sorry to have kept you," she said crisply.

Suzannah had waited thirty-five minutes.

"Had to fire someone. It's my own fault. Broke my own rule and hired a friend. Widow, needed something. Incompetent, though."

The waiter, who'd controlled his impatience for better than half an hour, brought over menus.

"None for me," Elaine Weiner said. "A green salad, no dressing. Perrier with a twist. And coffee, black. Yes, with my meal. That's it."

She appeared bored as Suzannah ordered fish and green beans. "Now," she said when the waiter left. "What do you have for me? We don't have to play men's games, do we? Discuss politics and sports before we approach what we're here for?"

Suzannah happily pulled two fat sheaves of papers out of her briefcase.

"I like your outfit," Elaine Weiner said. "Fine sense of color."

"Thanks. Coming from you, that's high praise."

"You accept my self-proclaimed credentials?" She chuckled. "All I have are very assertive saleswomen. They assert that anything I've stocked is correct for now. My customers are so insecure—most women are, anyway—that they become incoherent with gratitude. And you know what? They leave my shops with bargains. For the price of a blouse or suit, they purchase self-assurance. For a little while, they know how they're supposed to be." She put on glasses and studied Suzannah's lists. "Looks like a complete overhaul."

"Your present portfolio is as imaginative as you say your customers are. I might put an eighty-year-old widow on it, but even then, I'd shelter her more."

"What's this business here?"

"Well, until the inflationary rate slows down, we should keep risk exposure down. Maybe 25 per cent of your holdings. I suggest short positions in stocks there, if you want to speculate. We could hedge with covered options, gold—we can discuss that. Maybe commodity futures. I've listed several choices. Right now you're in a boring, safe, unprofitable group of stocks. You're not taking advantage of current conditions and you're paying too much in taxes."

"I'm impressed."

"But I'm not one of your dictator saleswomen. I want you to understand all your options and make the decisions yourself."

The older woman flipped through the pages. "I've never had anyone give me a presentation like this. You've analyzed what I'm holding, explained the theory behind taking new directions, listed suggested changes, a range of prices . . . tell me, are you this thorough because you're Suzannah Barnes or because you're a woman in a traditionally male field?"

"I don't know. I've been both for some time."

"Is it difficult? Has it been?"

"I assume you're talking about being a broker, not a woman. There's no overt discrimination any more. Too many lawsuits. But the attitude's still there. And you can't win. Either you're a bearable female—feminine and therefore too passive for the field or, if you manage to do well, then you're 'masculine'—only not in the fine ways they are. So there's a sludge of disapproval. I try to ignore it."

Elaine Weiner nodded. "I had to fight it even in women's wear. It was marketing and retailing and other male prerogatives. It was men controlling loans, deciding my fate. Well, I showed them."

Dinner arrived. Suzannah watched Perrier sipped and celery cubes speared. She resolved that after this meal, she would order dry salads, disregard menus, develop a will of iron.

"Are you married?" the thin woman asked abruptly.

"Not any more."

"Nobody counts early experiments." Elaine looked thoughtful. "I didn't think you were. It's too debilitating. Frankly, I think it's impossible."

"But—I don't—I've seen photos in the paper of you and your husband."

"Oh, of course. *Now* I'm married. Not while I was making my way, though. I mean for men, it's easy. Their wives help them up. But a woman with something going for her better stay unfettered. Nothing like a husband's ego to put weights on your ankles. Want advice?" She didn't wait for an answer. "When you're ready, marry a young one. They accept you as a finished product, don't work you over, don't try to mold you in their image, don't keep you in your place. Maybe they've got mother fixations, but who cares? They're attractive escorts, energetic, companionable, great in bed and they leave you alone. My husband's thirty-five. Seven years younger than I am. We have a most satisfactory marriage."

"I'll bear that in mind."

"You're how old?"

"Twenty-nine. Well, on the very verge of thirty."

"The biological time clock business getting you? Or do you have children from that early marriage?"

Sometimes, for no reason she knew, Suzannah's biology battled with her. Sometimes, she felt eviscerated. Emptied out. She became ovoid and hollow, a mournful cavern filled with echoes.

Sometimes, her breasts tingled with phantom liquid, the nipples stood erect, aching for release, for small mouths to suckle.

But that was an embarrassment, a primitive summons to the breeding ground. The womb and the breast, driven by their own instincts, ignoring her. The body, holding on since prehistory, sliding in its mindless juices, insisting on survival.

Preparing the trap. One had to be wary.

"I'm an aunt three times over," Suzannah said. "That suffices."

Elaine Weiner nodded. "I have twelve stores and no kids. My shops don't whine and ask for the car and tell me they hate me or get high on drugs. The business of children seems to be to drain our time and energy. To age and shove out the former generation. It makes Darwinian sense, but I'm not Darwin. Anyway, let's discuss more rewarding investments."

They ate as Suzannah discussed the records of a hospital management company, a semiconductor factory and a firm that man- ufactured dialysis machines.

As they finished coffee, Elaine Weiner smiled. "You are very like my saleswomen. I see what you've done. This is a complete wardrobe. Oh, I can pick the purple scarf or the aquamarine. The dialysis machines or the electronic switches. But you designed the look long before I entered the dressing room. Thanks, I feel like I'm getting a real bargain."

Thirteen

The next morning, Suzannah's joyful expression again provoked comments from Nick.

"See him again?"

"Not him. Her."

"Aha! You're officially coming out of the closet!"

"Her. Elaine Weiner."

"What did she do to make you so high? Give you the scoop on next season's hemlines?"

"I think she'll give me her business." But that wasn't it. Com- missions didn't account for the joyous aftershocks of last night's meeting. Elaine Weiner had given not simply income, but a benediction, pledges and assurances Suzannah needed to hear from lips other than her own. There was no way to explain it to Nick or anyone who, born male, inherited a plethora of role mod- els. Perhaps there was no way to explain it to anyone. She didn't care. It was her private possession, meeting a private need and it—life itself—felt grand.

It *was* possible to grab it all, to succeed, to be somebody. Her body temperature rose. Her touch, her instincts were back and as sure as were Elaine Weiner's. She could spin bright balls through the skies, juggle possibilities, make her dizziest dreams reality.

For now, business as usual. With zest, she dialed Donaldson Industries. She tolerated the receptionist's slurred "Delsundries.

Hold." And spoke to Keith Donaldson in a voice brimming with energy. "Stellercom's 22. It hasn't *thought* about 19½ since last week. What do you say?"

"Suzy-Q, I say it's even more overpriced than it was."

"Keith! You're losing money every minute you sit and insist on that. This isn't like you."

"I . . ." He capitulated. "Guess so. Buy it at the market."

She talked while she wrote his ticket. "Listen, there's something else to consider. A land company that . . ."

Keith joined well over a dozen of her other clients as part owner of Tydings and Roy. After she completed his orders, she wrote one for herself. Not all the thirty thousand, but the stock had again moved and she bought one thousand shares at 9½, humming all the while.

"At least keep your merriment silent," Nick said.

"Better than that, I'll share part of its cause. I've found a lovely bit of common stock for your consideration, sir." She explained what she knew about Tydings and Roy although not how she knew it. Instead, she stressed what a good buy it was for individuals or conglomerates.

"Slow down. I'm a salesman, not a customer. I'd have to investigate, watch it, read up on it. What turned you on to it?"

"I—I heard something."

He shook his head.

"That's irrelevant. Now it's my own thing. I have a gut feeling about it."

"Your guts have been addled since the weekend."

"C'mon. Never overestimate the power of a man." But she said no more because Elaine Weiner, having studied the suggestions overnight, called to give Suzannah the go-ahead. "And thanks," she said. "Thanks for being so thorough."

Suzannah wanted to repay the woman for existing. "At the risk of appearing less thorough, can I make a suggestion that wasn't on the list? There's a land development company . . ."

And the newest of Suzannah's clients put her capital into land and its developers.

"Think you might be hustling too hard?" Nick asked while she wrote Weiner's ticket.

"Oh, Nick, isn't your favorite sin greed, too?"

"Where you rushing so hard and fast?" he asked quietly.

She frowned at him, then shrugged. "To lunch, right now."

* * *

"She's marvelous, Abby. Gutsy and self-assured, and she knows everybody and she intimated that her friends also prefer dealing with women. God, I love her style of—"

"Suzannah, why didn't we eat at the deli? This hot dog's made of PVC. The napkin's the only tasty part of this meal."

"You could have stayed, but I have to buy a phone machine and this is my only time."

"Listen, I'm buying a pretzel to bury that plastic taste. Then I want to hear about the music man, not Elaine Whoosis. Why are you obsessed with *her?*"

"It's exciting, meeting an older woman you can admire."

"I never knew you were searching for a mentor with tits. Anyway, Elaine Weiner's a skinny businesswoman. Period. Is that something to bow down and worship? I've heard she could be replaced by a computer and nobody would notice except that computers don't have tantrums."

Suzannah waited until Abby slathered mustard over her thick hot pretzel and took a bite; then she spoke. "My mother said pretzel men suck their diseased fingers before they choose your pretzel and hand it to you."

"I've had worse in my mouth. I'm *sorry* I don't fully appreciate your new client. My compliments on snaring her even if I hate her stores, hate her ads, hate the way she wants every woman to be in her image and, from what I've heard, hate her, too."

Suzannah felt personally insulted.

"Ah, c'mon," Abby said. "Tell me your other stories. The salacious ones." She waited. "Cut it out," she said, and waited again. "Suzannah? Sulking produces cellulite. Ah good, you're smiling again. Now—how *was* he?"

"He . . . eats wonderfully well. And plays the guitar like heaven. And, ah, your theories about the correlation between those activities and others have been proven correct."

"Goodness me. Does that mean you had fun? Will you see him again?"

"Tonight. Literally a look-see. He has sitter problems."

"Uh-oh. Imperfection. The tragic flaw of custody."

"His wife's dead."

"Sadder still. He has a *permanent* squatter. You'll have to use your place. Personally, I like the freedom to leave. It's easier than throwing them out. But now I see the need for the phone machine. Not retrieving messages, are you, but stopping incoming calls. Guess he's really special.'' She suddenly sounded wistful.

Suzannah said nothing. She couldn't explain Coby to Abby or herself. And she didn't want to. She cherished her memories of the weekend, but they felt fragile, able to be shattered with too-casual handling.

And anyway, what if he turned out to be a fluke? A fantasy? A one-time-only special? If he did, then exposing herself, letting her emotions go public now, would create more pain and embarrassment later.

She waved to the right. "Store's one block over, Abby."

"Mind if I skip it? The wind's giving me a headache."

"There's no wind in a store."

"There's wind in my head. Run along."

Suzannah frowned. "Abby, whenever I'm with you lately, I—"

"Look," Abby whispered. "God. Look." She pointed at a nearby bench where a raggedy woman sat, legs wide apart, oblivious to the cold and the stares and comments of pedestrians. Intently, the woman ran a straight razor up one leg, studied it to be sure it was free of hair, then turned to the other leg. Still more upsetting than what she was doing was her head, which was covered with shampoo-style black hair dye.

"Jesus," Abby said, near tears. "Sweet Jesus. She wants to be pretty. She wants to be perfect, to be admired. And she's crazy."

Abby seemed hypnotized by the woman, who again shaved her legs rhythmically. "Jesus," Abby repeated, putting her hands over her ears as if shutting out a private message.

"Abby, come with me."

Abby shook her head. "She needs help, but I don't know what kind."

Suzannah forcibly took her arm and repeated her request. "Come with me. You can't stand on a freezing sidewalk and watch a crazy lady!"

"There are so many, aren't there? Aren't there more crazy ladies than ever?"

"Come on. I—I desperately need nail polish."

"*Nail polish?* Can you really see that woman, then go buy *nail polish*?" But she allowed herself to be led into the variety store near them. She stood by the cosmetic counter with the rows of bottles in their infinite gradations of pink, rose, red and purple.

"Abigail, what's the matter? What's happened to you?"

Abby looked at her with blank eyes. "Nothing. Zero. How do you handle that, doc? Zilch doesn't make for good stories."

"Is there a man? What about your gymnast?"

"Gone, godspeed. We—he turned me off. It happens lately. Men, all very so-what. Maybe the machinery's wearing out. Lord knows I've abused it."

"There'll be other men."

"Don't want them. I don't want anybody. It would only be more of the same, don't you see? It—it isn't fun any more. I feel like I shot up with Novocain, except my head, which hurts." Her voice had become hoarse and she cleared her throat and blinked. "The old cure doesn't work any more. I'm immune." She lifted a glistening apricot bottle. "This is your shade. Sexy Business-woman."

"Abby, you can't lock up and hide. You have to find out why—"

"Please. I didn't mean to say anything. Give me time. I'll work it through. Change jobs, take a trip. Something."

"Meanwhile?"

"Meanwhile, I want a layoff. Literally. From men, from you. From anything that wants to crawl inside me or my brain." She turned. "Where's a salesgirl?"

Suzannah watched Abby, all flash with jet hair and yellow tunic, bottle-green pants and high boots. Today she was Robin Hood as Samurai, but her skin lacked its customary shine and her voice was flat.

"There's the floor manager," Abby said. "One minute." She flipped her white coat over one shoulder and moved to a thin man straightening greeting cards. Suzannah watched Abby speak softly, watched her emit almost visible heat waves.

The manager was transformed. He became taller, sturdier. He patted his chest with dignity and rang up the sale himself, care-fully bagging the bottle and, with a brush of his hand over her skin, passing it to Abby.

"Nice to know the apparatus works, should I want to use it again," Abby said as they left the store. "Don't look so con-cerned. A week ago you were preaching chastity yourself." Abby turned and again found the madwoman with the dye and the razor and the naked outspread legs. "It isn't what she's doing, Suze. Only where. She's not that different, you know." She was silent a moment, then she turned to Suzannah. "Bye, now."

Suzannah couldn't let her go that easily, couldn't count on Abby's reaching out even if she were lurching and desperately needy of support. Abby had a history of hiding during black times. "Wait!" she said.

Abby's face was contorted. "Listen, Suze, you're the executive type. You love conquering problems, but if you can't, you get angry. You can't solve this one, so sooner or later you'll be pissed. Before that happens, back off, would you?" She shook her head and winced. "All this pressure makes it hurt more."

"I'm sorry. I—I'll see you. But please, don't hide just because you're not up for fun and games. Call me. And I'll call you, no matter what you say now. You have my permission to say 'fuck off,' but I won't stop trying."

Abby blew her a kiss. "Love you," she said, "and with your permission, I now say, 'fuck off.' " And she left.

During the afternoon, Suzannah's internal temperature, as well as that outdoors, reached a new low.

"Mr. Masterman wants to see you when you can." Didi, Masterman's administrative assistant, had a frosty telephone voice.

Having no alternative, Suzannah agreed to see him when the market closed. Which it did, all too quickly. She stared at the final reading on the tape. She had bullied Keith Donaldson into buying Stellercom at its all-time high of 22 and then it had given up the ghost and plummeted to 19½. Exactly where he'd thought it belonged. Kiss customer Donaldson good-by.

He was only one customer. It shouldn't have bothered her so, so sapped her energy. Those things happened, they were part of the business. Still, her shoulders sagged as she knocked on, then opened, Stewart Masterman's door.

He briefly discussed the business of Stanley Fisher's non-payment, although it didn't seem to trouble him much. Of course Suzannah would be fined. Of course caution was a virtue to be desired and innocent young, ah, brokers could be misled, but, of more importance . . . He picked up a sheet of paper. "You're putting quite a few people into Tydings and Roy, I see. Why? We aren't recommending it."

"I have a good feeling about it." Once again she gave her pitch, explaining its holdings and potential, her reasons for choosing it. Explaining everything except the rumored take-over.

"Still," he said, his voice a Santa-sugary boom, "still, it's incautious to base so much on intuition."

"I'm buying it myself."

"So I see." He tapped a manicured nail on the paper. "That doesn't concern me. You're not apt to sue yourself."

She knew she hadn't many clients left who were likely to make sizable purchases so she decided to please Masterman. "You're right," she said sweetly. "I'll hold back with my clients, but I'd like to still invest in it myself."

"Fine." He nodded approval. Santa would keep Suzannah on his route. "Precisely what I would have suggested." He pursed his mouth benignly. "You're a fine young, er, broker. Working out very well indeed . . ."

For a woman, she silently added.

". . . but you are, of course . . ."

Female?

". . . young. And, well, it's to be expected, but you have a tendency towards . . ."

The sort of erratic, insane behavior of your sex.

". . . impulsiveness. So sometimes we . . ."

Men. Possessors of wisdom and testosterone.

". . . older folk can lend a hand. We've had more time to learn, that's all."

She left his office and wiped away her humble smile. Stewart was a fool, a behemoth, a breathing fossil. His maternal grandmother was a Hastings and the firm respected Stewart's inherited stock, let him keep his position while the industry changed and administrative know-how replaced the old school tie as credentials for management.

Still, New York might laugh at the dodo in Philadelphia, but he was her dodo. Until he retired, Stewart was king of this fiefdom and she was a peasant.

Suzannah drove to night school cautiously, thinking of the day behind her, the night ahead. She smiled, anticipating Coby later.

But then she felt a mothy flutter of fear. Maybe you couldn't and shouldn't go back. Maybe he was just a one-time thing.

The flutters increased. Her mood grew darker, denser, irritations becoming corporeal, flitting across her face and blurring her vision like summer insects clogging a screen.

It had nothing to do with Coby, everything to do with the day, with the loss of her morning's exuberance. The genteel run-in with Masterman. The mess-up with Donaldson's stock. Josie's enigmatic behavior. Abby's unfathomable despair.

Her mother, isolated and withering away. And Isobel, senile.

And . . . and her birthday, looming darkly ahead.

She shook her head with exasperation. Look at her! She was worse than the ninnies who feared wrinkles and age. She feared the birthday itself.

But she wouldn't any more. She wouldn't set herself up, wouldn't put her hand back into the fire to see if—yes indeed!—it burned and hurt this time, too.

She was turning thirty. She wouldn't let one day out of a life's year ever matter again.

Suzannah blinked as a buried memory surfaced and spread slickly across the windshield.

Bonnie, her father's second wife, laughing loudly.

Suzannah had crossed the city on busses and subways to reach her father's apartment. Had swallowed hard and asked, clearing her throat, if he had again forgotten her.

She wanted him to lie if he had to. Wanted him to say his card must have been lost in the mail, his phone messages not transmitted, his gift never shipped from the store. Anything.

"It was my sixteenth birthday." Her voice was small with humiliation.

Bonnie, not her father, answered, first with a loud bray. "Your *what*, Suzannah? Your sweet sixteen? For heaven's sake—your birthday's in two months! It's in April—April 28!"

Suzannah's father, handsome face intent, watched with interest and said nothing.

Suzannah felt as if she were going mad. "February! February 15! The day after Valentine's!"

"April 28," Bonnie insisted.

"Don't *say* that! It's *my* day—*mine!* I know when I was born and you don't, Bonnie! You weren't there!"

But he had been there. Suzannah's mother always talked about how he arrived at the hospital late, how they couldn't find him, but how he finally arrived at the same time Suzannah did.

He'd been there. He simply couldn't remember, that's all.

Such an ordinary child she must have been. Such a standard baby. One of those faces you forget. Good old what's her name.

So he couldn't remember and he let Bonnie, his woman, usurp even Suzannah's birth date.

For years before that day, for years after, Suzannah honored his birthday with original poems and clever, expensive gifts. In code, she said she loved him a dozen ways each year. He was always pleased, always thankful—and always his thoughtless, forgetful self the rest of the year.

Now, remembering, Suzannah felt her old rage reheat, the rage that had kept her from freezing solid that night years ago. She had humbled herself, hands chapped in the cold, ice coating throat and lungs, frost chafing her vital organs by the time she left his house.

But she didn't cry. Burning, she didn't cry. Not until later, several blocks from his apartment, when she slipped on the ice and lay in the street sobbing until people helped her up, thinking she had broken something.

At least she had never exposed herself that way again. But idiotic, self-destructive fantasies kept resurfacing. Once a year, hot air balloons lifted off from nowhere, to be popped and deflated in the cold.

Now, she simply would not. She would be thirty and nobody's child. Nothing more offensive than an adult clinging to baby hurts. Time to pack them away. Her childhood was long gone as was that sixteenth birthday, sweet or sour. Nothing was the same. He was an aging man in an apartment across town; February 15 was just another day and she wasn't that needy kid any more. She was a stockbroker and tonight, a teacher. She had a class waiting. She inhaled.

"Common stocks," she said out loud. "Money market securities. Municipal bonds. Corporate bonds. Investment trusts. Convertible bonds. Mutual funds. Tax-deferred retirement plans. Deferred annuities. Options."

She recited the list twice, then a third time as she found a parking space near her building. She had all the headings and all the notes for her lecture neatly typed on sheets in her briefcase. But she walked into the building reciting them a fourth time and found the litany comforting.

She strained to project her voice because rough-hewn, definitely unmusical sounds cut through Coby's classroom wall.

"And so," Suzannah said, "we return to tonight's first question. What are you willing to risk? Security is a contradiction in terms if it produces anxiety. Naturally, we want to increase assets, but only you can decide what level of uncertainty gives you stomachaches, of what precisely keeps you secure."

The gum-cracker whose husband had left in a Porsche spoke up. "Does everything have to sound like my life? Jesus, risk and security. That's all I ever think about."

"I wish you didn't have to call it *risk*," a soft voice said. "My whole education was learning to avoid risk. I'm supposed to take care of things, to protect them. Never to risk."

Suzannah shrugged. "We were all raised that way if we were female. But look, you can minimize risk. You can concentrate on the predictable and the dependable. You can play it safe. Of course, in the market or anywhere, you'll thereby lessen your potential gain."

"Isn't it supposed to be a music class back there?" Myrna Tucker uttered her irrelevant comment, folded her hands and scowled.

They all listened to a sustained shriek, then a long downward whine. Then the pattern was repeated. "It's horrible," Suzannah agreed. "Why don't we stop shouting against it? It's ten o'clock. Next week we'll review annual reports and research data, and the week after, the panel's coming—the real estate broker, art and antique dealers, et cetera."

Satisfied, the class closed notebooks, pushed back chairs and left. Except for Myrna, who danced around Suzannah's desk discharging a volley of unrelated questions and opinions.

"Will you explain discount brokers?" Dance, shuffle, turn back. "Should I bring in my greeting cards when the antique dealer's here?" Move around, don't wait for an answer. "You want coffee?" Stop teacher before she declines. "Ever think about the risks in a gift store's inventory? I bought these adorable candy dishes. Gold canoes with the cutest paddles and the dearest Indians. Cost a fortune and nobody bought one. Go know, right?

And there was this incredibly darling coffeepot with even the sweetest cup attached to the most precious spigot—''

"I really must excuse myself," Suzannah said.

"I'll walk you."

"I'm staying in the building." Suzannah moved a pace towards Coby's still busy classroom.

"Him?" Myrna looked appalled. "Be careful. Never trust those big ones. Can overpower you just like that." She snapped her fingers. "Do you know self-defense?"

"I've been improvising all my life."

Myrna shook her head and left Suzannah to her dire fate.

Coby was completing his talk. Suzannah waited near the doorway, observing his students. Not by title as was her course, but by the destiny of uncertified night schools, his class was female-heavy. Women smiled up at him.

Women who spent days polishing mahogany until they could verify their existence in slick waxed table tops. Women who popped lemon room deodorizers into toilet bowls. Women who heaved sackfuls of children to pediatricians and soccer games.

Half the catalogue's offerings were home enrichment seminars designed for these women. Learn how to cook his favorite foods. Slim that bod to his requirements. With Wanda the exercise lady. Or Sally's disco shape-up. Or slimnastics, isometrica, stationary jogging, aerobic dance and who knows what.

Coby's women were the elite, improving their souls and saying to hell with the house. Suzannah watched them watch him.

Most wore the slightly bemused, soft expression of women willing to love.

Handsome men provoked such expressions. Not mere admiration, but a welcoming, tolerant, soft-lipped invitation.

A white-haired woman smiled, ready to mother him. A younger woman with straight brown hair absently stroked her lips. Her hungry expression was not maternal.

Suzannah moved to a more visible position at the door. Coby dismissed his class and she went to his desk while the women shuffled and buttoned and located purses. Finally, only the two of them were left.

"What, please, was that screaming and shouting about?"

He smiled. "Ah, yes. Well, I always wait for someone to ask how music started. No one ever does. So I ask, then I answer, best I can."

"Those screams were the beginning of music? Or war?"

"Maybe war, once. An example of pathogenic music—music born of passion. As opposed to logogenic, born of words, of the mind. What you heard was an Australian tumbling strain. Whatever it initially was, it felt good or signaled something clearly and it became ritualized to convey that emotion. That's all tumbling strains are—pure emotion, created somewhere near the beginning of musical creation, if not smack on the starting line."

He erased his blackboard. "We can't have digs to find ancient sounds. So we rely on contemporary primitive equivalents, like that tumbling strain." He turned to her. "I know you're dying to know what becomes of the pathogenic and logogenic strains which are, respectively, fierce sound—like what you heard—and monotonous text. And the answer is the merger of the two, called melogenic song." He sat down beside her. "Mind and passion combine and presto—music."

"No wonder your students look so dreamy. You give sexy lectures. But what are those words you erased? And those arrows? What does 'prenatal' have to do with screaming aborigines?"

"Listen, I can't stay here long. I have to make a tape for a lecture tomorrow. Want some coffee from down the hall?"

"Nope. But I want to know about prenatal tumbling."

He slouched in his school desk like a sophomore. "I'm less concerned with the sounds of the beginning than why and how music started. The blackboard doodles were my theory. See, music has no useful purpose. It isn't like words. They're for poetry, but they're also for how-to manuals. Paint creates the Sistine Chapel, but it also preserves wood and has a pragmatic, everyday use. But music, with no function except assigned ones, is universal. Why?"

"I give up. I can't answer knock-knock riddles, let alone this."

He leaned over and kissed her and they both, instinctively, glanced at the hall door, waiting for a vice-principal to spot them and assign detentions for necking.

"Anyway," he said, "I don't have the all-time answer. There are lots of theories. Gods presented music as a gift, man imitated birds, there's a music of the spheres some blessed men can overhear and repeat. More theories. But I think there's an intuitive, primal need for music." He gestured towards the ghostly traces of his blackboard notations.

"The fetus hears nine months of his mother's heartbeat, the rhythmic sound of life and connection. Physiologically, the newborn hears high tones first—his mother's voice. Then later, male tones. So we have rhythm and a range of sounds that are the first signals of nurturing, of life and love. Plus, there's no such thing as silence. Your nervous system makes a high-pitched sound and your circulating blood a low one. Wondrous trivia, yes? But I think the need and the sense of rhythm and range are inborn and instinctively connected with emotions."

He took out his pipe, again checking the hallway door.

"Don't worry," she said. "You only get in trouble for smoking in the bathroom." She lit a cigarette. "That was interesting. And somehow . . . comforting. I like being with you. Even not touching. Although frankly, I prefer touching."

He smiled. "What did I interrupt in your classroom with my pathogenic screams?"

"Investment possibilities. A sampler. Unfortunately, a taste for one's options isn't as instinctive as a taste for music. And certainly, risk-taking isn't. Not for women."

"But you're the exception, huh?"

"Any successful woman is. Any successful human takes risks."

"And are you?"

"Successful? Getting there."

"I meant a risk-taker."

"Of course. Have to be if you're after high stakes. Why? Do you have a risky adventure to suggest?"

He stood. "Perhaps. We'll discuss it in other places, other times. Now, I have to record examples of ballad drift."

"Sounds geological, not musical." But she, too, stood and they walked into the frosty night. "It's been short but sweet, Waldemar." She stopped. "What sort of name is that?"

"Ancient. Goes all the way back to Ellis Island. In high school, though, I heard about Danish kings named Waldemar. I adopted them as my ancestors, particularly Waldemar the Great, who helped Albert the Bear subjugate the Wends. Sounded much more heroic than a string of peddlers crisscrossing Europe."

"What's a Wend?"

"A magic t'ing de fairies wave. That's what my Zeyde Morris would have said. But then, he didn't know about Albert the Bear." He kissed her. She loved the smell of his skin.

She realized she was smiling as she drove home, savoring the aftertaste of Coby. The expressway was clear with only potholes to avoid. No longer remembered were the annoyances. She was reinvigorated, the debris cleared from her mind and vision. She pressed on the accelerator, hurrying to tomorrow.

Tomorrow, feeling good. With that money to invest. Another opportunity to ride the fast lane.

She drove recklessly, if anyone had been near to monitor, if anything created visible hazards. But the road was empty, the speed intoxicating and prudence, irrelevant.

Fourteen

Rachel pressed her temples and spoke softly. "I'd rather listen to the windshield wipers than that atonal clanging, if it's okay with you."

Coby snapped off the car radio.

"I don't want to probe," Rachel said, "but what's bothering you?"

He shook his head. "That music, probably. That's all." He was lying. He'd had moments the past five days when he sneered at the nagging guilt he felt. Sins of omission were no more a part of his ethnic heritage than was Albert the Bear. Yet he couldn't ignore the six rides he and Rachel had shared this week, the six missed possibilities for truth.

Monday, he's heard words squirreled at the back of his mind. Monday, he'd exhumed and examined them. "Rachel, I've met capital 'H' her."

Oh, but Monday was embarrassingly soon. He didn't trust himself to speak.

Wednesday, after another time with Suzannah, he was positive he should say something. Instead, he listened to Rachel discuss her difficulties with thirteen-year-old Nancy.

"I'm worried about what Nancy's learning from my experiences, my divorce," she said.

Suzannah, Coby thought. Explain Suzannah.

"I'm afraid she thinks she can't trust anyone. Can't count on anyone."

Rachel counts on you not to use her shabbily. Explain Suzannah, dammit.

"Do you think Nancy would trust men more if I'd left and David stayed? But then, what would she think being a woman, or a mother, meant?"

How the hell to explain? It didn't help that Rachel had accepted the possibility, had even broached it. She might call herself an old sweater, but echoing it would be cruel and what else would he be doing? Particularly so soon. It's like this, Rachel. After barely a week, I want and need this woman. I feel emotions I never felt—will never feel—with you, but nothing personal, babe. How would that sound?

And now it was Friday, the words still unsaid and he was racing through the rain, impatient to check in and be off again. Impatient to be with Suzannah. More guilt.

There was no language for his message without making it clear that Suzannah filled him in ways Rachel could not. That the sight and the smell and the rhythms of Suzannah were unique. That something fierce about her challenged him. Something less civilized, less humane than Rachel's almost maternal warmth. That the parts Suzannah had no control over, her face and her colors, her body contours and the shape of her speech, had been designed for him.

That even what felt wrong about her was right.

How in hell did one say that with grace? With the kindness and loving attention this woman, this friend, deserved?

Rachel wouldn't throw a tantrum. Rachel wouldn't sulk or be vindictive.

Rachel would understand. That made the prospect worse.

Rachel sighed loudly. "It's so easy dealing with other people's adolescents. Ah, physician, heal thine own teen-ager." She opened her pocketbook and hunted for house keys. "There's pot roast for dinner. Want to share it? I'll cook Adam a hot dog if he finds the roast disgusting. Nancy surely will. There's nothing I do lately that doesn't disgust her." She found her keys. "Have I thanked you for being such a help with her?"

"Me? How?"

"You've provided male attention. You have a gift for listening, for truly being there. You're important in her life." She leaned over and kissed him. "Thanks, from both of us."

Not her lips, but guilt lit upon his mouth. Tell her, jackass, he thought. Sure. How? By singing telegrams? You can't mean here, now.

"So. Pot roast?"

"Oh, I'd love to, and I'm sure it's delicious, but I've . . . made . . . another appointment."

Her dark eyes met his briefly, then veered to watch the rain splat and run down the windshield. "Well . . . leftovers, perhaps. Another time."

When she left the car, she waved without turning around to face him.

Suzannah pared away the tough purple points on the asparagus and boiled the frail remains precisely one minute, afterwards plunging them into ice water.

She smiled at her orderly kitchen, ticking off a mental list. The strawberries were macerating in kirschwasser, the veal scallops pounded tender, the mushrooms sliced and waiting, the bowl, beaters and cream chilling in the refrigerator. On the counters, a tall bottle of sherry, another, squat and curved, of curaçao and cylindrical jars of herbs and spices.

Everything standing one step before completion. When Coby appeared in an hour or so, she would be freshly washed and rested and her home as serene as she was.

In the living room, she appraised her table. "You belong in Bloomies, baby," she said, smoothing the hem of a cloth edged in wildflowers. The spring colors echoed in batik napkins, the trim on her translucent china.

Hotter tones lay at the center, pulsing from tapers in a pottery candelabra. A dozen flames would reflect in the facets of the Baccarat goblets and the silver's carved flowers.

She arranged harpsichord and flute selections on the stereo. Baroque and jazz, Renaissance and jet age. A night with no calendars, clocks or seasons.

She turned the machine on, much too soon for Coby's ears, but she gave the atmosphere a head start. Let notes cascade and pile, nestle in the pillows and echo off the parquetry.

A pity courtesans are in such disrepute, she thought, perfuming herself after her shower. It was fun enhancing the act of love. There were so many avenues, so many access routes to pleasure and the oldest were still the best.

She pulled her comforter close and drifted off, hearing the silver clusters of music as they floated through her room.

As avocation, courtesan wasn't half bad.

Coby gaped.

Mrs. Jennings was puce. He wasn't certain exactly what color puce was, but it sounded as disgusting as she looked.

She burped. "Don't know what hit me. Don't want to leave you in the lurch, but I sure don't feel good. Hope I haven't given it to the boy." She leaned heavily on the table as she stood up.

He wanted to punch her out, tie her down, insist she oversee Adam even if it killed her. You promised! he wanted to yell. It isn't fair!

He tried instead to find the long view, to accept fate, impersonate humanity. "Better get to bed!" he said loudly, covering internal roars of indignation.

She nodded, but slightly, as the motion seemed to dizzy her. "My boys are coming. One'll drive my car, the other has the pickup. I never get sick. I'm real sorry."

"Oh! Don't Be Silly!" He couldn't control his decibel level. It was enough he wasn't beating her to a pulp. *"Sickness is nothing to be ashamed of!"*

You fallible excuse for a Vermonter! Have you no sense of priorities? Your stinking microbes make me sick!

"Maybe it's a twenty-four-hour bug?" she said.

Twenty-four hours beginning Friday? FRIDAY? "Don't. Worry. About. It."

The doorbell rang and Coby greeted two worried young men. The Jennings boys ushered their mother out as if she were a terminal case.

Throughout the little scene, until Coby, having bellowed *"Get Well!"* closed the door and punched it, Adam watched silently. Occasionally, he murmured asides to Boots, who responded by licking Adam's nose and lips. Now, watching his father thrash the front door, Adam became a participant.

"Why are you punching the door?"

"I—I'm checking that it's closed tight." Coby held his fist with his other hand.

Adam turned to Boots. *Sotto voce.* "He'll play the piano now. Probly."

"Why do you talk to a dog? Why do you let that dog slobber all over you? Why would I play the piano of all things?"

"Because when you're mad, you play it. Crashy."

Coby spoke from behind clenched teeth. "I'm not mad."

Adam's eyes were dark and wide. "Do I have to stay home alone tonight?"

"Have I ever, one single time, left you alone at night? What's the matter with you?" His son wrapped his arms around the dog. "I wouldn't leave you alone," he added more gently. "Let's see what I can do about this."

He dredged an ancient, prehousekeeper list of sitters out of a kitchen drawer. Most of the names were now college age and long gone. Then he smiled. Hope and Faith McCluskey. The twins at the corner. So singularly unattractive no sane and sighted male would approach them.

Coby had considered the homely girls a lapse in the laws of natural selection, a brief rerun for Neanderthals, a double production of gnarled noses, sullen mouths, beetlebrows. With, alas, as the years passed, personalities to match. Now he'd see them shamble by, thick-waisted, stoop-shouldered, acne-scarred, scowling—and still, in high school, wearing matched outfits.

There was definitely hope. Or faith.

He dialed eagerly, only mildly ashamed that his motives and optimism were based on the wretchedness of the twins.

Their mother interrupted his introduction. "Sorry," she said. "They're busy."

"Both?"

"Yes." *"Really?* Doing *what?"* He knew his incredulity lacked tact, but he couldn't control it.

"What teen-agers do," Mrs. McCluskey said placidly.

He thanked her and hung up. Was it possible that God loved irony? That Hope and Faith could dally with the opposite sex while he settled for further adventures in child care?

Suzannah's greeting was groggy and confused.

"My housekeeper," he explained. "Stomach flu. I'm ground-ed for tonight, at least." Quarantined. Big scare notice on the front door. "*Fatherhood Inside. Acute Case*. Stay away. Debilitating and incapacitating. Lasts one full generation."

Suzannah's yawn was audible. "I was napping. What's that again?"

He repeated his story, glancing into the center hall at his son, now forcing one of Boots's legs into a parka. Explaining this side of his life to Suzannah felt like debating Matisse versus Picasso with Helen Keller.

Boots, exasperated with his costume, bolted and stumbled into the kitchen, but strait-jacketed by the parka, he was an easy tackle for Adam.

"Oh," Suzannah said. "I was really looking forward to . . ."

"So was I. So was I."

Adam freed Boots and put his jacket on himself, backwards. He circled the dog, flapping his arms.

"So I guess"—Suzannah seemed to be working through something complex—". . . you could bring him."

"Thanks, but I truly don't think it would . . ." Coby regarded his son, the plague. Adam had added an inverted colander to his outfit and with the silvery basket on his head, he continued his peculiar rounds. Boots watched, thumping his tail, not bothered in the least.

"Swakata!" Adam shot an imaginary bazooka, then bent to kiss his canine casualty.

Coby flushed with shame. That was his son, not a disease or disfigurement. His son, not an intruder.

That was the son he'd so wanted, the son who so wanted him. A part, forever, of his own reality. Meshed to his life irrevocably. It was shameful to consider a part without present function an obstruction. Sitting down, you don't condemn your feet because they aren't getting you anywhere.

If Suzannah were ever to be part of Coby's life, then all of Coby, including Adam, would be involved. This particular evening was too soon, an error of timing, but given that nature in the form of bacteria had changed the tempo . . . "Wouldn't you mind?" he asked.

"Well, the alternative is—I mean let's make the most of what's possible."

Not quite a wide-armed embrace of welcome, but no matter.

"We'll be there in forty-five minutes." He thanked her again and hung up.

"We? Me? You mean me?" Adam sounded as ambivalent as Suzannah had.

"We. You and I. We've got ourselves a date."

Perhaps a ménage à trois develops the ability to design intimate table settings. Suzannah lacked it. Even on a circular table, three was a crowd.

There was no way to avoid having the odd one sit between them.

How old was that child? She plumbed her mind back to their first coffee date. "I have a six-year-old son," he'd said.

What was six like? Certainly sufficiently civilized to eat with adults. Past high chairs and table banging.

She replaced the plain water glass with another crystal goblet. He could guzzle milk from Baccarat, damn it. The table, all settings now alike, looked less offensive. But there was more to an evening than linen and china. What the hell did you talk about with a kid?

Coby drove slowly, sluggish with presentiments of nonautomotive disaster.

"Dad, why won't other kids be there?"

"I told you. Suzannah doesn't have children."

"Isn't she a grownup?"

"Of course. Why?"

"Then why doesn't she have kids? What am I going to do?"

Coby chose question number two. "You can eat, read, watch TV or color. We brought plenty of things to do."

"I wish she had kids. Or that I brought Boots."

"Dogs are seldom on dinner party guest lists."

"That's *mean!*"

Coby heard his son slide low on the back seat, digging in to fortify an attack.

"He's my *friend*," Adam said. "You're supposed to be *kind* to friends."

They left the expressway at Suzannah's exit. "Suzannah's my friend, Adam."

"Like Aunt Rachel is?"

"Sort of. And like Tony and Michael are your friends."

"And *Boots.*"

"And I'm nice to your friends—"

"Not to Boots!"

Coby pulled over to the side and turned around. "Adam, there are rules in this world, whether or not they make sense to you right now or ever. And there are different rules for people friends and dog friends." He had to peer way over the seat because Adam was attempting to sit on his neck or shoulders. "Boots understands even if you don't. As for human friends, be polite and kind. Being kind tonight means not being angry Suzannah didn't invite the dog and behaving your best. It's special being included in a grown-up party."

"It's not a party; it's dinner."

"It's a grown-up party!"

"You don't have to shout!"

"I'm *not!*" He had been. "I'm sorry. I'm asking you plainly, will you behave? Because I'm your friend and it's a special kindness for me."

Adam attempted a shrug. It was difficult since his shoulders were where his rear should have been.

Coby accepted the aborted gesture as a pact and turned, moving the car into gear. They were late, having spent twenty minutes hunting busywork for Adam to tote. And then, noticing that Adam's jeans were mud-stained and raveling, he learned that Mrs. Jennings had been too bilious to complete the laundry. So there'd been another delay while Coby heated freshly washed raiment in the oven, wondering what was the proper baking temperature for red corduroy.

Behind him, Adam muttered darkly. Through the clacks of the windshield wipers, Coby tried catching what the child said. Only hissed sounds, beloved Boots's name and then, Coby thought, Adam's ultimate cry of defiance. "You're not the boss of me."

But maybe not. He couldn't be sure.

"I'm sorry we're so late," Coby said at the door.

"No problem. Come in, both of you." The shorter of them stared at her. Strawberry blond to copper curls, enormous eyes. He switched his beams to Coby, then back to Suzannah. Waiting. Checking.

She canceled a kiss of greeting for his father and stood straight and chaste. How charming. An in-house censor for the night.

"Hi," she said. She put out her hand.

He grabbed it and shook vigorously.

"Well!" Suzannah said, disengaging herself. "Make yourself comfortable. I'll bet you're starving. I'll be ready in two seconds."

"Isn't it pretty here?" Coby asked his son.

Adam sat on the white sofa, a small suitcase of Easy Readers and crayons on his lap. "It's empty. And the dining room table's in the living room."

"It's called a dining area. Why don't you wait here and I'll see if I can help Suzannah."

"Do I call her aunt, like Aunt Rachel?"

"Only if she asks you to. I'll be right back."

Suzannah was ladling soup.

"Need any help?" Coby kissed the back of her neck.

She stopped and smiled at him. "He's adorable, Coby. Like a kid in a cereal ad."

She meant the compliment, but she'd expected, somehow needed, something more resembling his father. The eyes were the same, lacking only dark frames to circle them, but nothing else was. Adam was a souvenir of someone else, and Suzannah wasn't particularly delighted by living monuments.

"Soup's on." She handed Coby a dish to carry in.

"Do you have a telephone directory?" Coby asked. "Otherwise, Adam becomes an old Kilroy drawing, nose stuck on the table."

Once seated on the Yellow Pages, Adam pulled his spoon through the soup as if measuring the plate's diameter.

"Delicious," Coby said. He watched his son paddle through the pale soup. Adam finally lifted the spoon to his mouth.

When it reached its destination, the child's eyes grew impossibly wide. He bunched his lips as if to spit, pulled the spoon away and squeezed his eyes shut. "It's—*thick*. And *cold*," he said with a gasp, then he gulped five times as if it were also lumpy and wedged in his throat.

"It's a cold soup called vichyssoise." Suzannah watched the child gaze at the soup plate with horror. "Not your soup-for-lunch favorite, hey? Hey, you don't have to eat it, or anything you don't like."

Adam put down his spoon and bowed his head.

The kid's odd, Suzannah decided. That doctor Coby said he sees. No wonder. She turned her attention to his father. "How's everything?"

"Terrific. Good news. I think I'm cutting a demo soon."

"Oh, Coby, that's really exciting!"

He shrugged. "The first time it happened, I thought so. Ten, twelve years ago. But there are lots of other steps, like making the record and having people buy it."

"Wait a minute—you've made a record?"

"Two. You mean you didn't know? You're not still requesting the greatest hits of Windfall, that spectacular local group of yore? You're not, then, just another groupie?"

"What I am is impressed."

"And surprised."

"Yes. Not because I don't think you're talented. I love your songs and your voice, but—" She felt something sear the air between them. Their glance was severed by a laser from planet Adam. Out of bounds! it shrilled, even if his lips never moved. Toe the line! Nothing fond, nothing intimate, nothing personal with this man! *My* territory! Do not approach or intimate you already have!

She cleared the table for the next course.

Twenty-five minutes later, Suzannah had a new age line etched between her eyebrows.

She had tried being a good hostess to Tiny Tim. She had avoided all sentences that would put him back on red alert. She had tried, also, to engage his teeny boy's brain. But after all, what did one say? Had any good books read to you lately? What's your opinion of this season's "Sesame Street"?

Questions that seemed brilliantly designed fell flat on the table along with crumbs and small dribbles of milk.

"What do you want to be when you grow up?"

"A daddy."

Biology was destiny once again. "Well . . . do you like school?"

"Some."

"What?"

"Recess. I have a dog. Boots."

There ensued one strained pause as Suzannah pondered the

connection between his two statements. Adam used the silence to become interviewer.

"Do you have a dog?" he asked.

"Nope."

"A cat?"

"No."

"Fish? A bird?"

"No."

He appeared amazed and a trifle disgusted. She offered a substitute. "I once wanted to *be* a cat."

He didn't find it as charming as his father had. He looked concerned for her mental health and, very patiently, enunciating clearly, he said, "People cannot become cats."

"True." She switched to his father, a man who looked as if he dearly wanted to sweat.

She had tried, also, not to notice what the boy did with her lovingly prepared food. She averted her eyes as he buried every mushroom under the untasted wild rice. She glanced away when she saw him sample a sliver of veal, chew once and stop, squirreling the meat in the corner of his mouth. She spoke energetically to cover his gags when he made contact with the asparagus. That vegetable was now lodged in his cheek with the veal.

She'd offered to heat a can of vegetable soup. It was the closest to childhood cuisine her cupboard came. But the Hobbit shook his head. A meal in the cheek is quite a speech impediment.

She beat the chilled cream, added curaçao and sugar and frowned. There was no avoiding him. Quiet, muffled by food and obvious promises to behave, he nevertheless loomed. Big Brother's short stand-in, perched on the Yellow Pages.

She nearly churned the cream into butter. She took a deep breath and smothered the strawberries with overstiff cream.

Her single goal was to end this evening with a semblance of grace, but the attempt felt overstrenuous, with too little ultimate gratification, like puffing a ripped cigarette.

However, she forced her face into a smile before leaving the kitchen. "You like strawberries, don't you, Adam?" She apportioned the dessert. "Everybody likes them," she added as a warning.

"Yeah," he said with real enthusiasm.

So, while she assumed normal children enjoyed whipped

cream as well, she wasn't miffed when he scraped it to one side of his dish or even when he spent an eternity picking all residual whiteness out of the bumps and prickles of the berries. But she was assuredly taken aback by yet another freeze-frame when he speared a strawberry and finally popped it in his mouth. He expressed fondness for the fruit oddly, rolling his eyes while holding his lips and teeth back from his tainted tongue. With cream and crushed berry at the lips, he looked rabid.

"I think," Coby said quietly, "there's ah, something different about this strawberry taste."

Adam nodded. Speech, nearly impossible anyway, would also increase the risk of contamination.

"Well," Coby said, "that means more for me and I'm glad."

The man's attempt to lessen the tension backfired, increasing hers.

A part of her knew she would soon laugh at what the courtesan's assignation had become. Right now, however, its humor escaped her.

"I hereby appropriate Adam's share." Coby reached for the dish.

At precisely the same moment, Adam grabbed for his milk.

Their hands collided in mid-air.

Suzannah watched with dull horror as Coby's forearm knocked a taper, unbalancing its pottery holder. A lime candle nose-dived to the cloth and Suzannah lifted her glass.

She didn't need to worry about that fire, because the Mexican candelabra and Adam's Baccarat both self-destructed on impact, releasing a flood of milk onto the flame.

But there were other tapers, fuchsia and orange, scarlet and cerulean, to ignite the cloth. Coby and Suzannah swatted, poured water and wine, fought mightily a series of crash landings and fire storms. They ignored the flames that spluttered in splats of whipped cream.

Adam bailed out as the conflagration and flood headed his way. The Yellow Pages thudded onto the floor, the chair loudly joining them.

"Oh," Adam said. "Oh, my."

Suzannah's table resembled Antietam Creek, only there were no victorious Union troops, no sense of unity at all among the survivors.

Shards of glass and bright pottery littered the burned and pockmarked field. Rivulets of milk, wine and water joined to form pale pink puddles. Crystal peeked from curaçao-flavored snow-caps.

"I think," Suzannah said after an intensive survey, "I think we'll have our coffee elsewhere."

Adam remained rooted to the spot, the war orphan, all eyes.

Suzannah sighed. "Don't be upset," she told the boy. "It wasn't anyone's fault. And it's nothing, really."

Nothing. Except one designer's cloth, replacement cost: eighty dollars, if inflation hadn't increased it. One Baccarat goblet, replacement cost: somewhere above fifty dollars. One Mexican pottery candleholder, replacement cost: pennies. Except for plane fare to Cuernavaca, where she'd found its maker on a side street. One potentially glorious evening, planned for, worked for, made possible. Replacement cost: nothing. She had no desire to re-enact it ever.

Coffee. And afterdinner liqueurs. And the child, yo-yoing out of the bedroom, bored with television, coughing, a-hemming, excusing himself as he repeatedly intruded, making sure no two sequential sentences were spoken, reluctant all the same to join them, station himself nearby and find occupation.

Suzannah stifled a yawn.

"I'd better go." Coby shifted his weight next to her on the sofa. "It's past Adam's bedtime."

"You think he's asleep?" There had been no interruptions for seven solid minutes.

"Probably. I'll wake him." But Coby didn't move, except to lean close and kiss her.

For a moment, the evening's static and strain erased. For a moment, she didn't hear the car chase on the bedroom television. Her apartment again became the citadel, the haven, the cushion on the hard surface of Suzannah's earth.

They sat quietly, holding each other. He was very fine, she mused. He gave laughter and music and a sense of adventure in small undertakings. He gave, when humanly possible, himself and completely. She liked that self, that gift.

If only there were not the flaw, the curly-headed antagonist. How divinely funny to be meticulous about birth control and then have your lover arrive with a prefabricated kid.

But, she reminded herself, father and son weren't joined at the hip. Other times, Coby traveled solo.

They kissed again and it was fine again. Fine in the remembered ways and new ways, underlined with emotions Suzannah sensed but couldn't identify. She held Coby closer.

"Daddy!" Horror. Outrage.

End of holding. End of kissing. End. "I want to go home," Adam said, walking to his father and clamping a hand on his arm. Once possession was demonstrated, he allowed his eyes to skit over to Suzannah.

"I thought you were asleep." Coby hugged his son. "How about packing up the books and crayons and turning off the TV? Then we'll leave."

Adam slowly removed his hand from Coby and walked, backwards, to the bedroom.

Coby sighed and stood up. "Can I please clean the mess first?" He waved in the direction of the pathetic table.

Suzannah demurred for the third or fourth time. She wanted to mourn her evening in private, hurl her own wreckage down the incinerator chute.

"Suzannah, you won't turn tonight into a *cause célèbre*, will you? He—this was strange territory. It was more my fault than his. I shouldn't have accepted your invitation, or I should have brought food, or plastic cups, or—"

"Coby—forget it."

Inside her bedroom, Adam experimented with the channel selector. Shrieks, bullet shots, basso voices singing beer arias, tire screeches and canned laughter bounced into the living room in rapid and painful sequence.

"Will you give us another chance?" Coby said.

She tried to ignore the background barrage. "Of course. We're good together, you and I."

"I meant Adam and me. Maybe on his home ground, where things would be easier."

The TV screamed in agony. She pressed a finger in her ear. "How about we take a rain check on—"

"How about tomorrow? Maybe a quick eradication of tonight's—"

If the man didn't whip the controls out of his child's hands, not only tonight would be eradicated.

"We'd have time alone," Coby said. "Adam goes to sleep

early. Please? It's important. I'd like to share my own life a little."

Around and around the channels spun, milliseconds of commercials, microshreds of scripts. And then, when her muscles were twitching to get to the boy, he noticed the other button on the remote control and there was blessed silence.

"Please?" Coby repeated.

"I have the feeling we played this scene before. That time it had something to do with getting past the beginning."

"It still does."

"You're kind of a middle-ness freak, aren't you?"

"If I don't see you tomorrow, it'll mean something I'd rather not know." He looked almost stern. And then his face began to warm, began a series of motions, moving towards a wide, somehow wicked grin.

She watched with amazement. He always seemed lit from within, but now, as he smiled, the light was raised to the surface, blazing through his eyes, flushing his skin. She could feel his heat. "I don't want to be any clearer," he added.

She wished she could paint, mimic and capture the colors, the darks and lights and shadings of this man. "What time does he go to sleep?" she asked quietly.

"Eight. Eight-thirty."

"How 'bout if I mosey over at nine?"

"Come earlier, please. Have dinner with us. Nothing elegant, but a meal with us both. I—it, too, matters." He kissed her.

"You kiss amazingly well," she said. "I'll be there."

Adam appeared, his blue satchel in his arms. "Thank you." He reached up for Suzannah's hand, and she knelt to be at his eye level. He seemed undersized for the son of a very tall man.

She saw tiny reflections of herself locked in the child's eyes, and she shook her head and swallowed hard. Polite social lies, closures for dreadful evenings, dried in her throat. "I'm sorry," she whispered. "Sorry that . . . sorry for . . ."

Perhaps for not counting him in. For pretending to entertain him and expecting him to honor the charade. For not having looked at him until this moment. Adam. For the first time Adam. Not Coby's son, not an uninvited third, but Adam. A little boy. A person. An other.

"I'm sorry." She looked away from the tiny Suzannahs in his eyes. "Sorry." For the ways things were, for what she wanted and who she was and what she didn't want to know about. "I wish . . ." She didn't know what. But she knew at least that her smile was, for the first time that evening, not counterfeit.

Adam's eyes almost swallowed her. His mouth opened with surprise and a small joyous sound. But then he shook his head, his eyes narrowed and his smile flickered and died.

They mirrored each other's confusion as they said good night. After they left, Suzannah sat and thought.

Coby drove carefully through the rain, hypnotized by the rhythmic whoosh and clack of the windshield wipers. He spoke to break his trance. "What did you think of Suzannah?"

Silence, then a yawn, and then, "Did I know her once?"

"No. Why do you say that?"

"When we were leaving, when she smiled . . . I thought maybe . . . I can't remember."

But Coby suddenly did. The first glance at the New Year's party before the woman became Suzannah and no one else. The shape of the chin, the coloring, and mostly, the smile and the lightning bolt shock of familiarity.

He thought of Adam's drawings, of the face Adam insisted he couldn't remember, and he had no sense of whether the stirred memories were portents of peace or war.

He glanced over his shoulder and saw his son curled on the back seat, asleep, dreaming his answers.

Coby drove on.

Fifteen

Winter-brave flowers struggled through the hard earth near Josie's front door. Snowdrops, Suzannah thought they were called. Signs of . . . more winter ahead.

"Hello!" Josie said. "Come in. We're wildly intrigued by your call for assistance."

"We?"

Josie smiled apologetically. *"Chère Maman et moi."*

"Damn. I don't want her along."

"She won't be. I know her better than you do."

"Don't rub it in. You're the good daughter and I am the one from whose mouth issues toads. Anyway, lead me to Herr Goering."

"Well, well," Nita said without delight as she was kissed. "Suzannah. Isn't your jacket too young for you? And it makes you look sallow. And fat."

"Want to come shopping with us, Mom?" Josie asked.

"I'd love to," Nita said.

Suzannah glared at Josie.

"Except for these—I don't know what you call them—these funny weaknesses I've been having." She shook her head. "I'd better stay put. Don't worry about me. I'll . . . I'll find something to do . . ."

Josie did not handle guilt well. She all but walked on her knees. "Can we pick something up for you while we're out?"

"I wouldn't want to spoil your day."

"Mother! It's no problem."

"I do need shampoo. Any brand."

The purpose of such vague instructions, Suzannah well knew, was to ensure that the selection would be incorrect.

"What's this big errand, Suzannah?" Nita asked. "Josie said something about a child?"

Suzannah carefully chose her words. "I have a friend who has a son. I'm having dinner there and I thought Josie could help me choose a gift for the boy."

"This friend, is it female?"

"No."

"This friend, does it have a wife?"

"A dead one. This game, is it Twenty Questions?"

"Does the friend have a name?"

"Coby. His real name is Jacob."

"Jacob? Jacob what?"

"Waldemar."

"What kind of name is that?"

"Are you suddenly into etymology?"

"What kind of—"

"A suspiciously Semitic kind of name, don't you think? And

with good cause, Mother. But relax. I'm having dinner with him, not marrying him.''

"Did I say . . . ?"

Josie kissed her mother. "We have to run."

"Now," she said, once they were safely inside her car, "who is Coby Waldemar and what's going on?"

"Nothing."

"Come on. You've never called in a consultant before."

"Okay. He's special. Terrific. Only problem is . . . six years old. For some reason, Coby wants the kid and me to—to interface. Last night, I screwed up. We all did. Nobody's fault in particular, but it's time to learn how to win kids and influence fathers before I'm with the kid again."

"Do you like him?"

"Adam. He's six! What's to like or dislike?"

Josie cruised the parking lot. "Kids are amazingly like real people. Only difference is they've had less time to develop neuroses, so there aren't lots of six-year-old masochists. That is to say, kids like people who like them."

"I don't dislike him. I dislike being the heavy, the intruder, the threat. It isn't conducive to good times. There's a space."

They walked into Wanamaker's bland suburban outpost, stepping around puddles on the blacktop. The air quivered, impatient to split into drops again.

"This is a six-year-old with one alliance on earth, so you *are* a threat." Josie allowed Suzannah first dibs on the revolving door. "Anyone would be."

The children's department swarmed with angry mothers, squirming children and saleswomen who strongly resembled bouncers.

Suzannah backed off a pace. "This is an underused symbol for hell," she said.

"Keep walking till you reach the book department."

"I don't think he can read."

"But you can. To him."

"Hey, Josie? I don't want to play the witch, but I'm not auditioning for Mary Poppins, either."

"You want him off your case? Then treat him as a human being. Interact. Interrelate. For Christ's sake, don't 'interface.' That's the most—"

"It's a perfectly acceptable term—"

"In business! We're talking about people, aren't we? Not commerce."

Suzannah thumbed through volumes until she nodded and passed one to Josie. "Finally, a short book that's not about frogs or pigs and has funny drawings."

Josie skimmed it, then slammed it shut. "A test of simple humanity," she said. She opened the book again, cleared her throat and read. "I love mornings, but Mom and Dad sure don't. In the morning, Mom wears a different face, all hanging down and unsmiley."

"Don't you think that drawing's funny?"

Josie flipped through the book. "The kid leaves home to find a saner household but discovers all families are pretty weird? Cute, Suze. Cute here where Mommy's hugging him, welcoming him home. Why give a kid whose mother is dead a book about a funny, intact family?"

"I didn't think of it that way. Anyway, the whole world can't turn around and grind to a halt just because he—"

"Correct. Be assured, it hasn't and won't. But if you want to be his friend, don't add to his pain."

Suzannah bit at her bottom lip. "Okay," she said softly. "Point me in the proper direction. Teach me."

"How about the classics? Something removed from everyday reality. Here." She handed Suzannah a red and gold tooled edition of Andersen's *Fairy Tales*.

Suzannah looked at the title page and felt peculiar, as if something sweet and fuzzy had lodged in her throat. She turned pages slowly, stopping at the subtle, somehow dated, illustrations. She'd seen these pages before, seen these very drawings. She stopped turning when she saw an English garden scene and she tumbled through time to land between the hollyhocks, at eye level with an odd little face peering through a hedge.

Into dusky bedtimes and a low voice lulling. Into magic and fairies, elves with ancient secrets and princes who found you and loved you forever because you were perfect.

"Will I ever live someplace wonderful?" she heard herself ask once upon a time and not so very long ago.

"You will," he'd said, bending to kiss her forehead like the prince with Sleeping Beauty. "You'll work magic and live in an enchanted garden. My Suzannah will live wherever her heart desires."

She swallowed hard and left the garden and old summer nights with the buzz of crickets and older children still allowed to stay outside. She turned the page and shook the overlapping images out of her head.

"Don't you like it?" Josie asked.

"No. Yes. I do. It's beautiful."

"So's the price tag."

"I'll leave it on. Maybe the kid'll be bowled over."

"Do you, ah, hear from Dad?" The book, wrapped in gala paper, nestled on Suzannah's lap.

"I call him. I want the children to know him. They're his only grandchildren unless, of course, you ever . . ."

Suzannah let the question dangle and sipped diet cola. "Does he . . . does he ever call you?"

"No. Ah, Suze, he still upsets you, doesn't he?"

"Nonsense. I'm too old for . . . yes. Stupid, isn't it?"

"Human. Somebody said we don't grow up until our parents die because then we have no choice. Maybe the boy you bought the book for is better off. He was given finality. You can recover from something that's definitely over."

"I don't know what you're talking about."

"Well, maybe I don't, either. Let's talk about Coby instead. What's he like?"

"Intense. Not in a tortured way, but when I'm with him, it's as if someone turned up the volume. Not loud, but—what's that grin for?"

"You. You've always had a gift for describing your men. You'd draw instant pictures—caricatures, really. Hawk nose and close-set eyes, you'd say. Or beautiful, a panther, all elegant dark lines."

"That was Seth. You've an excellent memory."

"But you followed a pattern. How he looked. What he did, where you'd gone. This time you tried describing a person. Oh, there is a difference, Suze."

"He's tall. Little nose, big eyes, glasses, high cheekbones, ruddy coloring. Doctorate in music, teaches at Temple, writes songs, sometimes records them. And we haven't gone many places except bed. And none of what I've said warrants that enormous grin."

"It's still different and I'm grinning because I'm happy for you."

"Why?" She leaned across the table. "I'm serious. Why be happy? When I mentioned the kid, you nearly tap-danced. When I said Coby was special, you—but if there's one thing you confirmed last Thursday at my apartment, it's the need to avoid the mess, the danger, the pretty trap. Who needs it?"

"Human beings."

"Not this one. Granted, the man's wonderful to be with. So I'll be with him—as long as it's wonderful. But not full time and surely not on a gimme-gimme basis."

"What the hell's a gimme-gimme?"

"You know. The way you live. All those hands out to Josie. Where's your time? Where are you? You're trapped, engine on idle, caught in a car-pool line."

"Don't laugh at the ladies in the car-pool lines. There are lots of ways to show love."

"But that's what I'm saying! It's your goodness, your lovingness, that's made you a sacrifice to home and hearth. I not only don't want that—it appalls me!"

"You didn't understand, did you? I was right. You can't understand."

"Josie, I'm not trying to hurt you. I'm complimenting you. You're good and giving and loving. But look what it costs! Look what it takes away from you!"

"Jesus, Suzannah, I get back in return! I can't explain it and nobody wants to hear, anyway. Nobody asks for marriage updates. Nobody cares about ongoing adventures. It's easy for you. With a new lover every few weeks, it's easy to sound exciting. But there are enormous gifts in staying power—trust, knowing someone so well, so thoroughly, you operate on a new level altogether. There are adventures, whether or not they thrill in the telling. There's almost a fusing—not losing yourself, but becoming something new and bigger. I almost forgot it myself for a while, it's such a well-kept secret."

"I surmise you've resolved your dilemma."

Josie nodded. "I've made a choice. I won't say I resolved much or ever will, but I made a choice."

"Which is . . . ?"

"My real life. No more games. It was special and exciting, because it was different, not because it's what I most need. I most need my people, my family. I'll find the rest, slowly. Meanwhile, I'm opting for nontransient pleasures."

Suzannah propped her chin in her hand and said nothing.

"Displeased?" Josie's features tightened. "I'm dull and unadventurous? Sure. Marriage doesn't get good press these days. No songs for the contented. No books, no films. The quiet joys are passé and growing's a solo affair. Having a partner means gimme-gimme. It's so much more exciting to couple midflight, keep it airborne and undemanding. Well, you're wrong! Maybe my joys are too subtle for movies or best sellers. Maybe happy people don't write. But there *is* something. Something real and fine and exciting that you don't know a damn thing about!" She pounded her fist on the table.

"Jesus! Are you defensive! Did I say a word? And anyway, where is this glorious wonderment? A week ago you were keeling over with the pain."

"So what? Do you want to anesthetize yourself like Mom? I know what you want. Easy answers and pat solutions. A man gives you trouble, dump him. Children make demands? Avoid them! Even sex—is it too complex? Then who needs a partner? Let your fingers do the walking, am I right? Those answers are everywhere and they stink. Remember the story about the Chinese man who burned down his house so he could roast the pig inside it? That's what your choices and answers remind me of. Talk about overkill! Slogans for T-shirts and nothing more because people can't stand complicated puzzles."

Suzannah dribbled soda through her straw. Who was this born-again housewife preaching the gospel of the submissive, proselytizing for passive dependency?

Her voice was strained as she attempted to avoid rupturing their new, untested bonds. "Josie, please understand. I'm not challenging you or your choices but I resent your missionary zeal. I'm not ashamed of my work or how I do it or the choices it forces me to make."

"I . . . I'm sorry. I'm so sure you disapprove of my life I do become defensive. It's difficult not to be. Nobody likes where I am except pink ruffled women I can't stand."

"Listen, we're both saying the same thing. We want to keep what we have. We've shaped our lives and don't want to wreck them. Maybe, to keep what we need, we have to give other things up. I need who I am, Josie. I like being strong and independent and competent. You shouldn't sneer at it.''

"I don't mean to. But everybody needs human connections, too. A complete person needs—''

"—to feel complete. You really think your choice is so complete? What will you do when your youngest kid drives off and you never have to car-pool again?''

"I don't know. I don't know how to go back to work now and still manage all the . . . I don't know how I can physically . . . I'm nearly forty, Suze. I'm tired and scared, and I have wrinkles instead of a résumé. I don't know.''

They were both silent. "Josie,'' Suzannah finally said, "do you know anybody who's worked it all out?''

"Sure. One. The perfume ad lady. The one who prances home, tosses her attaché case aside, tosses the kids a kiss, tosses up a quiche and then tosses around all night with Mr. Wonderful. Or did you mean in real life?''

"Hell,'' Suzannah said. "If we can't solve the problems of the world, let's increase them. Time to buy Mom the wrong shampoo.''

Nita frowned at the bottle. "This brand dries the scalp . . .'' She sighed. "What did you buy the boy, Suzannah?''

"A book of—''

"That's nice.''

"I bought him *The Joy of Sex*,'' Suzannah said loudly.

"Yes. What does . . . I can't pronounce that name—what does his father do?''

Suzannah narrowed her eyes. "He's a musician.''

"A *musician*?'' A reaction at last, the negative sort, Nita's specialty. One could almost hear the first tiny drumbeats of an imminent heart attack.

"He's a university professor, Mom,'' Josie said, bringing in coffee. "Complete with doctorate in music.''

"Not the kind who plays in bars?'' Nita sounded disappointed.

"Only when he's high on drugs,'' Suzannah murmured.

"I beg your pardon. I asked a civil question.''

"He's a marvelous, civilized, sensitive man. Unique.'' Suzannah waited for questions, civil or rude. Waited for interest. Waited for her mother to stop piloting her own channels of misery and look up to see her daughter waving on the shore. "He's really—"

"I'm sure he is," Nita said.

Suzannah waited awhile longer. Ask me something, Mom. For once, think about me, wonder about me. Pretend I'm a lady on a soap. Or a guest of Merv's or Johnny's. Wonder who I am and what I'm feeling.

Nita tsked at the shampoo and placed it near her.

"Really special," Suzannah said. "And I don't believe any of the rumors. He didn't murder his first wife. Even when he's desperate for a fix he isn't mean."

Nita closed her eyes behind her thick glasses. "Your husband visited me."

"He is not my husband and never really was."

"Brought me a gift from Hawaii." She lifted an arthritic hand.

"What gall!" Suzannah said.

"Not gall. Coral. Those flowers, those roses are coral." She finally opened her eyes.

"My mistake. It's a beautiful ring."

Nita pursed her mouth lest pleasure enter. "He said he thought of me the minute he saw it." She sighed. "He also said the two of you had a reunion last week."

"Lunch is not a reunion."

"I'll never understand why you—"

"I know. He's rich, Anglo-Saxon and has an easy last name. But he's labels. Nothing more. The Prince of Nothing. I wasn't happy with him, Mom. A person should feel special, or what's the point?"

Nita sniffed. "He's so handsome, he could be a movie star. Which reminds me, I saw such a good movie while you girls were out. This elegant man became involved with a servant girl who secretly—" Her voice became animated as it always did when reliving the videotaped dramas of her days.

Suzannah stood up. "I have to leave."

"You'll go change into something nicer, won't you?" Nita asked.

"My clothing or my personality?"

Her mother closed her eyes.

"The invitation specified jeans, Mom."

"Then at least put on more lipstick. You look washed out—even before you put on that silly, childish jacket."

Sixteen

"It was a good party, and look." Adam emptied a small bag onto the dining room carpet. *"A cowboy and two dinosaurs and bubble gum and a lollipop."*

Coby smoothed a green and yellow tablecloth. It had languished in the linen closet so long, time had perma-pressed its folds. He placed pepper mills and other weights on the worst of the creases. "Did Patrick like the crayons and coloring books?"

"Yeah. Until we used the crayons and some got broke."

"Broken."

"Yeah. And some kid ripped one of the coloring books, too. What are you doing?"

"Setting the table."

"In the dining room?"

"That's its purpose. A room to dine in. To eat in."

"We don't."

"When we have company, we do."

"We don't have company."

"Sure we—" Coby stopped. His son was correct. There had been a long pause between dinner guests. "Let's begin to."

"Who?"

"Suzannah."

"Again? We just saw her and her yukky food!"

"I'm making spaghetti, okay? You like that, so stop acting as if you'll throw up. And be nice."

"I already was nice once!" Adam stomped out.

Coby found him sitting on the kitchen table, dribbling salt out of the shaker. "Look, buddy, tonight's a bonus party. You had one today, I'm having one tonight. You're invited to both."

"Grownups have dumb parties. Anyway, Suzannah's weird. She doesn't even have an outside."

Horrible images flashed through Coby's mind and he won-

dered, with great fear, at his son's mental condition. "How's that
again?" he asked gently.

"No outside. No swings, no grass, no place to play."

"Oh." Relief. "You can't begrudge not having a . . ." Less
than total relief. The problem was, Coby was trying to avert
intergalactic war between two very different systems, and he
didn't speak either side's language. "You—you're right, Adam.
It's a shame. Let's show her what a real house is like, complete
with outside and toys."

"And a *dog*." Adam squinted. "You staying home all
night?"

Coby nodded.

"And her?"

"Suzannah's driving here, then driving herself home."

Adam nodded approval.

"You don't have to like her just because I do," Coby said,
"but give her a fair chance, will you? It could be fun sharing another friend, like we already do with Aunt Rachel."

Adam shook his head. "Aunt Rachel's different. She has
swings and she has Nancy—Suzannah doesn't even have a
baby—and she has a special Star Wars cup for me and toys and
. . . she *acts* different. I don't know."

"Well, if it seems a good idea, we could buy Suzannah a Star
Wars cup, okay?"

Adam shrugged.

Suzannah smiled as she entered the stone and clapboard
house. This expedition was a snap, a safari among bunnies.
She'd already survived the lioness.

"This is for you," she told Adam.

"Me? It's Patrick's birthday, not mine."

"Doesn't have to be a birthday to get gifts."

Adam held the package as if it contained explosives.

"How lovely," Suzannah murmured with surprise as they entered the living room. It had graceful proportions and an elegant
grand piano, but otherwise, it was a slapdash collection of ser-
viceable furniture. Not at all Suzannah's style, but its warm summer colors, framed posters and photographs, glowing fireplace,
brimful bookcases, record racks and abundant plants invited her
in, encouraged her to be herself and feel at home.

She moved a cluster of needlepoint pillows to make a comfort-

able resting spot on the sofa. Adam still studied the gift wrap.
Perhaps that medical problem was neurological. His synapses
seemed to wave aimlessly before connecting. But suddenly he
sighed and shredded the wrapping, letting pieces drift to the
floor.

"Thank you, Suzannah," he said politely, expressing less
than unbearable delight.

She decided she had to up the ante. "If you like, Adam,
I'll . . . I'll read you a bedtime story from it later." She fingered
the velvet binding of one of the pillows. At its corner, a small
"D.W." was needlepointed.

"Read to me?" Adam looked startled, and Suzannah felt a return of the night before's closing confusion. He blinked as if
clearing his vision, standing tensely, head to one side, listening,
waiting for something elusive.

What does he want of me? she wondered with some panic.
What does he expect, and why? She couldn't bear the intensity
and need in his glance and she lowered her eyes. And saw his
hand in the book. His thumb rested near the gnome's tiny face.
His hand covered the hollyhocks and the plank gate. For an instant, Suzannah was afraid she would burst into tears. She looked
away from Adam and the hollyhocks.

A beagle shuffled over, wheezed, and sat on her feet.

"That's Boots," Adam said. "His feet are black."

"Yes." Suzannah took it on faith because the dog's feet were
collapsed on hers and invisible. "That's a good name." If her
nose was functioning properly, another on-target name would be
flatulence.

"I named him when I was three."

Adam's sociable chitchat gladdened Suzannah. She must have
passed the admissions test. Now, Adam's father should an-
nounce graduation.

"We're eating in the dining room," Adam said. "We *have* a
dining room. And an outside."

On which cue the Patriarch stood. Suzannah was again impressed with his lean length, his flat hips and long legs and the
graceful but electric way he moved.

"C'mon," Coby said. "You guys can watch me fumble
around."

She tipped up her toes and pressed the dog's belly. Boots
leaped to his feet, flapping ears like castanets.

Can't win them all, she consoled herself as she followed father and son to the kitchen.

Copper pots hung from hooks and a ball and claw foot oak table filled the center of the room. There were indications all over of someone who loved cooking—and therefore sex, according to Coby's theory. The kitchen ghost depressed her.

"This is where we eat when we're *us*." Adam searched for another conversational gambit, then gave up. " 'Scuse me. Gonna get my dinosaur."

Suzannah expected something lizard-cold and scaly to shuffle in.

When Adam had gone, Coby turned from the range. "I love you for sure," he said. "See? I'm proving it. I'm cooking for you."

"I have some other proofs and demonstrations in mind," she said. She wanted to grab him, lift his navy sweater, kiss the down on his hard stomach, pull him onto the kitchen floor.

He lifted a wooden spoon and sampled the sauce. "This is good discipline. We're neither of us temperate by nature. Eventually, the eyes and the ears of the world go to sleep. That's why nature invented early bedtime for kids."

"I thought it had to do with dinner schedules, not sex. My mother's still angry because she put me to bed at six and I cried for ninety minutes every night before I fell asleep."

"Why didn't she put you in at seven-thirty?"

"I asked her that myself. She said she was too busy for a baby then. Had to make my father's dinner, which I then spitefully ruined by screaming. I remain the baby villain."

He stirred the pot of sauce. "It does not sound, from the little you've shared, like a winning childhood."

She shrugged and lit a cigarette. "Old history. Irrelevant."

"Smoking's bad," Adam said, re-entering the room.

She stubbed it out. Maybe he didn't want her to die?

He spread tiny figures on the oak table. Spacemen and tiny animals and cowboys and a lumpy Tyrannosaurus rex.

"I see cowboys," she said, forcing a show of interest. "But where are the Indians?"

"Native Americans are passé as antagonists," Coby said. "Aliens from outer space are the current heavies."

Adam pushed the salt shaker near the figures, then into one of them. "Blam!" He knocked over a spaceman. "Boom, bonk-

ada, here I come! Brrr!'' The dinosaur lumbered to the remaining astronaut. ''Yaargh!'' And the second astronaut bit the dust, or salt as it were. ''Eeeyow,'' he screamed as the monster pushed him off the edge of the table.

''Dinner's ready,'' Coby said.

''I'll be back,'' Adam whispered to his disaster epic.

In the dining room, seated around a table that could easily accommodate eight, Adam lifted strands of spaghetti as if unraveling the pile were the object.

''This is delicious, Coby. Great salad, really good sauce.''

''Dubrovnik special. Old family recipe. Two bottles of store-bought and lots of bravado.''

''What are you, Suzannah?'' Adam asked abruptly.

She stared, thinking of his plastic extraterrestrials and wondering if she struck him as that odd.

''Do you mean what does Suzannah do? Her work? It isn't the same thing, Adam.''

''Oh. I'm a stockbroker.''

''What do you break?''

''Not that sort of breaker, ah broker. I . . .'' Jesus. ''I find people with money to help companies grow. If they help, then they get money back.''

Adam looked as if he suspected a grown-up evasion.

Coby tried. ''Suppose the dinosaur company wanted to make elephants, but they'd used up their money making dinosaurs. Suzannah could ask you to lend them money to pay for new paint and plastic. If you did, and if they made lots of money selling the elephants, they'd give you back what you loaned them plus some of the money they made. Suzannah's sort of a saleswoman for the companies.''

''You mean you'd sell me a toy company?'' Adam asked.

''A part of it.''

''I want the dinosaur part. That's neat.''

''Not quite. Not the toys, a part of—''

''What part, then?''

Coby looked amused, then alarmed. He sniffed and bolted, shouting, ''The garlic bread!''

''You'd get a piece of paper. It's called a share of the company. It means you own some of it.''

''*Paper?* I'd give you my allowance and you'd give me *paper*? Nothing real?''

She accepted defeat. "Nothing real. But don't tell my customers, okay? They think it's real and as long as they do, it is."

Coby re-entered, carrying a plate. "A bit singed, but edible."

Adam switched his interest back to his dinner. After a long and intent search, he located one acceptable strand of spaghetti and loudly sucked it in.

By the waning of the children's hour, Suzannah knew several possibly useful things. Adam ate only bread and ice cream, discounting the three threads of spaghetti. He had an astounding range of nonverbal sounds and was, even on home turf, his daddy's protector. At every opportunity, he paid public homage to Coby. "My daddy's a good cook," he said, even while personally abstaining. "My dad plays piano and guitar and banjo and blike—"

"Balalaika," Coby corrected him.

"Balalaika and he writes music and he's a teacher, too." Adam was a tour guide, pointing out every scenic detail of his father, fearing she'd miss or undervalue them. "My dad's funny," he solemnly informed her while she was laughing at Coby's joke.

She never said that she, too, appreciated Daddy's many gifts. That wasn't Adam's message. That was, perhaps, the message he was intercepting and appropriating.

She sat in the living room, smoking, while Adam and Coby readied the former for bed.

It hadn't been dreadful. Certainly not a replay of last night's fiasco. It hadn't been a night to remember, either. Yet. It was only eight-thirty and there was life after bedtime.

Upstairs, freshly rinsed of spaghetti stains, Adam sat in his bed, the red wool blanket pulled up to his chest, rolling a small fire engine over his belly. "But do I have to?"

"It isn't a 'have to.' I thought, since she offered . . ."

Adam shrugged. "I don't like make believe."

"Since when?"

"Since now." He pushed the fire engine to the edge of the bed. "Scrrr . . . utch!" he said. "Booooooo—"

"Do you still think Suzannah's mean?"

"I don't know."

From overt hostility to ambivalence. Progress.

"Daddy, would you still come kiss me afterwards?"

"Sure. And before, too," and he stood and leaned to kiss his son's forehead.

"Do I have to kiss *her?*"

"Kissing is never a 'have to.' "

"Grandma makes me—"

"Grandmothers are exceptions. But the answer's no."

"Then okay."

"I'll tell her. And I'll tell you, you're one super kid."

They paused on the staircase. The changing of the guard.

"This is," she whispered, "the most intricate, ornate foreplay I've ever experienced."

She pulled a wooden rocker close to Adam's bed. "Your choice," she said, praying he'd opt for a short one.

He flipped pages. She was relieved but couldn't say why when he passed by the hollyhocks and the gnome. "This," he said, pointing to "The Emperor's New Clothes."

" 'There was once an emperor—' "

"What's an emperor?"

"A king . . . 'who was fond of beautiful clothes. He had dozens and dozens of suits hanging in his wardrobe, all as elegant and costly as—' "

"What's elegant?"

"Fancy. Terrific-looking. '. . . as costly as the other. Other kings and emperors spent hours—' "

"I can't see."

"There's no picture on this page. I thought I'd turn the book around when—"

"I like to see."

She adjusted her chair, pulling it close and turning it. " 'Other kings and emperors spent hours with their councilors—' "

"Do kings go to day camp?"

She took a deep breath. "It means advisers, here. People who help him decide what to do." She unobtrusively counted how many pages were left, then returned to the story, speeding matters by pretranslating every word that might not be part of his miniscule vocabulary.

" 'Two rogues'—two rotten men—" She glanced at him. His eyes were almost closed and he didn't challenge her definition. She read more quickly, editing, reducing, speeding the story.

Andersen's art was lessened, but Suzannah's artifice worked. There was a chance they'd complete the reading before dawn.

" 'That is indeed a lovely cloth!' " she eventually read. " 'What beautiful colors!' "

His eyes were open and aimed at the page. "It doesn't say beautiful. It says mag . . . magny . . . magnify?"

"Magnificent. Can you read, Adam?"

"Uh-huh."

She lifted the book. "Would you like to, then?"

"Uh-uh. But I want to hear the real story."

She honored the text as if it were revealed prophecy and they progressed a phrase, sometimes even an entire paragraph at a time.

When she staggered onto the last page, she was able to manage some vigor. " 'But a little child saw the emperor and shouted, "Look! The emperor has no clothes on!" ' "

"Wasn't he wearing underpants?"

"The artist hid that part behind the people, didn't he? But I don't think so."

Adam giggled. "That's so dumb."

"But he thought he was wearing something. He thought smart people saw gold and jewels. He thought the clothing was real."

"Like the stuff you break, right?"

"Who breaks? What?"

"The paper you sell, the stuff that's not real but everybody thinks it is?"

"Oh. No. I wouldn't say that. No."

"Anyway, it's dumb. A grownup who doesn't know what's real! A grownup!"

She didn't wish to discuss the nature of reality or varying rates of maturity with this child. There were only two paragraphs remaining. She read briskly as the crowd hooted and ridiculed the king. " 'And the emperor began to worry. Maybe he really and truly was naked. Maybe the spinners of gold had lied and fooled him. He was very ashamed, but he had no choice but to march down the street, all alone, pretending he wore a wonderful, beautiful suit.' "

"Thanks," Adam said. "That was good."

Suzannah, knowing she was irrational, decided she'd just read the saddest story ever written.

* * *

While she waited for Coby to descend once again, she scanned the titles in the bookcases, touched the wing chair to verify that it was real leather and examined the needlepoint pillows. They were exasperating to think about with their tiny, tedious stitches.

She wandered to the piano, a Steinway grand so mellow in its mahogany, so clean in its curving sweep, she wanted to own it even though she had no idea of how to play it. She gently pushed a key and heard a muted, reverberating tone.

She ran her hand over the ivory keys, the wood case, certain that the waxed patina had taken at least half a century to build.

The music rack held manuscript paper, scribbles and hatch marks, lines of notes unintelligible to her. But the inked-in words beneath them were legible between the dark blots and x's. "Suzannah," she read with a start. "Not of one season." There were notes beyond it but no more words. She looked behind the paper, found another sheet without the five-line patterning.

Words raced down it and up the sides. More cross-outs, more question marks, arrows connecting, then eradicated with squiggly lines. She again saw her name, bits of phrases. "Quicksilver evenings." "Thaw," crossed out, then written again. "Thaw?" Colors—apricot and coral. Combinations: "graygold" "summerskin" and, oddest, "moneygreen motions."

"Oh, mortification. Do you think leaving it out was Freudian?" Coby walked across the room.

She put one arm above her head, the other crookedly before her. "A moneygreen motion, I assume?"

He kissed her. "Your work—the night we met—I tried 'lectures' first, but that has an ugly click in the middle. I can't seem to . . ."

"May I have it?"

He shook his head. "When it's finished. When it's as close as I can get to what I want."

So she settled instead on the green sofa, enormously pleased by the idea of her own song.

"You're difficult to capture. 'Oh, Suzannah' surely isn't right, but I can't locate what is."

"Say my name again, please?"

"Suzannah."

"Ah, you have a way of saying it, doing it. I remember now why I'm hanging around."

They were silent, holding each other. "This is a good place to be tonight," Coby said. "Suzannah, was it difficult? Tonight, I mean. Was it awful?"

She kissed his neck, under his ear. "Shall I be painfully honest? I prefer less charcoal on my garlic bread."

"I didn't mean that."

"Forgive me. Flip is always my first choice. No. It wasn't awful at all."

"And . . . ?" He left the question unspoken.

But she heard it, resented it and answered it. "He's a likable kid. And bright, too."

"So . . . the evening wasn't bad?"

You're pushing too hard, she wanted to say. Enough. The child and I have a truce. But she said, instead, "The evening isn't over, one would hope."

Coby stood. "How about another log on the fire?"

"Setting the scene, eh? Act II. Upstairs, the child sleeps . . ."

"Well, until we're certain of that, might as well stoke the fire." Which he did. He surveyed his handiwork proudly. "Brandy?"

"And music, too, if possible." She removed her tooled boots and woolly socks and curled her bare feet under her.

Coby riffled through his records. "I gather from last night that you enjoy baroque?"

"In certain situations. That which I anticipated last night. That which I anticipate now. It's subtle. Less blatant than Liszt or old Sinatra. Or, oh, Ravel's *Bolero,* which would be tacky, like transparent blouses."

"I have Buxtehude, Pachelbel, Scarlatti, Vivaldi, Monteverdi, Corelli and of course, J.S. himself."

"Stop showing off."

"Lully, Hindemith—"

"Hindemith?"

"Wanted to know if you were listening. Rameau, Purcell, Han—"

"I didn't think you were like this. Bach. J.S. Bach."

He put a large stack on the turntable, then sat beside her, propping his feet on the coffee table. "I love that it's sleeting outside."

She smiled. "I'm a scene-setter, too."

"It's not a crime. We have to polish up the possibilities. Otherwise, life becomes—to borrow Adam's expression—drabbed out. I learned that early on, at my grandfather's knee."

"Tell me." She snuggled closer.

"Zeyde Morris would peer over the edge of his glasses like this." Coby pushed his own frames down to the tip of his nose and spoke in a gentle singsong. " 'Coby?' he'd say. 'I think maybe God only gave us the possibility of a soul, the tools to build one. Our eyes and ears, our hearts and minds. The rest is up to us. We can close our eyes or feast them on paintings, plug up our ears or hear concerti, learn or remain ignorant. And even if we do begin a soul, we can leave it tiny or help it grow. And what food would a soul grow on, Coby? Music and art and learning, of course. But to warm them and hold them together, it needs the most, love.' "

Suzannah thought of her childhood, where emotions were stains to be scrubbed away, where adults spoke word-puzzles whose solutions would have been, always, I am not happy. You are not sufficient. "Did your grandfather really say that wonderful thing?" she whispered, stroking his cheek.

"I'm not sure, but he probably meant to. Mostly, what I remember Zeyde Morris saying was, 'Coby? Don't aggravate your mama so much.' "

"Did he live with you?"

"Everybody did. Transients, refugees, distant relatives. It was a noisy, busy place. Unlike this place, which is sounding wondrously still." He turned to her.

And a telephone rang in the next room.

"Who . . . ?" He waited for it to stop, then reluctantly stood, and she listened with interest and surprise as his voice, coming out of the kitchen, became harsh, almost furious. *"What?"* she heard, then an erratically timed series of questions. "Why in God's name—where? Christ, are you safe? What an asinine—why can't you call a—what?" A muttering and what sounded like punches on the wall. "No! Don't move. Don't leave that—ten minutes, okay? Fifteen. Just stay there!"

He stormed into the living room, hands clenched. "That was a goddamn thirteen-year-old who ran away to live with her goddamn father who she couldn't find so she rode the goddamn busses and els until she had one goddamn dime left. And nobody answers at her house and she's locked out. So she called me, her goddamn last chance!" He bolted up the stairs.

Suzannah held her breath until she realized the impotence of such primitive control mechanisms. The world would unravel its surprises whether or not she asphyxiated herself.

"He's asleep," Coby announced when he came back down. "Damn this all to hell! It isn't even my own kid this time!" He grabbed his fleece-lined coat from the hall closet. "I won't be long. Thanks for watching Adam." He went to the door, then stopped to punch it. "Damn! Nobody's at her house. I'll have to bring Nancy here."

They kissed good-by, a friendly, drive-safely kiss and Suzannah leaned against the door after she closed it. Back to baby-sitting on Saturday nights, and she didn't even know the current rates.

She returned to the living room. Johann Sebastian still mixed passion with precision, superimposing patterns, one on top of another, locking and unlocking them tidily, neatly.

"How did you do it, J.S.?" she asked the stereo. "You, with your seventeen children. How could you hear anything, let alone anything so sane? Or did you leave the litter with the little woman and cut out for a quiet place? Did you hide, you son-of-a-bitch runaway father?"

She folded her arms and glared. Angry at Bach. Angry on behalf of his children and poor Mrs. Bach. Angry on his behalf, trying to forge art in the chaos of seventeen children. Just plain angry.

She sat in the leather seat and calmed herself. Coby would be back soon.

Accompanied by a thirteen-year-old.

Goody. The kid could baby-sit while Coby and Suzannah checked into a motel.

The music wasn't bad and the house was quiet. She enjoyed the "Well-Tempered Clavier," Benedictine and Brandy. The leather around her, warmed by the fire, smelled vaguely of Coby's tobacco. She closed her eyes and relaxed.

And heard pounding at the front door.

"I do not believe this," she muttered, retracing her steps. She peered through the small panes at the top of the door. Someone small was pressed close, trying to avoid the icy rain, banging and shouting, over and over, "Coby? Coby?"

Suzannah was bigger than it was. She could face it in person.

The woman outside was Central Casting's perennial victim. Anonymous face, hair sticking right and left in segments as if she'd raked her fingers through it. Her eyes skipped over Suzannah's face. "Coby? Is Dr. Waldemar here?"

Suzannah shivered as wet air washed the entryway. "Not right now. Is it urgent? Have you been hurt? Raped? Mugged?"

"Oh, God," the woman said, wringing her hands. Suzannah decided she'd never actually seen anyone do that before. She waved the woman in.

"My daughter," the woman said. "She's gone. I don't know where and it's night and where *is* Coby?" She went directly into the kitchen. "I'd better call the police."

"Listen," Suzannah said, "if your daughter's name is—"

"She's only thirteen!" the woman said. "I'll—"

"Listen!" Suzannah said, nearly shouting. "If she's named Nancy, she's safe. Coby's gone to get her."

The woman reappeared. "From where?"

"I don't know, but she's okay and she'll be here soon. Why don't you sit down, warm up?" It seemed the civilized, the only thing to do. But once Suzannah had taken her coat, steered her to the fireplace chair and poured her a brandy, she didn't know how to proceed. Etiquette books ignored entertaining crazies in the parlor. Particularly someone else's parlor and someone else's crazy.

"I'm sorry," the woman said after she stopped shuddering. "It's been awful. She left a note and her house key. Said she'd never come back again. I called all her friends, went to the movies, diners, pizza places . . ." She pressed her fingers to her forehead and said no more.

The woman was vaguely familiar, although Suzannah couldn't place her. "I'm Suzannah Barnes," she said.

They sat in silence again, letting Bach provide ambience, silver mazes glinting in the half-dark room. "Oh!" the woman said abruptly. "Sorry. I'm Rachel Kallen." She stared at the floor again. Then she sighed heavily and looked up. And then, she appeared mesmerized.

Suzannah followed Rachel's eyes as they studied the room. Clue, they said, pausing to register the single gleaming lamp. Take note, they said, focusing on the two brandy snifters, the records on the stereo. The woman's gaze crossed the floor to the fireplace, then over to Suzannah's boots on the floor and, finally, up to Suzannah's face.

Her cheeks became mottled. "You're not a baby-sitter, are you?" Her voice was thick with embarrassment. "I . . . I must seem . . . I'm so . . ."

Suzannah shrugged.

Rachel sipped brandy, breathed deeply and peered at Suzannah over the rim of her snifter.

Both women resumed their contemplations. Now that Nancy's welfare was established, the status quo revealed, there was only one remaining question. What claim have you, they'd ask—discreetly, obliquely—what claim on the owner of this house? Neither spoke, but Rachel answered it first.

"I teach with Coby," she said. "We're old friends."

Suzannah's smile was weak. "Guess we met the same way. I'm teaching at Main Line Night this semester."

"Oh, then you haven't known him long? I mean the semester started only a few weeks . . ."

Suzannah conceded the doubtful advantages of an earlier starting date.

"Is Adam asleep?" Rachel asked.

I know you've got seniority, cookie. No need to bandy proof. Next, you'll leap up to use the bathroom, anything to show you know the location and serial number of objects in this household. She nodded and said nothing.

"Have you met him?"

Translation: what is your role here? Do you share their daylight? Or are you summoned for after-hours sex?

"I met Adam last night and tonight, of course."

"Last night?" Rachel's eyes contracted, deepening the crow's feet around them. The most generous soul on earth wouldn't call those crevasses laugh lines.

They both glanced at their watches. Ten minutes or so until Nancy and her momma could be whizzed away, the door double-bolted and the night saved. Maybe.

"Would you like more brandy?" Suzannah asked.

"I'll get it," the woman said, as Suzannah had known she would. Rachel crossed the room, left and returned with another half-full snifter. It was difficult believing Coby was attracted to this person. She had weathered poorly, must be around his age, but older, aged from the inside out. And the outside was nothing to write home about.

He couldn't. He couldn't be the way he was with her with Rachel. Could he? And did she mind if he was?

Yes. There. Out of the closet at last. Yes. She retained the archaic flaw of jealousy. Possessiveness. Insecurity. Yes. Dammit, yes. She'd mind very much.

Rachel reseated herself and they listened to yet another ringlet of Bach. They had nothing to say to one another, or everything. They chose the first option.

"Daddy! Daddy! I had a bad dream!"

They both heard it simultaneously, both swiveled to the staircase, stood, then turned and faced each other.

It was the last thing Suzannah wanted to do, the last words she wished to utter. But there were, after all, territorial rights and boundaries to clarify.

"*I'll* go," she said crisply, and Rachel bit her lip, glanced again at the stairs and stayed in place as Suzannah brushed by.

Adam's room was lit only by a small light on the baseboard. She didn't know if flicking on the overhead light would startle him further, so she moved through a dark haze.

"Daddy?"

She could barely make out his small outline. He seemed to be sitting up, whimpering and clutching his blanket. Boots, a lump at his feet, looked on impassively.

"Shh, Adam. It's me."

"No! Where's my daddy!" His voice became alarmingly strong, with terror underlining it. "I want him—not you!"

"Your daddy had to leave for a few—"

"He said he'd stay! Where did you take him? I . . . want . . . Daaaaddy!" He threw his covers back, stood up on the bed, back against the wall, hands curled into fists. "Not you!" he shouted. "Not you!"

Boots, finally alert, shook his ears and growled softly.

Suzannah ignored the dog, moved to Adam, touching him gently to calm him. He felt clammy, but only for a second because he grabbed her hand and hurled it away.

"He'll be right back. He—"

"He said he'd stay! He *said* so! He tells the truth and he *said* so!" He breathed heavily, picked up a small metal truck and aimed at her head. She ducked.

Warily, she watched him wave his arms in a frenzy, then double over, clutching his stomach. "Where did you put him?" he screamed. "I need him! I need DADDY!"

"Adam," she said softly, but urgently. "Calm down. He'll be right back. It was an important errand."

"Don't talk to me! I don't want you any more! You're not my friend! You *took* him! Go back! Go back, *you!* He said—he *told* me—*you* leave again, not Daddy—*you*—"

His words became increasingly choppy, his breathing heavier, more desperate. He threw himself down, clutched his stomach and screamed incoherently.

"Five minutes. He'll be here in five minutes."

But Adam curled tighter and tighter, deafened by his own hysteria.

"Adam!" she said sharply, wondering if this were not the time for a slap, anything to shock him out of this incredible tantrum. "Adam! Listen to me! You must calm down. Calm *down*, do you hear?"

He swiveled his head in her direction. "Don't talk!" he screamed. "I hate you now! You're not the boss of me any more and you can't—you can't have my daddy back!"

He was insane; he was raving mad. She stood there helplessly, and then the overhead light was switched on and she whirled around. Rachel, small and smug, smiled. "Forgive me," she said. "I thought I might be able to—"

"Aunt Rachel?" Adam buried his head in his pillow and sobbed. "Make her *leave!*"

Suzannah stood frozen, watching Rachel move to the bedside and sit down, take the child in her arms, stroke his hair and croon meaningless sounds.

And then Suzannah regained the ability to breathe and move.

She could hear them while she sat downstairs, her mind racing, rejecting, backing up, considering. Upstairs, Adam cried. The words "her" and "she" whirred down the stairs like missiles.

There were times you had to admit you'd been dealt the wrong hand and wisdom was refusing to play. How had she detoured from her goal—a few hours of pleasure with a man—to this suburban cesspool? How had she become mired with a deranged, incoherent child and a visiting Goody Two-shoes? Who was she pretending to be, and why? For what?

Upstairs, she heard footsteps, a door closing, water running. She drank brandy. This was no longer amusing. Not any adventure designed for her. What was the payoff? Some stupid song of her own? A few hours of pleasure? Dear Lord, there were men all over the city. She didn't need this.

She thought with desperate homesickness of her pastel living room. Of silence. She would leave right now, let Rachel and the brat face-off alone.

Rachel and Adam, hand in hand, came down the staircase in the hallway. From a distance the boy appeared normal, a child stepping carefully in fuzzy blue sleepers. But even from the sofa she saw his swollen face, his free arm held against his midsection. She looked away.

"Adam's going to wait for his daddy down here," Rachel crooned, all treacle and pigeon-puff breasts.

Adam sat down on the bottom step.

"Don't you want to wait in the living room with me? It's warmer in there." Rachel bent over the little one. Jesus Christ kissing the lepers.

Suzannah lit a cigarette.

Adam glared into the living room, squinting.

Suzannah puffed smoke his way.

Rachel retrieved her snifter and walked to the sofa, seating herself at a discreet distance. "You understand, don't you?" she whispered. "Why this . . . happened?"

Suzannah shrugged. She intended to convey weariness, a worldly wise acceptance of whimsical fate. The gesture emerged as indifference, which at least was honest.

And Bach played on, insisting form and grace were possible, harmony natural, while in the hallway Adam snorted and hiccuped a coda to hysteria and beside her, Rachel whispered unrelentingly. "He has problems. He—"

"We all do tonight, don't we?" Suzannah checked her watch. Days had surely oozed by since Coby shut the door.

Finally, and Suzannah had to check her watch again before she believed only forty-five minutes had passed, Coby turned the key in the front door.

"Adam!" he said. Then, even while his son hurled himself at his kneecaps, screaming, Coby moved towards the living room archway. "Rachel! I saw your car, but I—"

Coby, his spawn locked on his legs, looked from one woman

to the other, opened his mouth, shook his head, looked down at his calves and said nothing, opting instead to lift Adam and hold him close.

It was funny, Suzannah realized. Too slapstick for her taste, but still, not without humor. Harpsichord music and Rachel rising, moving not to Coby but a bedraggled, defiant and drenched creature who slumped in behind him.

And Adam, screaming, "You said you'd stay!"

And Rachel, asking the creature, "Why?"

And the creature, dripping-wet hair, shaking her head, bursting into tears, shouting, "You *hate* me! You always pick on me!"

And Adam hiccuping and smothering Coby with hands and face. "I thought . . . you were . . . *gone!* I thought . . . she—"

And Bach, whistling in the dark.

And Coby, swiveling his head from Rachel to Suzannah, his son screaming in his ear.

And Rachel, hugging her daughter, who stood like a log, saying, "You're wrong, Nancy. I love you. Oh, you're wrong." And then, still embracing her wooden daughter, turning to look at Coby, and he at her, and then both of them at Suzannah.

And Suzannah, watching the command performance, acknowledging them with a small, regal nod.

And oh, for all the messages and meanings flying through the air they needed a sound stage.

Suzannah had the best seat in the house and she watched them untangle, dance between civility and madness as Rachel thanked and Coby thanked and Coby explained and Rachel explained and their children burst through with primitive counterpoint.

And then finally, Rachel and Nancy were gone, offstage in the wet night, leaving the real stars, Waldemar *Père et Fils* for the finale.

Which was dramatically weak because Adam became quiet, resting his head on his father's suede-covered shoulder, and Coby said simply, across the living room's length, "Stay there, please. This may take a while."

It did. By the time Coby tiptoed down the stairs, Suzannah had refilled her snifter and suspected she was a bit squiffed. By then, she had spent more than half an hour trying to remember what she was sitting and waiting for.

"You should have seen where I found her," Coby said. "Under an el station, huddled near boarded-up stores. Bars, massage parlors—she's lucky she wasn't murdered."

"Coby?"

"Probably because the weather's so bad, people weren't out."

"Coby?"

"Can you imagine an undersized thirteen-year-old in that—"

"Coby! I'm happy she's safe, but frankly, the particulars don't interest me."

He swallowed her. "Is it Rachel? Are you—"

"Rachel doesn't interest me, either. I suspect she does, or did, you, but that isn't my—"

"How did this *happen!*" He spoke with something near awe. "God, what a way for Rachel and you to, for—"

"Listen, I'd love to work out the logistics, but I'm tired, and I don't belong, and I'm going home now."

"Suzannah, please stay."

"There's no point." She pulled on her socks and boots and stood.

"Don't leave like this. Not this way."

She looked at the dark curls, watched him impatiently push his glasses up his nose. He kept his middle finger on the bridge as he stared at her.

"Coby, I feel like Dorothy in Oz, and I want to go home."

He put his hands on her shoulders. "Listen, could we—"

She shook her head.

"Ever? What are you saying? Never, Suzannah?"

"I'm not saying a thing except that I'm tired and I want to go home! I can't deal with anything now!" She saw his slaty eyes, felt his long fingers on her shoulders and softened her tone. "I like less complications. I like it when it's me and you. I'm not saying never."

"It's me and you now."

"But it's also too late."

He took his hands off her and walked to the bay window facing the street. "It's turning to snow. Driving's not safe."

"Nothing much is."

"At least let me give you coffee. You look bleary."

"Mother Waldemar." But she was chilly and confused. Hot caffeine wouldn't hurt.

Coby filled the copper kettle, his back to her. "I want to explain a little of why Adam—" He exhaled with a whoosh of air.

"There's no need," she said.

"There is." He turned around. "Or you'll leave thinking—I don't know what. I wouldn't mention it, but it's become relevant." He waited for the water to boil, then carefully poured it into two mugs and carried them to the oak table.

"When Dana died, when Adam was four, he was going through a pretty difficult stage."

She computed. At four, difficult. At six, more so. Even she had heard of the terrible two's. At thirteen, you ran away. There seemed no end to childhood's delights.

"We undoubtedly spoiled him. Overprotected him. See, he was—more than special. Dana had four miscarriages before Adam and when he arrived, we held tight for too long. Then, when we tried letting go a little, he fought it bitterly. When we'd leave him with sitters, he . . . reacted strongly."

Reacted strongly? Was that how Coby would define the witless scene upstairs?

"After Adam, Dana miscarried again. But when he was four—she was six months pregnant the night of the accident. Anyway, she was meeting an old college friend. I was out teaching. I—the sitter told me Adam had a full-blown tantrum, screaming for her not to leave him. But she did, and she never came back.

"I saw Dana again. She was in a coma for three days. But Adam never did. She was—a four-year-old couldn't see his mother that . . . he became, well, whatever. He was completely confused and I didn't help him. I didn't even see what was happening. I was blind, completely engrossed in my own loss. I lengthened his mourning and complicated it."

He stood and turned the range on again. Suzannah heard the stereo click off in the living room.

"I didn't know how to handle it with a four-year-old. I didn't know how to handle it myself. But how could I explain something meaningless to him? Should I have said, son, a drunk jumped the median strip and that's *it?* That's how life is? That's why your mother—and sister, which they told me when I didn't want to know—that's why they stopped being? Disappeared? For the reason of two bourbons, five beers, a bloody mary, what-

ever? Disappeared forever? What would words like that *do* to
him?''

Suzannah's skull contracted and pressed against her brain. She
concentrated on the graining of the oak table.

"I didn't say them, but he felt them." Coby touched Suzannah's hand. She was surprised his flesh was warm.

"He was messed up for a long time. All kinds of—anyway,
it's been long and difficult, but he's much better. He still has too
many boundaries, too many safety zones, but it's almost all past
history. But tonight—do you see what must have flashed through
his mind? A horrible replay, with a twist. Rachel told me what
she heard him saying. He thought I'd disappeared now, been replaced. Nothing could be trusted, not even his own mind. And—
well, he claims he can't remember Dana. He's more or less banished her image. But last night he—well, you look something like
her, okay? Enough to trigger a series of—oh, I don't know what
kind of hideous joke he thought was being played with his mind
when you walked in that room instead of me. I—I don't think he
knew it was you, Suzannah.''

The story saddened her. It confused her. But more, the phrase
"you look something like her" produced revulsion and she
shrank back, pressing into the hard rungs of the chair.

"The thing is," Coby said, "I have a son."

She put her hands on the side rungs, ready to stand.

"And he has me. That's the basic unit, the given." He looked
directly at Suzannah. "Whatever's happened is our history, but
the fact remains, I have a son."

She bowed her head, unable to meet his eyes.

"It will never be less complicated. It will never be me and
you, me and anybody. Not exclusively. Not that way." He
waited, then almost reached for her, but she'd moved too far
away.

"But I refuse," he continued, his voice raw, "I refuse to believe that means I can only be a father, not a whole man any
more. I refuse it, do you understand? I want my life back."

The silence in the house was suffocating. Outside, snow fell,
old whispers dropping from heaven. "You want her back," she
said. "Not me."

"No! I want my life. That one's over. I've mourned it."

She ached for the comfortable shape of her apartment, smooth
walls with souvenirs only of herself. "I have to leave." She

sounded drugged. "It doesn't mean anything, but I have to. Do you understand?"

"I hope so." He helped her on with her jacket.

She pulled him close and kissed him. The leaden weights of his story had dragged down the promise of their first, buoyant weekend. So she memorized the shape of his lips, tried to preserve their meaning. They were the only evidence the jury would have while she decided if, like Coby, she needed to get her own life back again.

After she had gone, he went upstairs and by habit and need, he walked into the red and white bedroom.

His son breathed deeply, his corduroy comforter gently rising and falling. Boots wheezed nearby.

Coby touched the red-blond curls, leaned to kiss Adam's temple, then sat back on his haunches and looked, feasting on this still-miraculous part of him set free to become something new of its own.

"I love you," he whispered in the dark. "I love you. You're my son and I love you."

But oh, he thought, standing, hearing his knees creak, must it cost so much? Must this loving cost everything else?

Seventeen

"Wouldn't need fur if you'd believe in something, lady. No!" Snowflakes melted on the man's face. "I got sunshine in my liver. Keeps me warm! Yes! I'm the Lord's solar collector. The sole solar collector. The soul's sole solar collector. Yes! The—''

Jimmy Sunshine collected sun and the coin of the realm. Suzannah placed a quarter on his palm and hurried on.

"Yes!" Behind her, he continued to preach although prospective congregants had chosen coffee, the Sunday papers and central heating while the storm played itself out.

Center City was embalmed, silent but for Jimmy's gospel.

Suzannah puffed clouds into the pale gray air until she reached the hardware store above which Abby lived. She pressed the bell inside the small alcove at its side.

"Company!" she called up when Abby's head poked out.

Abby shivered and pulled tight an old kimono. "Are you here to pry?"

"Me? I never pry on Sundays." Suzannah felt real apprehension. Abigail Song Newhouse's black hair, normally a seamless curtain, was snarled. Her eyes were bleary. "To be honest," Suzannah continued, now inside the apartment, "I need a sounding board. Ab, I'm all fucked up."

"Well," Abby said, going to the Salvation Army special she used as her best beloved chair. She snuggled into its secondhand lumps and valleys and pulled an afghan around her. "Well, well."

Suzannah noticed the glass of clear liquid by the chair.

"Well, well, well. You saw the music man again?"

"And his kid. And an ex-girl-woman-friend. And her kid." She explained as best she could, Friday and Saturday nights. The longer she spoke, the funnier the telling became, and she embellished it with gestures and finally stood to dramatize events, imitating the child's wrath, the runaway's stoniness, Coby's bewilderment, Rachel's detective business. She bowed at the conclusion of her act.

"Funny story, Suze. Maybe *Reader's Digest* would buy it. 'Life in These United States.'"

Suzannah had finally defrosted, and she hung her jacket on a bentwood rack. The closet intended for coats housed Abby's disorderly stash of books. Sartre and Baudelaire, Goethe and Freud, Sylvia Palth and *Tristram Shandy*, underlined and annotated and stored in piles behind a cheap flush door.

"Well, Suze, uncreating a kid's tough. So the question is—how much do you want the father?"

"I don't. I want Coby. They're not one and the same, are they? And anyway, I'm not sure I want him at all."

"Then drop him. What's the percentage? I thought you were the practical one of us."

But something about Coby made her—almost—want to believe poetry, not percentages. Want to believe, as he did, that a single thing, a person, could increase one's life, could—

"Look at you!" Abby said. "You *are* sure! He's got you by the—what do you say for a woman? Just plain 'gotcha'?"

"Nobody has me," Suzannah snapped. Then she grinned. "Nobody's had me, either. Think that's my problem?"

"You don't have a problem. Want him in your bed? Alone? Next time, don't invite the kid."

"It's that simple?"

"Yes, unless you're yearning for a church wedding."

"He's Jewish."

"Dammit, don't bother me with ethnic details."

"No wedding. No cohabitation."

"Then no problem." Abby put down her drink and slid deeper under the striped afghan. "You're lucky. I wish . . ."

"Abby?"

"Don't. That's your 'now it's your turn' voice. You said you wouldn't." She closed her eyes.

"I bet you haven't eaten. I'll make an egg."

"I'll throw up. You don't have to repay my wise words. My life's work is advice and counsel. Ask Abby. Everybody knows about that. A relief, actually, to have you ponder something other than fuck-face with the dresses."

"Elaine Weiner?"

Abby nodded and yawned. "I watched 'The Bachelor and the Bobby-Soxer' on the 'Late-Late Show.' Wasn't life nifty then? So simple, at least in Hollywood. Nobody had to think. Nobody had to figure out how to live. Everything was foreordained. Myrna Loy didn't have to make decisions."

"Do you think she kept her law practice after she married Cary Grant? Why don't they ever go past that big clinch scene?"

"The only thing she did was live happily ever after. That's what people did, then. That's why they're called the good old days." She yawned again.

"When did you sleep last, Abby?"

"My mother thought my father looked like Cary Grant. Only she said Cally Glant . . . he never looked that way. She was always wrong. The family knew. Didn't come near her till she was dead."

"Listen, I'll make tea, okay?"

"And me, too." Abby's voice was almost dreamy. "I was wrong. Not a real Newhouse. Not even to my father. To anybody. I wasn't anything. I never belonged."

"Have you seen him again? Is that what this is?"

"We had sherry and cookies." She shivered and pulled the blanket tight.

"Why did you go there?"

"We all wound up funny places yesterday, didn't we?"

"Tea? Would you like some tea?"

"You sound like Lucinda. I'd like a nap."

"You're frightening me. Let me stay, or come home with me."

Abby shook her head. "Will you knock it off? It's Sunday. Official day of rest. God was allowed, why aren't I?"

"All right. But . . . I'll see you soon, won't I?"

"Have I ever missed Tuesday lunch?"

Suzannah stayed outside until she heard Abby slip the bolt in the lock.

The snow had stopped and after two days of absenteeism, the sun frenetically used its makeup time.

Suzannah paused as she approached her apartment. The world was almost too bright to view without smoked glass shields. Sunbeams popped off drifts, hit windowpanes and leaped free again, diving into the snow and resurfacing to dance on top of it. Every shape on the landscape was outlined with light.

She stood at the circle near the art museum and surveyed the world. Slippery roads and poor visibility might have cosmic rationales, she decided. Might be worth it for this.

Until tomorrow, then the sun would slush the coverlet. When exhausts and wheels would darken and throw it sideways, when battle-weary workers would slide off its surface directly into the orthopedic surgeon's office. Tomorrow.

For now, she saluted the heavens. "Well done," she said.

Inside her apartment, she switched on her new toy and heard the recycled sound waves of her callers.

Potter Alexander had cataclysmic problems and hiccups. He shared both.

Then a breather. Suzannah couldn't believe it. A breather, getting off with an electronic audience.

Then Tully, who wanted to say hello. Indeed, he did what he wanted and said it.

The last caller didn't identify himself. "My housekeeper is no longer regurgitating." Coby sounded strained.

Abby, vodka-bleary and all, was correct. The business of Coby and Suzannah was laughably uncomplex. She dialed his number. "I'm delighted by the short duration of her virus," she said as soon as the receiver was lifted.

"What number did you want?"

Not Coby's many-toned voice at all. This was high, nasal and possibly drunk.

"Is Coby Waldemar there?" she asked, subdued.

"Oh, Sure. Hold on."

She heard the phone clunk against the kitchen wall and then a welter of vocal and instrumental sound. She and the phone dangled. She began to hang up, then stopped herself. Silly to be irritated. Of course Coby would have scores of friends, and of course they'd gather together, make music, laugh a lot. Why should it bother her?

"Hello?" Coby eventually said.

"This is Suzannah. I got your message."

"Good."

She'd expected more from voluble Jacob Waldemar. But the only sound was from the revelers in his house. She felt misused. She'd spent all night and half her day sorting emotions and deliberating futures and he—he threw a party and didn't have the decency to invite her!

"You never know," he said. "You send out messages and hope. No guarantee they're properly received."

"Are you talking about recording machines?"

"Nope."

She heard someone ask a question, envisioned him nodding or shaking his head. She cleared her throat.

"Did you say something?" he asked quickly.

"What is that noise?"

"That? An early version of 'St. James' Infirmary.' But don't you want to talk about, say, Mrs. Jennings' recovery?"

This was a new Coby. Careful, guarded. But maybe she'd earned this slowdown, listening last night, giving nothing. He wasn't a pushover and it wasn't completely her game. She grinned. "Hey, there. White flag time. I want to see you. When's Jennings coming back?"

"Tomorrow. Now listen, I'm heavy with theories. I want to

begin again—not past the beginning, but at it. I'd like to escort you to a quiet restaurant. I'd like to dine and listen. I want to begin to know you. How's that sound?''

Stupid. Forced and archaic. ''Fine.'' The noise in his house intensified. ''What's going on?'' she asked. ''Really.''

''It's my play group. Name sounded funny when we had kids in their own play groups. We lean more to beer and wine than milk and cookies. Want to join us? It'll go on most of the night.''

''Thanks,'' she said, ''but I . . . sing terribly and it's . . . you're too far away.''

''Well, then, I'll see you tomorrow. Around six.'' He barely disguised his pleasant impatience to rejoin his pals.

Even with the receiver back on the hook, she heard distant music and laughter. She cursed the soup for its refusal to heat.

She decided to unwatch the pot. When she returned to the kitchen with Marcel Proust, the soup was boiling. She sat at the white formica counter and focused on Proust's imagery, not hers, which was aqueous and clouded.

Eighteen

Rachel said nothing for most of the ride. When she did speak, her voice was hesitant, tiptoeing towards her topic. ''David's remarrying. That's where I was Saturday. He couldn't simply phone in the news. I had to have a surprise meeting with her. She's twenty-three. A model.''

''Oh. shit,'' Coby said. ''What a shit he is.''

Rachel bit her lip. David wasn't the only shit in her life.

''And I really added to the joy of your weekend,'' he said.

''I thought we decided to—''

''We didn't. Not really. We've skipped around it and tapped it lightly and backed off. And I still feel rotten about not telling you. Not being straight about it.''

"But I understand why. We all try to protect people we care for. Anyway, let's forget it. I need a friend."

"So do I."

She glanced sideways. "Isn't she one?"

"I don't know. I really don't."

Rachel touched his sleeve gently. "Be careful. She's not like you. She's not . . . generous of spirit."

"Oh, Rachel, don't base too much on Saturday. You're a mother and a psychologist and she—it isn't fair, really."

Rachel's lips tucked in to silence herself. "I don't want to see you hurt," she said, very, very softly.

"Thanks for the concern, but I'm a grownup. I know why you said it, but I don't intend to set myself up. I don't enjoy being hurt. I'll be okay. Let's take care of you instead."

"Not now."

"Not generous of spirit? Is that what you said? Why?"

"I won't repeat and I won't add. You know the woman. You know yourself. And I know when to shut up."

They reached Rachel's icy, sloping driveway. Coby leaned out when she left the car. "Be careful! It's really slippery ahead of you—watch yourself."

She blew him a kiss. "You, too, Coby."

He headed for Suzannah's apartment, sifting the last few days' overload of sensation, impressions, ideas. Rachel was correct. He did know himself. It was a happy, recent discovery. But Suzannah? Did he know her at all? He couldn't find words to describe her, not even in the privacy of his mind. Beautiful. Quick. Sensual. Prickly. Tough. Demanding. No. That wasn't Suzannah. There weren't words. He couldn't write the song, couldn't describe or capture her. No words, but sounds. Laughs, soft moans and sighs. And colors, warm and soft. Candleglow and flutesong, flame-licking platinum. Liquid ice, frozen heat, perfumes, tastes . . . Suzannah.

And she was all of that when she opened her door.

"You aren't dressed for our night out," he said. "What do you call that?"

"A thing." She pirouetted in her floor-length T-shirt, hands above her head.

He bowed and applauded. "Yes," he said. "I notice the absence of underwear, the abundance of you."

"That's the idea." She stopped being Salome. "You didn't

say where we were going and I didn't know the appropriate attire. It grew so wearisome deciding, I didn't.'' She nuzzled close. "I can always dress. I'm freshly laundered, and I've perfumed the most amazing places.''

"I brought you these.''

"Flowers! And candy, too?''

"A complete return to tradition.'' He handed her a bouquet and a red satin heart. "Couldn't remember if chocolates or roses came first.''

"I never knew. All I heard was 'candy's dandy but liquor's quicker.' Would you therefore care for something alcoholic?''

He shook his head.

"Then how about me? Would you care for me? You can skip the dinner, movies, stereopticon shows, ballroom dancing, fetes, whatever the old preliminaries were. Wooed with flowers and candy, I swoon. I am prepared to sacrifice a woman's most precious possession. Right now.''

"You're impossible,'' he said, laughing as she pressed close, became a vine, attached herself and grew out of him.

"I love your smile,'' she crooned. "Love those little whatchamacallits. Little rivulets attaching your cheeks to your chin. Love your arms, the way the hair curls here. Love your back muscles, the sweep to that almost aborigine rear, those flanks. C'mon, Coby. Traditions died for a reason. Today's much more fun.'' She unbuckled his belt. "Oh, and your stomach. I love it and I love . . . Coby? Are you going to insist on a restaurant now?''

"What restaurant? Who?''

"Didn't that beat the hell out of the old-fashioned hoopla?'' She threw back the sheets and left the room, returning with the chocolates.

"Did you know,'' he said, "that chocolates and love produce the same feel-good chemicals? Maybe that's why candy's a traditional part of courtship. If he couldn't get the stuff flowing— phenylethylamine—then maybe the chocolate would. I will risk overdosing by having both in one night.''

She put the heart-shaped box on the bed and opened her palm. "I bought myself a gift today. I want to show him to you.'' She passed over a small wood carving of an oriental man whose face swiveled, showing either a joyous or a mournful mask. "Isn't he dear? He's a 'congratulations-you're-on-your-way' gift. New holiday I invented. I've always loved netsukes."

He put his glasses on and studied first the little man and then Suzannah.

"They used them to clasp shut their moneybags," she said. "Isn't Japanese reverence for details lovely? Western pragmatism leads to zippers, not collector's items."

"On your way where?"

She chose a mocha-centered chocolate. "The Land of Deep Green. The Emerald City. I see its rich horizons even as we speak." She chose a second candy. She could pamper herself all she liked. Today she'd invested the last of her loan, no longer wanting any delay because T&R seemed hell-bent on rising. The price had been 8 when she began buying two weeks earlier. Today, with margin doubling her investment, she had $76,000 working for her and T&R was $13\frac{1}{2}$. Her $38,000 stake was now edging towards $100,000 and the split, the take-over, the doubling was still ahead.

God bless Tully's indiscretion. God bless greed. And God bless Suzannah for her smarts. She envisioned her money riding the high tides like an iridescent oil spill.

"And what will you do with your millions?" He handed back the netsuke.

"Laugh." She spun the face several times. The old man grinned and cried. "I guess I'll do and be anything I please. That's the point of money."

"What would please you? What would you want to do or be?"

"Successful. Somebody."

"You are already."

"Oh no. Those S's were capitalized."

He sat up straight and plumped his pillow into a backrest. "Seriously. If everything works as you hope, what will your life be like?"

"You don't want glittering generalizations?"

"No. I want to know what you dream about. Specifically."

She tilted her head and thought. "An old, polished townhouse. High ceilings and mellow wood. Beautiful, inside and out. Vacations. Travel. The world. When I have the capital, my own investment advisory firm. Mine. And . . . a beach house. Glass and cedar, on stilts, over a dune. And—"

"People?"

"What kind of question is that? Sure. Do you mean you? Are you being coy? You'd have unlimited passes, an open invitation. Oh, I can see you making music by the firelight, swimming with me in the ocean and then . . ." She leaned over, pulled the sheet down slightly and kissed the hard spot, close to the bone, in the center of his chest. Which action caused her to miss his sudden frown. She did notice his silence and she sat up again. "Why so glum? What is this? A delayed post-coital depression?"

"I just remembered the damndest thing. When I was in high school, my older brother Louis was seeing—quietly, at odd hours—a girl called Happy Mary. She was the official town tramp. It was, of course, the olden days, and we still had such archaic designations. Pathetic person, Mary. All tight sweaters and paint. Anyway, once she came over for a showdown with Louis, but I was the only one home. It didn't matter to her. Mascara running, nose running, stockings running, she said, 'He doesn't take me serious.' I had to turn my back to hide my snicker. She was ludicrous and she didn't know grammar or her proper place in the world. But she knew a lot more than I understood back then."

Suzannah put the netsuke on the night table.

"I take myself serious, Suzannah. Sand dunes and townhouses are prettier than the back of the bowling alley, but—"

"What on earth is happening? Aren't you happy? Aren't you enjoying yourself?"

"Right now?" He stroked a patch of velvet on the comforter. "I'm more than happy with you. Everything's too damned right and always is."

She again kissed the swirls of dark hair on his chest. "Is it such a turnoff that I'll be rich?"

"That's irrelevant."

"Then why this doom and gloom? Here, have more candy. Maybe your blood sugar's low."

"I thought and thought Saturday night. I know it's too soon. I don't presume to foretell events or feelings. But the thing I said, the thing I know for sure, is that I want my life back."

"Hey, Coby? Let go of this talk. Ready for dinner?"

"And—I don't want to set myself up. I'm not a misery collector. So if I can, even if it's rushing it, even if it's too soon—I want to talk. Because I'm afraid we're on a collision course, that sooner or later we'll crash and total each other."

"Dammit!" She stomped off the bed and pulled on her T-shirt dress. "You're spoiling everything!"

"I don't want to. I only want to talk."

"Well I don't! This was a splendid day in my life. I was high all day long and now look what you're doing!"

"The problem is, as much as anyone can so soon, I love you."

"Don't talk about love!" She clenched her hands into fists as she backed into the middle of the room.

He pulled the sheets off and left the bed, hunting his clothing and dressing as he spoke. "What should I call it?" he asked, zipping his pants. "Do I have to invent a new word?"

They edged away from the rumpled bed, the open heart-shaped box in its center, chocolates scattered on the sheets.

She stamped her foot. "You're spoiling everything!"

"Spoiling? Because I love you? *Spoiling?* Why is it so threatening?"

"Nothing's threatening!"

"Wrong. Something is. What is it?"

She backed up another step. "I don't . . . I've felt it from the minute you appeared in my office. From before then. I . . ." She pointed at him, suddenly realizing what had dragged at her, made her cautious, what she'd known all along. "You want too much. That's what it is. Too much!"

"Don't you want to be loved? Not only to be made love to, but to be loved?"

"I'm not a freak. Don't make me into—everybody wants—"

"You've got it then. Or do you prefer simply wanting it? Is that easier than dealing with it? So what if it's too soon to say the magic word? Knowing you longer will only add to what I feel. I already know you aren't perfect. I know you're running fast, you—"

"Cut out the—"

"Don't interrupt me. I also know you like choreographing the whole show, as witness tonight. But you can't. Not all the time or all the way. Not with me."

He bent to find a shoe, then put it on, hopping in place. "This is ridiculous! All the intangibles, the improbables, the chemistry, the things beyond our control are *fine*." He stood, the other shoe in his hand. "Aren't they? It's different. We touch the right way, laugh the right way. Am I wrong?"

"No."

"So what's so scary?"

She tiptoed back another pace.

"Suzannah, I need to know. I'll give this all the time in the world. But if your idea of complete happiness—of success—of being somebody—is counting cash under ten-foot ceilings—if you'll define . . . well, I don't know if I want to be . . ." He waved the shoe around, unwilling to finish his sentence.

She neared the bedroom door. "I'm not who you're making me, Coby. You're putting words into my mouth."

"Ah." He walked over and stopped her backwards progress. "Let's try other people's words. Imitation Rorschach. Instead of ink, a piece of poem. Ready? React. 'Come live with me and be my love and we will all the pleasures prove—' "

"No. I would . . . I would have to decline."

"That's what I thought I was hearing."

"And that's what I thought you were asking. And that's why I said it was ridiculous, much too soon for—"

"I didn't mean *now*. Are you saying that someday, if—"

"No. I'm not built for the role."

He dropped his shoe and worked on the buttons of his shirt instead. "Never?"

"Not in the foreseeable future. Might as well say never."

"Not with anyone? No matter who?"

"It has nothing to do with the other person."

"Not even to save gas?"

"Oh, Coby."

He smiled gently. "Listen, let's sit down and speak in the manner of civilized adults."

At oppostie ends of the sofa, facing the empty expanse of room and not each other, they waited for a conversational opening as tensely as teens on a blind date.

Suzannah finally cleared her throat. "What I resent is your surprise. Did I strike you as someone spinning wheels until she could enlist in the 'Brady Bunch'?"

"I thought you wanted . . . you were married once, after all. You made a commitment, a bonding. I thought . . ."

"He wasn't you." Each word needed to be pushed up her throat, over her tongue, and out. "Not at all. And I'm not the person who married him. And it was never what you'd call a commitment."

"It was safe because it demanded nothing."

"Not safe. I don't like your—"

"It was *wrong*. I thought you knew that and wanted more. Don't you? Don't you think you'll ever want more than splendid isolation, occasional stud service and good meals?"

She twisted on the sofa so she could face him, possibly help him understand. "Coby, what you consider more, I consider less. It's that simple." She touched his arm. "What's wrong with what we have? You can joke about candy and flowers, but you are honestly quaint. You're out of step with the times, not me."

He pushed his glasses up and sighed. "I know."

"I won't be boxed up. I won't be tied down."

"I wasn't thinking of a torture chamber."

She removed her hand from his arm. "I know. You were thinking of a flower garden with a little woman in the center and a child and doggy frolicking. Put me there and it'd be those old puzzles. What's wrong with this picture? I'd be what's wrong. You don't want me, Coby. You want an old-fashioned dream. You want the needlepointer back."

He looked ready to shout, but he didn't. "I meant *you*, Suzannah. No one else." He put his head in his hands and became silent.

"I could love you," she whispered. "I want to share lots of my life. But you're asking me to hand it over, give it up."

He looked at her, then returned to his head in hands position.

"Why not . . . let this go?" She waved her hand, dusting clean the air. "We have a fine thing going."

"We do." He sat up straight again. "I know I might qualify as a fool, pushing this way right now. But we're not talking about now, are we? We're talking somedays, and someday I want my life to cohere, becoming all of a piece. I don't want sitters forever, part-time people dancing in and out of my life. I want a friend, a companion as well as a lover. I know we're special. If we weren't, I'd never have begun this. It would be irrelevant. But, Suzannah, it's because you're special, because part of me is really scared. Things—bad things happen. I can't do much about that. But I can avoid self-inflicted wounds. I don't want to keep getting over things. I want to get on with it. So if a future's blocked out in advance, I need to know. I need to be able to decide."

"And what I need is to be Suzannah. Not somebody's wife or

mother or roommate. It erodes a woman, saps her. You don't understand what's expected, what's locked into the words 'woman' 'mother' 'wife.' You'd both use me until I was used up. You wouldn't mean to, but you would. It's the trap, the way things are."

He looked completely bewildered. "Are you afraid of losing your career, being chained to the kitchen sink? I have a housekeeper already. I don't need to live with her. What do you think I am?"

"A man. And a man with a ready-made family."

"I swear I don't understand. What would happen?"

"A million things. I can't afford children. I don't want them. Children fall off bikes, get sick, have parties I'd have to attend. Tell stupid jokes, long stories, need help with homework. Children . . . children expect. And as for husbands, or lovers, or roommates, whatever, there's no end to what that means. A department chairman needs entertaining. Moods don't mesh. There are obligations. I crave silence entire days. I don't want to hear your music or 'Sesame Street' in my background. I don't enjoy family fare—pot roasts and hot dogs and barbecues. Tot lots, dinner parties where married couples compare tennis scores. Family vacations. Coming home because a sitter needs to leave. Tolerating other people's friends—your friends—if I don't like them. All the—"

"Those are so negligible compared to—"

"That's my point! They're negligible to you, but not to me. Not as they pile and grow and never stop. The package is attractive as hell—that's why so many women buy it—but attractive as you are or not, it's a package and it's mined. I'd lose everything. I'd wind up like half the women around me, filled with nothing but hate and despair and dead dreams."

She walked to the picture window, staring into the night. Small wires spluttered and flashed in her head, short-circuiting her system. "This is stupid," she said. "This is so goddamned stupid." She gritted her teeth and stared, unable to see anything but the reflection of the room behind her. Her throat ached and she heard her blood whir in a frenzy through her veins. Her fingers on the sill became arthritic, each bone sick at its center, the marrow decaying.

He had done this to her.

"Stop!" she said, whirling to confront him. "Stop being stiff-necked, bullheaded. I offered you *me*—why haggle over the terms? You're insulting and irrational!''

"Me?" He stood up and limped to her, only one foot shod. "*I'm* bullheaded? *I'm* irrational? I've heard a great deal about men and life and the battle of the sexes. But nothing about me. Nothing about you. Is that rational?"

"So I used generalizations. What do you want? I have a difficult, demanding job I love. I have ambitions for more. I have only so much energy. I want to be somebody. That's specific. That's about me, Coby. And I see what happens to women. I don't have to relive their histories; I don't have to sink with them. I can use my brains to figure a way out. I wish it were otherwise, but it just plain isn't. So until the world changes, until some genius devises a new master plan, there's no other way. I understand the facts of life. I understand I have only now and I'm not omnipotent. I can't spread myself thin and waste my energies."

"I see. The country of coupling is dangerous so you'll detour it altogether. You know the future. You've *designed* the future. Damn it, Suzannah—you've written your script *and* you've written *my* script!"

"You don't have to shout!"

"Oh no? Well I believe in shouting! I believe in shouting and loving and fucking and living and making the most of my short time here! I believe in bellowing my lungs out if someone's too deaf to hear how stupid she sounds!"

"Shh! This is an apartment building!"

"I don't care where you live! I'm talking about your head! What is this rhetorical bullshit? How did I become a dangerous beast? For Christ's sake, what the hell is going on? You know—you just plain *know* how I'd be because I'm male? You have to keep me and all men in our place because otherwise we'd destroy you? Suzannah—you and I—we're the same species!"

"Don't punch my wall!"

"God but you make me mad. You'll retreat, is that it? You! Gutsy, risk-taking you!" But he halted in mid-punch and breathed deeply, pacing around and around her sofa and carpet.

She rubbed her knuckles and listened to his horrible one-shoe stomp, one-sock shuffle. Then, he again threatened to shatter the plaster, this time verbally.

"*Liberté, Egalité, Fra*—whoops, sorry. *Sororité!* Off with your head, sucker. Only good man's a dead man. You, Suzannah, are like my brother Louis. Only difference is he's a specialist on *women*. The two of you . . . 'Women,' Louis says, 'snick, snick. Dumb—all they need is a good—' ''

"How *dare* you compare me with Louis?"

"But you'd *like* him, or at least have a lot in common with—"

"Stop talking about Louis!"

Coby silently circled the Aubusson, punching the sofa each time he passed it.

"And put on your other shoe!" she shouted. "You look like a damned peg-leg!"

"I have room for a career and a family. Why couldn't you?"

Goddamn him for his stupidity. Goddamn him, baiting her in her own living room, shouting and pushing his weight around.

"Huh? How come I can handle it and you couldn't? How come? I have room for both. Why don't you?"

The muscles in her neck became drawstrings and she didn't care who heard what because this man hadn't heard a thing. "YOU'LL USE A WOMAN, THAT'S HOW COME!"

His mouth opened in awe.

She couldn't stop. "MEN ARE FATHERS, YOU FOOL! FATHERING IS EASY! HUSBANDING IS EASY! MEN MADE UP THE RULES AND THAT'S WHY!!"

He waited until she stopped shaking. "Me," he said. "Not some abstract feminist dartboard."

After a time, the ligaments of her neck stopped twitching and her skin temperature returned to normal. But, no longer supported by rage, she nearly fell, and she pushed by him to clutch the sofa back and lean on it for support.

He looked at her sadly, then shook his head and spoke gently. "Suzannah, how did I become your enemy?"

She lost small chambers of her mind, heard cell walls crumble, felt their contents dry.

He walked to the door. "But you're right, I guess. If there could have been a future, I would have used you. I would have expected you to use me. I thought that was the deal. I might have welcomed another child. Ours. And with all the good will in the world, with all hopes for the end of roles, I'd still have used your body to grow the baby. And then your time would have been used to nurture it. Mine, too, but I take it that doesn't count. So you're right. Only what you think of as a pound of flesh, I think of as loving. And being alive."

He opened the door, but then noticed his shoeless foot and stood in confusion until he sighted his shoe and walked to retrieve it. "You've added up what you've seen, Suzannah, but you've added it up wrong, so that you wind up with zero. Nothing. Don't kid yourself. You can cover it with whatever rhetoric's in style today, but involvement is what's scary. Your philosophy's too fashionable, too pat, too damned much today's best seller. Anger and sighs. Renunciation of the possibility of happiness. Dammit—stupid people who don't know what's chic, who haven't read the right books, taken the right courses, spoken with the right people, found out that it's impossible for men and women to do anything but destroy each other—those unenlightened fools are out there right now being happy!"

"I think you'd better go."

He nodded, and went to the door. "Okay. Maybe I just don't understand. Jews aren't into renunciation, denying the pleasures of earth for some great heaven to come. Jews don't have saints and don't find them alluring. I don't. Not when they starved in the desert and not now when people like you keep the pleasures of the flesh but give up being human. The new saints. Saints who fuck. Fucking saints. I'd rather be human."

And then he was gone.

Stupid. The center of her brain said stupid. Stupid, if repeated as she clutched the back of the sofa. Stupid. *Stupid.* More and more loudly, tolling, a clanging iron bell swinging in ever larger arcs. STUPID. STUPID. Sound waves spreading, circling, her, the room, the building. STUPIDSTUPIDSTUPID!

Vibrations in the air colliding, enlarging, re-entering the bell tower inside, replacing marrow with iron. Stupid! Echoes, icy metal inside, rigor mortis as she clutched and stood unbending, too brittle to bend again, ever. Stupid . . . hewas stupidhe was . . . cobystupid . . .

Cold. The room was freezing. Something about thermodynamics. Heat couldn't reach this high in the sky? Did it ever? She shivered but stood straight, the armature of steel and iron supporting her and echoing in dull trills to the peals sounding from her center.

"Enough!" she shouted. "No more!"

And the bell stopped.

She was surprised by the cracked sound of her voice. Her throat was dry and her stomach empty.

She went and opened the refrigerator. The apples were too hard and thick-skinned, the cheese too flabby, the eggs unthinkably viscous. She settled for two glasses of water and pictured Coby's leave-taking. From a distance, she mentally watched him search the underground parking lot, find his car, bend his large frame low, enter and slam the door shut. Then he drove off, the VW dwindling into a speck on her mind's horizon, small enough to begin forgetting.

She poured the last of her water down the drain and stood, breathing deeply.

There were hours of evening left and she suddenly couldn't bear spending them alone in this chilly, empty place. She reached for the phone, for Abby. Abby would know how to laugh and dismiss the idiocy, the exhausting wrongness of the last two hours.

She waited as the phone rang and rang. Please be home, Suzannah silently mouthed. Please. There was no one else on earth who knew how things were. No one else who, with a reach of long red nails and a wisecrack, could put events into perspective. Suzannah's disappointment was acute as the phone continued ringing.

She decided to give up when through the receiver she heard a harsh, distorted cry. "Stop it!" Then a slam.

Stop what? The ringing? With a mounting sense of fear, she dialed Abby's number again.

This time the phone rang only once. Then Suzannah, feeling her limbs freeze and numb, heard the receiver be removed, then clunk as it was dropped.

"Abby?" she shouted. "Say something! Abby? Please— something?"

But she heard only dull noises shuffling the air. They—cries, sobs, murmurs—she couldn't say—terrified Suzannah more than screams would have.

"Abby?" But only the raw, half-audible sounds.

She hung up, raced to find her cape and left her apartment at a run.

Coby stopped her midway down the hall. "I forgot my coat. I—where are you going?"

"I think Abby's—"

"What?"

"I don't know. I can't talk. I can't stop. Something's wrong."

"I'll get my coat and take you there."

"No. I'll go *myself*."

"Oh stop it. Stop it just for now. You're either overreacting to nothing or wasting time. Open your door."

"I don't know why you're doing this."

He kept driving. She saw his jaw clamp tight, the bone at its side press against the flesh. "I know you don't. If you did, then the whole night's . . ." He shook his head and again clamped his mouth tight.

She cried with fear as they raced up the flight of stairs. "Abby!" she shouted, pounding on the door. "Abby!"

They heard nothing, pounded again.

"Suzannah, find a phone booth. Call the police. I'll try to—" He rammed his shoulder against the door, backed up and rammed it again. "Go!" he shouted. "For God's sake, move!"

She stood frozen, her mouth still open to scream.

"What's the racket?" a voice said. Across the landing, an elderly woman peered out of her chain-locked door.

It took time. It took convincing and patience Suzannah lacked, but the woman, while forbidding admittance to them, did promise to call the police.

By the time they arrived, sirens flashing, paramedics racing up, Suzannah was hoarse from crying.

She heard the door give and turned away. Finally, she forced herself to enter and to look.

Her mouth opened and her lungs heaved, but no sound came out.

Abby was sprawled in the chair. Next to her, on the end table, vodka, a pill bottle and the telephone, its receiver dangling to the floor, buzzing.

Suzannah watched in horror as a drop of blood hit it.

Abby was dead. As dead as anything had ever been, blood leaking still, oozing onto the slipcover beneath her wrists, onto her cornsilk blouse, onto her arms, onto her fingers.

And Suzannah, mute and paralyzed, also died. Her flesh constricted and burned away. Every muscle became rigid, her chest collapsed and she suffocated. She shut her eyes, shut it out, stopped it, unmade it.

"NO!" she screamed. "NO! She's dead! Oh, God, not dead. NO!"

She pulled at her hair. "The blood—oh, the blood, she's dead. God! The blood!"

"She's not dead," a paramedic said. "It's messy, but she's not dead."

They followed the ambulance to the hospital. They waited, answering the clerk's questions as best they could.

"I'm calm now," she said to Coby. "I'm calm. I'll call her father now." She opened her purse to find change, found it, dropped it, and burst into tears.

"Sit down. I'll get you coffee," Coby said.

"You should go home," she answered. "Thank you for . . . thank you. But you don't have to stay."

He looked sad. "Suzannah—"

"Thank you, but it isn't your problem. You've been unbelievably kind, but it isn't, she isn't even your friend."

He bit his lip and said nothing and he stayed.

"I'll call her father later, when we know more." She finished her coffee.

"Don't you think he'd want to know? To be here?"

"No." Her voice dwindled to a painful whisper. "No. I think he'd be annoyed. We'd wake him up."

Coby looked at his watch, then put it to his ear. "It isn't late. It only feels that way. I'll call."

"But—"

"I know. But I'll call." He walked down the hall.

"She'll be okay," a white-jacketed resident told them. "You her family?"

"They'll be here later," Coby answered.

"Lucky you arrived when you did. She was full of liquor and pills, but it was early enough."

"The blood," Suzannah whispered. "All that blood."

The resident shrugged. "Superficial cuts. I don't know what she had in mind. They weren't deep. Lots of them, though." He shook his head. "Nope. The pills and liquor would have done it. The rest was . . . decoration."

"She'll live? Are you sure? Will she—will it affect—"

"She'll be fine if she stays away from booze and sleeping pills."

"Can I see her?"

"Tomorrow." The doctor rubbed a hand over his eyes. "When did you say the parents would be here?"

"Later," Coby answered. "They were—they were in the middle of dinner."

The doctor yawned and shook his head. "She's lucky she's got friends."

While Coby drove her home, Suzannah tried and failed to make sense of it. "She's so beautiful, so talented. She's brilliant, but she's hidden it for years. She could have . . . she could be . . . I don't understand."

"I remember her from New Year's," he said. "She was beautiful."

"Is. Is beautiful. She's alive."

"Yes. Beautiful and alive and under hospital care. So I'm worried about you now."

"Oh, I'm nothing like her that way. I love her and we're friends, but I'm not like her that way. Is that what you're afraid of?"

He leaned over and kissed Suzannah gently. "I'm not sure what all I'm afraid of. But call me if you need someone. Any hour. Even if, if I'm, if we're not—even if. Now, good night." He looked at his watch and sighed.

"Thank you for everything." She left the car and walked into the building slowly, like an invalid.

Nineteen

Suzannah sat at her desk, head in hands. "Abby's alive," she repeated softly. "Last night's over."

All morning, she'd needed to hear herself insist that all was well. Abby was alive. So was Suzannah.

The night had been so long, filled with demons poking at her flesh, accusing her of crimes and endless mistakes. But the night was over. She'd outwitted it and survived because she was strong and she knew who she was. Abby had asked men to define her. That, not vodka or pills or razors, that was the suicide and Suzannah would never copy it. No man, no love, none of the male seductions would become her drug, dulling and weakening her defenses.

She forced herself to work, placing orders, buying and selling, wheedling and insisting until her pulse strengthened and she lost that tremor that had plagued her all night and morning.

"You all right?" Nick asked at one point. "You keep sighing."

I'm okay." She began believing it. She wrote a series of numbers on her yellow legal pad and they comforted her.

Words were pushy. Words weaseled, whined and intimidated their way through your brain. Spiny words and malicious words and foolish, stupid words. She wrote numbers instead.

Numbers were clean. Abstractions with solid reality to back them up.

"30." Her number for today. Her age, as of this day.

"523." Her apartment number. Where she lived.

She calculated the commission dollars she'd generated in the previous hour, computing the figure with the devotion of a Cabalist who believed there was a code to break, one number that would tell her everything she wanted to know about the world.

She glanced at the tape, nodded as she saw T&R at 16. She wrote down that number as well. Then she recalculated her holdings, her profit.

She'd purchased 7,000 shares at five different prices, but all were lower than the stock's present high.

Numbers. She loved the shapes of the zeros. She drew commas with the care of an artist.

She'd spent $38,000 to purchase $76,000 worth of Tydings and Roy on margin. Tuesday, at ten forty-three, her holdings were worth $112,000.

She subtracted the $38,000 owed her company for margin plus some for commissions. She subtracted the $30,000 plus bank interest she owed on the loan. She subtracted the $8,000 savings she had first invested.

She remained more than $36,000 ahead on this bright winter day. And the split, the take-over, the doubling of that at least— still glowed in the future. Double $112,000 and you had $244,000. Take away the loan—still $68,000 in margin and bank loan—take away her original $8,000 . . . and she would have $148,000 profit. She drew a box around the number, doodled sunrays bursting from its sides, underlined each number and put exclamation points next to it. $148,000!!!

Even if the precise figures changed a bit, she was sure she was going to make something in the neighborhood of that figure.

Let there be a few such events in her life and she'd be free. Strong. Never again beholden, never anyone's employee, never paying rent for space she didn't own, never following rules she hadn't created.

"You ready for me?" Sara Pratt, in faded housedress and eau de tuna, seated herself next to Suzannah's desk. "I'm a little nervous. Not used to this."

Suzannah made soothing sounds while they completed the formalities of a new account. Numbers, sparking like comets, flashed through Suzannah's brain. Unknown, stellar numbers soaring to infinity. Sara Pratt, the bag lady with the stash under the mattress. Sara Pratt, eccentric heiress, gap-toothed widow using stock certificates as antimacassars.

Sara passed over a piece of paper. "Sell it."

"This is it?"

Sara nodded and smiled.

"One share?"

"A piece of the company. A stake in its future. That's what Mr. Calloway said to my late husband. Well I say my husband's been gone seven months and Mr. Calloway's future ain't mine no more. So I say let go of it. Oh, I know it's up a buck, but I think I'd like to try something else."

"You know you'll pay commission and with a stock selling at twenty dollars, you'll—"

"Pff." Sara brushed away the tariffs of the capitalistic system, annoying though they were. She now wished to invest in a dress company, to buy one new share and spring for an additional three dollars.

Bullish Sara was really purchasing residence in the visitor's gallery, a place to be between sunrise and sunset.

It shouldn't have bothered Suzannah so. It was only the souring of her own fantasies. Nothing real. But her fingers resumed last night's trembling as she wrote the order. She misspelled a word and stared, unable to remember its proper shape.

After Sara, Suzannah began a new column of figures, convincing herself she was perfectly fine.

The night before receded, dimmed to a faded negative in the white glare of day. Abby and the blood—but she'd been there, she'd saved her, she'd done the right thing. And the other? How quickly she'd become addicted to the pleasures of Coby, how prematurely she'd designed calendars on which he'd regularly appear. How childish she'd been.

He was different. She could still admit that. His forthright emotions, his ease in living with them, that was different. And pleasurable. And bothersome. And ultimately, destructive.

She had done the right thing despite her sense of dread all night long, despite the nagging sore spot inside that wouldn't stop aching.

She checked the tape. T&R still read 16. She wrote the number down again and circled it several times.

She reached for Patty Luboff's questionnaire. The woman's deadline was this week. She located her stopping point, Question 94. Nice number. "What, if any, life experience (as opposed to academic instructions, texts, etc.) best prepared you for your current position?"

She shoved the inane questionnaire away. Preparation? She'd had none. Not in a class, not outside one. None. She'd taken every step on her own, beginning at point zero, and every day, she started back there again.

What did they think, those scholars and spectators pondering her profile? Did they think there were guidelines, crib sheets telling you how to get on with it? How to be something new in an old world? Academic fools. Know-nothing idiots. Just because there were requirements and qualifications didn't mean there was preparation.

Her hand shook wildly but became sturdier when she put it on her ringing telephone.

"Suzannah? This is Carl Diamond."

"How's Phoenix?"

"I'm home. Walked in half an hour ago. I'm a little confused. I found a confirmation? It says you sold fifty Xerox a week ago Monday."

"Sure. I remember."

"But I asked you to *buy* fifty, not sell them."

"Oh, Carl, I'm sure you—" She flipped through her daybook, her heartbeat suddenly audible. And there it was in her angular, rapid script. "Buy fifty Xerox." How . . . ? "I—I stand corrected. I don't understand why this—but we'll take care of it."

"It's up three points. Would almost pay one of our plane fares."

"You'll have that—you'll have your shares at last Monday's price. And of course we'll make up for the fifty you already had that I sold. I—I hope you'll forgive me, give me another chance. I . . ."

"Of course. Sure we will."

She hung up feeling as if she'd spun around and around in her swivel chair until her insides were as blurred as her vision. How was it possible? How could she have made such a primitive, insane error?

She turned her chair around, facing the back of the board room and its street-level window. How? Carl had called . . . and then that snotty lawyer. About Katie MacPherson. That's how. That officious toady had rattled her brain while he tried to rake her over and use her.

She closed her eyes. "Oh, God," she said weakly. Her hands were shaking again.

She opened her eyes and met the glance of a man on the street, winking at her, wiggling a finger as if she were a specimen in a zoo. Tears welled up and she blinked furiously.

The asshole outside cocked his head, playing some safe game behind the glass shield.

"Fuck you," she growled. She lifted her hand, then her middle finger.

He opened his eyes wide, grimaced and laughed out loud.

"Fuck all of you!" she said, more loudly, and she stood, pushing her chair so violently it skidded off its plastic mat and banged into the divider.

Nick found her in the lobby. "What's wrong?" he asked.

She had hoped the impersonal lobby would return her to herself. Instead, she'd dissolved, become a blurred shadow in the stream of passers-by. And her hands, her arms, her shoulders, shook.

"Please, let me help you."

Nick's voice was kind and she couldn't stand it. It weakened her further, freed the tears to surge over the edges of her eyes.

"I made an error!"

"That's all? Suzannah, we all make them."

"I made an error! I made an error!!"

"Shhh—you don't want these strangers to know you're fallible, do you? Suzannah, you're worrying me. Talk about delusions of grandeur—I never mixed you up with God. You're allowed an error now and then, so calm down."

"You don't understand. He said buy Xerox and I heard him and I wrote it down and I sold it!"

He shook his head. "Mama," he said softly. "So what? It's only money. Oh, and maybe another trip to Masterman's office, and you'd better be calm for that. If he saw you like this, it'd feed his prejudices. You know how he'd be."

Nick lowered his voice an octave. "What's the matter, Ms. Barnes? Female problems? Is it—That Time of Month?"

"Don't be funny. I made an error!" She swiped at her nose with her hand.

"I think I'll have you committed if you don't snap out of this." He pulled a handkerchief out of his breast pocket. "Here, freshly ironed by Amelia." He wiped her eyes, then handed it to her.

She blew her nose loudly. Several times.

"Stocks are not to cry over," Nick said softly. "Save your tears for real things."

She blew again furiously. "You don't understand."

"Correct. But I don't think it's about stocks."

"I told you! I made an error!"

"Frankly, I can live with that better than with W.C. Fields in drag. Look at your schnoz! How can I proposition a soggy mess? Come back, Suzannah Barnes, wherever you are."

She sniffed and shook her head to clear it. "You don't understand, do you?"

"Nope. And I don't think you do, either. But when one of us does, let's share the news, okay? Meanwhile, go wash, breathe deeply and return to your post. And no more tears. Oh, for love and death and pain, okay. A scene now and then. But not for this. Absolutely not for this.''

"Better?" Nick asked when she returned to her desk.

She nodded, but she wasn't sure if numbness was better or worse.

She worked methodically. Only now and then did the word "error" wrap its talons around her cerebral cortex and squeeze.

At eleven forty-five she saw Michael Tully saunter in, squint and head her way. "Suzannah!" He had the false camaraderie of a brush salesman. "I've been trying to reach you!"

She stood instantly on her guard. "I'm sorry I didn't return your message, I've been—"

"No big thing. Let's talk now."

"I'm in a rush."

"It's important, Suzannah. I—"

"Not now. Honestly, it's impossible." She pulled on her cape.

"Then when?"

"I'd have to check my calendar."

He leaned closer. "About that stock business . . ."

"Oh, is that it? That you didn't buy from me after all? Don't sweat it, Tully. It doesn't matter." She picked up her briefcase and closed her center drawer.

"You'll be sorry," she thought she heard.

"What?" She stood very still.

"I didn't say anything." He put his leather gloves back on. "Except good-by."

He seemed to have relaxed completely. Even his perpetual squint was missing. The calm façade terrified her.

"Hey," she called as he walked away. "Maybe some other time? Maybe lunch, soon?"

"Check with my secretary," he said, and he left.

She felt nauseated, chilled to her center, shaking again with cold and mindless fear. "Error!" the hawk inside screamed, diving, beak first, for her brain. The room closed in, each telephone ring stabbed through her head.

"How long will you be out?" June asked.

Suzannah shook her head with confusion, clutching her cape tightly. "I don't think I . . . June, I don't feel well. I'm going home after I visit the hospital. Nick will cover."

* * *

She waited for the bus, feeling shorter, crumpled like the black-coated Social Security women who stood in lumpy stockings, their bowed heads covered with kerchiefs.

Across the street, a sweet-faced bald man waited at the light, hands at his sides. When he saw the green signal, he put one hand, palm up, above his head and rotated it as he walked. Around and around in flapping circles went his hand, fingers beating against the wind.

He reached the curb, whirred in her direction, then waited for the bus, resting his propellor-hand by his side. Suzannah stood as far away as possible, trying to avoid contamination by madness, however cherubic its face.

The man entered the bus first, his motor reactivated, his fingerblades spinning.

She controlled a strong urge to scream.

She despised hospitals. Hated the smell of disinfectant, loathed the look of institutional paint and shrank from the knowledge that somewhere down the corridor, death was guaranteed.

Abby's door swung open on its own.

"Mr. and Mrs. Newhouse." Suzannah extended her hand to the pale female half.

"Suzannah." Lucinda Newhouse acknowledged the greeting and quickly reclaimed her gloved hand. "We meant to ring you up, to express thanks for your quick thinking last evening."

Peter Newhouse also shook her hand. "Ummph," he said, meaning, she supposed, "thank you."

He didn't look like Cary Grant. Never could have. More Gary Cooper, but maybe Cary and Gary were confusing sound-alikes to a Korean.

Gary Cary frowned. "This is so—I don't understand this business."

"Why, we had the loveliest visit with Abigail this very Saturday!" Lucinda curled her mouth into a self-satisfied pout. "I even baked my special cookies." You see? she seemed to want to add. After I baked sugar cookies that spiteful ingrate slit her wrists.

"What do the doctors say?" Suzannah asked Mr. Newhouse.

"Oh, some psychiatrist suggested Abby was depressed. That's ridiculous. You know she's always joking. If anything, she's unduly frivolous, not serious enough about life. Depressed indeed!''

"What treatment do they suggest?"

He shrugged, dismissing their ideas. "This staff wants to blow an accident completely out of proportion."

"She—she seemed pretty serious last night." Suzannah's voice crumbled under her. "If you'd seen—"

He didn't want to see, didn't want to remember, didn't want to consider Suzannah's words. "Even the hospital said they were superficial cuts," he said.

"But the fact that she thought of it, that she tried it—"

"She had too much to drink and behaved irrationally. We all tipple overmuch now and then, act foolish."

Lucinda leaned towards Suzannah and spoke confidentially. "And it's so like her to do something dramatic. She always was a bit flashy."

Panic cut at Suzannah's veins. "She really needs your support."

"Support? Of course. It may be immodest to say it of myself, but I consider myself a generous man."

Lucinda's smile of agreement was exceedingly tight. With pursed mouth, she glanced at her husband and sighed. And then, miraculously, without a rip or fissure opening, Lucinda mutated, melted into Scarlett O'Hara, her face and demeanor completely changed. She swayed in place, and as she spoke, Suzannah almost smelled magnolias. "Suzannah," she said sweetly. "Oh, but we're selfish and inconsiderate, detaining you this way. Now you rush along. I'm sure you girls have all sorts of things to chat about!"

"I—" Suzannah silenced herself and entered Abby's room.

Abby looked weary, but smoothly combed and beautiful once more. "Welcome to the palace. Looky, a private room to keep the scandal secret." She touched Suzannah's arm as Suzannah bent to kiss her forehead. "I'm sorry. I never meant for anyone to see me that—"

"Don't bother with sorriness, please. But, if you can, try to explain. Because I love you and I want you to stay alive."

Abby put her hands on the sheet covering her, palms up. "There isn't any why. I didn't plan it. I couldn't stop the headaches, couldn't sleep. Movies were playing in my head, but backwards, or spliced oddly. They didn't make sense and they wouldn't stop. I wanted to sleep. I wanted the pictures and the noise to stop."

"But . . . the . . . the cuts?" Again Suzannah felt her throat seal against rising bile and nightmare images.

"Ah. The cuts." Abby looked at her bandaged wrists. "I guess that was crazy. Maybe the vodka. My mother—when I found her, my mother looked peaceful. I always wondered about that. Always wanted to know how it had been, what it was like. I didn't want her way out but still . . . I was numb, you know. I thought I could find out without hurting. Funny, isn't it?"

"What?"

"Well, I told you. For months, when a man touched me it stayed on the surface like a sponge bath. Suzannah, before, when I was with a man, that was the only time I knew my shape, felt my outline. I knew I existed then, and then it was gone, and I didn't. I was shut down, boarded up and abandoned. No sensation at all." She sighed heavily. "So why would a razor hurt? I couldn't feel anything else."

She exhaled, puffed like a winded runner. "The joke is, it hurt. I tried lots of places, always surprised because it still hurt and then I passed out. I'll never know why she looked so peaceful. So. That's the whole story. Dumb, huh? Oh, to have a reason, a final note, a message for the world." She tsked at the condition of her nail polish.

"How do you feel now?"

"Fine. They removed my drugs and put in their own. I don't feel intelligent, but the pictures have slowed down. I don't miss them. Some were pretty grotesque."

"Well what are we going to do about you?"

Abby rolled her eyes. "I think they'll release me into Daddy and Lucinda's care. Which means the booby hatch. God, Suzannah, if I could once see that man unbend, once have him look at me—why didn't he leave her in Seoul? Why didn't he let me pick garbage with the other round-eyes' kids? What did he do, drag her back to be ostracized? Why? *Noblesse oblige?*" She looked near tears, and Suzannah held her bandaged hand.

"Don't do this, Abby. Don't torture yourself."

"I thought, if I searched, I'd find something. A spark of life, of passion. I'd like—I'd like to believe in feelings. I wouldn't like to think he incurred a debt in Korea. That I'm payment, a long-term mortgage. I need to believe there could be something . . ."

She shuddered, ran long-nailed fingers through her hair. "I'm a fool. To be this old and still . . . but I am, and I do. I would like to believe . . ."

"Me, too."

"I know."

They were silent for a while, then Suzannah felt a rising rage. "Dammit! Damn them! They're fools, Abby. Your stinking aunts and you ice-cold grandparents and your father and anybody who ever made you feel worthless. I say they're all—"

"Shh!" Abby looked frightened. "You're crying. Hey!" She waited. "Oh, boy, I'm not sure I can handle . . . this isn't the time for . . . listen, Suzannah, don't cry." She waited again. "Are you crying for . . . ? Do you realize there's a song for this scene? Your own personal song?"

"What? My song? What do you know about my—"

"You aren't quick today, love." Abby lifted an imaginary banjo and strummed imaginary strings. " 'Oh, Suzannah, don't you cry for me . . .' "

Suzannah cried anyway, although she didn't know for whom she gulped or sniffled.

" 'Cause I'm gone to Alabama . . .' " Abby stopped singing and spoke softly. "Alabama. Gone to Alabama. Sounds fine. Can I borrow your lyrics?"

"What are you talking about?"

"I won't stay with Daddy. Will not be put in his care. I'll cut out. He won't mind at all."

"Alabama?"

"I don't know. Is it warm there?"

"You're moving away?" The idea was a fist in Suzannah's solar plexus, a punch that would leave a permanent hollow.

"Moving on. I should have long ago. Maybe I needed last night, needed to know I wanted to live. The thing is, I don't know how. I have to go where nobody knows me so I can start from scratch. When they ask me who I am, I'll have to answer. And I'll aim for the truth, whatever that is. My family taught me what I wasn't—wasn't one of them, wasn't like anybody else. And school did pretty much the same until boys said I was something else. Significant, finally. As big as my tits. Terrific.

"I want to start over without any of their answers. No more

snappy patter, no more cover-ups, no more hiding behind my mammaries and letting the men feed me lines. Because if I could be honest, if I could find out what I am and who, and like myself, maybe I'd find someone else who did, too. Like you have.''

"Me?"

"Coby. I know he brought me here and called my parents. He doesn't know me. He was with you, doing it for you. That's nice, Suze. Everything about him sounds nice, Suze.''

Suzannah checked to see if Abby was sarcastic, but nothing in her face indicated that.

"That's what I want. Something real. I want to feel something. I'd like to . . . to love. Why should that sound so obscene? But I . . . after you left my apartment Sunday, I realized I'd never felt that way. Never cared enough to worry about strategy, to try and figure how to make something work. Nothing— the kind of guys I picked, or picked me . . . nothing seemed worth it. Nothing special's ever happened to me. Not that way. I thought it was because nothing special was possible. Now I think . . . I think I wouldn't let it happen, wouldn't let it exist. But there *are* special people, aren't there? I'm real good coping with creeps, but what if a winner came my way? Like Coby. He must be different, he—''

"Cut this out or I'll have them cut off your supply of brain softeners. You know, you don't have to be with your folks or leave the city. You could stay with me until you knew what you wanted. I'd sign or whatever. Accept responsibility. Give you time and space to think this through.''

" 'Come live with me and be my love,' huh?''

And Suzannah saw the doorframe, his long hand on her shoulder, a face of graceful shadows and light and those words, the verbal Rorschach. She inhaled sharply. Why did it have to be this way? Split with survivors on one side, lovers on the other? Why was the world so fucking damned sad?

Abby didn't notice her changed expression. "Thanks, Suze, but it isn't a matter of state requirements. It's a matter of being on my own. Freud says sanity is the ability to love and work. Something like that, but I haven't managed either one. I want to tackle both.''

"I'll miss you.''

"Me, too. That's the bad part.''

"Well. I'd better go.'' Suzannah stood with difficulty. Her

legs were numb, her arms, leaden weights. "I don't want to exhaust you."

"I wish you could stay and share my life of leisure awhile longer. But oh, you career women." Abby smiled, but she seemed wan and small on the high bed.

Nothing sounded as lonely as a hospital room after visitors went home. Or home itself, this particular day.

"I could stay," Suzannah said softly. "To be honest, I'd like to. I could use a friend today."

"You know I could. Let's make it National Friends' Day. Now there's a hot idea. Why hasn't Hallmark rushed to start that holiday? Why don't we? What's the date?" She thought, then looked upset. "Damn! It's your birthday! Oh, Suze, I'm so sorry. Screwing up your very own day. Go. Go out and celebrate. You don't need a hospital room."

"If it's Tuesday, this must be where I lunch. With you, remember? Weekly friends' day. I'll go buy something to smuggle in. Besides, I'm avoiding heavy-duty celebrations. This is the biggie. The great divide."

"Does it bother you?"

"No. Maybe it's scary for women who set value by their skin tone and womb condition. But not for me."

"Suze, why aren't you celebrating with the music man?"

Suzannah shrugged. "Who knows?" she said softly. "Who really knows?"

Twenty

Suzannah delayed her class break until music resumed in the next room. Then she freed her students and sagged on her chair, bewildered, dislocated and in pain.

She was having trouble maneuvering this day without repeatedly stubbing her toes and tripping. Someone had rearranged the props; someone had changed the lighting, and nothing had its familiar shape. Wherever she moved, she stumbled.

Her visit with Abby had been pleasure in a dark outline, each minute marked as one of the last. There were no substitutes for their bond. One such friend per lifetime, and Abby was her allotment. Now, long distance, they'd have to shout even to hear each other.

She yearned to sleep, but that would have to wait, so she stood and went in pursuit of the only available stimulant, coffee.

She glanced through Coby's open door. His disciples, twenty women in heat, ogled him. They laughed excessively after he spoke.

Well, so what?

Attractive men attracted.

Coby would find his little woman.

She braced herself against the cinderblock wall, and then she moved on.

Luckily, tonight's lesson was untaxing. Back in the room, with half-full coffee cups on their desks, her women studied quarterly reports, statements, confirmations and research reports she'd explained and distributed earlier.

The minute hand slowly moved nearer ten. She rushed through her final instructions, her assignments and encouragements, interrupting herself to yawn three times.

She packed her materials while music still played behind the connecting wall. He'd graduated from those screams and shouts to something Middle European and folksy.

Then the music behind the wall stopped and Suzannah left quickly, rushing to the parking lot to avoid a post-mortem. She'd been through enough rehashes already. Whines, snarls, whispers, pleas. Each time a tiny divorce, a redistribution of blame, settlement of what little they'd shared. Each one an autopsy, whether they'd died of natural causes or been murdered.

There was a note under her windshield wiper. On its back she saw music. On its front, "Please Wait. C."

He was not the type for recriminations, accusations or dissections and they'd said everything, all in one lump, last night.

There was nothing left, no new ideas. Unless his old ideas had withered in the morning light. Unless he'd realized he'd been foolish.

She waited in her car, hugging her cape close, less fatigued than she'd been in her classroom.

When he knocked at her window, carrying a white box tied in gold ribbon, she welcomed him cautiously.

"How are you?" he asked. "Did you sleep at all?"

She shook her head.

"Neither did I." The blue shadows beneath his eyes looked like bruises. He cleared his throat and pushed up his glasses. "The hospital said Abby's recovering." He relapsed into silence, seemingly unable to think of another sentence.

She would ease his discomfort, give him his clue. "If Abby can do it, why can't we? Recover, I mean. I spent all night long thinking."

"And . . . ? You've come up with . . . ?"

The soft light in the car eased over his cheekbones, darkened the hollows beneath them and smudged the clean line of his jaw. She loved his face. "Nothing new. But I still can't see why our differences have to mean anything. They're only—"

"Don't." He turned and looked out the windshield again, and she watched his profile tighten. "They're large differences, Suzannah. Basic. They're who we are and where we want to be. Let's not dredge them up. We'd add pain and wind up in the same place."

Her throat suddenly felt scraped raw. "So. It's like that?"

"I think so. Maybe we're an error in timing. The right people, the wrong moment. I wish—well, I'm the fool who believes in . . ." He made a noise of irritation with himself. "Nothing."

She pressed her cheek against the cold glass window and closed her eyes. His voice was weighted and tired, his tempo unfamiliar as he continued to speak. She could hear nothing of what she would define as Coby. Cobyness. Not that rhythm or sound or warmth, none of that something he had, that heightening, that intensity, those colors that splashed their walking and talking, eating and loving, that music and shine he brushed over the ordinary. All that was gone. He'd emptied his voice and moved away.

She interrupted him. "Why did you ask me to wait?"

"Oh—I forgot why I was—your car was locked and I didn't want to leave this."

She opened her eyes. "It's—did you know it's my birthday?"

''No. Happy birthday. But this isn't a gift. It's more . . . reparations.''

And all her anger ripped out. ''Stop that! Stop harping on the goddamn war business! It's over, Coby. Didn't you just say that? There's no more war. There's no more anything between us so declare a goddamn amnesty, would you? Why reparations? Why?'' She could hear her voice traveling on tighter and tighter vocal cords.

''I didn't mean to—I'm sorry. I meant to bring it last night so, as Zeyde Morris would say, 'It shouldn't be a total loss.' ''

She accepted the white cardboard box, her anger replaced by a lassitude so complete, it threatened to become paralysis. ''Guess it's not my song,'' she said. ''I'll open it later, okay?''

''Whenever.''

They sat in awkward silence. ''Well, then,'' he said. ''Well, then. Happy birthday.''

She watched her lap, kept her eyes on the package instead of Coby. He left her car and her life and dissolved into the night.

''I don't understand,'' she told the air. ''I don't!'' she insisted loudly. She hit her fist on the steering wheel, then turned on the ignition. ''I don't understand!'' she screamed, her words ricocheting off the windshield.

''Nothing makes sense any more!''

She pounded accidentally on the horn, and the blare shook her into action. She began her trip home.

She threw her cape on the sofa and poured herself a snifter of Remy Martin's finest, lifting her glass in the quiet room. ''A toast to Suzannah,'' she said with vigor. ''Suzannah, now truly among the Elders.''

She ceremonially seated herself and lifted a small stack of mail.

Chris had remembered. Of course. She frowned at an envelope addressed to ''My Old Lady, Apt. 523.'' He hadn't chosen a prefabricated card, but had drawn a wizened gnome on a small square of yellow posterboard. A cartoon balloon said, ''Gnome is an island. Silver threads among the gold's okay by me.''

Clever Chris. She tossed the square onto the coffee table.

Her mother and sister remembered. Unnecessarily, because Friday they'd hold that annual semblance of celebration. False, obligatory festivities, so close to Valentine's Day the two merged into a heart-shaped Suzannah cake, a rosy Jell-o mold on white doilies, a bloodshot dinner.

And Suzannah, tensing as her mother asked, "Did your father remember?"

And Suzannah, lying. Assuring her that of course he had.

Once, when she turned twenty-three, he had. She never discerned why that particular year mattered, what obscure significance it held.

So. Saccharine sentiments from her mother, a funny card from Josie, two bills and a circular advertising a private coat sale.

And a letter on lined paper from one A D A M W. Awkward print thanking her for "the good book. I like the dumb king. Maybe he was blind."

Onto the table.

She gulped brandy. Breathing was slightly difficult.

She opened the white box. Inside, a Baccarat goblet. Her pattern. Coby had fine visual retention.

Inside the goblet, a tiny white plush unicorn. The creature there never had been, attached by its blue bow to a card. "With apologies from the Waldemar demolition team. Bear with us—there's more to follow. We're weaving floral cloths and shaping clay into candleholders. For now, a beginning. And love."

He's obviously written the note, put the unicorn in there before Monday night. The creature that never was, like the two of them, wouldn't be. Not going to be fed with the possibility of being this time.

He should have changed the note.

She rose, holding the new goblet in one hand, her snifter in the other. "It doesn't matter either way," she said as she approached her bedroom. She was thirty goddamn years old. Into a new classification, checker of one box lower when questionnaires demanded age groups. Grownup.

So it did not matter.

She put the Baccarat on her night table and pressed "playback," sitting on the edge of her bed and sipping brandy.

Potter first. Potter always, just as she'd feared. She yawned through hiccups and laments.

Nick next, but it was too late to wake his household and find out what he'd wanted.

Cards didn't matter. Remembering, any way, was all.

Aunt Isobel, sweetness itself. "Keep a finger open."

When Suzannah was small, she'd admired a filigreed ring Isobel wore. "It was my great-aunt's," Isobel had said. "She gave it to me when she was very old. I'll give it to you when you're grown up and I am very, very old."

Suzannah drank more brandy. So. All unaware, they'd passed the ritual markers. Suzannah thought of the time she'd remove the ring from her own gnarled fingers and transfer it to someone else, and she shuddered.

Then she listened again.

A magazine solicitor so optimistic, he left a number to call.

Then nothing but the empty whoosh of tape.

She ran it through again, shaking her head in disbelief.

"Not even this year?" She drained the snifter, then stood and paced her bedroom, returning to stare at the inert slab of machinery. "Not even a lousy phone message? Sorry I missed you? Not even that?"

She put her hand on the phone, then withdrew it. "Not even after I've told you it matters?"

She craned her head towards the ceiling. She wouldn't cry, dammit! Not for him. Not for any of them. Not ever. She was thirty fucking years old and had lived too long for this!

She stormed to the window and looked outside. The icy breath of the pane hurt her skin.

She'd told him. Year after year she'd broached the subject, said it mattered, made her feel sad to be so totally forgotten, so constantly. Year after year he looked confused, suggested she was somewhat tedious about formalities.

Formalities?

"My birth, my life . . . aren't they important? It's such a small—just once a year—you could lie, could pretend it mattered. This was a big one. A landmark. And I told you! What did I ever do to you? I try so hard, I buy you gifts and visit and I remember. I call you. But you . . . why?"

She could die and he'd never know. Not unless someone checked her records and phoned him, forced him into attention. She could die!

Jesus. She sounded like her mother.

This shouldn't matter. This was nothing. She knew it would happen, so why, time after time, did she skip home, flooded with hope, believing in fairy tales, convinced she'd find the garden where everything was right? Why? Why did she do that?

She didn't run the rest of her life on such infantile, groundless optimism. Why this exception?

But once a year? Surely once a year he could stir, remember that at some point it mattered. It must have, once upon a time. Couldn't he convince her of it?

She could die, burst her heart and lungs with the trying and it wouldn't matter, wouldn't reach. Her mouth had been taped shut as had his ears and his heart.

She had burned through, turned ashen and floated off.

For all it mattered, she was already dead.

It *didn't* matter! Who was he? Who was *anybody?* They were all—not for him, not for Chris, not for—those fuckers! When you're there, dancing out your heart, they applaud and smile at each other. Then they take a break, forget, find another act.

Why did it hurt so much?

She blinked furiously. She'd be damned, die before she let her juices run free as tears for them.

"Goddamn you—*you're* dead, do you hear? I'm sick of this! Sick of needing, of begging—I deserve more than that!"

She lifted her snifter, then realized it was empty and replaced it on the sill so violently a small edge broke. So what? What was crystal? Fancy glass? What the hell was anything?

"I never needed you," she hissed in the dark. "Not for a minute. I won't be her, sitting and mourning and waiting for a man to rescue me. Don't need you or your man games, the traps. Don't need your women, the fake marriage vows, the—"

She stormed into the living room and shredded Chris's card, picking at the slick coating of the posterboard, breaking her nail on its stiff back, retrieving dropped pieces and ripping them until she clawed at pulp, reducing it to fluff and filament.

"*None* of you with your wheedling and demands and fucking everything in sight, leaving me alone and wanting to erase me with kisses. Liars! *None of you!*"

Back in her bedroom, she glared at the answer machine, then ripped the wires from the wall. "I don't need you!" she screamed. "Don't need a goddamned thing!"

The Baccarat and the unicorn sat by her bed. "Not this! Not you! Not the lies, the ties, the traps. *Nothing!*"

She hurled the crystal against the wall, watched the winter enter, ice crystals form, fragment, swirl, shatter and hail onto the answer machine, the night table, her boots.

She threw herself on her bed and became smaller and smaller, a tiny sea animal burrowing furiously into the sand before the surf washed in and drowned her.

"I deserve more," she said, deep inside her pillow. "I deserve attention. I . . ."

Then the foam covered her nest and the walls shook loose to swallow her.

Twenty-one

She entered the office late the next day, logy from a thick, drugged sleep. She had had the dream again, the suffocating dream, the dance and the slip and the broken bones. The laughter and derision and worst of all, the drop into invisibility, the unbecoming and dissolution of Suzannah. It had taken three glasses of wine to still herself and fall back asleep.

Hung-over emotionally and physically, she nonetheless entered her office eagerly, craving the imposed rhythms of work, the busyness of business.

June, filling in a form and munching a carrot stick, had a sign on her desk. "Smile," it said. "Today is the first day of the rest of your life." Suzannah smiled.

"Thanks for covering for me yesterday," she whispered to Nick. He was on the phone, and he waved away her thanks.

She sipped black coffee and opened her *Wall Street Journal.* She had fifteen minutes before market opening. First she checked prices from the day before. T&R had closed at 16. Good enough.

She thumbed through the paper, reading quickly. Until a headline so startled her, she splashed coffee over it. Through the stained, nearly transparent newsprint, she read again:

TRADING SUSPENDED IN LAND STOCK

Philadelphia: The New York Stock Exchange announced

suspension of trading in Tydings and Roy Development, a Philadelphia-based land development company specializing in large tract holdings.

Chairman Marshall Roy requested the suspension at 12:30 Tuesday afternoon, pending an announcement concerning rumored manipulation of company shares.

Roy, speaking at market closing Tuesday, said there was no factual basis to the rumored acquisition of his firm by a chemical conglomerate. The origin of the rumors is being investigated by the Securities and Exchange Commission. There is speculation that misinformation, possibly disseminated deliberately, accounts for the company's recent and dramatic climb.

Trading is expected to resume shortly.

Suzannah reread the damp newspaper twice, mouthing the words like an illiterate. But they read the same way. They said the same thing.

Nick hung up his phone. "Feeling any better? You really had me worried yesterday."

"What does this mean? Tydings and Roy. What the hell is—"

"They suspended it. I saw it on the tape. Called your house and left a message. Guess it's that take-over you talked about." He lifted his phone again.

"The—what are you talking about? Didn't you read the paper? Didn't you see his announcement at market-closing?"

"No, I—"

"How can you say 'take-over'?"

He put down his receiver. "I left early yesterday. Amelia's mother had a heart attack.

"They say the stock was manipulated! That it's all a deliberate *lie!*"

"My mother-in-law is doing well, thank you. How is your friend?"

"My—what? He's no—who?"

"Your *friend* in the hospital."

"I—Nick, I'm in trouble. I—you knew where I was going. You should have called the hospital!"

"For Christ's sake! Suzannah, listen to yourself. Lately, you're—I don't know what! Sobbing about errors, hysterical over suspended trading. What the hell's happening to you?"

She turned away with sudden fear. How much had she told him? What had she spelled out? If the SEC investigation touched on her—how much would Nick remember and choose to tell?

She looked at the news story again. Perhaps there was something she'd missed. Something reassuring.

". . . pending an announcement concerning rumored . . ."

Had Tully become suspicious of the rumors? Was that why he'd called and visited? To try to tell her?

". . . manipulation of company shares."

And she realized with disgust for her bumpkin-like innocence, she realized who'd been the rumor-monger, the manipulator of shares and of Suzannah.

She'd kill him! The son of a bitch had deliberately set her up! "Soul mate," he'd called her, knowing what she'd do with his "secret." She dialed his number in a fury.

He was away from his phone. She pondered that. He was at his office, not in hiding. Did that mean he was innocent? Or guilty as hell, but avoiding the shadow of suspicion? Did anything mean anything?

"Do you honestly think it's nothing?" she asked Nick.

He shrugged and remained engrossed in his own concerns.

Screw him. Ignore him. Find something to do. Expectation was always worse than reality.

But reality proved sufficient. T&R resumed trading. At ten points lower than it had closed. At six. She shivered. Please, God, push it up again or I'm screwed.

The stock fell another point. Five.

FIVE. Suzannah furiously recalculated her worth. She had put up eight thousand dollars of her own savings, borrowed thirty thousand from the bank, doubled the sum with a further thirty-eight thousand through margin from Sherwood Hastings. Sixty-eight thousand borrowed—and hadn't she just worked this out a few days ago when she *knew* she was on the verge of a fat six-figure profit? Sixty-eight thousand borrowed and now, at five, her shares were worth only thirty-five thousand.

She broke into a cold sweat. She was going to be sick.

No. There had to be . . . there had to . . . a way . . . there had to be, given time, given thought, there had—

There was, instead, a margin call. Notice that she owed the firm more than her shares were now worth. She had no way to cover the balance. Dully, she agreed to sell.

Dully, she stared at the tape. A mouse awaiting the boa constrictor's next move.

And dully, she saw T&R fall another point. Her shares sold at four. Twenty-eight thousand dollars. God. Oh, God. She still owed forty thousand dollars!

She moaned. "Nick?"

"Too busy now. Sorry." His voice was crisp and not the least bit sorry.

Well. So. Where had everyone gone? Even her? Where was the Monday lady? The almost Somebody awaiting that fat profit? Buying expensive toys, wearing jewels and gilt robes? Stripped naked Wednesday. The profit, the wealth, only make-believe after all. The Empress' New Clothes would come from the thrift shop.

Oh, God.

Her skin remained clammy, tiny prickles rising to wave the fine hairs on her arms. She shivered and concentrated on breathing. In, raggedy half-gasp. Whoosh, out. In, with difficulty. In, more. Halt—lungs stuck. In, dammit. Stop the spasm now or the brain would also die.

She trembled when her phone rang, touched the receiver tentatively. If she lifted it and spoke, she'd forget to breathe.

But that was her job, that phone. That was *her*.

"Elaine Weiner here," the voice snapped. "Suzannah, much to my surprise and regret, I'm forced to bring suit against you. Advocating that land company was more than ill-considered. It was unprofessional and, most important, costly to me. In the light of today's news story, considering how you rushed me into it without the slightest caution—"

"I wish . . . you'd . . . reconsider." Suzannah sounded near death. "Not all"—she gasped—"stocks can"—sharp gulp—"work-Icouldnot—"

"It's your business to know something, isn't it?"

"Please. I . . ." Suzannah checked herself. She was near tears and that wouldn't do. Would not do at all.

Elaine Weiner's voice softened a bit. "I'm ashamed to say so, but I may have helped the fiasco. I bought additional T&R through my former broker—a sop, a final bone for him. And he went and told other clients, and—"

"I'm not—you can't blame—"

"I know. Nonetheless, I intend to recoup my losses. I called as a courtesy. My lawyer will contact your manager."

It would never end. Suzannah had tripped over a snare and would fall forever into the abyss.

A lawsuit. A personal lawsuit.

Others, perhaps.

A forty-thousand-dollar debt.

A lawsuit.

Laws. Laws. Loss. Lost.

Lost job. Fired.

Lost everything in the crash. Lost income, lost position, lost title, lost place, lost Suzannah.

Betrayed. All around. Complete. Coby, sniping and forcing her out of happiness. Abby, somehow. Tully for sure. And Elaine Weiner. God—she had worshipped that woman!

Her face solidified into a bitter mask, a door slammed against the world. Unconsciously, she rocked in her swivel chair, blind to the room, deaf to its sounds.

Betrayed.

Not fair! For an honest mistake, for trying too hard!

Not at all fair!

Fair? When was fair a heavy thing with you, Suzannah?

Fair is foul and foul is fair hovering on . . .

Take-away. Endless take-aways.

The man, the pleasure.

The friend.

The money.

The job.

THE JOB!

Suzannah! Suzannah to dwindle, becoming nothing? Nobody? Trashed and abandoned?

"Nick, I have to leave." She grabbed her briefcase without explanation. "June, I have to leave," she said again. She glanced over at Masterman's closed office door, at Didi, filing her nails outside it.

"I have to leave," she repeated.

Behind that office door, Masterman might be listening to Weiner's lawyer. Behind that office door, Masterman might be planning to eradicate the bothersome Suzannah, to clean up this mess with walking papers.

"No!" she whispered, hurrying outside, fighting the winter

wind. "No!" she said to verify her existence with sound. "No." She wouldn't be reduced to shadow and memory.

To be in debt, poor and jobless?

To be nothing? Nobody. A file clerk, an executive trainee. Euphemism for nothing. Making payments on her debt, making spaghetti and Spam? Making ends meet? Making do?

Never!

Oh, but he'd warned her and he'd remember. "Unwise, Suzannah. No lawsuits wanted," he'd said, smacking her hand, prying her fingers from the pie.

"I am Suzannah Miller Barnes. I will be somebody."

A woman gaped, stepped aside, but Suzannah didn't care.

"Suzannah Miller Barnes," she repeated, stumbling.

"Stay near me," the woman told her child. "She's crazy."

Who will want me? A second-rate house. A throw-away, a stop-off. Second-rate clients with second-rate dreams.

"And I am bright and capable."

Nothing of her own, ever. No base on which to build a thing.

"Crazy!" the woman hissed as she passed her.

"I am, I will be, I can be—"

Reduced to nothing, skeletal Suzannah, tripping over chipped cement. A corpse refusing to lie down.

Once inside her apartment she fought the urge to capitulate, bypass reality with drugs or drink.

She would figure it out. She reached for a yellow tablet and her pen. She'd make order. Lists. Numbers.

1) Stock sold for $28,000. Sherwood took that. Owe Sherwood $10,000 more.

2) Owe bank $30,000.

She carried the pad to the kitchen and opened the refrigerator. Muttering, she calculated repayments. She opened a blue-lidded plastic container and ate the cold cauliflower it held. It was possible. Start with the Sherwood debt. Ten thousand wasn't overwhelming, opening a box of Special K and eating dry fistfuls while writing. On her salary, it could be—oh, Jesus! What salary? What if, what about when she lost even that?

Oh, and she *would*. That was Masterman's method of handling annoyances.

She washed down the Special K with orange juice. The job was separate, its own problem. Make it a different entry. Don't muddle them. Suzannah opened the freezer, poured fudge sauce into a container of rocky road and spooned the combination into her mouth.

It was so cold in the apartment. Her bones ground against each other, their cartilage and muscles, springs and cushions, missing.

Forty thousand. But only ten right away. She could string out the bank. So separate the two.

She could sell something. The Aubusson. There was that.

Her midriff flashed and ripped. It was *her* Aubusson, the first post-divorce purchase. The hallmark of her independent success. It was hers. HERS.

So was the debt.

Then another bank, another source. Borrow from Peter to pay . . . she pushed circular pretzels into her mouth and concentrated on their crunch and salt. Borrow and repay Sherwood.

But oh the job. The job. The Job!

Think about the money. Settle the money first.

She spread sweet butter on a slice of bread. There was still the thirty, the goddamned inflated interest charges as well, month after month. Impossible. If she had no job, who would lend her money?

Oh, the humiliation of walking the streets, searching for someone to want her. With not a shred of support for her claims of significance.

Selling herself at five million times earnings.

She pulled the tab on a soda and washed down the bread, gulping from the open can, shaking her head.

No book value, she.

The. Money. The money. Themoneythemoneythemoney.

She lit a cigarette and dialed Tully's office. Again she was told he was "unavailable."

She puffed on her cigarette, reaching into a tall glass canister for jelly beans which she ate by the fistful.

Damn him. Damn him for what he did to her. For what reason?

Then she shivered, remembering that snowy Tuesday dawn and wondering whether her abrupt dismissal had prompted this. Knowing, then, that it had. That he'd planned it in the shower, come out and set her up. And she'd fallen for every bit of it. She wondered how many people, like herself, had been victimized.

"I didn't deserve this!" she shouted, pounding on the counter. "Not this!" She dialed his number again, again heard his secretary, who sounded peeved, say that Tully was unavailable. "Tell the bastard I *know!*" Suzannah shouted before she slammed the phone down.

She was shaking. The jelly-bean level fell until sugar bubbled in her blood and nauseated her. She swayed against the counter top, weak, impotent and defeated.

So what if she "knew"? She was Tully's co-conspirator, which *he* knew. As greedy, as guilty as he was, should anyone find out.

She was certain Tully had saved himself, had bailed out with his bundle earlier. She'd been left to drown. Lost. Used. Betrayed. Insulted. Abandoned.

And broke.

Themoneythemoneythemoneythemon

Killing her. All of them. Draining her until she cracked and dried up.

Money. Money. Money.

And then she had it. Chris. Money. Chris and money, twins from birth. A two-for-one special. A package deal. So obvious she'd missed it until now.

And what was the harm? There wasn't time for ethical debate. This was a matter of survival.

The money! She dialed.

Whore.

Who said that? Who had the right?

"Chris?" she said when he lifted his phone. "I need you."

"Didn't I say I was your fate?" He was still bronzed and his white teeth gleamed when he smiled.

"You did. And about my fate in general . . ." She presented her dilemma with the light touch of an artist, framing it in a way he understood and accepted. "I've made lots of mistakes, been wrong about so much. Some things cost me cash, others . . ." She let the suggestion float over to him on the afternoon air.

They sipped wine and he nodded and smiled with contentment. He was the man who'd known the future, been correct in his predictions and self-esteem because what else did her summons confirm? He was irreplaceable, this Christopher Barnes. Who else was such a scholar of pleasure? Who else so generous in its distribution? Didn't he know where to go, what to say, what to do and how and when to do it? Wasn't his timing perfect, his technique worth an Oscar? Weren't special effects his specialty?

Was he not the lover the women of the world craved and couldn't find and wasn't Suzannah the lucky winner?

And now, with Suzannah half clothed, then nude on the sofa, as he cupped and stroked, lips and fingers, tongue and hand, as he perfectly attended each part of her body, wasn't it therefore her fault, something missing in her that made it sawdust and ash, a meaningless bump with a stranger?

It certainly wasn't Chris's fault that she wished he'd speed his performance, be less the virtuoso and write her a check for forty thousand dollars. It wasn't his problem if she felt like a butcher's chart, erotic zones marked with broken black lines. It wasn't his problem or fault and she'd best learn to love it because it was a large debt she'd have to repay.

But what was wrong with her? Had Abby's numbness become epidemic? He was doing it right, wasn't he? But it was nothing like the way it was with—she stopped herself. That file was sealed.

He tried to hard. He remembered. There, that place on her side where a touch, a light run across buried wires sent sparks. Only . . . they fizzled, sputtered and died.

This was different. This was moves, parts, pieces and physiology. That had been something more. Something outmoded and wonderful. Something happening with, between. But this . . . this was not to think about. This was now. This was afterwards. Her tomorrow. Her choice.

She arched her back and felt Chris enter and with each stroke, each in and out and in and out he stitched her close and it wasn't his fault she felt nothing but distant pressure.

Her body accepted guilt and quickly accommodated him. In and out, tailoring her to him.

He speeded his stitches and she, too, performed, moaning as he shuddered, smiling slightly afterwards, sighing softly.

"You have a fine way of welcoming someone back," he said.

She felt pity, then a sharp sense of superiority. Men were pathetic. Primitive, uncomplicated, oblivious.

But then she was overwhelmed by sorrow. For joining with someone so far away. For his not knowing or wondering. For her disguise, her borrowed body.

"About the money," Chris said, picking up his clothing. "Stop by the office any time. I'll have a check waiting."

He left the room and she let her tears flow, resenting them mightily.

Why should she feel so soiled? He hadn't meant to trigger this response. He was gracious and giving in his fashion. Gallant. Generous. The Prince of Nothing, yes, but where was the big something? There were only irrational expectations, large and imaginary white chargers and only in poems were possibilities infinite.

Chris was okay. He'd never trouble her soul or stretch her to the breaking point.

He reappeared, washed, glowing and fit. "I have to run now," he said. "I'm keeping a client waiting."

There had been years when a suddenly sprung prior appointment infuriated Suzannah. Years when she snapped and bristled because Chris sculpted their time, knew its contours and kept them his secret. As he had just done again.

The difference was, she no longer cared.

He bowed as he left to sell real estate. "A delight, ma'am. Rest assured, I shall be in touch."

It didn't matter when. Not like it once had. Whenever was fine. Whenever. And in between, whoever.

They were equals now. Both only mildly interested. A balanced, bearable match.

She stood up carefully. The sofa was stained with his semen, their juices.

She gagged.

Did so again in the bathroom, gagging and soaping, washing and gagging.

And then, heaving. Way down, down near where he's pushed and insisted they were related. Down in the numb zone, suddenly alive with revulsion and loathing. An earthquake. A volcanic belch, the reshaping of the globe. She bent over the toilet, letting loose the lava of her life. Jelly beans and bread and butter, fudge sauce and Chris, indifference and hope, Coby and forbidden mourning, Tully, decisions made, corners turned, bad judgments, missed cues, humiliation and cold, Abby's blood, night sweats and terrors, cold childhood, lukewarm life, stumbles and wantings and

She clutched her stomach because of the pain, something fierce dying, something horrible clawing up, crawling through intestines, slithering through heart, something fearful and freezing icing her throat, something stinking and foul, aborted tissue and decayed hopes, something exploding into the toilet over and over again.

She sat back in a hollow in space and waited inside, waited and rocked until she crawled out. Light, with none of the weights she had carried. Newshaped, newformed, newborn. And empty.

She hugged her fragile shell, wondering at her escape from gravity. If she let go of herself, she'd pull away from earth, so weightless was she, so filled with airy space. But she knew, if she held on, she'd fill again, this time with strength, with solid reinforcement. Not with dead issues, daydreams and nostalgia this time. She'd walked into the trap, lowered her defenses and let them enter her system to fester and decay. Never, never again, and praise be for her survival and narrow escape.

She washed and brushed and rinsed and then went into the kitchen. With lips set tight, she crossed out problem one. Money. "No problem," Chris, her fate, had said.

Problem two remained but now, cemented back into shape, she was stronger than it was and she could see its logical solution. Let Elaine Weiner sue, but let her sue the company, not Suzannah.

There was all the difference in the world. The world, the one she must have, *was* the difference.

As for the convincing of Masterman, hadn't she played Sweet Sue and stopped selling the moment he mentioned it? Didn't such obedience earn certain courtesies?

She wouldn't wait for his summons. She'd confront him herself, this day. She was strong. She'd roll over him, flatten his objections, convince him their fortunes were intertwined.

She applied makeup as carefully as a screen star. The ingenue, not a Joan Crawford career-woman type with football shoulders and visible claws. Nothing but veiled edges, soft shadows, pale pinks, gentle blushes, sweet lips.

She chose a soft knit that hugged enough and no more, and composed her line of attack.

The dimming sky surprised her out of her meditations. Half-past four. More than time to move on.

The street was damp and menacing, the sidewalks unshadowed steel. It would snow again shortly, compounding the dangers, the leftover hazards, the slicks of ice patches, solidified drifts and hard channels.

Storm warnings had obviously reached her office. The work force evacuated quickly, trying to outrun snow-stalled expressways and umbrella gorings in subway stampedes.

Masterman's door was closed and Didi away from her desk. Suzannah waited until only those with official hours and inconsiderate superiors remained at their posts.

And then she could wait no longer. Didi, the guardian of the gates, was still absent. Perhaps Masterman hadn't wanted his top-heavy assistant to tumble face-down into a drift and had sent her home early. In any case, Suzannah needed to act now, while the wondrous strength was in her.

She knocked once and opened his door.

Stewart Masterman's eyes were regrettably small and pig-like. But they grew round and large when she entered. His mouth formed a silent "O."

Suzannah audible echoed it. She couldn't see if Didi's mouth mimed theirs, but she suspected it did. She couldn't see it because Didi's back was to her, her head buried somewhere in Masterman's open zipper.

Stewart Masterman gaped at the door. Suzannah closed it, then realized she most certainly should leave.

Didi sensed her employer's waning enthusiasm. She stopped her rhythmic head movements and turned. Then she, too, became mesmerized by the doorknob. Her eyes reeled from it to Suzannah's hand, up Suzannah's arm then down again. She fixated on the little button that should, by all rights, have locked the room tight. She crouched, slack-jawed.

Masterman swiveled his chair so that his privates were away from his staff. He faced the console behind his desk and the portrait of his large and unattractive family.

Suzannah watched a tremor run through Didi. Her cheek quivered, her neck pulsed, her chest heaved and her arm shook.

The spasm ended on her ring finger, grounded by the plain gold band.

Then, flushed like spotty spoiled fruit, Didi left.

I should leave, too, Suzannah thought. Tactless to stay. But we have to talk about my job.

My job?

Would New York retain the sorry manager now recuperating

from fellatio interruptus? Wasn't there official policy concerning even more discreetly handled employee interminglings? Hadn't Masterman told her so? Would she now tell New York? Would Masterman think she would?

He swiveled back and seemed surprised Suzannah was still in his office.

She felt as uncomfortable as he appeared. Should she back out and pretend it never happened?

Hell no! This was funny! Men! Those silly primates, those early experiments.

But this particular man was her boss. Manager. Ruler.

This particular man was intrinsic to her fate.

As she now was to his.

Masterman pushed his chair in so his offending parts were tucked beneath his desk. He waited.

"I think we should discuss a lawsuit," she said.

He appeared ready to faint.

"Against me."

Yes, the correct approach was to ignore the obvious. Everyone knew what everyone saw what everyone did. It, his cock, job, shame, wife, secretary's husband, power, prestige, credentials—everything was a stronger weapon if a silencer was kept upon it.

"Yes." His voice cracked while traversing this one-syllable word. Without his customary booming, he continued. "I . . . know about the suit."

"Then you *must* agree she's overreacting. We're *all* fallible, aren't we? A person shouldn't be thrown into jeopardy because of a single slip, should he?"

"He?"

"Grammatically speaking. He, she, whatever."

"Hrrmmm. Yes. Well, no. I . . . you are suggesting . . . ?"

"That the office be named in the suit. That I be protected. I mean there's a great deal involved here."

His eyes were glazed, rabbity.

She enunciated carefully. "Mr. Masterman, do you realize that one hysterical woman can destroy an entire career?"

He seemed desperately aware of that. "Everyone makes mistakes," he mumbled. "I'm sure we, that is, we're only human, aren't we? And our legal department could, certainly . . . that is if . . . ?'' He waited, watching her, checking whether they had a deal.

"Of *course!* Thank you! I'll never forget this. *Never!*" She wasn't feigning her enthusiasm; she wasn't lying about that promise.

Messages received and accepted. Truce.

Survival!

Didi's chair was empty. She and the entire remaining cast of players had fled. Suzannah stood among fifty brown desks, fifty beige blotters, fifty charcoal chairs, the only warm color under the cold fluorescents.

She'd saved her neck. Amazing. With no help from Sir Launcelot, the Royal Canadian Mounties, the Lone Ranger or Superman. Suzannah to her own rescue. Oh, with some help from precision timing, lust and flabby marriage vows.

She let her laughter bubble and flow over the rows of desks. "Thanks," she said, saluting the heavens, now hiding above acoustical tiles. Up there, the mothergod held her quivering belly, chortling at how biology became Suzannah's slingshot against Goliath.

It was over. By a funny route, over hurdles and around detours. Luck helped, but even with a less priapic office manager, Suzannah would have triumphed, and she knew it. Masterman's afternoon delight merely saved time and energy.

If you wanted things enough, life delivered them. Anything. Suzannah's want was potent, and she wanted it all. Everything. And soon. Not for her the far horizon, promises for the distant future, but now, or in the near future.

Her thoughts triggered odd echoes until she remembered the first night with Coby and the ambivalent fortune cookies. Something about futures . . . she shuffled through her wallet until she found the slip of paper.

"The near future may bring everything you have always wanted. Then again, it may not."

Well, it had.

Not instant riches as hoped for, but not destruction either. She had her job, her future, everything she always wanted.

Didn't she?

She thought again of Masterman, of how he'd be more apt now to give her generous shares of new offerings, help her in the ways managers could, and she laughed out loud. She had everything she always wanted and she'd soon have more. She laughed again.

And choked off the laugh, suddenly hearing madwomen laughing, alone, in empty rooms.

She sat down at her desk and stared at windows the night turned into mirrors.

Why did she feel so curiously flat? Why wasn't having everything more fun? Wasn't "fun" part of one's basic "everything"?

She glanced towards Nick's desk, a joke shaping on her lips. But office hours were over, his desk was locked and she remembered his face, as closed to her as his desk now was.

"What's happening to you?" he'd asked with contempt.

She shook her head. What *was* happening—now? What defeatist trip was she embarking upon?

She would celebrate instead, crack open champagne, toast her salvation and reaffirm her future. She would go home to her lovely, her uncluttered apartment where none of the mess and confusion of the past few weeks were visible.

She heard her words—mess and confusion and uncluttered—and she blinked. She was sounding a great deal like . . .

Screw it. She refused to think about that. Instead, back to celebration plans. Champagne, soft music, the apartment safe against tonight's storm.

And she'd toast herself.

And hear her voice bounce off the wall and echo. Then she'd kiss herself good night.

She shivered.

No more of this! For God's sake! She shook her head. She sounded like—truth was, a person made her own fun and didn't sit around wallowing in self-pity. Didn't become sedentary, inactive. Didn't stare at one's reflection and sniffle like—so help me just like—

Her phone rang. Somebody. She answered it eagerly.

"Mother!" she said, her surprise honest. "I can't believe it. I was just thinking of you."

Her mother didn't particularly care. "I wanted to know . . . well, Josie said I should ask . . ." Nita Miller sighed, already depressed about something yet unsaid.

Suzannah began an apology even though she hadn't a clue as to her crime.

"Josie thought, about your birthday dinner, she thought you

might want to bring that . . . musician." She sighed again, loudly, exhausted at the thought of more guests although Josie did all the work. "Oh," she forced herself to add, "and his child. Josie said I should ask about both of them."

Well, well. It was the evil daughter's chance to shine, to do her single good deed. "Thanks for asking," Suzannah said, "but there's no need."

"I want to do what's right even if my place is small and these dizzy spells are—"

"Mom, there's no need. I'm not seeing him any more."

"You're *not*? That's *wonderful*!"

Suzannah could not remember ever hearing her mother's voice that animated when it was discussing her. "Mom?" she said. "Point of interest. You never met him, so why is his departure such a joy?"

"Oh, you know why. Why say that? You know why or you'd still be seeing him. He's not our kind, Suzannah. So much wrong with him. No future there. A musician—what kind of provider would a musician be?"

"I don't need a provider, Mother."

"Anyway, what kind of grown man makes music his work? And they're all odd, anyway."

"Grown men?"

She heard her mother gasp with annoyance. "Why are you picking on me? I'm *agreeing* with you! And then there's the child. Who *needs* that? Believe me, Suzannah, children are no picnic."

"I believe you." The message had been etched on Suzannah's frontal lobes. For the first time, she pondered its source and substance.

"And someone else's child—"

"Sloppy seconds, right, Mom?"

"You said it."

"No."

"No?"

"I meant you'd say it, wouldn't you?"

"Suzannah, I know you. You're self-centered. What kind of mother, let alone stepmother, would you make? You'd be *terrible*."

"I would not! I'd be . . . I'd be . . . ." She shook her head, unable to see herself as a mother. She couldn't be a mother. No.

Why? She couldn't take care of, raise a child, because . . . because *she* was the child. No. Stupid thing to have entered her mind. How a child? Forever?

"You would never sacrifice your life the way I did."

"Mother, cut it out. My break with him had nothing to do with money or children." But she was left with the question of what it *had* had to do with. Reality, as she'd insisted? Being self-centered, as her mother said? Or angry and fearful, as Coby had said?

"Will you ever understand what I went through with the two of you? What it did to my health? Do you know how it is to be all alone, doing your best, but all, all alone?"

Suzannah glanced around the enormous board room, at the dark night shadows, and she said nothing.

"You don't understand anything about me, about the way a man can hurt you, about being stranded forever! Being alone is like being dead!"

But you *chose* isolation. You sought it as your grail. You shunned life and worshiped two-dimensional simulations on a flickering screen. You let no one—not even your daughters—close. You wanted isolation and you got what you wanted. Everything you always wanted.

Suzannah's stomach fluttered and she looked around again only to find Nick's desk and new shadows. She considered the evening ahead, her solitary celebration.

She would celebrate survival.

Economic survival, the sort her mother understood. The sort her mother had probably also celebrated. Also alone. Her route had been different—courtrooms and lawyers and bleeding him dry for deserting her, but . . .

"You'll never understand me," her mother whined.

"I'm beginning to," Suzannah whispered. Scenes from her childhood reran in her head but with a changed camera angle. Not every shot was from Suzannah's viewpoint this time. The flutters in her stomach increased, flew up and became words.

"Mom, we're both scared, aren't we? We become nuts and focus on what's less scary. I work here, you work there, but I *understand.*"

"I don't know what you're saying. The only thing I do know is that you love hurting my feelings."

"I—" Suzannah softened her voice because now she was sure

she did understand. Just a bit, just a first glimpse, but a beginning all the same. Her stomach calmed, she became lightheaded. "I don't want to hurt you. Truly. I'm sorry."

Her mother sniffed. "You're never nice to me. Never do a thing to please me."

Suzannah felt anger, then she relaxed. There was no point. And today, she could hand her mother a bauble. "I saw Chris today. Not . . . not really for business." It wasn't pure truth, not complete truth, but it was the best she could offer, and it would please her mother.

"Ah," Nita said. "Well, so things have changed."

"Yes." Indeed. Most changed of all, Suzannah. Back to Chris, or was that change at all? She was, as he'd predicted, "ready" for him. Gamy, like birds English hunters would hang until they decayed and were considered delectable.

She was changed. Diminished. Ready to live in small dwellings, flimflam constructions that looked great if you didn't lean on them. Chris.

Ready to feign affection, sham excitement, lie down and bed a man because he'd pay her debts? Oh, God, she couldn't have, no matter how distraught—she wouldn't let her mind label the act, she—

"I am so glad," her mother said. "I want the best for you."

I want the best for me, too. Everything I always wanted was the best. Which I have, which the near future brought, or will. Which may be brand-name guaranteed best and still—oh, God . . .

"There are worse fates than a handsome, good provider. Search your heart. See if you can't forgive him. I know he roamed, but men will be men and nobody ever said it was easy. Profit by my mistakes. I acted in haste. I wouldn't bend. I'm ashamed to admit it, but I've learned, after it was too late. Believe me, the path of true love never did run straight."

More and more often, her mother sounded like Mary Worth.

"Remember," Nita continued, her borrowed words giving her a volubility she usually lacked. "Remember, a good man's hard to find. Believe me, I've wondered where my stubbornness got me. At the time I thought I was right, but . . ."

She continued speaking, but Suzannah heard only herself. "Like mother, like daughter," she heard. "God help me."

But it wasn't a curse at the cradle. It wasn't a terminal affliction. It wasn't inevitable. It wasn't inescapable.

For a moment, she rose above her life, hovered under the acoustical tiles and had an aerial view of her terrain.

She'd thought herself a trail blazer. She'd thought herself a pioneer, but now she saw tidy patterns and well-worn paths. She heard the voice buzzing over the telephone giving directions for familiar destinations, even if Suzannah renamed them.

She didn't want that map any more.

Then she goddamn well didn't have to keep it. There'd been no witches at her christening. The only gifts she received at birth were choice and chance.

Chance. Once or twice a lifetime—chance in disguise. Something small on the sidewalk. Something subtly dangerous, designed for the brave.

A news item on the last page, a slip of the tongue at dawn. A stock deal that doesn't work. A person who could. The one person who could.

Chris/Daddy didn't have to be her fate. She didn't have to insist on being ignored, insulted so she could keep on feeling sorry for herself. She could move quickly, jump to new ground.

She had a profession. She didn't need the world's oldest to pay off losses. She had something less desperate to sell than herself. She still had $30,000 equity left in the building she and Chris owned. Why hadn't she thought of it earlier? Why would it have been unthinkable? Now she could let go of it, sell him her share and repay most of the debt that way. Let go and be free. And pay the remainder to the bank the hard way. The right way.

It might take longer to have an enormous bank account, the way she was moving. So she'd just have to live longer, that's all.

She felt lighter, as if the building, the debt, the old maps and guidelines had been removed from her back.

"Mom," she said, "listen. I'm going to invite him for Friday."

"Chris? What a wonderful—"

"No. Coby. Coby and Adam."

"What? A minute ago you said—"

"*Ten* minutes ago. I was a lot younger. Things change."

"I'll never understand you, Suzannah."

"But you do. That's just it. You do. Thanks, Mom," she said earnestly. "You'll never know how much you helped me."

She dialed his number with rising excitement, whistling

tunelessly. What luck to have a ready-made party as a face-saver. Age as alibi. We grow too soon old and too late smart, right?

After twenty-seven unanswered rings, her enthusiasm and confidence were gone.

It had been a stupid impulse. She would have seemed a mindless fool. After all, everything she'd told him was still true. She'd invented no new solutions, so why do a turnabout?

But all the same, where was that man with a child on a stormy Wednesday night?

Wednesday.

Coby had mentioned Wednesdays. He was always downtown, he'd said. Adam had a doctor's appointment.

Where?

She hadn't asked who the doctor was, where precisely he was located. Hadn't even asked why a weekly appointment, although now she knew it was therapy.

But she hadn't wanted news of Adam or childhood pain, of loss and truth, parents' disappearances and lingering sorrows. She had her own version, after all, and she wouldn't easily share center stage. Oh, time to grow, Suzannah, she thought with revulsion. Time enough by now.

In her teens, pale and chubby, bookish and laughed at by girls whose fathers weren't screwing the neighbors, Suzannah had remodeled herself. She had forced on self-confidence like armor, learned to strut and talk fast and had done such a hell of a job her audience bought the act as authentic. So had she for the longest time.

Right now, she couldn't remember the trick of doing it.

She used to be smarter. Now she didn't know a damned thing except that she was stranded in an empty office after-hours without answers of a place to go.

And under her elbow, the still-incomplete Luboff questionnaire. "Oh, babe," she muttered, "were you mailed to the wrong address!"

She carried it to June's typewriter.

Dear Patty,

I'm returning this, incomplete, because I've run out of answers.

You and Hawthorne want to know if I know a happy woman. Offhand, I'd say no.

But if you'd hum a few bars, maybe I could learn it?

"Scared the living daylights out of me, you did! I thought the place was empty!" A woman with a mop and a security badge put her hand on her large bosom.

"I'm sorry." Suzannah typed an envelope and put the questionnaire and her note inside.

The cleaning woman pointed the mop as if it were the long arm of the law. "And what *are* you doin' in this office at this hour?"

"I work here."

The woman's expression softened. Suzannah was not a thief but another poor working stiff. "Ah, so the sons of bitches have you workin' late while they're by the fireplace with their fancy wives. Take advice from someone older, dearie. Quit. There's other jobs, but there's a storm comin' and only one life to live." She rearranged the objects on a desk, stood back and looked proud. "Workin' girls gotta take care of ourselves. No one else will. Not a man alive, and for sure no big egg-zek-u-tive. Not those men. Like they say, a good man's hard to find."

"God but they say that a lot. Do they say what to do if, by a fluke, one is found?"

The cleaning woman, reading a memo retrieved from the wastebasket, didn't hear her.

"I'm going to find a good one." Suzannah covered June's typewriter and left. "I *found* a good one, dammit," she said at the door. "I just . . . misplaced him. Have to find him again."

Outside, the street was a study in slow motion rushing. Bodies bent forward, pressed into the spray of snow as if heads and torsos refused to wait while feet gingerly maneuvered the slippery paving.

Suzannah felt every icy step through the thin soles of her shoes. She profoundly regretted her romantic footgear. As events had worked out, she could have worn scuba fins on her feet and Masterman wouldn't have noticed.

But delicate slippers had seemed imperative, so she now moved carefully, skin smarting in the swirls of snow and wind, and she tried to avoid those patches where old ice increased the hazards.

"Eighteenth Street," he'd said. They'd gone to that bar on

Chestnut Street and he'd said he was around the corner from it every Wednesday, right about this time.

She walked more briskly and turned onto Eighteenth Street before it intersected with Chestnut so that she could cover the area on both sides. She scanned storefronts and small businesses for three blocks and then saw, in the distance, the building where she had her annual Pap smear. A medical building, she knew, and the odds were high, were surely in favor of its being . . . "Be it," she muttered, walking double-speed.

In front of the brick building, still a half block away, a news vendor clapped his hands and blew on his finger tips, then spoke to a small boy with copper curls.

Suzannah squinted through the snow flurries. "Adam? Adam?" But the wind swallowed her voice.

She became desperate. If that was Adam, she couldn't lose him. Not today, not now while she still understood why she needed to reach and touch him. "Adam!" she shouted. "Hey!"

"Adam!" she screamed, running, craning her neck to keep the curls and green parka in sight.

And then the concrete tilted, rose and smacked her side, flipped her, twirled and disappeared, leaving only white glare and all-over hurt.

In the nightmare again. In the spotlight. In the pain.

But she was awake. Still, she heard the first, predictable sharp laugh. A titter. A giggle. She pushed with her head, to escape them, but she couldn't move and she slipped below the wave of mockery and drowned in shame.

Her breath came in gasps as she tried again to save herself. She opened her eyes to dredge herself out of it, to find sanity and freedom—and found instead she was trapped inside her dream. It had taken over, stamped her life forever. She was still surrounded by the hazy nightmare faces wrapped in gauze, blurred and sneering while Suzannah fell apart and died. They would laugh, they would merge, the mouth would devour her—

"Suzannah? Get up, please. Suzannah?"

That was not the sound of night terrors. She opened her eyes again and saw the green parka and Adam, fuzzed as was everyone through the snowflakes.

"Oh, Adam. It *was* you! Oh, I'm so glad, I—" She tried to stand but she couldn't. As irrational as it was, as ridiculous as it was, the horror returned full force. She was ashamed of herself because her lapse was over and she knew what was real and what was imagined, but she had to check whether her leg had fallen off and melted into the sidewalk.

It had not, but it hurt terribly.

"Are you hurt? Is that why you're crying?"

"I'm not crying," she said. "It's the cold that's . . ." She tried to stand and finally admitted she couldn't. Something critical had snapped. She made a cushion of her cape. Adam, staring, blew a large pink round of bubble gum.

"I lied," she said. "I just lied to you. No way to begin, is it? I was crying. I thought—please don't laugh. Until I heard you say my name, I thought I was stuck in the worst dream I ever had. The one that scares me the most. You understand?"

He nodded.

"I thought you would."

He popped his bubble gum and sucked it in. "You dream about falling in the snow?"

"Not exactly, but about falling. And freezing. More . . . about messing up. Having people know I did. Trying hard and not making it. I used to think it was the worst thing in the world."

"Why?"

"I'm not sure any more. So anyway, I guess the worst thing just happened to me, and I found out it's not so horrible. But the joke is, now that I'm not as afraid of falling down, I can't stand up."

Adam extended a mittened hand.

She put it inside both of hers. "Thanks," she said. "You're one of the good guys."

"Adam? Why are you—" Coby's voice died away. "Suzannah?" He knelt beside her. Adam followed suit. "Suzannah? Are you all right?"

"No," she said, and she smiled. "But that's not news, is it? Isn't that what you tried to tell me? Usually, I'm only nuts. Tonight, I'm crippled, too." He reached over to help her. She took his hand and put it next to her cheek. "It's good to have friends," she said.

He grinned and hugged her, nearly toppling from his kneeling position.

"Lunatics! You want pneumonia?" The news vendor blew on his finger tips and shouted. "This ain't Miami Beach to sit and make chitchat. What's the matter? You crazy?"

"Not me!" she yelled. "Not any more, mister!"

"Shouting in the streets weakens your claim," Coby said softly. He put his arms under her cape and helped her to her feet. She tested her right leg and winced, then leaned on him.

"What happened?" he asked.

"Oh, I was . . . well, actually, I'd been . . ." She laughed loudly in the frosty night and it didn't make her feel a madwoman at all. "It was charades, Coby. I was acting out a proverb I just invented. I mean it's so brilliant your Zeyde Morris—or you—might have said it. And you didn't even guess it."

"I give up. What were you miming, crumpled in the middle of the pedestrian right of way?"

"That you can decide where you want to be, you can run like hell and do all your tricky steps and still wind up flat on your ass in the cold."

"Funny. That's—you say you invented that one?"

She nodded. "I'm going to patent it. Make samplers."

She held Coby's right shoulder and, less heavily, Adam's left. Slowly, lopsidedly, she hopped and they progressed.

"Do you think this dependent stance is suitable for a feminist?" Coby asked.

"Do you think remarks like that are fair?" She hopped silently, then said, "Facts are facts, man. Use your eyes. I can't make it on my own."

"And when you're no longer lame and that statement is only a metaphor?"

"I'll make a new statement. Change it to I don't *want* to make it on my own. That's truer, anyway. I mean it's fine from nine to five, but have you ever been all alone at night in an enormous office building?"

"No."

"It's not a real convivial spot."

They hobbled towards Walnut Street. "I'm going to be— I've been pretty stupid at work, too, lately. I'm going to have to give enormous attention to it. I have to clean up some messes I made." She sighed loudly. "And I still can't see how two people with two careers . . . and I'll be so involved and exhausted . . . I don't see how with that, and a kid . . . I don't know how to . . ." She shivered.

"Neither do I." He pulled her closer.

They followed Adam around the corner. "Where we heading?" Coby asked.

"For trouble, betcha," she muttered. "I don't know anyone who's really done it. I mean worked it out so it's fair and happy for everyone. I don't even think it'll happen for a few more generations." She shook her head and followed Adam.

"You're probably right," he said, apparently not troubled by the fact.

"I bet we fight a lot," she added.

"Possibly. That isn't the worst thing in the world."

"I'll mess up. I know I will. I don't know how to take care of—I'm scared of—I don't know anything about any of that. I'll mess up."

"Probably. And I will too, and that isn't the worst thing in the world, either."

"What is?"

"Not trying. Being so stupid you buy prefabricated answers. Not believing in the possibility of being."

"Ah. The creature there has never been. Us."

"Well, why not?"

Adam led and they continued walking. Every few steps she tested her leg and eventually, she could put gentle weight on it.

"I'm hungry," Adam said. "There's the McDonald's—"

"I don't think Suzannah likes—"

"Suzannah hasn't been liking Suzannah all that much. A deal, okay? If now and then I could taste veal and vichyssoise—"

"Yuk," Adam said, but softly.

"Then in all fairness, we could now and then sample somewhat more . . . heavily advertised food products."

She limped across the street, holding both of them tight as they navigated the packed snow at the curb.

"Coby?" she said. "If—well, if it works, even for a while—if it—do you think now I might really, someday have my own song?"

"That's a biggie with you? Then sure. Someday, Scheherazade. I'll write a few notes every year, keep you dangling. And meanwhile, you can write one for me."

"Me? I don't even know music. I can't play."

"Come on, Suzannah. Nothing's been written for us. We'll both have to improvise and play it by ear."

"So will I," Adam said. "Whatever that means."

"So will we all. Whatever that means."

About the Author

Judith Greber lives in the San Francisco Bay area with her husband and two sons. Her humorous articles and short stories have appeared in several magazines.